TIMETABLE
AMOS ELON

Amos Elon, one of Israel's leading journalists, has covered every major event in Israel
since the 1960s. His previous books include:
Israelis: Founders and Sons, *Herzl* and
*Between Enemies: A Compassionate Dialogue
between an Israeli and an Arab*. Mr Elon lives
in Jerusalem.

Books by Amos Elon

HERZL: A BIOGRAPHY (1975)
HERZL: A PLAY, with Dore Schary (1976)
BETWEEN ENEMIES: (with Sana Hassan) A COMPASSIONATE
DIALOGUE BETWEEN AN ISRAELI AND AN ARAB (1974)
THE ISRAELIS: FOUNDERS AND SONS (1971)
JOURNEY THROUGH A HAUNTED LAND,
THE NEW GERMANY (1967)

TIMETABLE

Amos Elon

ARROW BOOKS

The events described in this book happened. The main protagonists are called by their real names. The letters and telegrams are genuine and can be found in the official archives cited in the notes. For easier identification the letters have been set in a smaller type and the telegrams have been set in small caps.

Arrow Books Limited
17–21 Conway Street, London W1P 6JD

An imprint of the Hutchinson Publishing Group

London Melbourne Sydney Auckland
Johannesburg and agencies
throughout the world

First published by Hutchinson 1981
Arrow edition 1982

© Amos Elon 1980

This book is sold subject to the condition that it shall not, by way of trade or otherwise, be lent, resold, hired out, or otherwise circulated without the publisher's prior consent in any form of binding or cover other than that in which it is published and without a similar condition including this condition being imposed on the subsequent purchaser.

Made and printed in Great Britain
by The Anchor Press Ltd
Tiptree, Essex

ISBN 0 09 930420 1

FOR B.

Contents

Departure, 18 May 1944   1
Another Planet   10
Arrival, 18 May 1944   43
19 May 1944   53
20 May 1944   74
21 May 1944   88
25–26 May 1944   91
26 May 1944   107
Excerpts, 15 May–3 June 1944   113
26–29 May 1944   118
29 May 1944   137
30 May 1944   144
2 June 1944   150
3–7 June 1944   156
Excerpts, 6 June 1944   174
6–9 June 1944   177
10 June 1944   190
11 June 1944   196
12–25 June 1944   203
2–26 June 1944   213
27 June 1944   230
28 June–4 July 1944   234
5 July 1944   242

6 July 1944	244
8 July 1944	249
The Prisoner	256
Concert of Nations	288
Disclosure	292
Cairo	309
Jerusalem	331
Postscript	344
Notes	347

TIMETABLE

Departure, 18 May 1944

They left Vienna early on the morning of Wednesday, 18 May 1944. Behind the barely visible rooftops and spires of the city, bleak clouds hung in the charred hills that only a week earlier had been ablaze in the fires of an American air attack. The three-engined Junkers-52, on its regular weekly flight from Vienna to Istanbul, had taken off after an hour's delay. It was now heading east at a low altitude. The sky was gray. The airplane lurched in the ashen mist. The growl shook the fuselage and the great metal body shuddered in the frost.

Jenö Brand (or "Joel," or "Jo," as his friends called him, or "Eugen Band, Ingenieur, Erfurt" as it said in the crisp new German passport issued him only a few hours earlier by the Gestapo) sat in the front row by the window. He felt nauseated. The seat belt pressed against the muscles of his stomach. A taste of gall rose in his throat. He leaned back. The headache that had been with him for many days pounded at his temples.

On his right, Andrew Gyorgy stirred in the narrow seat. "Not a bad way for two Jews to slip out of Nazi Germany, eh?" he said with a grin. "Not too many have gotten out in such comfort!" Gyorgy stretched his legs. Brand said nothing. His eyelids fluttered. Then he turned his head back to the window. He was a robust, youngish-looking man in his mid-thirties, squarely built, clad in the casual grace of fine

tweed and flannel. The face was broad. The squat, square,
peasantlike features contrasted oddly, but not unpleasantly,
with the elegance of his dress and the apparent felicity of
his manner. Had he been able to walk about, his gait would
have been that of the sailor he had been in his younger
days: not heavy, but swaying, with both feet solidly on the
ground. His hair was burnished, brown to bronze, the forehead wide. The ears were delicate, the lips pale and sensi-
tive against the softness of his cheeks, the large eyes
grayish brown but vivid.

He shut, and opened them again. The window flickered
in the glare of distant lightning. His eyes strained at the
spectral sight outside. The airplane was flying almost parallel to a wide highway below. At first Brand did not recognize it. The road was straight as a line, and without traffic.
Then he realized it was the main highway from Budapest
to Vienna on which they had motored in the day before.
The fields on both sides of the road were dotted by little
mounds. In the glassy, ghostly pallor, Brand recognized the
vast cemeteries that ran adjacent to the road for miles. The
flat expanse of tombstones extended in the slush far into
the distance, to the lots of the stonemasons, where more
tombstones—still blank—and more crosses, funeral plaques
and statues formed yet another, uninhabited graveyard.

The plane shook. There were only a dozen or so passengers on it. Flying abroad in wartime was a rare privilege,
granted mostly to high-ranking functionaries on official
missions (and, occasionally, their mistresses), couriers,
diplomats and businessmen trafficking in arms and raw materials between the belligerent and the neutral. Gyorgy was
right, Brand thought. It was certainly an odd way to be
leaving. He still only half believed in it. He glanced at the
fellow passengers. In the seats behind were several officers
in the field-gray uniform of the Wehrmacht. Immediately
across the aisle, a young man unfolded a Swiss newspaper.
His owlish face glowed in pinks and yellows; the warm,

good-natured eyes were rather docile. He sat next to another civilian, a slim, slight, bony sort of man, bald as an egg. A little golden swastika was pinned to his lapel. His sharp aquiline face was bent over a book, and by his gaunt look he might have been taken for Dr. Goebbels himself. Brand swallowed. A sudden wave of heat ran through his flexed limbs, and his back was wet with perspiration.

The plane struggled through the shreds of clouds and bumped through another air pocket. The young man across the aisle gripped his armrest to steady himself.

Gyorgy called out, "Have a little patience, sir. I've flown this route before. We'll soon be out of this foggy mess."

The young man smiled back weakly. Brand turned his face back to the window. Pangs of pulsating pain pounded at his brain. His mind reeled backward to the day before. The short scene at home, his wife and children kissing him good-bye. The departure. The brief stop at Komárom, on the way out from Budapest. The railroad depot—the slimy concrete platform—the train—the huddled mass of people packed into cattle cars. The stone-faced guards—the monotonous bureaucracy of the head count. In the rarefied cool air of the airplane the reek of coal and steam at Komárom still stung his nostrils. And in the roar of the plane's engines he discerned the rumbling roll and screeching steel clatter of the departing train.

A steward picked his way down the narrow aisle with an uneasy step, offering drinks from a silver tray. Gyorgy pressed a glass into Brand's hand, and raised his own slightly in a little flourish. "Come on, Jo. Drink up."

"Yes."

"Not bad, eh?" Gyorgy said. "Yesterday, Hungary. Tonight, Istanbul. Lobsters and lights and ladies on the Golden Horn. And now, this." He sipped his drink appreciatively.

"I shan't be there long enough to enjoy it," Brand said. "I'm coming back as soon as I can."

"Dear boy, you must be joking."

"You know I am not."

"Oh, come on."

"I have a job to do. As soon as it's finished I go back."
The last few words were drowned in the roar.

"Speak up, Jo. Don't worry. Nobody can hear us in this racket. Anyway, they don't understand Hungarian."

"I said I'll be back in Budapest in two weeks."

"I say you'll be making a mistake."

"No. I hope I'll be able to rescue thousands, tens of thousands of people."

"You should have tried to rescue your wife and your children first. Why didn't you take them out with you?"

"I couldn't."

"Ridiculous."

"It was part of the deal. The Germans promised they wouldn't touch them."

"I got my wife out."

"How?"

"I have my ways, my dear. She is waiting for me in Ankara. And we are staying there. For good."

"I thought . . . But you are always going—uh—back and forth."

"I'm finished with that."

"You're no longer working for . . . ?"

"The Germans? Yes. But I am retiring."

"They sent you along, didn't they"—Brand searched for the correct word—"to keep an eye on me?"

"Don't you worry. *You* do *your* job—if you can. I'll see to my own. Maybe I'll help."

"I doubt I shall need your help in Istanbul. My friends are waiting for me there."

"Don't expect too much. I know them."

"They are not the usual people that you know. Chaim Weizmann has flown to meet me."

"Ah. The king of the Jews. No more, no less."

"He'll sign the draft agreement and we'll make the first deposit."

"How much?"

"The Germans didn't tell you?"

"Not exactly."

"Perhaps they have less confidence in you than you think," Brand said sharply. He regretted his tone immediately. There was no sense in picking a quarrel with Gyorgy at this point. Gyorgy was, after all, working for the Germans. He was not a man likely to retire from so lucrative a business. Even if he did not go back, he still might be able to cause harm.

"Let us stay in touch with one another in Istanbul," Brand said in a more conciliatory tone. "I'll keep you informed, I promise."

"I wish you all the luck in the world, my dear Jo. I really do. Perhaps you will succeed." The lines of Gyorgy's face, usually quite bright and debonair, suddenly collapsed. "Do you think I am made of stone? I hope you succeed. I hope so very much. I only wonder . . ."

"What?"

"You're too tame for this job. You'll get hurt."

"I cannot get hurt. Others will get hurt . . . if I fail. In one way or another we'll find an arrangement."

The steward came along with more drinks. Brand swallowed another cognac. He did not want to talk. He was weary with fatigue. He forced his eyes shut. After a short while he fell into a light sleep. He surrendered willingly to its dark embrace: a moment of oblivion he had not had in the past twenty-eight hours.

* * *

He was startled out of it by a sudden jolt from below. The aircraft touched down for a landing at Belgrade. The passengers filed through the puddles into the grim shell of a terminal building. Its windows, shattered in a recent air

raid, were blocked with sandbags. The premises swarmed
with steel-helmeted troops. The ill-fitting uniforms hung
like sacks on their skeletal adolescent bodies.

Gyorgy was greeted effusively by a German sergeant
clad in heavy worn-out boots. "Doktor Gyorgy! Always
on the move." Brand sat down on a wooden bench, while
Gyorgy went off to make a telephone call. He watched the
slim, supple figure disappear through the dark frame of a
side door. Who was Gyorgy calling in this ravaged place?
He liked Gyorgy in a way, even envied him his easy non-
chalant manner that he seemed never to lose, not even in
the most trying and dangerous situation. Gyorgy was an
adventurer all right, greedy and unscrupulous. He has
never let me down though, Brand thought. No, never. And
was he really bolting now? I must be on my guard, Brand
thought. If he bolts, he could spoil everything.

Presently Gyorgy came striding back from the telephone,
which, he said with a shrug, was out of order, as usual in
the Balkans. He offered Brand a cigar. Then his tone became intimate once more.

"I might as well tell you, dear boy. I am not just running
off. I have a new job. It's very big," he added in a whisper,
"and it may put an end altogether to this war."

"Gyorgy, I know your type of work."

"This time it's different. Honest. High politics. Top
officers in the Wehrmacht and the Waffen SS. Hitler's own
entourage! Important contacts with the British Government. But my lips are sealed. . . . Perhaps in Istanbul . . ."

"Oh, come off it. I know you better than that."

"Just wait. You'll see."

"What are you really out for?"

"To survive, of course. Aren't you?"

Brand only nodded. A small commotion had picked up
in the room. The passengers were called back to the

departing airplane. A sentry was checking off names and carefully inspecting each passport.

In a little while they were strapped into their seats and the airplane departed. Brand pretended to sleep. Gyorgy was chatting in German with two civilians across the aisle. They were discussing night clubs and restaurants in Istanbul. The little bald man with the gold swastika pinned to his lapel seemed to know a good number of them. His voluptuous lips were set in the bony tallow of a narrow emaciated face, and the names of exotic pleasure haunts rolled voraciously off his tongue.

The three men introduced themselves to one another. The bald man's name was Dr. Volker Mann. He was in charge of Turkish affairs at the Propagandaministerium in Berlin, on his way to Ankara, he said, to address the annual conference of the German-Turkish Friendship League.

The young man was Swiss, his name was Corrado Vitin. He was traveling to Ankara for the Red Cross on a problem of refugees. Gyorgy introduced himself, giving his name only. "Hungarians like to play mysterious," the German said, and they all laughed.

"I am just a businessman," Gyorgy said. "Nothing very exotic." The steward came again with drinks. They downed another round and agreed to meet in a week's time at Abdullah's cabaret on the Bosporus shore. The German looked curiously over at Brand dozing in his seat. He had not overlooked the extreme courtesy—even deference—that Brand had been accorded by the authorities at the Vienna airport.

"Your companion—if I may take the liberty . . . ?"

"My companion is an engineer from Erfurt. We are traveling together."

Brand opened his eyes slowly.

"We are not disturbing, I hope," said the German. "Oh, I am terribly sorry."

"I was awake."

"Naturally, in this racket. Are you with the ministry?"

"Not exactly," said Brand slowly. "But in a manner of speaking, yes. The Erfurt Engineering Company."

"I see," Mann said eagerly. "Is it machinery?"

"Uh—machinery? You could say so, yes."

"I am very pleased to meet you. The future of German technology is my favorite subject. And it is the theme of my lecture in Ankara—as I was just telling your friend. If you should be in Ankara, *Herr Ingenieur,* I should be pleased if you could attend."

"Thank you. I am only going as far as Istanbul."

"Perhaps we might discuss it sometime."

"Certainly."

"I often come to Erfurt."

"We'll meet before that," Gyorgy said lightly.

The aircraft was approaching the landing strip of Istanbul. It was growing dark outside. The plane reached the islands in the Sea of Marmara and crossed the mouth of the Golden Horn. A million lights were sparkling in a sea of darkest Prussian blue. Brand was startled by the unfamiliar vision of a city fully lit up. They were over neutral territory, circling over peace. He was transfixed by the very marvel of its presence.

The airplane braked to a stop in front of a brilliantly lit terminal building. The heavy door was pulled back. A draft of wet air blew in, saturated with the stench of fuel. The passengers descended the slippery ladder in the blinding glare of a powerful searchlight, and were ushered into an unkempt hall. Turkish security officers were seated behind an elongated bare table.

"You are coming from Vienna, Herr—uh—Band?" The security man spoke German. He leafed slowly through the passport. The crisp new pages crackled.

"From Budapest, actually." The policeman carefully went through the passport once again. In the yellowish light of the overhead lamp his face was full of curves and shadows. For one long moment they held each other's gaze. Then the officer stood up.

"You will please follow me."

"Oh?" It flashed through Brand's mind that Weizmann would want to greet him in discreet privacy. The other passengers were already being waved toward the exit.

"Your papers are not in order. You must go back to Vienna. The plane turns around in the morning. Until then you are under arrest."

Another Planet

This is a true account. Hungary, where Brand's journey had begun on the day before, was still a rather special place in wartime Europe. An ally of Nazi Germany, its troops were of course fighting alongside the Germans on the Russian front, where they often surpassed their German allies in sheer ferocious bestiality. Yet for the hundreds of thousands of Jews who lived under Hungarian rule in 1944, the country was still an enclave of relative safety, out of time and place in the inferno of Hitler's Europe. Elsewhere on the continent, Hitler's war against the Jews was almost won. Every country had been combed, every city searched, every hamlet sifted for its last surviving Jews. Millions had already been annihilated in the gas chambers of the Polish death camps.

Of all the great Jewish communities on the continent, only that of Hungary had been spared. It was one of the oldest in Europe. Jews had first settled in the Hungarian plains in the seventh century, before the arrival of the Magyars.

Severe anti-Semitic laws had been enacted in Hungary too. But until May 1944 the Jews of Hungary had only been disenfranchised, plundered, terrorized and forcibly resettled and enslaved in the Ukraine, whereas in the rest of Europe most Jews were already dead or about to go up the chimneys as gray, acrid-smelling smoke.

This unique situation had begun to change in the second half of March 1944. On 19 March, German troops marched into Budapest to prevent the Hungarian Government from seeking separate peace with the Western Allies. On that day, eleven august Jewish noblemen were still, theoretically, members of the Hungarian Senate, and were assured by the government that it opposed the deportation of Jews to the Polish death camps. But the *Final Solution* was being prepared here too, and despite the protestations, with the active support of the Hungarian Government. Slowly at first, not always very consistently, for even within the government, conflicting forces were at work, leaving the murderers, as well as any potential rescuers, room for maneuver.

Joel Brand, who flew to Istanbul on 18 May to save, as he hoped, thousands of lives, was no idle dreamer. He had some reason to believe that he might at least achieve a delay in the timetable of the charnel house, for, meanwhile, the Russians were advancing toward the Hungarian plains and approaching the death camps themselves.

He was a level-headed man of quick, perhaps too quick, intelligence. He was not essentially a political person but a businessman. Like many central Europeans, he had a facility for languages. He was a native of Hungary, but had attended school in Erfurt, Germany. As a young man in the early 1930s, he had roamed the world as a merchant seaman. He was a man of certain means. An engineer by training, he owned a small textile plant in Budapest, which through a series of shrewd maneuvers he had saved from sequestration as Jewish-owned property. His father had been the founder and first president of the Budapest Telephone Company. Brand still occupied a minor post there. He was married to a buxom, good-looking woman of uncommon intelligence named Hansi. The marriage was not a success. But in times of war, people tend to put personal problems aside. Both Brand and his wife were active in the underground.

They had stumbled into it almost casually. Early in 1943 the Hungarian police had deported Brand's sister and her husband to Kamenets Podolski, to what was called a "resettlement area" for Jews but was in reality a slave labor camp. Brand, as a former cadet officer in the Hungarian Army, had not been touched. In a fashionable cafe in Budapest he happened upon an old acquaintance who was currently employed by the Hungarian secret police. An underpaid civil official not adverse to making money and, as he put it, "a friend," he offered to bring Brand's sister and her husband back to Budapest for a consideration of ten thousand pengö. Three times the man traveled to Kamenets Podolski. Each time he somehow brought back the wrong couple. Each time Brand, or the family, paid the ransom. On his fourth trip the man finally brought back Brand's own kin.

From this inauspicious beginning a network of rescue activities had spread. It was directed by the newly formed, clandestine Jewish Aid and Rescue Committee, of which Brand became a prominent member. The others were Otto Komoly, a civil engineer, the committee's leader, the journalist Rudolf Kastner, who was the committee's political officer in touch with foreign consulates and liberal Hungarian politicians, and Saul Kleinmann, a broker on the diamond exchange who served as their treasurer. They were odd men, whom the infernal circumstances had tossed up almost by chance, men of a bohemian bent, gamblers, but of strong character and integrity nevertheless. At almost any time, each one could have saved himself and his family, with relative ease, by escaping to Switzerland or Turkey. And yet they had remained behind to help and save as many as they could. The main Jewish body, the officially recognized Council of the Jews of Hungary, was paralyzed by surrealistic notions of legality, which continued to inspire and disable its rich and timid dignitaries. Brand and his colleagues proceeded from the assumption that in the new order of bestiality legality was obsolete. They would save whoever they could by whatever means.

The committee produced false baptismal certificates and passports and established contacts with similar underground groups in Slovakia. By autumn, 1943, the activities of the committee were reaching across the frontiers of Hungary. Its volunteers penetrated the ghettos of Poland and Slovakia, and some of their inmates were smuggled into the relative safety of Hungary. Brand was in charge of these forays.

They were accomplished through daring and ingenious means. Not the least important of these was the forging of links with professional smugglers, underworld types and certain pliable members of the German and Hungarian security agencies. Budapest was a hotbed of corruption, intrigue and interservice rivalries. Brand found himself pursuing relationships, even cordialities of a sort, with German diplomats and officers stationed in the Hungarian capital. One was a German Gestapo man named Dr. Schmidt who was attached to the German legation as a "Hungarian expert." They first met in the Budapest night club Imperiale. Brand knew one of the house girls there. She had told him that Schmidt was a heavy gambler and badly in need of money.

"So you are the famous Jenö Brand," Schmidt said, and sent the girl out of the room. "I hear you want to bring over some children from Slovakia?"

Brand said, "I'll help anyone."

"Very well," said Schmidt, "but the code word is children. How much will you pay for each?"

A working relationship was established. Brand periodically met Schmidt for business lunches at the Opera grill room to barter for passes and information. Schmidt confided to Brand that he was "inwardly" opposed to the mass killings and to prove it he was ready to serve Brand here and there for large sums of money, which he needed with ever-increasing urgency, for he was a heavy gambler.

Another of Brand's contacts was Josef Winninger. Winninger was a German counterintelligence officer. He claimed to have access to the higher reaches of the Nazi military establishment, and on various occasions he proved it. He told Brand, after swearing him to secrecy, that in the embattled upper echelons of the army and the SS there were men—perhaps even Himmler himself—searching for alibis to serve them after the war. They would be prepared to spare the Jews now in order to save their own skins later on.

Contacts were eventually established with the free world also. It was still possible to cable and speak on the telephone with Zurich or Istanbul. A convenient middleman was found to carry in, from Switzerland or Turkey, the funds the committee needed to oil its way through the corrupt bureaucracy. This was Andrew Gyorgy, Brand's traveling companion on the flight to Istanbul. His nickname was "Bandi." He was a black marketeer in hard currencies. Many a Hungarian politician had used him to smuggle his money out to a safe place. On such missions and others (it was said he also worked for several espionage agencies, including the Gestapo) he traveled regularly between Budapest and Istanbul. He carried a Hungarian diplomatic passport. His versatility, coupled with his usefulness to his various employers, had made him a rich man. His pass enabled him to travel the German Reich to the very ends of its shrinking confines.

Because he had once been a Jew (before his conversion to Catholicism as a child) and was eager to make even more money, Gyorgy was ready to assume the risk of bringing in from Istanbul the large amounts of currency and gold intended by Jewish organizations abroad for rescue work among the entrapped Jews of Hungary and

Slovakia. For this he charged a 10 per cent commission. But "as a patriot," as he put it (or perhaps as a realist), he was willing to defer payment until the end of the war.

More funds were needed all the time to smooth the work of the committee through the labyrinth of greedy German officials. As the fortunes of war changed, the number of corruptible Germans increased considerably. The committee was able to exploit conflicts of interest—between the army and the SS, and between the Gestapo and military counterintelligence (long infested by opponents of Hitler). By the end of 1943 some three thousand deportees had been smuggled back to Hungary by the men of the committee. They were a small force facing the most unrelenting machine of death ever devised by man.

When the German Army occupied Hungary in March 1944 that machine was already being geared up with scientific precision to annihilate the last more or less intact community of Jews left in Nazi Europe. A special staff of handpicked experts, led by Adolf Eichmann, had gathered early in March in Austria to plan the logistics of the vast operation, down to the smallest detail.

They divided Hungary into five "zones of operations"; a sixth was the city of Budapest. In each zone the Jews would first be herded into ghettos, then freighted by rail to Auschwitz, where four new crematoria had just been installed. Twelve were already in operation. The aim was the destruction of 700,000 Hungarian Jews within the shortest conceivable time.

Time was a crucial factor in the calculations of both the executioners and the handful of men and women bent upon last-minute efforts at rescue. The first Russian patrols were just descending from the Carpathian Mountains; it was not unlikely that the Red Army would soon begin to advance toward Budapest. On 19 March, Adolf Eichmann and his staff arrived in the Hungarian capital. They moved into new field headquarters in the Hotel Majestic. It was a coincidence that only a few hours earlier Brand had vacated a suite in that same hotel. In the past months the suite had served as a decoy address for the work of the committee.

* * *

Brand had not simply signed out. He had been lingering in the bath that morning at 9 A.M. when the door flew open and Josef Winninger rushed in. "Get dressed! Otherwise you will be arrested! The Gestapo is here! Hurry!"

Brand dressed quickly. The two men left the hotel by a side door. Eichmann's little convoy of cars and light trucks was parked outside the main entrance and porters were unloading wooden crates and typewriters and folders and files. Winninger drove Brand to his own office on the Danube embankment. Here Brand was conveniently placed in the "protective custody" of the German Army counterintelligence agency. He spent the next few hours in Winninger's room quietly collecting his thoughts. Winninger had disappeared. Brand telephoned his wife that he was safe. She told him that German troops were encamped in the park outside their home. Through the window Brand looked out at the pleasure boats on the river; downstairs on the quay there was a fruit and flower market; life was continuing as usual. He waited for word from Winninger.

After a considerable time, the rotund, smiling Dr. Schmidt, in the full regalia of a Wehrmacht officer, appeared through a side door.

"You are free to go," said Schmidt. "I've fixed it up." He drove Brand home through streets teeming with German mobile patrols. Schmidt was amicable and obeisant. His fat little face quivered as he said, "If I can help in any way, please feel free to call—at any time you wish." Brand was not fooled. He sensed immediately that his "arrest" had been engineered by the resourceful Winninger and Schmidt. Now that so many more Germans had arrived in town, Schmidt and Winninger wanted to ensure that if any-one would get paid by the Jews it would be themselves.

"We'll soon have much to talk about," said Schmidt.

"Thank you very much."

"Not at all. I shall always be glad to be of service."

That evening, members of the committee crept through the darkened streets to meet in Brand's home. The grim situation was discussed at length. There was little doubt that the deportation of the Jews of Hungary to the death camps in Poland would soon start. Komoly proposed that a messenger be sent to Istanbul to warn Jewish representatives there of the impending disaster. In their desperate isolation, the men of the committee still believed that it was only the ignorance of the outside world that prevented it from taking more effective steps to save the doomed Jews. But if they could alert the outside world, Britain and America might yet threaten Hungary with severe reprisals. And perhaps the deportations, which the Germans could not carry out efficiently without the support of the Hungarian gendarmerie, would be averted, or at least delayed. Saul Kleinmann happened to be in possession of valid travel documents. Trains to Istanbul were still running via Belgrade. The committee decided that Kleinmann should depart immediately.

"There is little time left," said Kastner. His voice dropped dejectedly, for he had specific news. Eichmann had made a first move. Earlier in the day the leaders of the official Council of Hungarian Jews had been summoned to meet with Colonel Hermann Krumey, Eichmann's deputy. The president and his counselors had come to the meeting with packed bags. But Colonel Krumey had allayed their fears of immediate arrest with charming reassurance. ("But, gentlemen," he had said, "what on earth has entered your mind?") He requested only that they supply lists of addresses and a small quantity of blankets and mattresses for use by the German garrison. He had also asked for a piano, for he wished to continue with his music practice. Otherwise, everything "will continue as usual."

It was a pattern all too familiar to Brand, Kastner, Komoly and their friends. In one form or another it had been repeated all over Europe. Part of Eichmann's diabolic skill—born of years of experience—was to gain the involuntary co-operation of the official Jewish leadership. Within a week, in fact, the first ghettos were created in the northeastern provinces closest to the line of the Russian advance. On 29 March all Jews were ordered to wear a yellow Star of David on their outer garments. Brand and his friends were exempted, thanks to the solicitous Dr. Schmidt, who provided them with special passes.

There was not much, however, that they could do. They did manage to smuggle a bit of money into the ghettos. Two runners succeeded in penetrating the virtually sealed-off towns of Košice and Ungvár in the Carpatho-Ukraine to warn the occupants that they were marked for death. Their warnings were ignored. The victims were too demoralized; some simply refused to believe. On 5 April the first trainload set out from the northeastern corner of Hungary in the direction of Poland.

It so happened that on that day Brand and Kastner were lunching with Schmidt at a restaurant on the banks of the Danube. A part of the building had collapsed in an American air raid two days before, but the elegant restaurant, noted for its fine fish, was open for business as usual. They sat on the terrace overlooking the river. Schmidt glanced at the damage behind them. "They have made a bit of a mess, I admit," he said offhandedly. "But it doesn't cause us much harm, does it?"

A small orchestra was playing on a raised platform. Schmidt was in a good mood, for he had just been recommended for promotion. He grew talkative over a bottle of Tokay. "I have something that might interest you." Schmidt's voice fell to a conspiratorial tone. "This will cost me my neck if you give me away, but I tell you, there are all sorts of odd tricks afoot. All kinds of confusion. Eichmann is getting the run-around. One day he is ordered to get on with it as quickly as possible. The next he's told by Berlin to go slow. Himmler's new theory is that the Jews are our soundest investment right now." Schmidt smiled. "To yield any dividends, of course, they must stay alive. . . . The question is, gentlemen, can you make the new policy worthwhile?"

"I think we can."

"Then we are in business, so to speak. I must tell you another thing—in great confidence, of course. . . . My old friend Wislizeny has just joined Eichmann's staff here in Budapest. He subscribes to the investment theory, you know. And now he is here. That should interest you, shouldn't it?"

Wislizeny was the SS officer in charge of Jewish affairs in Slovakia. They had heard of him before. He was known to have pocketed fifty thousand dollars as an advance against the lives of ten thousand Slovak Jews, and had kept the bargain.

Brand said, "We will pay you three million pengö if you arrange a meeting with Wislizeny."

Schmidt sipped his wine appreciatively. "Good," he said, "but a bit too dry." His small eyes shot up. "Let us say five million. That's fair, isn't it? And another million for Winninger."

* * *

They met with Dieter Wislizeny in the same restaurant a few days later. Wislizeny had brought another man with him, whom he presented with a slight flourish: Colonel Hermann Krumey, Eichmann's first deputy. The two officers were elegant in their pearl-gray uniforms with matching kid gloves, which they did not remove during the entire meal. Krumey was taciturn. Wislizeny led the conversation.

Before his posting to Budapest, Wislizeny had been the butcher of the Jews of Austria, Slovakia and Greece; at this point in the history of the charnel house his brutality was matched only by his greed. He seemed to be quite well informed of the activities of the committee and of its links with Jewish welfare organizations in the West. He hinted at all this nonchalantly, as though it were the most obvious thing in the world. And he quickly came to the point. What were they prepared to pay?

"A lot," Kastner said. "But we have our demands."

"Let's hear them."

Brand spoke. He put forth four demands. First, no mass killings in Hungary. Second, no deportations to Poland. Third, no ghettos and concentration camps. Finally, he requested exit facilities for Palestine—and for emigration generally. For this they were prepared to pay Wislizeny two million dollars in cash.

"Only two million?" Wislizeny said deprecatingly. "I wouldn't even consider such a sum. That's less than two-fifty a head. In Slovakia I was paid five."

"The sum could be increased," Kastner said quickly. "At any rate, we would pay two hundred thousand immediately as an advance."

"Ah, now you are talking," said Wislizeny. He agreed to accept the advance, which they promised to deliver at the earliest possible opportunity. Wislizeny then began a discussion of Brand's four requests. Yes, he was prepared to promise that there would be no deportations, and, yes, no mass killings.

"But, gentlemen, let us be realistic about that too. When one planes, shavings are bound to fly—some fifteen thousand or so may die." He balked only at Brand's last request. "A mass emigration of Jews, yes. But not to Palestine. We don't want to offend our Arab friends."

Kastner said they could be flexible on the destination of

the émigrés as long as lives were spared and the survivors permitted to leave.

Krumey suddenly spoke up. Before they could commit themselves further, he said, they would have to consult their superiors. And he added that their negotiations had been authorized by Himmler himself.

The discussion broke off. The Germans insisted on paying the bill.

"You will soon hear from us," Krumey said. "You will be summoned to another meeting."

* * *

The green Mercedes pulled up outside the Opera Cafe. A uniformed SS man stepped out to hold open its door. Brand settled into soft leather cushions. He felt strangely light and spry. A few minutes later he walked up the marble stairway he knew so well to the entrance of the Hotel Majestic. The doorman recognized him and bowed. Brand crossed the lobby with its velvet drapes and gilt cupids floating over the carved doorways. Now that it was the lair of power, the air somehow seemed thinner. Behind the wrought-iron grill of the former bar, the little marble tables had been rearranged into straight lines, like soldiers on parade, to serve an assortment of uniformed secretaries and their typewriters. But along the paneled walls the potted camellias, azaleas and sprigs of unseasonal hibiscus and jasmine were flowering as though nothing had changed in the life of the great hotel. Brand was led to a suite on the second floor. Through the open door he saw Krumey and another man standing at the tall french windows.

"Ah, Herr Brand," said Adolf Eichmann, moving toward the center of the room. "Here you are! Just as you have been described to me!" He gestured with his right hand in an air of consummate politeness. He was a medium-sized man, slender, his thin hair combed back. The narrow face was bland, and marked with no notable characteristic other than a constant twitching of the mouth, the result of a skin disease that was periodically infesting the inside of the cheeks. "Please sit down."

Brand was little prepared for the courteous reception. He seated himself in the proffered armchair. Eichmann and Krumey reclined opposite him on a sofa. Their legs were smartly fitted into high polished boots. The adjutant remained standing. On the table between them were the remnants of a rich breakfast.

"Would you like a drink, Herr Brand?"

Brand shook his head. Krumey filled two glasses.

Eichmann spoke. "We've made inquiries about you. Thorough ones."

"Sir?"

"The results were positive. Yes. You are the so-called Jewish Rescue Committee. It is illegal. Et cetera, et cetera. You smuggled Jews out of Poland. Not very many." As he spoke he folded his legs comfortably on the coffee table.

Brand clutched the carved armrests. "We just do relief work, sir. Everything is within the law."

"You discuss that with the legal department, will you? Now, let's agree to speak absolutely frankly. . . . Good. At this moment you have no reason to be upset. We know everything. You get a lot of money from abroad. Clear violation of paragraph eighty-four. Paragraph thirty-one. Et cetera. I admit, I quite admire you and your work. Don't you, Hermann?"

"Absolutely."

"You are a Jewish idealist," said Eichmann, almost amicably. "I like that. We should be able to come to an understanding. As two *idealists*." He lingered on the last word almost lovingly. To Eichmann an idealist was a man who did not let his own feelings interfere with the line of duty.

"Yes, an understanding. In everyone's interest," echoed Krumey.

"I expect you know who I am," Eichmann continued in

a harder tone. "I am the man whose duty it is to solve the Jewish problem. I *have solved it*—in Poland, in Germany, in Holland . . ." The names of half a dozen countries rolled off his tongue. "Now I must solve it in Hungary as well."

Brand stared at him, saying nothing. He was surprised at his own calm and lack of fear. He noticed that Eichmann's fingernails were carefully manicured. A pungent smell of leather hung in the room, from the boots of the two men. Eichmann's revolver belt was casually thrown across the silk back of the sofa. He swung his arm around it to reach for a sheaf of papers.

"How many Jews are there in Hungary just now?"

"Some six hundred thousand, I think," Brand said.

"You are cheating a bit. There are at least two hundred thousand more in the border areas."

"Sir, I don't think there are so many there."

"I would not argue if I were you," Krumey said. "Colonel Eichmann is an expert on Jewish matters. He has been attending to nothing else since 1938. He could even speak Hebrew with you."

"After the war, maybe," Eichmann said. "Right now we have more urgent business at hand. I offer you an honest bargain. There are over eight hundred thousand Jews in Hungary. Another million in the rest of Europe, give or take a few. We are ready to sell them to you."

"I understand," said Brand. His throat was tight.

"It's a good clean offer," said Eichmann. *"Blut gegen Ware. Ware gegen Blut.* Blood for goods. Goods for Blood. I can't sell you the whole lot, but, say, a million. Take them and go. Against payment!"

"Take them to England," Krumey said lightly. "Get in touch with Churchill."

"Sir?"

"You heard him," Eichmann said impatiently.

"Yes, sir." Brand had more or less expected something of the sort. Not in this form, though.

"What category interests you? I suppose you'd want first and foremost to take out young material, men and women —able to reproduce. Yes? Is that so? Speak up, man. Do you want the children, or the old?"

"Sir, it is not for me to choose who should live or die. I want them all to live."

"More than a million I can't give you. Later perhaps. Is that clear?"

"I understand."

"You are ready to deal?"

"Yes."

"We'll close Auschwitz if the price is right. You have heard of Auschwitz, Herr Brand?"

"I have heard of Auschwitz, sir."

"I knew you were an intelligent man."

"How much do you want?"

Eichmann laughed. He turned to Krumey. "Did you hear that, Hermann? That's rich. These people think of nothing but money." He turned back to Brand. "We'll need some money too. But we want *goods*."

"We have very little property left that could be of any use to you, sir. Anyway, you can confiscate what you want."

"Come now, Herr Brand. I think I said before you were an intelligent man. Didn't I?" He paused. When he was not speaking he was chewing his mouth. "We are not interested in your old rags. You get us raw materials from England and America. Chemicals. Medicines. Soap. Trucks. Et cetera. How much does a truck cost these days in America? A thousand dollars? Eleven hundred? Let's compute one hundred Jews for each truck. That's ten dollars a Jew, give or take a few cents. Can you get us the trucks? Yes or no? Damn it, yes or no?"

Brand knew very well that he could never procure English or American trucks. But the question required an answer. At the very least it suggested a possibility of delay. It was safe to say:

"Yes, I can."

"How soon?"

"I think we can find a way," Brand said slowly, sorting out his thoughts as he spoke. "Of course I must first consult my associates." •

"You may consult whom you like."

"Naturally we cannot find these trucks in Hungary," Brand said. The perspiration was running down his back. But his brain was clearer now, as though a fog had lifted from its cells.

"The Jews in America will get them for you," said Krumey.

"Yes," echoed Eichmann. "They've more money than all of us. The money that gives us so much trouble, the Jews have got it all."

A transient light was flickering in the blunt brownness of Eichmann's eyes. The ferocity that animated the man's life, Brand thought, was really a kind of fear. Eichmann considered Jews as vermin, to be exterminated. But at the same time an omnipotent master race of millionaires that controlled the world. And yes, he would gamble on these paranoid illusions.

"Yes," he said confidently. "Yes, I imagine we can raise considerable amounts of money. Our people and Mr. Churchill will . . ." Amazed at his own fluency, he spun out a fantastic yarn of various possibilities. "Of course we might have some difficulties," he added.

"Difficulties?" Eichmann's voice was acid. "What kind of difficulties? If we can dispose of sixteen thousand Jews a day, it should not be so difficult to find some trucks within a few weeks."

"I mean difficulties in arranging transport. And currency transfers. There are currency restrictions everywhere."

"Don't serve me up any legal crap, will you. Who do you think we are? Fools?" Eichmann reached down for the black leather case that nestled on the carpet by his foot. He snapped it open and tossed a brown envelope on the table.

"Open it. It's for you." The envelope was franked with Swiss postage stamps and addressed "Family Brand, Bulyobdki 18, Budapest."

Brand lifted a silver knife lying on the tray and sliced open the envelope. There emerged a wad of Swiss bank notes wrapped in a letter.

"We intercepted that just the other day. Forty thousand Swiss francs from your—ah—associates in Geneva. They don't seem to bother too much about—ah—currency regulations."

Brand placed the envelope with its contents on the table before him.

"No! Take it! It's yours. We don't mind." Eichmann turned to his standing adjutant. "Bauer, have Herr Brand sign a receipt. Not now. Later. For our records. Forty thousand francs. But you'll need much more if we are to complete our bargain. This will buy you only a hundred Jews or so."

"I must go abroad to get you what you want."

"By all means," said Eichmann. "Go to Switzerland."

"I'd rather go to Istanbul. It's nearer to Jerusalem. And from there I can contact London—or New York."

"That's all right, too. Telephone. Tell them you're coming." He turned to Krumey. "See that he gets all he needs. And book a seat on the plane. Charge the ticket to the office. You'll be our guest, Herr Brand. Bauer! Inform IV B-Four in Vienna. Copy to Berlin." He was quickly clicking off more details. "Make a note of it, Bauer." To Brand he said, "Do you have a passport? I assume you are a Hungarian citizen?"

"Yes, sir."

"We don't want the Hungarians to know about this. If

they did, they would want the money for themselves. Et cetera. Krumey will get you a German passport."

It was all happening too quickly for Brand. "Our people in Istanbul will want some sort of guarantee," he said. "They will want to be sure that you keep your side of the bargain."

"Man, you are not on Jew Street here! You are speaking to a German officer!"

It was the first time that Eichmann had raised his voice. There was a shrill grinding tone to it. In his rage he had knocked a glass from the low table. But in his violence Eichmann seemed to arrive at the truth of his madness, and at something like a cure, for he calmed down immediately. He could reason again. "What do you mean by guarantees?"

"It is not I who need convincing, sir. But, quite naturally, my colleagues abroad will want some reassurance before they pay. Stop the deportations, sir. If the deportations continue nobody in Istanbul will believe me."

"No. The deportations continue. Otherwise your—ah—associates will think they can get their Jews for nothing. And then never pay up. The deportations will teach them we mean business."

Krumey spoke. "Excuse me, Colonel. If I may say so, it is none of my business, but Herr Brand may have a point there. Why not approach the arrangement in stages? If one stage succeeds, we start on the next."

"I will make only one concession. While you are gone, the deportations continue. But I agree to reroute them, to, let us say, Austria. I'll keep your Jews there for you—on ice." He grinned. "But you must return quickly with a positive answer."

"I shall."

"I give you two weeks."

"Sir, two weeks is not enough . . ."

"I don't expect the trucks in two weeks. Just a simple

'yes' or 'no.' If it's 'yes' I show my good will and give you ten thousand—no, twenty thousand—as an advance. Children, and some old women. We'll put them on the Swiss border for you."

"We will take them to Palestine," said Brand.

"No. They go to Switzerland. Or you take them to Spain. After that you start the deliveries. We begin ours. For each truck you deliver I'll give you a hundred Jews. Fill the trucks with chemicals, or coffee, I'll give you even more Jews. Is that clear? More goods, more Jews! And tell them the trucks will go only to the Eastern front. Word of honor! They don't have to worry about them being used in the West."

"You must give me more time. Even if my colleagues in Istanbul agree immediately, they will need time to get Allied approval."

"You have two weeks. That's enough for a simple 'yes' or 'no,' yes? Fly to London if you have to." Eichmann rose. "I don't want the Hungarians to know about it. Is that clear? Cable me at the Hotel Continental in Vienna."

"Yes, sir."

"Don't use my name. I have a splendid idea! Cable me under the name—Herzl."

"Sir?"

"Yes. Herzl, care of the Hotel Continental." Eichmann smiled. "Herzl. Now there was a great Jew. But he is dead. Buried in Vienna."

"You see," Krumey said, "the colonel knows everything."

Eichmann was still grinning. "I gave instructions that his grave be kept up. Nice and tidy always. You cable me under his name. Is that clear?"

Brand swallowed.

"I said, is that clear?"

"Yes, sir." Brand stood up. He felt slightly dizzy. Two waiters had materialized through the walls and were clear-

ing the table, silent as ghosts, emptying ashtrays and
straightening cushions and chairs. Outside the clouds had
burst. The rain beat down against the french windows.

Eichmann spoke. "I don't think there is anything left to
discuss. Ah, yes. One small matter."

"Sir?"

"You have a wife and two children?"

Brand nodded.

"They remain here. To guarantee your return. But they
will be under my protection. Bauer!"

"Yes, sir."

"Make out three special passes."

"Yes, sir."

"For the others the deportations begin tonight. For your
information, Herr Brand! To a transit point in Slovakia.
Good-bye, Herr Brand."

The adjutant opened the door. Eichmann and Krumey
remained standing at the windows. Brand walked out. As
the door closed behind him he heard Eichmann picking up
the telephone. "Schöller! Call the estate. I want to ride this
afternoon. . . . Yes. Never mind the rain!"

* * *

He crossed the vast lobby, past the concierge hovering
over his elaborate carved box of keys, the secretaries and
typists and uniformed doormen. He stepped out into the
rain. The paved drive was grimy and slippery with puddles.
The sun had not been seen for days. He walked down with
an uneasy step. The steep hill, falling from the front terrace to the banks of the Danube, seemed a deadly precipice
under his feet. As he walked toward the waiting limousine,
he grasped at the white railings to steady himself. An unseasonal cold wind was sweeping up from the road below.

Inside Eichmann's heavy car it was stuffy and hot. He
wiped his face with a handkerchief. There was a faint smell
of perfume in the car. He lowered the window. The car was

just crossing the river and slowing down. Brand knocked at the glass partition. "Here," he said hoarsely, "I'll get out here."

The great chestnut trees along the quay were in full bloom. There were few people about. Brand buttoned his coat and hurried up Andrassy Utza. Outside of Gerbaud's pastry shop, where the windows were filled with gleaming Easter eggs, he found a taxi.

A few minutes later he ran up the three flights of stairs and let himself into his apartment. Hansi was waiting by the door. Her hair was bound into a bun and her eyes were dark with worry. He handed her his wet overcoat.

She said, "Kastner and Komoly are in the living room."

He walked quickly past her and went in. The men embraced. Brand heaved himself into an upholstered chair. For a moment he looked at them, saying nothing. Hansi and the two men waited. The room was filled with cigarette smoke. Brand began to speak. Slowly, in a hollow voice, he gave them a dry, matter-of-fact account of what had happened in Eichmann's suite. Hansi was hardened by her work in the underground. Like the two men, she remained mute.

When Brand finished, there was a long pause. Finally Kastner said, "This is sheer madness. The Allies will never allow them trucks in the middle of a war. And chemicals, yet."

"But maybe coffee and medicine," Brand said. "And money! I tell you, they want money! It ties in exactly with what Schmidt and Wislizeny told us." His forehead was covered with perspiration. "I tell you, it will work!" he cried.

Hansi said, "To me it looks like a trap."

"We don't risk anything!" Brand shouted. "All is lost anyway! I shall go to Istanbul!"

"What will you tell them?"

"I'll tell them that they want money."

"Eichmann wants trucks."

"We'll promise him trucks. We don't have to be in any rush to deliver them."

"You think you can fool him?"

"Yes."

"Not for long."

"It may give us an opportunity to delay . . ." said Komoly. "The Russians may be in Budapest within a month. Every day we delay Eichmann, we save thousands of lives."

"Tens of thousands," Brand said, more calmly now. "I must go to Istanbul. If I don't there is no hope. If I do, maybe there is an outside chance. Let's telephone Istanbul now."

The others exchanged glances. "I will speak to them," said Kastner. He agreed that even the slightest delay would be a gift from heaven. Yet Kastner was not sure that Brand should be the one to undertake the mission.

Not that he disliked or distrusted Brand. On the contrary, he appreciated Brand's ingenuity and courage. No one in the network was more adept at forging Swedish passports or smuggling Slovak and Polish Jews into Hungary. But Kastner thought that as the committee's political officer *he* should have dealt with Eichmann, not Brand. When they had paid Wislizeny his advance, Kastner had expected himself to be called to the Majestic. But instead Brand was summoned.

Aloud, he said, "Don't fool yourself. It's going to be very tough for you in Istanbul. They'll laugh when they hear you want trucks."

"I know that very well."

"Perhaps we'd better send a man who has had some legal training. And a certain amount of diplomatic experience."

But Komoly said firmly, "We don't need a lawyer. We need a man we can trust." What is even more important,

Komoly thought, Brand is a man *others* trust. He is that kind of man.

Hansi protested. "Joel is needed here. You can't ask that he leave his children as hostages."

But Komoly brushed her aside. "Joel goes."

Kastner, as usual, deferred to Komoly, and guessing the real reason for Komoly's preference for Brand, he thought, yes, he is without guile. Aloud he said, "Be on your guard in Istanbul."

"Don't worry. I know the Germans."

"I don't mean the Germans. I mean the British. It isn't every day that Eichmann sends out an emissary to a neutral country."

Komoly said, "The first thing you must do in Turkey is get in touch with the American ambassador. He will understand. You'll be met by our own people at the airport—Steiner and the others. They'll put you in touch with him."

Brand said, "Kleinmann is already there. It's a good thing we sent him. He'll help to explain the situation here." He was speaking more calmly now but his face was pale. The scene in Eichmann's suite lingered in his consciousness, unassimilated, threatening. He sat upright and very stiffly in his chair. He lit another cigarette. He closed his eyes briefly and saw the two uniforms and boots outlined against the tall french windows. He opened his eyes, the same ghostly view remained imprinted there, as on a doubly exposed film. A wave of wild, perhaps blind, courage mounted within him. He looked up almost imperiously at his colleagues as if he had suddenly brought them within his power.

Hansi booked the telephone call to Istanbul. "Person-to-person, please. Mr. Steiner. S-t-e-i-n-e-r . . ."

Two hours later, Kastner shouted into the receiver. "Joel is flying out to Istanbul! On a most vital mission! Can you hear me?" The connection was bad, the voices drowned in mysterious Morse signals. "No, not Joseph! Joel! Joel

Brand! Did you get that? Ask Kleinmann. . . . What? I can't hear you! Can you hear me? It's a matter of life and death. He must be met. Steiner—do you hear me? Inform London! And Jerusalem! Tell them he's coming, they must meet him! Everything here depends on it! . . . What? Yes, we'll cable you his arrival. . . . No! He must come back in two weeks! . . . What? Hello! Steiner! I can't hear you! Hello! Hello!"

The connection was broken off. Kastner put the receiver down. "He said something about Kleinmann."

"What?"

"I don't know. I couldn't hear what he was saying. But he got our message. At least the important part of it."

When the two men had left, Brand and Hansi returned to the small sitting room.

"You don't want me to go."

"That's not true. It's clear you must go."

"I can stay. Kastner might go instead. He seemed rather anxious."

"No. The Germans want you. You must go."

"Perhaps he'd do a better job."

"No."

Brand looked at her through narrowed eyes. It suddenly seemed to him that she looked relieved. She wanted him to leave. Her dark eyes were large and her face was smooth. No, he thought, no. It is her way of hiding her emotions.

"You want me to go, then," he said a bit petulantly.

"I didn't say that."

"When I come back," he began, "we two might try . . ."

"Yes, of course," she said quickly, and turned to go to the children's room. Brand followed slowly. They looked down at the two boys sleeping in their beds.

The doorbell shattered the heavy silence, followed by rude knocking. Brand rushed to open the door. Two Hungarian policemen pushed into the flat.

"Who's been making telephone calls to Turkey from here?"

"I have."

"What's your name?"

"Brand."

"You're in contact with the enemy."

"No. It was a normal business call."

"We'll see about that. Now you come with us."

The two men grabbed Brand roughly by his arms and pushed him out. The stairway was badly lit. Brand bumped his foot against the balustrade. A sharp pain rushed through his leg. He stooped to rub it with his hand. The policeman pulled him up and dragged him down the stairs. Hansi watched from the doorway. As soon as they had reached the next landing, she ran back to the telephone.

* * *

Schmidt drove him home the next morning shortly before lunchtime. The rain had ceased. The city was cast in a yellowish haze. Schmidt was jovial. "It seems to be my job these days to get you out of jail," he said. The fat little eyes winked in the folds of the fleshy face. "It's a good thing your wife reached me this morning. But it's getting more difficult every time."

"Oh?" said Brand, a little absentmindedly, rubbing the palm of his hand against his unshaven face. He had been questioned for hours by the Hungarian security police, but as soon as Schmidt had entered the commissar's room and flashed his identification, they had allowed him to go.

"What did you tell them?" Schmidt asked casually. His eyes were trained on the road ahead. "I hope not too much."

"Nothing."

"They questioned you for a long time."

"I kept saying I was calling Istanbul on business."

"That was the only reason they pulled you in?"

"Yes. But I said nothing about our—affairs."

"Good," said Schmidt, pursing his lips. "The less they know, the better for all—of you."

The car stopped at an intersection. Schmidt turned his head. "I understand you had an interesting talk with Colonel Eichmann."

"It was just a preliminary chat."

"I would hope it was worth the—ah—expenditure."

"Certainly we are very grateful to you."

Schmidt dropped his usual bonhomie. His voice came out hard. "Listen, any financial transactions—all deals—go through me. Is that understood? No deals with anybody from now on except through me!"

"I wouldn't dream of doing anything behind your back."

"Then you are well advised. Eichmann's days as top man on Jewish affairs are numbered anyway. The Wehrmacht is taking charge. If you people want something done, you'd better deal with us."

"Of course."

Schmidt accompanied Brand to his flat. He bowed over Hansi's hand. "It was nothing, *gnädige Frau*. Pleased to have been of help." When the door was shut, Brand said, "He warned me against making a deal with Eichmann. He wants me to deal only with him. The rats are already fighting over the booty."

"What are you going to do?"

"I'll stick with Eichmann. He runs the slaughterhouse."

The doorbell rang. Hansi started. Brand opened the door cautiously. A lanky youth dressed in a long leather coat stood outside. Brand sighed with relief. The boy was a runner for the committee who had been sent to Bratislava a few days before. The boy slipped a coded note out from between the soles of his shoe.

Hansi went to her desk to decipher it. Brand looked on as she worked out the short message.

WE ARE TOLD BY RELIABLEST SOURCES THAT
THURSDAY AGREEMENT WAS SIGNED BETWEEN
HUNGARIAN, GERMAN, SLOVAK STATE RAILROADS
ADMINISTRATIONS TO RUN 180 SPECIAL FREIGHT
TRAINS FROM HUNGARY TO AUSCHWITZ BEGIN-
NING MAY 15. POLISH COMRADES REPORT EIGHT
NEW GAS CHAMBERS COMPLETED SECOND WEEK
MARCH. WE ARE TRYING TO OBTAIN LAYOUT.

* * *

The next ten days were spent in agonizing anticipation.
It was up to Krumey to set the exact date and manner of
Brand's departure. For some reason the Germans were taking their time. Brand had another meeting at the Hotel
Majestic. This time Kastner went along, and the proposed
deal was discussed once more at great length. One million
Jews. Ten thousand trucks. Eighty tons of coffee, twenty
tons of tea, fifteen million bars of soap, or alternatively,
gold and hard currency. On 15 May they were told that a
seat had been secured for Brand on the weekly plane leaving Vienna in three days time. They wired Istanbul and received a cable back on the next day.

JOEL SHOULD COME CHAIM AWAITS HIM.

Hansi looked up, puzzled. "Chaim?" If it was a code
name she was not familiar with it. "What does it mean?"

"What a question!" Brand said excitedly. "It's Chaim
Weizmann!" This augured well for the success of his mission. Chaim Weizmann was president of the World Zionist
Organization, the unofficial leader of all the world's Jews,
and a close friend of Winston Churchill. He was obviously
flying from London especially to meet him. They would
work out the agreement together. Weizmann was taking
the matter seriously, as he should.

To further enhance Brand's status, Komoly and Kastner
decided to approach their timid adversaries on the board of

the official Central Council of Hungarian Jews to solicit
their formal support for the mission. It was readily granted.
Hofrat Samuel Stern and Philip von Freudiger (both
members of the Upper House of the Hungarian Parliament) gave Brand a formal "letter of accreditation." The
letter emphasized Brand's selfless and courageous contri-
bution to the cause of rescue and confirmed that "Herr Joel
Brand undertakes his journey in the interest of the entire
Jewish community of Hungary and we urge all those concerned to assist him in his efforts [in the task] which he
will explain in person. . . ."

On the morning of 17 May he packed a small suitcase.
The family sat around the living room. The blackout cur-
tains were lifted, but the drapes remained drawn. The light
was diffused through their burnished pattern. Hansi had ordered them from Paris before the war.

He looked at her. "You are still not sure I should go."

"I didn't say that."

"You don't really believe that it will work."

"I have to believe it."

He thought he sensed a certain sarcasm in her retort.
No, it was not sarcasm. It might be resentment, yes. Aloud,
he said, "I love you."

"What about me?"

"You are safe. And the children are safe. I'll be back in
two weeks."

"Yes."

"Yes." He held her hand, trying desperately to smile. She
shook her head. He withdrew his hand. It was covered with
sweat. The children were told that their father was going
off on a short trip and would soon return. Just before
eleven Brand rose to leave. The tension in Hansi's face dis-
solved into sobs. Brand held her wet face in his hands.
"There is nothing to worry about. I will be back in two
weeks."

There were no taxis. He walked the fifteen blocks to the

Cafe Opera—the Nazis seemed to know of no other meeting point. Punctually at noon a black Opel drew up alongside the curb. Colonel Krumey was in the front seat next to the driver. In the back was another man, dressed in a light beige overcoat. Brand started.

"You know Andrew Gyorgy, don't you?" Krumey said.

"We have met, yes. Hello."

"Mr. Gyorgy is going to be your traveling companion."

"Oh?"

"I'm sure you two will get on splendidly. But you look surprised."

"Not really," said Brand, and settled back in his seat. He was seething with fear and confusion. Why was Gyorgy coming along too? To make his 10 per cent commission? To inform on him? In all his negotiations with the Germans there had not been so much as a mention of a shadow.

Gyorgy seemed completely at ease. He was leafing through an illustrated magazine. They drove on in silence. The narrow streets of Buda gradually melted into open farmland. Soon there was nothing but rolling vineyards, orchards and pasture on both sides of the road. A light drizzle fell. At Tato the wide expanse of bright-green corn seedlings spread out over the wet plains as far as the eye could see. Gyorgy was doing a crossword puzzle. "A very rich country," commented Krumey. "Put a stick in the ground and it grows into a tree."

"Good firewood," Gyorgy said casually. They reached the outskirts of Komárom. The pink turreted walls of the old medieval town alongside the Danube hugged the low hillside. As the car passed through the center, Brand's eyes nervously searched down the narrow lanes. There were very few people about; it might be because of the bad weather. Reports had reached the committee just before Brand's departure that the Jews of Komárom had been rounded up and locked into a pen surrounding the ancient synagogue.

Krumey suggested a short break for lunch. "A very good idea," Gyorgy said, and put his magazine down. Brand said nothing. It occurred to him that in their deliberately casual manners, the three of them were acting out a sort of shadow play. Each played his own part in his own way; layers and layers of shapes and designs were carefully scissored and trimmed upon the screen of make-believe. It reminded him of something he had once seen as a young sailor in Japan. The real protagonists were offstage, locked behind the boarded-up alleyways of a thousand ghettos.

Over lunch they spoke of airplanes. Gyorgy ordered a round of *barack,* the heavy, dry plum brandy that was a specialty of the region. Krumey grumbled at the unavailability of coffee. He told Brand, "You must bring me a few kilos from Istanbul." Afterward he ordered his driver to make a short detour. The car drove past dilapidated tenements to an old railroad depot. Before the war it had served as a siding for local food-processing and bottling plants. It was unexpectedly alive and crowded with human activity. A heavily armed ring of Hungarian field gendarmerie parted at the sight of Krumey's official car and waved them through. There were no Germans to be seen. The deportation of some two thousand Jews was being handled by Hungarians only.

The car stopped short of a long loading ramp. It was packed with dark clusters of men, women and children. They were being herded into cattle cars, and as each wagon filled, the doors were boarded up and nailed tight. Other than the hammering and occasional shouting of the guards there was not a sound. The deportees had a blank look, beyond terror or despair, expressionless, like dead fish.

Krumey got out and slammed the door behind him. The car was filled with a sharp stench of steam and coal.

Brand's eyes followed Krumey as he hurried through the rain up a short flight of steps. Krumey shook hands with a stout Hungarian officer. The two men conferred briefly. Then Krumey rushed back into the car. A look of satisfaction spread across his face.

"I thought it might be a good idea to pass by here, Herr Brand. You did take a good look around, didn't you? Fine. It should make your colleagues in Istanbul shake a leg."

Then he settled back comfortably. They heard the loud rumble of a train. The car moved on. Krumey lit a cigarette. It would not be true to say that he was driven by hatred. He was a careerist. From the humdrum and poverty of a *petit-bourgeois* family in a dreary little upper Austrian town he had worked his way up through the ranks. If until now the murder of Jews had bolstered the career of a man of his background and élan (the policy-makers in Berlin were all too elegant to soil their hands in sordid detail) he hoped that the new policy from Berlin—to gain economic advantage by keeping the Jews alive—might further his career even more. Yes, it might even seriously improve Germany's fading chances to win the war. In the back of Krumey's mind there was also a vague notion that he might emerge from all this a very rich man. And with that disingenuousness which is essential to a long uninterrupted chain of successful crimes, he even felt virtuous.

It was in this frame of mind that his manner suddenly changed to something like charm. He said warmly, "But please, this was only a temporary diversion you just saw." He drew a little circle in the air. "I assure you, Herr Brand, Colonel Eichmann will keep his other promises, too. These people are not going anywhere terrible. We are sending them to Waldsee, in lower Austria. A beautiful spot in the woods. Fresh air and a cool mountain lake to swim in. They'll be well taken care of. Until your return."

"I understand," Brand said hoarsely. His face was taut and strained, as though he were facing a strong wind.

"You will be back in time, won't you?"

"Yes."

"Good."

"If you keep your promises," Brand said, "we will keep our side of the bargain too. My associates are waiting for me. Professor Weizmann has flown to Istanbul especially. This should show you how seriously we take the offer."

"Fine. I hope the professor is well. We can settle all this in a decent way." (The word Krumey used was *anständig*.) "And, gentlemen, be sure this is all just temporary. For the war. Afterward we can all be *gemütlich* again."

The rest of the journey was uneventful. There were no guards on the Austrian border. They drove straight through to Vienna without a stop. Krumey put them up at the Hotel Continental, which was the Vienna headquarters of the Gestapo.

Early next morning he returned and drove them to the airport. Brand wore the gray overcoat and red-striped woolen scarf by which he knew his friends in Istanbul would recognize him. This too had been prearranged.

Krumey was all smiles. He handed Brand a letter addressed to Dr. Hoffmann, at the German Legation in Istanbul. "He is your contact there," he said. "Stay in touch. He will help you." He took out their tickets and a crisp new German passport for Brand. "Do you like your new name?" Krumey grinned. "They've called you Band, not Brand. I don't know why."

"It will do," Brand said. He reached for the passport and tickets with an outstretched hand, as across a chasm.

"I must ask you to pay me for the tickets," Krumey said.

"Right now?" Brand asked. He had assumed it was being charged to Eichmann's office.

Gyorgy sensed his hesitation. "It's only money. You should be very indebted to Colonel Krumey."

Krumey stuffed the money into his coat pocket. At the foot of the plane he made a special show of introducing Brand to the chief pilot. Everyone bowed. It was like the end—or the beginning—of an official state visit.

"*Auf Wiedersehen.*" The plane warmed its engines and took off into the mist.

Arrival, 18 May 1944

Two men had been watching Brand's arrival at Istanbul airport through the window of an adjacent waiting room. The beam of the powerful searchlight threw a bright crescent over the port side of the plane. The two men leaned forward eagerly. When Brand, whom they recognized by the red-striped scarf, came down the stairway together with Andrew Gyorgy, one of the men turned sharply.

"Mark! What in hell does this mean?"

The other man did not move. "I don't know, Steiner. Relax."

"Something is foul."

Mark said nothing. He was the younger of the two. His hands were thrust into the pockets of a trench coat and his face was half hidden under the raised collar.

The older man squeezed his arm. "How can you be so damned calm? Don't you see? It's a trap."

The younger man still said nothing. He edged away slightly, to free himself.

"Damn it, Mark! Don't you recognize him? I'm sure it's Gyorgy. The Gestapo man. He was mixed up in the break-in at the British Embassy. Everybody in Istanbul knows him. What is Brand doing with that rat?"

"We'll have to see."

"Let's get out of here."

"Why?"

"Damn it, you know why! I can't afford to be seen with him. It would ruin me!"

Brand and Gyorgy were walking across the tarmac toward the security control. Brand seemed to be explaining something to Gyorgy.

"Don't panic, Steiner," Mark said calmly.

"I should have known better than to take you out here with me. Okay. Do what you want. I'm leaving." Steiner turned abruptly and quickly walked toward the door.

"All right, all right," Mark said. "I'll get the car. We can always find Brand later on."

In the car a few moments later, Steiner said heatedly, "I don't understand you. It was clear. They are traveling together. As a pair."

"Perhaps not," said Mark. His eyes strained through the rain-swept windshield at the dark road ahead. "It could be coincidence."

"It is more likely a trap," said Steiner. "I shall have nothing to do with that man. You people deal with him, if you must!"

"All right, all right!"

"Keep me out of it. I cannot risk my position," Steiner said with finality. "I have no right to. I could be thrown out of Turkey on a day's notice."

"Don't exaggerate."

"Oh, damn you," Steiner said, buttoning up his raincoat with nervous little fingers. He was a lean fussy man in his early fifties. His thin frame was crowned by a mane of white hair which he was continually pushing back with the palms of his hands. As the Istanbul representative of the Jewish Agency for Palestine (a charitable organization) he had no official standing. His delicate task was to maintain whatever contact possible with Jews in Nazi-occupied Europe, but without violating Turkish neutrality or arousing the suspicions of British counterintelligence.

The harsh, though often erratic, laws of Turkey re-

stricted him to welfare work among the handful of refugees
who managed each month to escape to Turkey. The
Turkish Government, when it did not send them back to
Nazi Germany, was forever pressing Steiner to get them
out of the country. Yet the escape route to Palestine, which
was Steiner's other main responsibility, was blocked by the
British authorities, who had imposed severe restrictions on
Jewish immigration.

He was a diplomat without status or protection, negotiating (pleading would be a better word) with Turkish bureaucrats, foreign consuls and Red Cross officials. His personal position in a country where the pro-German party
was still quite strong and pro-Arab sympathies were ramp-
ant was precarious in the extreme, and his diffidence was as
much a part of his character as it was a requirement of his
job. In his efforts to step on no toes, he rarely moved in
any direction at all.

"Damn you," he said again. The rain was beating at the
windshield.

"I'm sorry," Mark said, "I didn't mean to be offensive."
Mark was one of a dozen clandestine Jewish agents from
Palestine who had been sent to Turkey at the beginning of
the war under various convenient disguises. His cover was
that of foreign correspondent for the Tel Aviv daily newspaper *Davar*. He was not as exposed as Steiner, less en-
cumbered by notions of legality or status. He and his clandestine companions—men doubling as commercial agents,
shipping representatives, teachers, even agents of British
intelligence—had volunteered for tasks that were as demanding as they were dangerous. Their job was to save as
many Jews as they could, through whatever means they
might. For years they had been smuggling Jews into Turkey and out to Palestine, a handful here, a small boatload
there. Mark's instructions came not from Steiner but from
the illegal defense organization of the Palestinian Jews
Haganah.

By role and temperament no two men could have been more dissimilar. Mark was at home in the murky labyrinth of Istanbul harbor, the shady nether world of smugglers, spies, double and triple agents. He disdained the legal niceties and inefficacy of Steiner's bureaucratic world. And although they frequently had to consult, Steiner was careful to disassociate himself from Mark and all his works.

Steiner had been perplexed by Brand's sudden and mysteriously heralded arrival. He had never heard the name before. Kastner, yes, but Kastner's voice on the telephone had sounded so strange. And had it really been him? It was difficult to tell.

Brand's arrival on the arm of Andrew Gyorgy made it all look even more suspicious. Gyorgy was known in Istanbul as a smuggler who doubled as a German agent and was moreover involved in shady business deals with certain Turkish politicians. When the butler of the British ambassador had recently been exposed as a German spy (not before escaping with the secret contents of the ambassador's safe) Gyorgy was said to have been one of his accomplices. The British were known to have put a price on his head. He was also said to have doubled-crossed a branch of Turkish intelligence known as Bureau D.

The car was approaching the city center. "How do we know Brand is really a Jewish emissary?" Steiner said.

"We don't. But we got Kastner's message, didn't we?" Mark said. "Kastner made it quite clear."

"Maybe . . . but this Gyorgy . . . he is up to something with Brand. I'd like to know what it is."

"Money, of course." Mark paused. "Gyorgy works for us, too, you know."

"You must be out of your minds! A Gestapo man?"

"So what? He does what we need. We owe him fifty thousand dollars."

"Don't tell me. I mustn't know about these things."

"Okay. By the way, Gyorgy is a Jew. Did you know that?"

"A Jew?"

"Yes. A Jew. Well, maybe not really. He's just Jew-ish. Not the whole hog."

Steiner grimaced. He disliked these trite flippancies. Why does he always have to clown, he thought. Everything was always a cabaret act. Aloud he said, "But what is he up to?"

"I told you. Money."

"And Brand?"

Mark shrugged his shoulders. Brand was an enigma.

* * *

The subject of these suspicions and concerns, meanwhile, had just been placed under arrest and faced the security officer with a bewildered eye.

"But you don't understand. I am on an official mission. There are important people waiting for me here in Istanbul. I'm sure some of them are here right now."

"Oh?" The officer leafed through the passport once again. "It says here you are an engineer."

"What it says is beside the point. I tell you I am on an official mission."

"We've had no word from the Foreign Ministry about that. Would you like us to contact the German Embassy?"

"I am not a German courier. I am being met by the Jewish leader Chaim Weizmann. He's flown especially from London to see me."

"I don't know what you are talking about. Let us call the German Embassy." He reached for the telephone.

"Don't!"

The officer put down the receiver. "You go back to Vienna early tomorrow morning when the plane turns around. You'll find a Turkish Consulate in Vienna. If they give you a visa"—he sounded doubtful—"you come back. Follow me now."

"One moment, please. Let me explain. My friends here will . . ."

"I have other work to do. Follow me now."

He led Brand to an adjoining room and closed the door. There was a wooden desk with an old typewriter and a dusty telephone. Brand sat down heavily in a rickety cane chair and looked at his watch. It was close to 11 P.M.

Presently the door flew open. Andrew Gyorgy strode in, lively and officious, followed by the security officer. Gyorgy's face was beaming. "My dear fellow," he said, "wherever would you be without me?"

The security man closed the door firmly and leaned against it. Gyorgy handed him a bundle of bank notes.

The guard looked down at his palm. "I am not sure . . ."

"I am," said Gyorgy confidently, and handed him another note. "Two hundred fifty Swiss francs! Really now." He pointed to the telephone. "Is this the outside line? Thank you so much."

Brand stirred nervously. "Who are you calling? Not the German Embassy?"

"Of course not. I am calling my friend Kuzuk, in Bureau D." He nodded toward the security man. "He is his friend too. You will like him. Very much."

* * *

The restaurant was crowded in spite of the late hour. Clouds of cigarette smoke hung in the hot air over tables laden with dirty plates and bottles and glasses and ashtrays filled to the brim. The room was saturated with the pungent smell of charcoal and grilled meat. They were crowded at a table too small for four, too many for the tired waiter who, harassed by the owner, was at this moment contemplating his resignation. The food arrived lukewarm after a long wait.

Major Kuzuk accepted the long delay and disorder with the sardonic air of one content in the discreet, sweeter exercises of power. His dark face was smooth, with just a touch of insolence. He leaned forward intimately.

"What you say sounds most interesting, Dr. Gyorgy."

"More than interesting," said Gyorgy. "These officers are at the top of the German Army. Himmler is one of them. They will make a decisive move within weeks."

"How do you think they'll proceed?"

"Eh, who can tell?" answered Gyorgy. "My hunch is that they'll knock off Hitler. After that, who knows? They'll sue for peace. But one guess is as good as the next."

"Peace where? On all fronts?" asked Kuzuk.

"Oh, don't worry. They only talk about the West. Then they hope you'll all join and help run down the Bolsheviks."

"We are strictly neutral, dear sir," Kuzuk said officiously. He was a patriot of the New Turkey.

"Just in case their plan goes wrong, my contact in Vienna gave me this nice long list of names." Gyorgy unfolded a piece of paper that had been pressed between the bank notes in his wallet. "You'd be surprised who's on it. They all want to be treated nicely when the war is over. They want you to know they're men of good will. They tried their best."

Kuzuk took the paper, looked at it cursorily and folded it into his breast pocket. "And what do you think, Herr Band? I understand you are very well connected in your country."

"I am in little position to tell, sir," Brand said carefully, "but things are moving, there's no doubt." He was grateful to Gyorgy for the intervention at the airport, which had brought about his temporary release, and in some way grateful to Kuzuk too. He wanted to please. "They realize, I am sure, that their ship is sinking. Naturally they are all looking for means to get off." Brand looked down nervously and poked at his dish of burned meat drenched in tepid oil.

"They want a meeting with the Allies," said Gyorgy. "That's the real reason why I came out." He turned smilingly to Brand. "You were just my cover."

"I shall speak to the British," said Kuzuk. "You will hear from me tomorrow. Thank you for the list. It was my pleasure to help you, Herr Band. But please remember, you are only on temporary shore leave, so to speak. I am afraid you must remain at your hotel until this matter is cleared up. We have booked you a room at the Pera Palace. I hope that will be convenient."

"Perfect," said Gyorgy. "An excellent hotel."

"You have understood me, haven't you?" Kuzuk said.

"Certainly," said Brand. "I fully understand." His head was dropping from exhaustion. It was close to 3 A.M. They had left the airport with Kuzuk two hours ago. He was desperate to leave this murky place, to find Dr. Weizmann.

Brand and Gyorgy drove off in a taxi. The wet streets were deserted. The driver nosed the car through the fog that drifted over them in waves. The car bumped in and out of potholes in the road.

"Remember, dear boy," said Gyorgy, holding on to the strap, "you owe me two hundred fifty Swiss francs."

* * *

The Pera Palace was a ramshackle old building built in the nineteenth century as a luxury hotel. Its plush splendor had since frayed and faded; the humidity was peeling the paint off the walls. Brand registered. The light in the hall was dim. The night porter weighed Brand's passport in his hand as though it were a sheet of precious metal.

"How long will you stay with us, sir?"

"Two weeks. Possibly less."

"But this is the best season, sir. Why not stay longer?"

"In this rain?" said Gyorgy. "Ask him again when the

sun is out." He turned to Brand. "I am off. See you in the morning."

The elevator was not working. Brand followed a bellboy to the marble staircase. From somewhere in the shadows, half hidden by a pillar, a man rose from a threadbare armchair. He whispered in English:

"Brand? I am Raskin."

"Who?"

"Jewish Agency."

"Ah, finally." Brand sighed with relief. His drowsiness fell away and he grabbed the man by his hand. "Why weren't you at the airport? I was almost arrested! Didn't you know I was coming?"

"Yes, yes, we know. It's all right. But not here . . ." The stranger looked around worriedly. "We cannot talk here. Let us go to your room."

"Where is Weiz . . . ?"

Raskin hissed, "Not here." He took Brand by his arm and firmly maneuvered him up the two flights of stairs to the landing where the bellboy stood waiting. As soon as he had tipped the boy Raskin closed the door securely on its lock.

"Is Weizmann staying in this hotel too?" Brand asked immediately. "Can we go now to see him? We must not lose any time."

Raskin raised his eyebrows. "Weizmann? Here? In this hotel?"

"But of course. He has been here for days. You cabled us last Tuesday that Chaim was awaiting me."

"Chaim? Oh, but you mean Chaim Steiner. He heads the Jewish Agency office here. He was at the airport this evening but left when he saw you with that man . . . Gyorgy."

Brand was standing frozen in the middle of the room. "You mean . . . you mean . . ." he stammered. His right hand clasped his tie, which he had been about to loosen. For a moment he clung to the hope that perhaps Weizmann had come to Istanbul secretly. Raskin was likely a minor office hand, not fully informed. Then the realization of what Raskin was saying, and his tiredness, hit him like a blow.

"As far as I know, Weizmann is in London. Why on earth should he be here?" Raskin looked at his watch. "Oh my God! Listen, you must be exhausted. I'll let you relax now. Have a bath. Get a good night's rest. I'll come back in the morning. Then we can talk."

"But there's no time. Where in hell is Steiner? Call him now!"

"I can't. Not at this hour."

"But you must! Why can't you?"

"It's three A.M."

Through the large window a deep rumble came in from the direction of the Golden Horn. The parquet floors shook slightly. The roar of the unseen train reached a crescendo, and then died away, as in Komárom the day before.

19 May 1944

It was almost dawn when he sank into a kind of sleep. He tossed about on the bed. Toward seven, the traffic noise outside grew louder, drifting in through the windows with the pale and dusky light. Brand pulled himself out of bed. Torrents of rain were gushing down at the windows and the tiled rooftops on the hillside below. The city was discolored in eerie shades of fog and ash, gray, almost achromatic, and there was no telling where the hillside stopped and the waters of the Golden Horn began. But across the deep gulf of leaden vapor and rain, the minarets of the Blue Mosque protruded out from under the mist like thin daggers.

He showered and put on fresh clothes. The waiter brought him a mug of black coffee. He had not tasted its like in years. At nine there was a gentle knock on his door. It was Raskin.

"I have been expecting you for hours," Brand said. "Where are the others?"

"Mark and Landau are on their way."

"Who are they? Why isn't your man Steiner here?"

"He thinks it's better you talk to us first. You'll like Mark and Landau. They are Palestinians on special duty here."

"They don't interest me. Where is Steiner? He is the head man."

"He is busy this morning. But the others will be here soon."

"I have no time for idle talk. Don't you see how urgent this is? I was sure Weizmann would be here. We must act immediately . . . get in touch with Churchill and Roosevelt."

Raskin stared at him blankly.

"Yes. Churchill! Immediately. Where is Steiner?"

"He had a meeting this morning with the Swiss consul. What do you mean, contact Churchill and Roosevelt?"

"I mean the lives of a million human beings are at stake. This is why I flew here."

"I see," Raskin said slowly. "I don't know what Steiner's other plans are this morning. But he . . . I think perhaps he will call, or drop in later."

"Why isn't Kleinmann here? He knows me! We sent him to Istanbul to be our liaison man here."

"He *was* the liaison man," Raskin said uncomfortably. "But you see, he had a disagreement with Steiner. A week after he arrived Steiner sent him home."

"What?"

"I mean he sent him to Palestine."

"I don't understand."

"You'll understand when you meet Steiner," Raskin said hesitatingly. "He is not the easiest man to get on with. And his responsibilities are very great. Kleinmann gave Steiner too much advice. Steiner—uh—felt he had enough advisers already." He paused. "I hope you have had a good night's rest at least."

Brand swayed lightly on his feet. "Yes," he said in a dry voice. In the awkward silence that followed Raskin walked to the window.

"It's an eerie place, this hotel . . ." he began. "Would you like us to move you to the Majestic? I'm sorry, is something wrong?"

"Nothing. Nothing. Anyway, I can't move from here. The Turks have confined me to this place."

"Ah yes," Raskin said. "I noticed the odd-looking fellow loitering on the staircase. Bureau D. You mustn't worry about him. He is the harmless sort." He looked up at the cracked ceiling. "This was once a very elegant hotel," he continued. "It's part of our history, you know. Theodore Herzl stayed here in 1899. Perhaps in this very room. When he was here to talk to the Sultan about a Jewish state in Palestine."

"You are still only talking! Now it's our turn! The Jews of Hungary go next!"

Raskin swallowed. He didn't want to get into a political argument, especially one so futile. He was a shy young man, and although he was anxious to learn the purpose of Brand's voyage, he did not know where or how to begin. He was also waiting for the others.

Instead, very seriously, he said, "It's really true then. The Germans are killing the Hungarian Jews."

He did not speak in disbelief—Raskin was no innocent —but sadly. He was standing by the desk gazing at Brand with his clear blue eyes. Yet there was something in his voice, perhaps its very gentleness, that grated unbearably upon Brand's nerves.

"What?" he yelled. "Don't you know they are killing us all?"

"Of course I know," Raskin said, perhaps too quickly. "You don't understand. I didn't mean to sound that way. . . . It is just that you are the first man I have seen in months who has managed to get out. Like this." He glanced down at Brand's German passport, which lay on the desk beside him. "The others had to swim across . . ."

Brand pushed the passport aside roughly. Under it lay a yellow sheet. He unfolded it. Raskin saw a sketch of thin lines and arrows drawn in pencil and marked here and there with little inscriptions in ink. It might have been a surveyor's rough sketch of a farm. The creases were frayed from many foldings and unfoldings.

"Take a look at this instead of making silly remarks," Brand said. "It's a sketch drawn by a Slovak Jew who escaped last month from Auschwitz. We got hold of it just before I left. I trust you've heard of Auschwitz?"

"I'm sorry, Brand, I . . ."

"It shows all the new furnaces and gas chambers that were installed there last winter. And the railroad lines leading in from the south. The Allies must bomb them immediately. The railroad lines must be destroyed before it is too late. And the furnaces too. The man who brought out this chart said he'd overheard a German guard telling another, 'Man, we'll soon be getting a fine lot of fat Hungarian sausages. . . .' Do you hear me!" Brand yelled. "A fine lot of Hungarian *sausages!*"

Raskin swallowed again. He picked up the chart and looked at it carefully. "This . . ." he said, and stopped. Then he put the chart back on the table, blinking as though he had just glimpsed into some deep terrible hole. He sat down mutely. The telephone rang. Raskin answered it.

"Yes?" There was a lengthy pause while the caller spoke. "No. I think you are wrong . . . he is not here. No, Brand is alone . . . Fine."

"That was Steiner," Raskin said as he hung up. "He was worried that Gyorgy might be here. But he is on his way over now."

Shortly after eleven Steiner arrived. He was accompanied by Mark and another man. Steiner shook Brand's hand and then turned.

"This is Teddy Mark," Steiner said. "And this is Landau." Landau was an athletic-looking man in his late twenties. He ignored Brand's proffered hand.

Steiner said nervously, "I could not meet you yesterday. You arrived with that seedy Gyorgy."

"It was not my fault. The Nazis forced him on me."

"Why?"

"As a watchdog, of course."

"He is not here now, I hope." Steiner peered at the closed bathroom door.

"No."

"Good."

"Why are you so upset? I know Gyorgy is rotten. But *you* have worked with him before."

"I have never had anything to do with him."

"But . . . but . . . he brought us the last two batches of money."

"That's neither here nor there. The man is dangerous."

"Anyway, I am on my own. Gyorgy has nothing to do with my mission."

"And what is your mission?" Steiner said harshly. His voice cracked a little as he spoke. "You told the Turks you're a German emissary."

"I did not. I am a member of the Budapest Rescue Committee." Brand took out his wallet and produced his letter of credentials.

Steiner inspected it carefully and handed it to Mark. "Anyone can produce a document like this."

"It looks genuine enough," Mark said in a controlled voice. "And after all, Kastner told us on the telephone that he was coming."

"Damn it!" Brand flared up. "And you cabled back that Weizmann was expecting me here!"

"Yes, Raskin told me. I am really very sorry about this." Steiner suddenly looked sad. "It was a misunderstanding."

"A very costly misunderstanding. Call Weizmann now. He must come here immediately. Do you hear? Immediately! We must contact Churchill."

The others exchanged looks. Oh no, Steiner thought, we have another hysteric on our hands. Another Kleinmann.

"Let's not get ahead of ourselves," Mark said wearily. "Tell us first about your mission."

Brand took a deep breath. "Are you sure we are safe here?" he asked. "I mean, are you sure the Germans haven't wired this room?"

"I doubt it," Mark said. But he was not sure. He went over to the radio and switched it on. The room was filled with the sound of string music.

The rain drummed against the window. Brand looked at them questioningly. Then he began to speak, sparing them none of the details and grim side plots. The messenger from Slovakia. The scene at Komárom. Eichmann and Krumey. The certainty of total destruction. The offer of trucks. *Blut gegen Ware. Ware gegen Blut.* Money. The two-week time limit. Kastner. Komoly. The men of the committee. The wife and children he had left behind as hostages. Gyorgy.

The three men listened. Brand continued to talk. No one interrupted. There was something compelling in Brand's telling of this most fantastic of schemes, and in his apparent courage as well. His final words were, "I must go back with an answer. Whatever happens, I must go back within two weeks." He looked around at the stunned faces.

Steiner drew himself up. Behind the bony skull his silver mane rose like a small cloud of smoke. (No, he thought, no, this is not another Kleinmann, come to meddle and impose himself with scenes of futile hysterics. It's a good thing we packed Kleinmann off to Palestine, though, he would have made this situation even more difficult than it is. This man is different. He seems serious.)

Only Landau continued to regard Brand with an oblique and suspicious eye. But he said nothing. All remained silent for a time. Steiner clutched his head in his hands, running his fingers through his hair. His first question was, "Where is Gyorgy now?"

"Don't worry. His room is on another floor."

"Stay away from him. He is dangerous."

"He is only a poor wretch trying to save his skin. Which is more than most of us have been able to do."

"I tell you he is dangerous. He could wreck everything."

"Forget Gyorgy," Brand said tersely. "What is more important is this. . . . Can you decide? Do you have the authority?"

Steiner slowly shook his head. "No."

Brand cried, "You see what you have done! Weizmann should have been here! Eichmann has made us the offer. We must give him an answer. Even if you cannot decide, or if we decide to delay, I must cable Eichmann. Today. At the latest tomorrow."

Steiner shook his head again. "No. I am sorry. This is not something for us. We don't have the authority. This is a political affair. It's too big. Too big for all of us. For you, too."

"We must contact Jerusalem," Raskin said.

"Don't fool yourself," Steiner said. "Nobody in Jerusalem is going to get to Churchill in two weeks. Or even to Roosevelt!"

"Telephone Weizmann!" Brand said. "He is Churchill's friend, isn't he?"

"I am sorry. There are only military phone lines between here and London. They won't let us use them."

"But in God's name! In the meantime tens of thousands will die!"

"There is another possibility," Mark said. He was looking at Steiner. "Let's try to gain time. Brand could go back to Budapest right away. We could bluff our way through the next few weeks. Brand will tell Eichmann that his offer is accepted on principle. The Allies will meet his emissaries in a month's time in Switzerland to work out the details. In the meantime, maybe the killings will be stopped."

"Eichmann is shrewder than you think," Brand said. "He

is not going to take my word for it. I promised him Weizmann's."

"Let's write a letter right now. I'll sign Weizmann's name," Mark said. We don't lose anything, he thought. Weizmann can always deny it. He couldn't be held responsible for a forged signature. Aloud he said, "The Nazis will never know it wasn't him."

"Stop this nonsense!" Steiner said angrily. "I am responsible here. We can't afford to act on our own. It is not in our jurisdiction. This thing is too big. I'll cable Jerusalem."

Brand jumped up. "No! No! Cables take days. Your decoding clerk in Jerusalem will be away for the weekend! Why can't Weizmann come here right away? He hasn't even been told of my arrival! Do you want thousands to die because he didn't hop onto a plane in time?"

They had been speaking English. Steiner suddenly threw a few curt Hebrew words at Mark.

"What's that? What did you say? What are you keeping from me?"

"Brand, please. Don't upset yourself. We were only trying to think of another way to get the message to Jerusalem."

"We have no time to lose! Don't you understand? There must be some telephone line to Jerusalem. Tell them to send someone right away. Someone who *can* decide. Weizmann!"

"Weizmann is in London . . ."

"Well, Ben Gurion then. Or Shertok. Some famous name everyone knows. The Germans here follow my every move. They must tell Eichmann that somebody important has really met me here. It's essential. Then I go back."

He paused, gasping with frustration and impatience. The headache was returning. "I will cable Eichmann myself. I'll tell him the offer is accepted in principle provided the deportations are stopped."

"You must *not* cable Eichmann before we hear from Jerusalem. You have no right . . ."

"But we must tell them *something*. They've given me the name of a certain German here . . ."

"Who?"

"Werner Hoffmann. He's a diplomat at their embassy."

"For God's sake, stay away from him. He is the local Gestapo chief."

"But I must. They've given me a letter . . ."

"You will do as we say. Don't contact that man."

"Then telephone Jerusalem now!"

"Dear Brand, this isn't something I can discuss with Jerusalem on the telephone." Steiner resumed his patient tone. "I don't give Ben Gurion orders. Please understand my situation. We must be patient. We must cable and wait."

"But we lose time! I cannot lose more time! Eichmann gave me two weeks! Two days are already wasted! Every single day twelve thousand Hungarian Jews are driven off in cattle cars. Eichmann promised to keep them in Austria —'on ice,' he said—until I come back. If we don't give him an answer, these people will go straight to the furnaces."

"We can't possibly deliver him the trucks in two weeks even if Churchill himself agrees to the transaction."

"But we don't have to deliver the trucks! Don't you understand? Mark understands. Why can't you? We say we agree *in principle*. Then we say we'll meet them next month in Switzerland. To work out the details. We offer them food. Or just money. I know them. They *want* money. The ground is falling away from under them. They *want* to strike a bargain. They'll stop the killing, at least for now. And meantime the Russians advance into Hungary. We win time. And time gains lives!"

Landau rose. He had not uttered a word throughout the

entire proceedings. "Mark and I have an appointment at two," he said with a slightly embarrassed air. "I am sorry."

Mark shook Brand's hand. Landau did not. The two men left the room. Steiner and Raskin remained seated.

"But this is awful," said Brand. "You don't know what you are doing. Their blood will be on your hands. Let me fly to Jerusalem now, this afternoon!"

"The next plane leaves day after tomorrow," Steiner explained quietly. "I doubt whether you can get a seat. You don't have the necessary papers, or priority clearance. And even if you do get on the plane, the British in Jerusalem will arrest you as a German spy."

"We smuggled Jews out of the Polish ghettos! And you are telling me you cannot get me to Jerusalem? Or don't you want to?"

"Brand, I must make you understand. We are not a government. We are here on sufferance, on good will. Mark and Raskin and Landau are here under false cover. I am the Jewish Agency, yes, but I tread on thin ice. The Turks can throw me out at a moment's notice. Jerusalem does not belong to us either. We are on sufferance there too. We depend on the British in every way. Some things we can do. And some we cannot."

Steiner paused, searching his mind for more words. Could it be that we have another Kleinmann on our hands after all, he thought. If he was no longer suspicious of Brand's integrity, he was beginning to be impatient with his manner. He thought, this man thinks he is the Savior himself. There were no Saviors in Steiner's world.

Raskin opened a window to allow fresh air into the stuffy, smoke-filled room. The whistle of a train came in through the fog. Brand started.

"What's the matter?"

"Nothing."

"I understand," Steiner said gently. "Listen, Brand. You are overwrought. It is natural. You haven't had a decent rest. You have been through hell. Have a bath. Take a nap. Please. We shall do our best. There is little we can do at this moment but wait. I promise you, we'll hear from Jerusalem in a few days."

"And if we don't?"

"We must report your mission to British intelligence here anyway. I hope they'll contact London directly. That way we'll bring Weizmann into the picture. They'll pass the message on to him."

"Are you sure?"

"Almost certain."

"I thought you said they'll consider me a German spy . . ."

"They will. But they'll pass the message on. They may not like us, but they are gentlemen. It's never failed before."

"I hope you're right. Surely they are in instant touch with London?"

"Of course they are. The question is, will they communicate instantly? They have a different set of priorities."

"You mean they'll likely send a postcard . . ."

"We can do one other thing. Send a messenger." Steiner turned to Raskin. "I'd like you to go to Jerusalem. We can't put you on the plane, but you'll get there by train in two or three days. That way, they will have a firsthand report and bring the matter right to the top of the British Government."

Brand felt his heart beat violently against his ribs. He looked at Raskin. The man seemed trustworthy enough. He looked more intently at Steiner. Steiner's face was smooth and calm. Steiner troubled him. He seemed so petty in his bureaucratic concerns and small fears. Yet his resignation gave an impression of maturity and something like the wisdom of experience as well. Brand could not figure him out.

Raskin stood up. "I'll have a letter ready for you in an

hour," said Steiner. Brand took the folded chart of Auschwitz and placed it carefully in a white hotel envelope.

"Take this with you."

"Better leave it here," Steiner said. "I'll keep it. You
don't cross frontiers in wartime with maps in your pocket.
If the Allies decide to bomb, we can always get the chart to
them through the British military attaché's office."

"At least tell them about it!" Brand cried. "If all else
fails, let them at least destroy the gas chambers and furnaces. And all the railroad lines from Hungary. They must
drop commandos to blow up the line. I'll jump with them,
and lead them in if they'll let me."

"I'll tell them."

"On the back of the map is a detailed list of all the
major rail junctions. We have contacts everywhere in the
Slovak and Polish undergrounds. I can give you names,
addresses of people who will help."

"It will not be easy," Steiner began. "They would have to
operate hundreds of miles behind enemy lines. How would
they get back?"

"It can be done! By God, let us throw some sort of
wrench into their machine."

"I am going home to pack," Raskin said. He shook
Brand's hand. "I hope to have news for you soon."

Steiner remained seated for a few minutes longer. He
met Brand's gaze, then he sighed and his head dropped.
Brand remembered his late father once saying that there
were sighs as long as the diaspora. But what good are
sighs? They go unheard and lead to nowhere.

He lit another cigarette and puffed on it in continuous
spasms. The two men stared at one another through a
cloud of smoke. It was growing dark. They had not turned
on the lamps. In the dim light their figures were outlined
against the outside fog, gray on gray. Nothing in their lives
had prepared them for the task they faced. They were a
fragile little force wholly dependent upon the good will of

others. The others cared about other things. There was an immense gap between the forces of death and those of salvation.

* * *

On his way down from Brand's room, Mark was stopped by Andrew Gyorgy.

"Hello, Teddy," Gyorgy said in a lame voice. "I know what you're thinking. But it isn't true. I swear it. I delivered that money to the contact as I said I would. What happened after, I don't know. Remember, we were dealing with a Rumanian."

"Okay, Gyorgy, okay," Mark said. "Now excuse me, I must go."

"You've just been with Brand. He is an odd chap, don't you think?" A narrow smile played across Gyorgy's smooth and elongated face. As he bent forward he exuded a mixture of bad breath and eau de cologne.

"Why do you ask?"

"I give you my advice. Pay no attention to him. He wishes well. That's why I agreed to help him. But he is out of his element."

"Oh?"

"Kastner sent him here because he wants to sleep with his wife. That's all."

"Is it?"

"Look, he is a naïve child. I fixed this trip for him. I invented this stunt. For a greater purpose. It wasn't easy, but I did it. I needed an alibi myself, to come to Turkey on a mission of *real* consequence."

"And what would it be this time?"

"Dissident German Army officers. Top people. Hitler's own entourage. They want me to arrange a meeting with the Allies. If that works we can save your Jews too."

"Why should the Nazis send out a little smuggler like

you to arrange meetings with the Allies? They've got an ambassador here."

"Ah, but they don't trust von Papen. He is a Foreign Office man. This is strictly a military scheme. Heinrich with the spectacles [Himmler] *is behind it.*"

"I see."

"Brand probably told you of his own scheme to rescue the Jews . . ."

"What about it?"

"Pure fairy tales," Gyorgy said airily. "Pay him no mind. Come along with me. I have been with the British all morning. They are offering me all sorts of goodies."

"For example?"

"My lips are sealed. Why don't you talk to them yourself? You're thick with Colonel Roberts."

"Yes. I will."

"My scheme is far better than Brand's. And it will save more Jews."

"Have you mentioned this to Brand?"

"Of course not. He wouldn't understand. He is a megalomaniac, in the grip of childish fantasies."

* * *

"How do we know Eichmann isn't lying?" Steiner asked Brand.

"We don't. But what is there to lose?"

"I still don't quite understand the whole thing." As a raw young man Steiner had joined a Socialist commune draining swamps and plowing virgin soil in Lower Galilee. He had grown up in the rigors of Marxist ideology, and was a man who believed that one cannot understand *something* unless one knew a good theory that explained *everything*.

"A good number of high Nazis apparently want to strike a bargain," Brand said. "Himmler. The generals. A lot of smaller fry, too. It's not surprising. They know they are losing the war. They don't suddenly indulge in humanitarian fancies. They are being realistic. We should be realists, too."

"But good God, Himmler himself? After butchering four million Jews? Surely he cannot believe that if he stops now he'll be considered a Good Samaritan after the war?"

"Don't apply normal human logic to these twisted minds. Himmler does it for his own distorted rationale. Not ours. He thinks he is serving German destiny by sparing the Jews' lives. Just as he was serving it before when he was butchering them."

"But surely Hitler isn't in on this, so how can it work? What if he discovers that Himmler and the others are plotting behind his back?"

"Let them destroy each other. In the meantime, we save lives. Maybe thousands and thousands of lives. Then, who knows? Another gang comes to us with another deal. We negotiate with them, too."

"You think you can fool them. But maybe they are really bluffing us. They know damned well we can't send them trucks in the middle of the war."

"They are sure we *can*. They think the Jews own the whole goddamned world!"

"But if we don't send them trucks, what then?"

"I told you, they'll take money. And alibis."

"For money alone they'll stop the killings?"

"How can we tell before we try? The same sort of deal worked in Slovakia a few months ago."

"But how is it possible? After all, Germany is run by one man. It's a totalitarian state."

"If that were true they might still win the war," said Brand. "But it isn't. Sure, Hitler is the Führer. But he is more like an oriental potentate now, surrounded by a court of lackeys and intriguers. And opportunists. They're all running around like headless chickens looking for alibis. And Swiss bank accounts. There is our chance."

"Only a miracle would save us now."

"We can make miracles," Brand said awkwardly. "I am certain of it."

"I am afraid we are very overdrawn in the bank of miracles."

* * *

By the time Steiner left night was falling, and from the bay below foghorns from unseen ships were wailing in the dark. Brand put on his overcoat and carefully opened the door. There was nobody in the corridor. He crept to a fire exit and raced up to the next landing. Here he wrapped his face in the woolen scarf and rode down the elevator to the ground floor.

The lobby was crowded. Brand walked quickly through the revolving door. The street was wet and windy. He broke into a trot and, turning right, followed the labyrinth of filthy narrow little streets. He came upon a lit sign, FERNAND CHAVAL BARBIER FRANÇAIS, and rushed inside. A small man in a white jacket was standing by the sink.

Brand said breathlessly, *"Pouvez vous m'indiquer le plus proche office postale, s'il vous plait?"*

The man looked at him blankly. He did not speak French, nor did anyone else in the shop. *"Poste*—Telegraph—*poste . . ."* Brand repeated.

A light of recognition dawned in the barber's round and friendly face. He put on his overcoat, took an umbrella and led Brand back through the alleyways to a post office on the main thoroughfare.

Brand took a telegraph form and wrote:

HERZL, HOTEL CONTINENTAL, VIENNA
NEGOTIATIONS SUCCESSFULLY BEGUN STOP YOUR
PROPOSAL ELICITS GREATEST INTEREST STOP MY
ASSOCIATES ARE PREPARING DRAFT AGREEMENT
STOP RETURN BUDAPEST IMMEDIATELY DRAFT
COMPLETED STOP RESPECTFULLY BRAND, PERA
PALACE HOTEL.

The man behind the little barred window peered at him through thin steel-rimmed glasses. He carefully counted each word, then counted again, and a third time. A German-speaking clerk was summoned from the back room.

"Do you want this telegram to go as a night letter? It is much cheaper."

"No."

"You want the regular rate?"

"Yes, the regular. No, not the regular. Urgent."

"That will again double the cost," the man said doubtfully.

"Send it off. Send it off immediately."

Brand had no Turkish currency. The clerk protested that he did not know the rate of exchange. Finally he said, "Give me fifty dollars. That should be all right, more or less. If it is too little, I'll add to it from my own pocket."

Brand gave him a fifty-dollar bill. He walked back into the street. The rain had stopped. The wet air reeked with the stench of open sewers and brown coal. He wandered aimlessly up the street, then turned down a wide public stairway to the wharves below. A little steamboat was anchored at a wooden jetty, waiting for passengers with some destination along the Golden Horn.

He started across the greasy boards, slipped and suddenly fell on his face. Two sailors helped him to his unsteady feet. Brand looked at them vacantly; he could not quite understand why they had. He felt apart from them, full of resentment for their solicitude.

The skin of his cheek was scraped. Blood dripped on his right eye from a cut on the forehead above. He wiped his face with his sleeve, and limped back up the wide stairway, through the maze of little alleyways to the hotel. The plainclothesman was on the landing. Brand pressed a bank note into his palm. The man stared at the blood encrusted on his forehead.

"*Merci,*" he said. "*À propos,* you have a visitor."

Brand opened his door. Mark was sitting by the window, smoking a cigar.

"I was sure you wouldn't mind," he said. "I came back to see how you were. I was sorry to leave so abruptly before."

Brand placed his wet coat on the wing chair. A stain of water spread over the beige silk cushion.

"The door was unlocked. So I just walked in."

"I know. The Turk outside told me."

"Don't concern yourself with him. I've made an arrangement with him. He'll get his daily retainer."

"That seems to be about the best you people can do," Brand said. "In Hungary we go for higher stakes. But then you are much more comfortable here." He made a broad gesture with his arm.

Mark was about to answer testily when he noticed the blood on Brand's face. "What happened?"

"It is nothing."

"You are bleeding."

"I said it is nothing."

"Where have you been?"

"I went for a walk and I tripped. That is all."

"Where did you go?"

"Am I under interrogation?"

"Brand, you are being very difficult. And a little unfair. I understand. You are overwrought and tired. You ought to have a bath. Come, let me help you with this."

"Will you, for God's sake, stop commiserating with me!" Brand shouted. "Damn all of you! And stop telling me all the time to take a bath!"

"How long were you gone?"

"It's none of your business."

"You went to cable Eichmann. You should have listened to Steiner. Now you make everything much more difficult."

"Is that so? *I* make things more difficult, eh? *I* am the one paralyzed by fancy notions of legality. *I* am wallowing about in all sorts of bureaucratic niceties, upper ranks, lower ranks. Jurisdictions. You listen to me, Mark. I got three men out of a Polish concentration camp last June. They didn't mind that it wasn't done through proper channels."

"Brand, I understand how you feel. I have plenty of problems with Steiner myself."

"Damn you, we face the most vicious monsters in the whole of history and all you do is fight among yourselves."

"It is not all we do. Still you should not have cabled Eichmann."

"I had to."

"Why didn't you ask me?" Mark said softly, "I would have found a better way for you. You went to the post office?"

Brand nodded.

"In this city the walls have eyes. I'll have a good bit of explaining to do when I see Colonel Roberts in the morning."

"What will you tell him?"

"The whole story. Well, almost."

"You will?"

"I must. What else would you expect me to do?"

"I expect you to help me."

"Of course. But don't you see? We depend on the British almost entirely. Try to understand our limitations, Brand. You are a courageous man. You must also be wise."

"The wisest thing would be for me to fly right back to Budapest. Make out that letter for me. And sign it Weizmann."

"We can't do this on our own, Brand. We need Steiner and his bureaucrats and busybodies to follow you up. Otherwise Eichmann will call your bluff. You'll be a dead man within a day."

Brand rose from his seat. "You bastard!" he yelled,

"Why have you changed your mind? And so soon! You are working for them!"

"Hold on . . ."

"Admit it, you are a British agent. You're working for them!"

"Listen, Brand . . ." Mark opened another package of cigarettes. "Listen, Brand . . ." he began again. Then he paused. His patience was a form of despair which he did not bother to disguise as a virtue but displayed openly like a public announcement of bankruptcy.

"Listen, Brand. Yes. You are right. But it isn't all that black and white. Of course I also work for the British. Who would you expect me to work for in the middle of this war? The Germans? If I didn't work for the British, I wouldn't be here. I'd be pushing pencils. Like Steiner. We don't have anyone else. We have no people. No money. No trucks. . . . I must go now. Try and get some rest. Please."

Brand stared after him as he disappeared into the corridor. He took off his clothes and fell onto the bed. He stared at the concentric lines of light cast by the lampshade on the ceiling. What should he do next? He did not know. It was obvious that his mission was foundering. Nothing was working as he had hoped.

With a shudder he realized that if Eichmann only knew how poor, how impotent they really were he would never have offered him the "bargain." With a shudder he remembered that in his eagerness to confirm Eichmann in his delusions he had half convinced himself that the Jews had power, riches and political influence in the free world. Yes, he had come to believe it himself. He had only himself to blame.

* * *

Later that evening Raskin boarded the Ankara express. Steiner's letter was rolled up and hidden in an empty tube

of toothpaste. Halfway to Ankara the train was unexpectedly blocked by Turkish military movements and
pushed to a side railing where it idled for five and one-half
hours. When he finally arrived in Ankara, he had missed
the connection south. He had to wait there a full day.

20 May 1944

On the following morning Teddy Mark rose early. Breakfast was not yet being served in the little pension where he was living, on a narrow lane behind the White Mosque. He dressed quickly and gathered his papers in his briefcase. By eight o'clock he was driving up the hill toward Taksim Square. His throat was chafed from too much tobacco. On the previous night, after leaving Brand, he had gone back to his room and worked until 2 A.M., hammering out fourteen pages, single-spaced, on his portable typewriter. Teddy Mark was a clandestine Jewish agent, but he also had another job, as interrogator (in three languages) for the Istanbul liaison office of British Military Intelligence. He had just concluded the interrogation of two Bulgarians who had crossed the Black Sea in a little sailboat. At nine-thirty he was meeting Colonel Roberts of M.I. 11 to hand in his report.

He parked his car on Taksim Square. He had more than an hour to spare. The weather had improved. For the first time in days the crowded square was bathed in the yellowish, lurid light of a distant sun. Mark entered a cafe and ordered breakfast. His thoughts kept running back to Brand. He was pleased that he had not lost his temper the previous night. He was intrigued by Brand, and on the point of actually liking him. This did not happen very often in his work. Among the men he had met in the past two years who had broken out of the inferno, Brand was impressive, if enigmatic; and the sheer audacity of his fantastic scheme appealed to Mark's imagination and sense of high adventure.

It was likely that Roberts already knew of Brand's arrival, through his own sources, if not through Gyorgy. Mark wondered how he might best broach the subject. He looked out onto the busy street; the sun felt pleasant on his ruddy face. He was a fair young man; at twenty-eight he still had the clean, lean look of a college student. As he sat at the little marble table—tanned, alert, good-looking—he might have been taken for a tourist, or a scholar of Byzantine art, had not the war made such a possibility highly unlikely. There was an air of melancholy in his deep-set dark-brown eyes. With a gay spirit, he had the most desolate nature (an association more frequent than is imagined). His father had been a prominent Viennese surgeon. Mark had last seen him in August 1939 just before leaving Austria on one of the last permits for Palestine issued by the British consul to a Viennese Jew. His parents had been refused permits and had remained in Vienna. Mark had not heard from them since.

He finished his breakfast and drove slowly along the wide esplanade, listening to the BBC on the car radio. The soothing, gentle voice, that of a silver-haired gentleman standing by a fireplace, exuded an air of infinite civility and calm. The news was good this morning. It would put Colonel Roberts in an agreeable frame of mind. In Italy the Allied advance west of Cassino was continuing; Field Marshal Rommel was bracing his troops in Normandy as a vast Anglo-American armada gathered off southern England for the invasion of France. The invasion might take place any minute now, but it would not necessarily help the Jews of Europe. It would only be the beginning of the end.

Mark's links with British intelligence in Istanbul were of an informal nature. The activists of *Haganah* were under strict police surveillance in Palestine, and some were locked up in prisons. But in Turkey, a working arrangement had developed between *Haganah* agents and certain branches of British Military Intelligence. It was more the result of personal relationships that had grown over the years than of official policy directives. It was never clear whether London was even aware of it. In Istanbul, *Haganah* agents were part of the British intelligence establishment. The Turks did not mind the presence of foreign agents so long as a certain parity was maintained, for the sake of neutrality, between the number of German spies and English spies. Colonel Roberts had placed Mark and his men on the British quota, for he regarded his little arrangements with them as extremely useful. It was not one-sided. Mark and his colleagues were instrumental in the rescue of Allied pilots shot down over Greece and Bulgaria. In return Roberts helped Mark's men to smuggle Greek and Bulgarian Jews into Turkey. Mark interrogated them for Roberts, and in return, Roberts tactfully closed an eye afterward, when Mark was sending them on to Palestine with false papers. Roberts was inclined to regard this as only a minor infraction of the immigration rules. Once or twice a month he even felt vaguely virtuous about it. In any case, there were never more than a dozen or so each month who slipped through the Palestine immigration controls in this way.

Roberts was an easygoing, slightly phlegmatic man in his early sixties. He had lived in Turkey for years as a businessman before joining Military Intelligence at the beginning of the war. He was fond of Mark personally. As an interrogator Mark was especially effective with refugees from central and southern Europe. His reports, garnered from endless, often conflicting hearsay, were appreciated by everybody in the service. On one recent occasion, Mark's careful and precise questioning of a Rumanian engineer had given Roberts the first clear picture of the extent of damage caused by Allied air attacks on the Ploesti oil fields.

And yet, whenever Mark offered Roberts additional bits and pieces of information picked up in the course of his interrogations regarding the mass deportations of Greek and Rumanian Jews to the reputed death camps of Auschwitz and Sovibor, an odd thing happened. Robert's regard for Mark's precision and reliability somehow became less pronounced. On certain occasions he was totally incredulous. He was too polite, and too fond of Mark, to say so openly, but he was sure (and Mark knew it) that Mark was exaggerating his tales of horror for purposes of Jewish propaganda.

It was a natural reaction to the stories coming out of Nazi-occupied lands, shared also by many a Jewish leader in Palestine, England and America. The crime was too enormous, it staggered the imagination and paralyzed the mind.

As for Colonel Roberts, he required no special prodding to believe that the Nazis were monsters. But he was strongly aware of Mark's double function and he suspected that Mark—perhaps under instruction from the Jewish leaders in Jerusalem—was deliberately magnifying the case in order to elicit concessions from the British regarding the future of Palestine after the war.

Robert's office was located in an annex of the British Consulate, on a hill overlooking the Golden Horn. His official title—and transparent cover—was Chief Passport Control Officer, and his desk was cluttered with stamps and stubs and paper clips and unsharpened pencils and daring novels printed before the war in France that he regularly smuggled into England for distribution among his friends.

He received Mark cheerfully, with that unmistakable tone of playful irony that until recently was the hallmark of a certain class of English civil servants. He was always pleased to see Mark. Of the dozen or so agents in his direct employ, Mark was easily the most civilized. The two shared a passion for Modern German letters.

"Did you hear that speech of Rommel's?" Roberts said. "Not the best prose style, but full of interesting hints."

"They're pretty nervous," Mark said. He handed Roberts his typewritten report. The office was flooded in sunlight. Roberts was in a good mood also because he was looking forward to his weekly game of tennis in the afternoon. An orderly appeared.

"What will you have?" Roberts asked.

"Coffee," said Mark.

Roberts said, "Tea."

A large wooden tray of cups, pots, biscuits and Turkish sweets, spoons and saucers was brought in. Mark pulled out a cigarette. The orderly lit it for him. "I would like to talk to you about a man who flew in from Budapest the other day," Mark said. It came out less casually than he had hoped.

Roberts said, "Ah, yes. Brand. He has been sending telegrams to a man called Herzl at Gestapo headquarters in Vienna. An odd affair."

"Did you say Herzl?"

"My dear Mark. You look disturbed."

"It must be a code name."

"Do you know who it might be?"

"I know that Brand . . ."

"I don't know about Brand—or Band—or whatever his name is—it's probably neither—but I know Gyorgy."

"I wouldn't trust that man too far, sir."

"I thought your crowd was working with him."

"We've used Gyorgy in the past, yes, sir—up to a point. Not as a source of information. Just to deliver money. On that score he never let us down."

"As far as you know."

"As far as we know."

"I am sure you know he has been working at one and

the same time for the Germans, the Americans and the Hungarians. He has cheated them all. It would be rather out of character if he'd left you out."

"Sir, Brand has nothing to do with Gyorgy. He says that the Germans forced Gyorgy on him as a watchdog. It was not Brand's fault. To the contrary, it means the Germans don't trust Brand."

"Do you?"

"Yes, frankly, I do."

"Well, you place a certain trust in Gyorgy, too."

"We can't always be choosy. Brand strikes me as different."

"What does Mr. Steiner think about Brand?"

"He takes my view, sir."

"Steiner wasn't so happy with the other man who came out of Budapest last February. Quite rightly. Our men are still interrogating him in Cairo."

"I never thought that Kleinmann was really worth all your trouble, sir. The fact that he got out doesn't prove he was an enemy agent. But I am convinced Brand is different."

"You are an incurable romantic, Mark. Nothing is more dangerous in our trade. Believe me, I have been in it long enough."

"Sir, I spent a few hours with him yesterday. He is not overly intelligent. But he seems sincere. He is part of a Jewish underground group with which we are in touch. They are men we know from before the war, and we trust them." He paused, uncertain how to phrase his words. "Brand brought us an offer from Eichmann which could save innumerable lives if we use it properly."

Roberts' finely fashioned English face—a touch of Lord Chesterton, a touch of Noel Coward—was furrowed by deep lines. He slowly shook his head. His job was to gather and evaluate information, not to negotiate with the Nazis.

"Adolf Eichmann, eh?" Roberts said. "No less? The butcher behind the scenes?"

"Brand says he's no longer hiding behind a desk. He is out in the open now, in the lap of luxury. He's living it up at the Majestic Hotel. Drinking and playing cards. His work elsewhere in Europe is—finished, he says—or almost. And all that know-how he's gathered he now plans to use to liquidate the Jews of Hungary. In one blow. But before he begins he offers us a deal."

Roberts' eyes were wary. "What kind of deal?"

"He'll trade trucks for Jews."

"My dear Mark," Roberts said, "surely you don't believe that? Of all possible things—trucks! To transport even more Jews more efficiently to the concentration camps."

"We don't have to send him trucks. Brand says the Nazis are so hard up they'll be content with money. He wants to go back to Budapest with some shrewd answer."

"He should not try to be too clever."

"Sir, he only wants to delay Eichmann. He'll tell Eichmann that his offer is being considered. Just *considered*— nothing more. The talk can go on for months in some neutral country."

"You must not contact the Germans, Mark. Not before M.I. hears of this, anyway."

"I am not going to contact the Germans. Brand will. He commits nobody."

"What does Steiner think about this scheme?"

"Frankly, sir, he is being circumspect. Perhaps too circumspect."

"He is wise."

"I am not sure."

"Have any of your colleagues been in touch with the Germans?"

"I can't be sure. But I doubt it."

"I hope for your sake you're right. You and Steiner are British subjects. The Russians will know immediately.

They'll think we are negotiating a separate treaty with the Nazis."

"The lives of hundreds of thousands are at stake."

"They are not the only ones who face death in this bloody war."

"They are the only ones nobody seems to give a damn about!"

Roberts softened. Mark had never used this tone of voice with him before. "I am sorry," he said, "I didn't mean to sound heartless. This man really wants to go back to Budapest?"

"Most definitely."

"Very courageous."

"I beg your pardon?"

"One might say even desperate."

"We are all desperate," said Mark. "The only recourse we have is a strategy of desperation."

"Perhaps you are right," said Roberts, hesitating. "But no, I don't believe you are. Come to think of it, this crazy scheme is beginning to make some sense. If you see it in conjunction with the mission of his accomplice, Andrew Gyorgy."

"Sir, there is no connection between the two."

"Gyorgy has been talking to my men all of last night. He says he came out on behalf of certain Wehrmacht officers to arrange a separate peace. But we mustn't take advantage. Fancy that. They would like to keep all their conquests in the East. They're also calling for a meeting in a neutral country."

"It is a coincidence, Colonel. Brand has no idea of what Gyorgy is up to. He was negotiating directly with Eichmann before Gyorgy showed up."

"He flew in on a German passport."

"He is a Jew."

"Are you sure?"

"Yes. I trust him."

Roberts changed his tack. "Perhaps he's in the pay of the Hungarian Government. They've wanted to go neutral for a long time. Maybe they have hit upon this new approach. Through the Jews."

"May I suggest, sir, that you talk to him?"

"I don't see what there is to talk about," said Roberts. "I will, however, cable London a detailed report."

"How soon do you think you might have an answer?"

"Hard to say."

"Eichmann gave Brand only two weeks."

Roberts gazed at him silently. He felt sorry for Mark. Why should a sensible man like Mark be falling for this wild fantasy? And yet he seemed to feel very strongly about it. As a special favor Roberts promised to send a copy of his report to British intelligence in Jerusalem, with the request to forward it to Sir Harold Macmichael, the British high commissioner to Palestine.

"Macmichael will discuss it with your own people immediately." He met Mark's eyes with quiet irony. "That should get *you* off the hook, shouldn't it?"

"With your permission," Mark said tightly, "I must leave now. I am lunching with someone at the Grand Hotel."

"If it's not Adolf Hitler," Roberts said cheerfully, "it's all right with me."

Soon afterward Roberts spoke on the telephone with Captain Kuzuk. The best course of action, he suggested, might be to ask Brand to cut short his stay in Turkey. The suggestion was made in an offhand, oblique manner. Roberts was not about to take any risks. Who would have imagined it, he mused. Now it is the Jews who want to negotiate with the Nazis! And so close to the end.

Or could it be, perhaps, that German intelligence was trying to penetrate Jewish relief organizations? Even Mark's own band of overzealous Palestinian desperadoes?

It's worth an inquiry, Roberts thought. No, not Mark

himself. Perhaps the others. Roberts wondered whether he had not gone too far, officially speaking, in his collaboration with them.

* * *

Brand had a nightmare. He was in a rowboat with Eichmann, in the middle of a lake. A crowd of people lined the lakefront in a great arc around them. Eichmann was pulling at the oar, making a great splash. When the water struck Brand, it turned out to be sand. The sand was rising in the bottom of the boat, covering Brand's feet, his thighs, up to his chest. Brand screamed and woke up, covered with sweat. It was after nine. The sun was coming in through the curtained windows.

He bathed and paced impatiently in his room. For a while he stared out the window at the minarets and domes. The saucers left behind from his sparse breakfast were littered with stubs of half-finished cigarettes. When he finally went downstairs, it was time for lunch. He felt something like hunger and entered the vast dining room. The floor was of white and pink marble, the ceiling a placid pool of blue and gold reflecting the glories of Paradise.

At the sound of a shrill voice calling out his name he wheeled around. "What a pleasant surprise, *Herr Ingenieur!*" Dr. Volker Mann, the itinerant propagandist from Berlin, rose from his table. "You here at the Pera Palace?" Brand stopped dead. "If only I had known," said Mann. "And this is my last morning in Istanbul. I must leave for Ankara within the hour."

"I . . . I . . . I was also just leaving."

"But I shall be back. In four days' time. And now that I know where to find you . . ."

"Yes indeed," said Brand. "I shall see you then."

"How are you doing with your machines . . . ?" Mann began, but Brand had turned abruptly and walked quickly out, up the stairway, into the corridor leading to his room. The detective lingering outside his door gave him a friendly nod.

"Your visitor is here, monsieur," he said.

"I am not expecting anybody."

"I know, monsieur. But he insisted I let him in."

Brand opened the door. Mark was standing in the middle of the room. The telephone was ringing. Mark reached for the receiver and handed it to Brand.

"This is the porter, sir. There is a gentleman here to see you."

"Yes? Who is it?"

"A Captain Kuzuk, sir."

"I'll be right down."

"He is on his way up," said the voice, and rang off.

Brand looked about the room. There was nothing but full ashtrays on the table and the debris of an unfinished breakfast. He went to the bathroom and straightened his tie. He was suddenly relieved that Mark was here. There was a light knock on the door and Kuzuk entered.

"I am very sorry to disturb you, Herr Band." Kuzuk spoke German with but the slightest of accents. "Oh, Mr. Mark, you are here? I thought you were lunching at the Grand Hotel."

"I was indeed. Are you having me followed, Captain?"

"Heaven forbid. On second thought, it is not surprising to find you here so soon. You have much in common with our visitor here, don't you, Mr. Mark?"

Brand said, "Your visit is a bit unexpected, Captain. What can I do for you?"

Kuzuk assumed an air of slight exasperation. "Germans are always so abrupt!" he said, and sat down. "In Turkey we never expect to come to the point so quickly, Herr Band. Or is it Brand?"

"I am sure you are not going to make difficulties for Mr. Brand because of a little misprint," Mark said.

"God forbid, no. Bureaucracies are nowhere perfect. Not even in Germany."

There was a short silence. Mark said conversationally, "Well, at least the weather has improved. The first sunny day in weeks."

"It is truly delightful," said Kuzuk. "May is always the best month in Istanbul. Or should be. What a shame for you, Herr Band, that you won't be able to enjoy it for much longer. And perhaps miss some of the sights. A pity."

"I could not possibly stay beyond my two weeks."

"Ah, but this is why I have taken the liberty to come to see you. I am afraid you cannot stay even for that long. On Thursday when you arrived, I was able to arrange your temporary release into our custody."

"I am extremely indebted to you, sir."

"Now, I'm sure you would say that a visa is a mere technicality, and of course it is. But only in peacetime, Herr Band. Wouldn't you say so?"

"Yes."

"Yes. Not in times of war. Don't you agree? Ah, I knew you would understand. I have tried to be of help to a friend of André Anatole Gyorgy. But you see—you *do* see, do you not—I am only a captain! And I have been overruled."

"I will go back on the thirty-first, at the latest."

"Alas, I am afraid you cannot stay that long. You must leave Turkey. Please. You may go wherever you like. Germany. Or Vienna. Or perhaps Mr. Mark will take you with him to his—Holy Land?"

"I cannot go to Palestine. You know that, Captain. I am, at least technically, a German citizen."

"What do you mean by 'technically,' Herr Band?"

"It is not important. The fact is that I cannot at the moment go to Palestine."

"He is right, Captain," said Mark.

"Well, in that case, go back to Germany. You need not wait for the next plane. There is a daily train which connects at Salonika. I should be happy to drive you to the station tomorrow morning."

"Captain, I cannot take that train. I'd be taken off by the first SS guards at the border, and sent to a concentration camp."

"But why? You carry a valid German passport, don't you?"

"He is a Jew, Captain Kuzuk," Mark said. "The German passport is only a convenience granted to Herr Brand by a certain German agency with which we are negotiating."

"Ah, this affair is even more complicated than I suspected. It's a pity André did not warn me. I am very sorry. Believe me. But my hands are tied."

"Give me only a few days more," Brand pleaded. "We are at any moment awaiting the arrival of a very high official from Jerusalem. I need only a brief conference with him. After that I'll take the first direct plane to Vienna."

"How soon do you expect the arrival of this—ah—personage?"

Mark spoke. "He is due at any moment. I would very much appreciate it, Captain, if you would give me an opportunity to speak to Colonel Roberts before you take any action."

"Colonel Roberts? Didn't you spend the morning in his office?"

"We discussed other matters."

"I daresay I am most certain Colonel Roberts does not consider Mr. Band one of his, how shall I put it, one of his protégés. Of course, if you wish to speak with him again, it is still early in the afternoon. But no—today is Saturday. The colonel always plays tennis on Saturday afternoons."

"I will reach him before the night is over," said Mark.

"I'm not sure he can be of much help to you. This is strictly a Turkish affair."

"I fully appreciate that. Please give us another twenty-four hours."

Kuzuk examined his fingernails. "Believe me, I very much dislike limiting visits to Turkey in this way. Most visitors never stay long enough anyway. We are a very misunderstood people." He looked up sharply. "Twenty-four hours, then."

"Thank you very much, Captain," said Mark.

"Before I leave, do you mind if we—um—examine the briefcase and things? Only a formality. I am sure you will understand."

"Go ahead," said Brand. "I have nothing to hide."

Kuzuk opened the door and called in the detective, who began to empty Brand's suitcase on the bed. Kuzuk held up the suitcase to look for a double bottom. A book was lying on Brand's night table, *The Three Musketeers*. Kuzuk slowly leafed through it. He looked up appreciatively.

"A very good book. But Zola is so much better. Do you like Émile Zola, gentlemen? Upon my word, the greatest writer who ever lived."

Mark glanced through the book, guessing its real purpose, while Kuzuk continued his search. No, Mark thought, no, it can't be his code book. Not this, of all books. The matter is too serious for melodrama.

Kuzuk was leafing through Brand's other papers. There was only a passport and a stamped paper exempting "the Jew Joel Brand" from wearing the Jewish star. "By order, [signed] Hermann Krumey, Sturmbannführer, SS."

21 May 1944

"How do we know he is not a Nazi provocateur?" Landau said. It was Sunday, he and Mark were playing poker in the sitting room of their pension.

"Steiner seemed to think so at first," Mark said, shuffling the cards.

"Hold it, man!" Landau cried. "You pay the fine again."

"All right, all right." Mark laughed. They had a long-standing joke in the pension that whoever mentioned Steiner except by derisive indirection—"Mr. Nervous," "His Excellency," "Sir Top Bloat," and the like—paid a fine of ten Turkish pounds. Mark pushed a bank note across the table, but his laughter was a bit strained.

"The bloody pedant," he said, dealing out the cards. "He is afraid of his own shadow. He is now saying he never expected we'd use Gyorgy as a courier. As if we could have sent the money by postal order!"

"Is he going to push Brand across the frontier into Palestine? I mean, get rid of him like he got rid of Kleinmann?"

"I don't think so. He takes Brand seriously. Kleinmann was a different cup of tea. And he's heard that the British threw Kleinmann into jail as a German spy. That bothers him."

"Kleinmann is still in jail, is he?"

"I think so."

"They probably know what they're doing. Do we know that Brand isn't a Nazi agent too?"

"I know."

"I don't trust him. Here, I'll take two," Landau said, shifting his cards. His lean fingers were bony and long. He was ten years older than Mark. Under the cover of a timber merchant, he had been at work clandestinely in Istanbul since 1942. Landau was so accustomed to Byzantine intelligence intrigues that Brand's open arrival by air seemed to him more suspicious than it would have been if he had suddenly popped up from a manhole in Taksim Square wearing a diver's suit.

"I think he is honest. He's done great things before in the underground," said Mark.

"What better cover could he pick?"

"It's not a cover. I'm convinced of it."

"The first rule in this work, my dear Mark, is 'Always Distrust Appearances.'"

"I tell you, I am sure. He is not a provocateur."

"You've been wrong before."

"This is different."

"Three jacks."

"You win."

"Look, Mark, it doesn't make sense. Let's assume you are right. If the Germans wanted to strike a bargain they wouldn't have sent out this Boy Scout. Somebody at their embassy would have telephoned our 'Distinguished Resident Diplomat.'"

"They know as well as you do that 'His Excellency' wouldn't accept their call."

"I'd take it. Wouldn't you?"

"Yes. I would talk to them."

"Then why didn't they call *me?*"

"They probably think you're really in the timber business."

"Be serious, Mark."

"Maybe they're not as bright as we think."

"You're hedging."

"Perhaps they're split among themselves. Maybe they don't trust their ambassador here. Roberts says Himmler used his masseur to contact the British. Through some Swedish fairy."

"Don't try to convince me. Convince Roberts."

"I'm trying."

"I can see you're not being very successful."

"I'll be happy if I manage to keep Brand here until Shertok arrives."

"Roberts promised you that he won't be thrown out?"

"I didn't ask him. I went back to Kuzuk. After some prodding he became more amenable."

"You had to promise him something?"

"Not yet."

"Why should you have to use Kuzuk? Roberts is your friend."

"They're all my friends."

"The trouble with having you as a friend, my dear Mark," Landau said, "is that one never knows when you will turn around and stab yourself in the back."

Colonel Roberts did not cable London immediately on Saturday as he had promised Mark, but rather on the following Monday. The message was not marked "Urgent" and suffered a further delay at the Cairo relay station.

The copy, however, that Roberts sent to Jerusalem arrived on the same day, and was placed in the special leather folder on the high commissioner's desk intended for secret communications. Here, however, it lay unread for two days. Sir Harold Macmichael, His Brittanic Majesty's High Commissioner in Palestine and Transjordan, was away on a tour of inspection in the southern desert. The message had been marked for "H.E. eyes only."

Sir Harold returned to Jerusalem on Wednesday night. On Thursday, the twenty-fifth of May, at 9 A.M. he settled down at his comfortable, wide, dark-grained walnut desk. Sir Harold loved this desk. It was a beautiful eighteenth-century English piece that had been presented in 1921 to one of his predecessors by the Right Honorable Winston Churchill, then Secretary of the Colonies. Churchill had just passed the better part of a long weekend in Jerusalem to clear up—"once and for all," as he put it—the nasty muddle in the Middle East.

On the final day of his visit, around lunchtime (he had just risen following a long night of heavy drinking), Churchill hit upon the solution for which others had vainly been groping for so long. He called for charts and more whiskey and cigars, and with a blue crayon on a royal ordinance map carved out the rough confines of a new Arab emirate on the high plateau across the river Jordan. The scale of the map was 1.500,000 (two mm. on the chart equaled one kilometer on the ground), and the thick crayon he used would later give rise to bitter territorial controversies. Churchill was sorry afterward that he had not sharpened it, but he had been in a bit of a hurry. So the modern kingdom of Jordan was born in 1921—of a blue crayon—to clear the muddle for all time, and also to honor a pledge made long ago in the Hejaz when they had promised the young Bedouin Prince Abdullah a crown.

And Churchill saw everything that he had made that afternoon, and behold, it was very good. Now everybody would be happy. Bedouin warriors, native Arabs, Jews. The Jews would not have Transjordan, as promised them —rashly, Churchill felt—during the war when promises had been thrown wildly about Whitehall unmindful of consequence. On the other hand, they would be able to build their homeland west of the river, in Palestine proper. The Arabs would satisfy their national aspirations east of the river, under the mild, benevolent gaze of Abdullah. The arrangement was less perfect than T. E. Lawrence had envisaged for the Arabs, when, in his own words, he "wrote his will across the sky in stars to gain them freedom." Still even Lawrence approved of it in the name of peace. And the deed was sealed.

Then Churchill lay down his crayon and rested from his labors. Abdullah received his emirate and a subsidy from the British Crown. West of the Jordan, however, it was not so simple. The Arabs rejected Churchill's compromise and remained violently opposed to a Jewish homeland. Before long, Churchill was out of office. Over the years, many factors, good and evil, had combined to frustrate the success of Churchill's 1921 compromise. But good, evil, or both,

by now, twenty-three years later in May 1944, they were
all too complicated for anyone, in the obscure and con-
voluted chain of cause and effect, to remember.

On this side of the Jordan, the only tangible remnant of
Churchill's effort was the high commissioner's desk. It was
stained dark, and was smooth. Sir Harold leaned on it wearily. He was the fourth to occupy a thankless post that had
embittered all of his predecessors, and was causing more
trouble and heartache than any other colonial post in the
realm. In his years in office Sir Harold had reaped nothing
but ingratitude. The Arabs hated him for having ruthlessly
crushed the armed rebellion they had staged in the late
thirties with the active support of Fascist Italy and Nazi
Germany. In the aftermath of that rebellion Sir Harold's
main task had been to appease the Arabs at the expense of
the Jews and win them over to the Allied cause.

For this he was detested by the Jews—unfairly—for he
was merely the administrator of policies that had been decided by others in London. Yet with that total mistrust
which Jews often feel for any adversary, Macmichael was
accused of being an anti-Semite as well. In truth he had little sympathy or antipathy for either side. He dismissed the
Arabs as shallow Levantines: "They are no more true
Arabs," he used to say, "than I am a South Sea Islander."
If he tended to overestimate and resent the power of the
Jews, he took great care to be fair and just in his dealings
with them. But since he also believed, like most civil servants, that they were exaggerating their woes, he saw no
harm in locking the gates of the country against Jewish
fugitives from the slaughterhouse at the very moment, in
1939, that the slaughter had begun.

He was a good administrator, lacking less in good will
than in imagination. His great passion was the ethnology of
the Sudan, a subject upon which he had written many a
learned discourse. In Palestine he felt constrained. Its size
was that of Wales, its problems those of a continent. He

was ill at ease in this quicksand of ancient history that kept sucking one into a morass of romance and folklore and mysteries, and where rival litigants struggled hopelessly in a mire of prejudice and taboo.

As Sir Harold saw it, the conflict between Arab and Jew seemed to admit to no logical solution. He had little understanding for either side's incessant howls for freedom. Freedom was something he was so accustomed to as an Englishman that on his palate it had become quite tasteless, like water. He had no tolerance for the demagogues of either side. They were always invoking the sacred name of History. In Sir Harold's long career, history had merely been one damned thing after another. He had been high commissioner now for almost seven years, and was looking forward to his next posting, which was due shortly.

Sir Harold was sleepy. He had had only four hours of rest. His party had been entertained until midnight by the chief of a hospitable Bedouin tribe. Sir Harold yawned. He shielded his eyes against the blazing fury of the light that streamed in through the large windows.

Sir Harold sighed. He opened the brown leather folder on his desk with a harassed air and began to read. The uppermost document was an estimate of illegal arms and ammunitions amassed in Palestine by Jewish and Arab civilians. The quantity had quadrupled during the past two years. In a conclusion the authors of the report raised the possibility of a civil war between the two communities as soon as the war against Germany was over and British forces had been sent home. Sir Harold laid the estimate aside.

The next document was a message from the Colonial Office in London informing the high commissioner that his request for a special detachment of riot policemen had been granted:

"A first company of men with previous experience in riot control in Ireland will be sent out to Palestine as soon as shipping space for them can be secured from the War Department."

The third paper in the file was Colonel Roberts' report from Istanbul. Sir Harold glanced through it with growing unease. Roberts' message was couched in the vaguest of terms: "a man purporting to be a Jewish emissary" . . . "the company of a notorious con man and double agent . . . suspected of participating in break-in at British Embassy here . . . now under arrest" . . . "an offer from one Adolf Eichmann said to be in charge of anti-Semitic measures in Hungary" . . . "trucks to bolster German war effort" . . . "there are grounds to suspect Nazis may be trying to infiltrate Jewish relief organizations, perhaps even Jewish Agency" . . . "advising GHQ, M.E., M.I.5, and H.C. Jerusalem at their request."

As he continued to read, the high commissioner's eyes narrowed, his mouth grew taut. The fine silver mustache quivered slightly. He at once recognized the explosive potential of this suggested barter, whether it was to be accepted or rejected. If it were accepted, where could one possibly accommodate one hundred thousand, two hundred thousand, three hundred thousand Jews? Sir Harold knew that all hell would break loose among the Jews if they were not admitted into Palestine, and among the Arabs if they were.

On the other hand, if the barter offer were rejected, Britain would be accused of callousness toward the victims of persecution. There would be the usual hysterics in the American press and nasty questions in Parliament.

The high commissioner leaned back heavily. He picked up the telephone and called the buttery for some hot beef tea and Makintosh crackers and jam. He decided to tackle the matter diplomatically. He must delay the decision for as long a time as possible. And he must call in and consult the Jewish leaders, Ben Gurion and Shertok, if only to avoid a future scandal. The idea of seeing these two men greatly depressed him. Shertok was wily, Ben Gurion rude and abrupt. What little politeness there had been before the war seemed to have been placed in mothballs for the duration. His last meeting with Ben Gurion, only a week before, had ended on a note of mutual acrimony. Afterward, the high commissioner had told his wife at dinner that it had been like having a tooth extracted by one of the Indian dentists they had known in the Sudan, with a B.Sc. (failed) degree from the University of Calcutta.

On second thought he decided to wait, at least for a few days. After all, Roberts had alerted London. Why must *he* take the first step? Why here? In this hotbed of emotions? Better leave it to London. Let Whitehall summon Weizmann for a consultation about this most astounding offer. Weizmann was a much more reasonable man than either Ben Gurion or Shertok. The high commissioner touched a button on his desk. There was a light knock on the door. A secretary entered.

The high commissioner dictated a short letter to the director of prisons requesting him to reject a demand by Jewish youths imprisoned in Acre Fortress for training in illegal arms, to be allowed to join combat units of His Majesty's forces in Europe. They were to stay where they were.

Next he instructed his secretary to draft a cordial note to their gracious hosts of last evening. The secretary looked at her pad.

"On another matter, sir. Mr. Shertok rang. He requests an urgent meeting with Your Excellency. Possibly this morning. Mr. Ben Gurion wishes to come too.

"I should have known," murmured the high commissioner. "Ask them to come this afternoon. No. Make it tomorrow morning."

"Would there be anything else, sir?"

"Yes. Please call the Flower Show. Lady Macmichael has agreed to lend her patronage."

* * *

Moshe Shertok was the head of the Political Department of the Jewish Agency, a kind of foreign minister in the Jewish shadow government. He was a man in his late forties—prudent, rational, eschewing all extremes, with a religious devotion to his task. The dark brooding eyes in his fine oval face were a true index of his wistful, ponderous character. The dark mustache lent his smooth face a curious resemblance to that of Charlie Chaplin. The forehead was high. On Wednesday, 24 May, Shertok was arriving home late at night from a concert when he stumbled on the figure of a man fast asleep on the stairway outside his door. It was Raskin, who had arrived in Jerusalem a few hours earlier with Steiner's message rolled up and hidden in a tube of toothpaste in his bag. The train voyage from Istanbul normally took three days. But Raskin had missed the connection in Ankara and had been further delayed for a day at the Syrian-Turkish frontier. Seven days had passed since Brand's arrival in Istanbul. Of Brand's two-week period, one week had elapsed.

Shertok was thoroughly surprised. He had not been advised of Raskin's arrival. He knew Raskin vaguely and invited him into the flat.

His face turned stony as he listened to his visitor's brief account. It was the first he had heard of Brand's mission. He was flabbergasted by the delay, and furious at Steiner. Why had he not been told before? Then he read Steiner's letter. It was couched in a mixture of bureaucratese and rhetoric.

> The cup overfilleth . . . indeed, the proposal designated to alleviate the burden and rescue the doomed has been submitted to us as a Satanic project which we could not take upon ourselves to consider without first relaying it to you. . . . The courier will supplement the details that speak for themselves. . . .

There followed a list of complaints about other Palestinian agents in Turkey, their insolence and lack of discipline, and other routine office matters. Shertok crumbled the letter in his hand into a ball.

"I should have been told of this before."

"Steiner thought it too delicate a matter to telegraph."

"Why didn't he go through the American Consulate? The Americans were willing in the past to relay our messages through the diplomatic wire."

"I don't know. Steiner felt it was safer this way."

"Do the British know about this story?"

"Colonel Roberts does. At M.I. Eleven."

"Since when?"

"I think Saturday. I'm sure Mark asked him to pass the information on to you."

"They haven't so far."

"They don't think too much of it."

"Do you?"

Raskin looked down at his hands.

"Well, do you?"

"Brand certainly does. He seems serious enough."

"Do you trust the man?"

"Yes. We know he has done tremendous work in Hungary. He has been smuggling Jews out of the Polish ghettos. But there is the other man, this scoundrel Gyorgy. He is the dark figure here. He is a black marketeer. He's worked for half a dozen spy rings in the past, including the Germans."

"Isn't that enough to discredit Brand?"

"Yes and no. That's the mystery. Gyorgy is a special kind of scoundrel, too. He is a Jew, you know."

"What? And working for the Germans?"

"He's also worked for us. We have used him to send fairly large sums of money to Budapest and into the ghettos. He always delivers—as long as he gets his ten per cent. You might say he is a rat with a Jewish heart."

A look of annoyance spread across Shertok's face. He had a fine sense of the ridiculous but little sense of humor. Like many hypersensitive people, he regarded his compatriots as grotesque caricatures of himself.

"I'm sorry."

"And they must go back together?"

"According to Brand, yes, since the Germans planted Gyorgy on him as a watchdog. But Gyorgy doesn't want anymore to go back. He's certainly got enough money to retire."

"What if Brand goes back alone?"

"I don't know. If he offers them a bargain, it may yet save thousands and thousands of lives. What do *you* think?"

"I don't yet know what to think," Shertok said. "I should have been told about this sooner." His quick mind raced through the possibilities. "If we can delay the Nazis, through this or any other means, we certainly must do so."

"Steiner would like you to look this man over."

"I'll fly to Istanbul as soon as I can."

"Excuse me, but must you really?"

"Yes. I want to get my own impression of Brand."

"Please don't mind my saying so, but wouldn't that be a mistake? If you go, aren't you likely to raise too much dust? I mean internationally? Why not let Steiner, or Mark, handle it discreetly? If you go you can't avoid telling everything to the British. Wouldn't it be safer if you didn't?"

"We must not engage in any subterfuge," Shertok said firmly. "We cannot circumvent the British."

"If there is a scandal later on you could blame us. Wouldn't it be better that way?"

"No," Shertok said. "No. That's not our style." He asked Raskin to come back in the morning and repeat his report at the meeting of the Jewish Executive Committee.

* * *

The Executive was the governing body of the World Zionist Organization, a movement which in the beginning of the century had set out on a course at once realistic and utopian: to lead the persecuted Jews of Europe into the safe haven of their own land. The Zionists had foreseen the coming disaster in Europe, for they were hard-boiled men. But being also singularly naïve (a combination more common than one thinks), they believed at the same time that once in their own land all Jews would be six feet tall, free, happy and secure.

Various political groups were represented on the Executive: the ruling Laborites, the Conservatives, the Liberals and a religious party. They were as antagonistic to one another as factions of revolutionary movements often are, and for as obscure ideological and personal reasons. Their jealousies and frustrations were also fueled by tragic failure. Their revolution had been delayed too long. The very people who in the flush of youth and optimism they had set out to save and give a new dignity in their own land were systematically being wiped out in the gas chambers and crematoria. They all sensed their impotence to affect its fate. Faced with a disaster they had somehow foreseen, they had no means whatsoever to prevent it, nor any power for independent action save through appeals to the conscience of mankind, a recourse which had proven highly ineffective so far.

News of the disaster in Europe had reached them intermittently over the past three years. The first versions were garbled, as unco-ordinated intelligence often is, and caused more confusion than enlightenment. Europe was a charnel house of the improbable. An over-all view was obscured in a flood of unrelated Job's messages. When in 1943 the true nature and design of the holocaust slowly began to emerge, the sheer magnitude of the crime was still beyond human comprehension. Because it was incomprehensible, some could not fully believe it. For those who did comprehend, the horror was in some way disembodied and surrealistic. The few who saw clearly did not know what to do.

The Executive met early on the following day. A heat wave had struck Jerusalem that morning. The members of the Executive arrived covered with perspiration. The chairman was David Ben Gurion, a sturdy, stocky man of small stature, with an immense white mane of hair, in his late fifties. He was the agency's chief executive officer, a politician of great popular appeal and authoritarian manner. He was one of the early pioneers who had arrived in the country in 1906 in the wake of the Russian pogroms. His single-minded aim was to lead the Jewish community of Palestine to self-determination and independence. He was a pragmatist heading a body of inveterate ideologues. In his ninth year as chairman, he was a man of few illusions, and adept in the art of power politics. He craved special measures to rescue the doomed Jews of Europe, but could not believe in their practicability. He believed that only statehood would bring about radical change. Every other task, therefore, was subservient to its achievement.

Ben Gurion sat at the far end of the oval table. Sitting next to him was Shertok, whom he appreciated as an able diplomat, but not (as everyone knew) as a policy-maker. Next to Shertok was Eliahu Dobkin, a Laborite like Ben Gurion and Shertok, formally in charge of the Immigration Department, which in recent years had had few immigrants to worry about. Next along the table was Dr. Emil Schmorack, a Liberal Conservative charged with the economic affairs of the Jewish National Home. Schmorack was a mild man with a passion for parsimony and proper bookkeeping methods.

Across from him sat Yitzhak Gruenbaum, a former Jewish deputy in the Polish Parliament, who had escaped from Poland just before the war. His large, round face was lined, the mouth, above a short, pointed beard, drooped in a bitter frown. He headed the National Commission for the Rescue of the European Jews. This melancholy public body, frustrated by an inability to save any but a handful of escapees, was composed of a dozen public figures excelling mostly in oratory.

Next to Gruenbaum sat Rabbi Y. L. Fishmann. He was the leader of the religious party, a man of relentless zeal and a passion for splitting hairs in argument, of whom it was said that his God was in the sky and therefore more troublesome than terrestrial bosses who, on occasion, could be induced to compromise. On his left sat Dr. Werner Senator, chief administrator of the Hebrew University of Jerusalem. Senator was not a party man. He was the representative on the Executive of the wealthy American Jewish community, whose support for the National Home was boundless as long as they themselves were not asked to settle in it. Raskin was at the far end, opposite the chairman. He was the only man in the room in shirt sleeves.

Word of his arrival had spread earlier. The air in the room was heavy with anticipation. Shertok introduced Raskin as "one of our most trusted workers in Istanbul. I have full confidence in him."

Raskin spoke. "The subject of my report is both serious and at the same time fantastic," he began. "The Germans seem ready to barter a million Jewish lives for ten thousand trucks, eighty tons of coffee, twenty tons of tea and fifteen million bars of soap." The men around the table stirred.

"They have sent a man to Istanbul to make the offer, a Jew whom we trust, a known worker in the resistance. He tells us they are ready to release ten thousand Jews in advance against our agreement in principle to the transaction."

Raskin spoke in a slow low voice. The room was very hot and brilliant in the harsh white light that came in

through the large french windows. Everything in it stood
out in sharpest detail. The nine men around the table listened in silence.

When Raskin had finished his report, a waiter came
around as usual, with cups of tea and biscuits and dates.
The established routine struck Shertok as ludicrous. With
mute nervous gestures he motioned the waiter to withdraw.
Then he looked across the table at Gruenbaum, who was
glowering over his cup of tea and shaking his head in short
spasmodic movements.

"This is a satanic provocation," Gruenbaum said. His
cheeks were mottled purple with anger. "A satanic trick,"
he repeated. "It will make it even easier for the Germans to
slaughter the Jews of Europe. . . . I am opposed to the
payment of any ransom." He conceded, however, that
Shertok must go to Turkey immediately to interview Brand.

Gruenbaum continued to make his objections in a confused, rambling manner while Shertok twisted uncomfortably in his chair. He regarded Gruenbaum as a
narcissist, prone to cultivate the most minor of differences.
Shertok tore a small sheet from his pad. "If power cor-
rupts," he wrote, "the total lack of it breeds irre-
sponsibility." He passed the note on to Ben Gurion. Gruenbaum was now saying that even if it were possible to
ransom lives for money, he would still be opposed, for
"where would the money come from? I ask you, gentlemen, how could we ever pay?"

"We have some funds," Eliahu Dobkin interjected.

"We do not," Gruenbaum said angrily. "The funds we
have were collected for other purposes. They are conse-
crated to the upbuilding of Zion. We cannot touch this
money!" It was not the first time that Gruenbaum, the head
of the Rescue Commission, was pursuing this argument.
Once more he was pleading for assurances that Jewish
funds collected for settling immigrants and planting trees
and building schools in Zion would not be diverted to other

purposes. He felt very strongly about this. "These funds are sacred!" he said, "our main task is *here*. However much it hurts we must resist this recurrent temptation to relegate our task *here* to second rank."

The others contested this point, some calmly, some heatedly, in anger, all speaking at once. Shertok made an effort to interrupt.

"It is a moot point," he argued, "as long as we don't know where we stand." The question of funding the ransom could be dealt with later. If the offer was a serious one he had no doubt that new funds could be collected in a hurry. He agreed that Eichmann's offer might well be a devilish trick, but until they knew for sure they must make every effort to explore it. Shertok was aware of recent peace feelers by the Germans and he suggested that the dissensions within the Nazi hierarchy might be used to save lives. He would go to Turkey immediately to see what could be done.

Eliahu Dobkin spoke. The concern he felt was of a special nature. In his opinion efforts ought to be made to ransom first of all those Jews who were Zionists. It was only fair, he argued. The others might come later.

He added that the few whom they had managed to bring out of Hungary in recent months had turned out to be just rich people and fewer than a third were Zionists.

The chairman followed the discussion with an inscrutable face. He rarely looked directly at a speaker, but stared down the long green velvet tablecloth. His silence was of the palpable kind. He was considered charismatic, that is to say, his mere presence in a room did something to the normal critical faculties of others, as though he moved in a magic field of mythic energies. When he finally spoke, briefly, his words were followed with concentrated attention.

"I warn you," Ben Gurion said, without looking at Gruenbaum, "this is no time for futile indignation. Let us

not waste our breath on talk of devilish design. We speak
of the devil himself. We will deal with him if we must. If
this is an opportunity to save lives, we must use it. Of
course we cannot do it alone." He paused. "We must consult the British."

"Yes," said Shertok. "Without the British we can do
nothing."

Gruenbaum raised his hands dramatically. "Consulting
with the British will ruin everything even before you
begin!" he cried across the table at Shertok.

"We cannot circumvent the British," Ben Gurion said.
"In any case they must be consulted. We are together with
them in this war and the proposal comes from the enemy."
Ben Gurion was a sharper, perhaps more cynical man than
Shertok, and even as he spoke he foresaw only more frustrations and disagreements with the British and few new
opportunities to rescue. But he did not voice these doubts.

The proposal was put to a vote. It was agreed that Shertok and Ben Gurion should seek an urgent meeting with
the high commissioner. Until then the ransom offer must be
guarded carefully as a deadly secret. It was also resolved to
call a general strike on 5 June, and hold mass meetings
throughout the country to protest the threatened extermination of the Jews of Hungary.

Then Ben Gurion turned to the proposal that the Allies
bomb the death camps of Auschwitz.

Schmorack cried, "This is nothing we should even discuss! We cannot ask the Allies to bomb a concentration
camp full of thousands and thousands of helpless Jews!"
Again everyone spoke at once, and so heatedly that the
recording clerk lost track. Ben Gurion begged for order,
and again called on Gruenbaum.

"This is not a new idea," Gruenbaum said. "Our representative in Switzerland made a similar proposal last
month. He was relaying requests he'd received through the
underground, from Poland, Hungary and Slovakia. They

are begging for an attack on the gas chambers. To put them out of operation."

"They can't possibly pinpoint targets from such heights," Schmorack said.

Raskin interjected, "May I say a word? Brand brought out with him a chart. It is very detailed. And it shows all the railway lines leading into the camp."

"I'm sure the Allies would insist upon making their own aerial photographs," Gruenbaum said. "I am strongly in favor of asking them to do so—and launch the proposed air attack."

Again everyone spoke in great agitation. Schmorack repeated, "We cannot take this responsibility upon ourselves. It is monstrous. An air attack on Auschwitz might kill thousands and thousands of Jews."

Dr. Werner Senator added, "No, we cannot in good conscience do this. We cannot instigate the death of even one single Jew."

Ben Gurion and Shertok voiced no opinion. The matter was not put to a vote. It was clear where the majority stood.

Ben Gurion closed his leather folder. "Gentlemen," he announced, "the Executive resolves that we must *not* suggest to the Allies the bombing of concentration camps and other locations where Jews are likely to be the victims."

26 May 1944

Government House in Jerusalem was the local headquarters of that great power which, in the words of T. E.
Lawrence, "had thrown a girdle of humor and strong
dealing around the world." It was a large fortresslike villa
in pink stone set upon a narrow rock. The site was known
since Roman times as the Hill of Evil Counsel. A
magnificent park of olive trees and rolling English lawns
was surrounded by barbed-wire fences and concrete pill-
boxes manned by fuzzy-cheeked guards. Shertok and Ben
Gurion drove through the main gate. Behind the blooming-
rose hedges Sir Harold's daughters were playing tennis on a
clay court.

The high commissioner strode toward the two men as
they entered his spacious book-lined study. The bright light
streamed in through the arched windows at his back. Sir
Harold knew that the Brand mission would be the main
topic of their conversation. But he calculated that he would
be in a stronger position if they brought it up first, by way
of a plea.

"I am pleased you called. I meant to have a meeting arranged with you anyway this week," he said after the usual
introductory remarks.

"Your Excellency knows we put great store in having
these routine consultations," said Shertok. "We believe in
close co-operation."

The high commissioner sat down, feeling rather awkward. He knew there would be a disagreement. There always was. His discomfort was compounded by an arthritic pain in his left knee which always bothered him on hot humid days.

"Ah, co-operation," he said. "A nice word. What co-operation can there be between you and us? We are a wretched colonial administration without funds and power. You on the other hand represent a great international force. You have enormous means. Whatever you want, you get. When you don't, you fight."

Ben Gurion flushed. This was not a promising beginning. "Your Excellency has an odd way of phrasing our woes," he said. "I am very sorry about what you just said. You have been among us for six years but I am afraid you still know very little of the Jewish community in this country." Inside he seethed with anger. In the six years he's been here, he thought, he never once agreed to visit a kibbutz.

Shertok, foreseeing a needless clash, said, "I am sure Your Excellency knows that in these difficult times we are fully co-operating with the authorities to maintain law and order."

"But of course, I do appreciate *your* efforts, gentlemen. We all wish to maintain a measure of sanity in this country. I am sorry I must say this. I realize you are in a delicate political situation. One only has to look through the daily papers to see where your constituents hope to push you. It's clear the terrorists enjoy at least passive support within the Jewish community. This is what worries me so."

"It worries us too."

"It should frighten you. Last week they tried to blow up the Jerusalem radio station. Fortunately they didn't succeed. I'm sure you've seen the placards they posted in Tel Aviv with my picture and the 'Wanted for Murder' inscription. The next thing will be an attempt on my life, don't you agree?"

Ben Gurion said, "Your Excellency knows perfectly well that these leaflets are the work of small dissident groups. We have never hesitated to condemn their methods publicly. We've gone so far as to provide the police with lists of suspected terrorists and their addresses. A considerable number of extremists have been arrested as a result. This we did at no little political risk and personal discomfort. The terrorists after all claim they are fighting for free immigration and for a Jewish state. We condemn their methods. But may I remind you, sir, that this country was promised us as a national home by His Majesty's Government? People find it harder and harder to understand why its gates remain locked. I can't understand it either. If the present policies continue, it will become more and more difficult to restrain young people from acts of desperation."

The high commissioner glared at him. "I cannot accept that at all," he said. "Whatever we do, it is never enough! You always accuse us! I am fully aware of the tragic consequences of the war for the Jews of Europe. His Majesty's Government is not lacking in sympathy and has given ample proof of it. We are the only people who help the Jews and yet you go on insulting and throwing mud at us. You know that we have informed the Turks that any Hungarian Jews who arrive in Turkey will be admitted to Palestine. Even though the quotas are filled. Even though the Arabs will raise havoc when they hear of it. But however much we exert ourselves, in your eyes it is nothing." He raised his voice. "Nothing!"

Ben Gurion said calmly, "I am sorry we provoke you to such harsh language. We are not ungrateful. It is a fact that Jews could get *out* of Hungary almost freely until March. But no country was ready to take them in. The Turks did not give them transit visas because they could not enter this country. Now at long last you offer them entry permits. But it is too late. The Germans aren't letting anybody out anymore."

"It was the fault of the Turks," the high commissioner said. "We didn't delay. They did. I have not yet heard of any threats of terror against the Turks! I will tell you what the trouble with you is. You are too clever. Too clever."

He was sorry as soon as he had said these words. But why was it, he thought, that Jews always had such a proprietorial air regarding their misfortunes? As if others never suffered. He could not understand the connection between the Nazi persecutions and the growing fury of young Palestinian Jews against their British protectors. He was not a heartless man. But certitude being the child of custom rather than of reason, he was convinced that he was absolutely correct. There was little in his past experience as a colonial administrator that had sensitized his mind enough to carry his imagination further. Wherever he turned he recognized a new aggressiveness. He longed for a distant past. It was gone and now he heard only its "melancholy long withdrawing roar"—Matthew Arnold was his favorite author.

This is going to end badly, Shertok thought, and we have come to achieve concrete results. He offered a conciliatory word. "Your Excellency, we pray that some Hungarian Jews will be able after all to escape to Turkey. I appreciate the new right they now have to proceed to this country. And I wish to reassure you as well that we shall do our best to uphold law and order."

"I certainly hope so," the high commissioner said. He was very tired. Discussions with the Jewish leaders, he thought, always get out of hand. How I long to move on to another place, he thought. Nothing, nowhere, could be as bad as this.

Shertok shifted in his chair and, as the high commissioner had expected, turned to the Brand mission. In carefully rounded phrases, delivered in a respectful tone, he repeated Raskin's report, adding little, leaving out only

Raskin's complaints about Steiner. Sir Harold listened intently without a hint that he already knew about it.

When Shertok had finished, the high commissioner appeared deep in thought. The soft bell tinkle of sheep grazing on the rocky slopes nearby came in through the open window. Then Sir Harold spoke, carefully pronouncing each syllable:

"There is obviously—more here—than meets—the eye."

"We are well aware that this might be so," Shertok said. "Just the same, we feel the offer should be explored. With your permission I would like to leave for Istanbul immediately to see this man. Your Excellency may rest assured that I shall report everything to you and to the British Embassy in Ankara."

"You wish to negotiate with the Germans in Istanbul?"

"No," interjected Ben Gurion. "We think Brand should be permitted to return to Budapest with some agreed answer."

"What kind of answer could you suggest that would not seriously damage the Allied cause? In my opinion this smells of nothing more than Nazi intrigue. It is based on other motives than the apparent ones."

"We don't know," said Shertok. "The Rumanians have been selling us Jews for months. Mr. Hirschmann of the American War Refugee Board was recently paying them two hundred and fifty dollars a head. The nearer the Russians get to Bucharest the lower the price gets. Most recently they've asked next to nothing."

"I was not aware of this," said the high commissioner.

"Why not try the same system in Hungary too? All I ask is to be able to speak to this man. We could then decide what steps to take."

"I see," said the high commissioner. "Yes, by all means. Go to Istanbul to look this man over." He paused. His pale eyes were focused upon the pile of papers on his desk. "Yes. Certainly. Go. This way we shall at least not be giving ground for later accusations that we may have missed a chance of saving people."

"There is a small problem, sir," said Shertok.

"Oh?"

"I went to see the Turkish consul general this morning. I am sorry to say, he would not issue me a visa."

"He refused?"

"It seems odd, doesn't it?"

"I should certainly say so."

"It's a fact. He said he must refer my request to Ankara. He said he did not have the authority."

"Very strange."

"Perhaps Your Excellency might impress upon him the urgency of my trip. The Nazis have given Brand two weeks. There are only six days left."

"He does not take his orders from me. But I will certainly do my best. I'll telephone him this morning."

Excerpts, 15 May–3 June 1944
(A Random Selection from the Tel Aviv Newspapers)

RED ARMY POUNDS AT GATES OF HUNGARY

* * *

. . . As many as thirty trainloads of deported Jews arrive daily at the concentration camps of Birkenau in Upper Silesia. . . .

* * *

"I bring you greetings not from the living but from the dead." These are the words of a man who arrived in Palestine this week after a long and arduous journey from Poland. Only five months ago he was in Bendyn, Poland. . . . He states he is revolted by the questions put to him here by many people who ask whether reports from Poland are not grossly exaggerated. . . .

* * *

ALLIES ADVANCE ON ROME

* * *

The Hon. Basil Davidson of the British Council will speak on Byron and the Romantic Imagination at the Menorah Club at 8 P.M. . . . Entrance is free. . . .

. . . The YMCA, Jerusalem, at the request of
the Women's Auxiliary Territorial Service, has
agreed to open their swimming pool to members
of both sexes on Thursdays and Fridays. . . .

* * *

In the afternoon, led by Their Eminences, the
Chief Rabbis Herzog and Uziel, the convocators
marched to the Wailing Wall where special
prayers were intoned for the salvation of the Jewish people in Europe.

* * *

FIGHT BACK. You too can beat disease-car-
rying germs by observing strict cleanliness and
hygiene with the aid of Shemen's Carbolic Bath
Soap. . . .

* * *

ANGLOAMERICAN ARMADA GATHERS
Invasion of Europe Imminent

* * *

Two thousand bombers flew sorties over Occupied Europe last night, according to Reuter's Air
correspondent, Michael Ryerson. Flying For-
tresses and Liberator bombers penetrated the
Posen area in western Poland and attacked targets at Krysinev in Lower Silesia. . . .

* * *

1944: BEST YEAR FOR GRAPES IN DECADE

* * *

THE CRUCIAL QUESTION

". . . Is our Workers' Party splitting apart? Are we going to remain a united party? This is the crucial question that faces us today, as workers, as Zionists, as Jews," David Ben Gurion said at the Labor Party conference in Petah Tiqva.

* * *

CHAMBER MUSIC ORCHESTRA A SUCCESS

* * *

. . . of June 12, maritime insurance rates in the Mediterranean will be reduced from 6% to 4⅜%.

* * *

. . . Mr. Mintz of the National Rescue Committee told reporters that in July 1943 the British Government had privately informed the Jewish Agency that henceforth every Jew who escaped from Occupied Europe to Turkey would be admitted into Palestine . . . but the decision was relayed to the Turkish Government only in March of this year. During the delay of nine months, more than one million Jews were exterminated by the Nazis. During that time an average of nine visas a month were issued by the Turks to Jewish refugees. Mr. Mintz added that if the British note had been submitted to Turkey earlier a great number of lives might have been saved.

* * *

. . . the payment of half a pound each month
into the special savings account enables deposi-
tors to receive an electric refrigerator at the end
of the war. . . .

* * *

BLACKOUT REGULATIONS RELAXED

* * *

. . . Lieutenant C.K. of the Free Polish Army,
who left Poland via Sweden last autumn, said he
was stunned that in Palestine life was so "normal." People swarm to the beaches, night clubs
and cabarets are crowded each night. If people
here really knew the situation in the Warsaw
ghetto they would not go to night clubs and
cabarets. . . .

* * *

At the Eden: Johnny Weismuller in *Tarzan
Against the Nazis*. Nature itself seems to be
fighting the German war machine as Nazi para-
troopers threaten Tarzan's kingdom of the jun-
gle. . . .

* * *

LABOR PARTY FACES SPLIT

Mr. Ben Gurion, who demanded the immediate
expulsion of the dissidents from the party, interrupted his speech to welcome four party members
who have recently escaped from Occupied
Europe. One had left Hungary only two months
ago. . . .

* * *

AIRPORT CAFETERIA STRIKE

* * *

. . . The British Government has asked the Pro-
tecting Power (Switzerland) to make full inquiries into the deaths of seven RAF officers who
were killed on May 28 while attempting to escape
from captivity in Germany. . . .

* * *

NATIONAL FOOTBALL CUP CONTROVERSY

* * *

RED ARMY ADVANCES ON MINSK

* * *

Brand idled at the Pera Palace, upstairs in his room, or in the lobby, whenever he felt sure he would not run into any Germans. He was no longer counting days, but hours. The night far surpassed the day in anguish. He lay awake for hours on his bed. With each day that passed he felt more depleted, worn and wasted.

The delay was his fault. He had failed to convey the true state of affairs and its urgency. Another man, a better man, might have been more successful. Kastner, Komoly. Time also weakened his own resolve. In the half-consciousness of sleep and wakefulness he was suddenly terrified by the very idea of going back to Hungary. The fear crept through his body like an arterial pain. He lay on his bed, bathed in cold sweat. The smell of his own body disgusted him. I am not made to be a hero, he thought, why must I be a hero, in Hungary today, where the only contact with life is the certain expectation of death.

He thought of Hansi and the children. Did she still have the special pass? He closed his eyes. His limbs grew heavier and heavier against the rough and humid texture of the sheets. He lit a cigarette, then another, and another, and waited for the day.

One morning Mark came and convinced him to come out for a little walk. The two men strolled down to Galata Bridge and crossed over to Stamboul. The harbor was thick with tugboats and launches. Heavy wafts of black smoke rose over the dirty surface of the water. The stench hung in the market place among the garbage and dead fish, and rags and carcasses hung on iron hooks. Ratlike clusters of beggars huddled on the grand staircase of a mosque.

Further up the hill the air cleared, the domes and minarets soared into the clean sky. They walked into the Hagia Sophia, which until recently had been a mosque and was now a museum. Fresh grass was growing between the crumbling stones as though nature were slowly recapturing the work of man. Inside the basilica the sunlight streamed in through the high windows, on vaults of dazzling gold-leaf mosaic, but it was icy cold.

The solemn voice of a German guide echoed through the dome. "Hagia Sophia—Holy Wisdom—built in the year 547. It has been in constant use for fourteen centuries. . . . *Meine Herren und Damen,* it has withstood hundreds of earthquakes, survived the rise and fall of empires . . ."

In the small crowd of listeners Brand recognized the thin, slump-shouldered figure of Dr. Volker Mann. He gripped Mark's arm.

"Let's go," he hissed.

"Now?"

"Yes."

"Are you all right?"

"Damn it, I said, let's go. Now!" He ran out by a side door. Mark caught up with him in the large square.

"Please excuse me. I'm sorry I rushed you out."

"No harm done. I have been here before."

They walked on through the park to the garden of Topkapi. The palace was closed. They stopped at a small outdoor cafe. The sun came through the leaves of the olive trees and the air was full of damp freshness. Mark spoke of Shertok's imminent arrival. They had had a cable that morning that he might be arriving on the afternoon flight from Cairo.

"He is a kind and understanding man," Mark said. "Tough and able, too. A born diplomat. If we get a Jewish state one day he'll be our foreign minister."

Brand breathed deeply. Their little outing was doing him good. If Shertok would only arrive it could redeem the wasted time. Time might actually run backward. He could return to Budapest on Thursday.

They walked slowly down the hill through the gardens and parks to the shore of the Sea of Marmara. Under a stone gateway Brand was approached by a youth dressed in a thin, threadbare coat.

"Dollars? Sterling? Swiss francs?" the man said casually, clinking a few coins in his coat pocket. "I give you good rate."

Brand looked at Mark, who said, "Why not?" Brand slipped a twenty-dollar note into the youth's palm.

"Attention!" the youth exclaimed. "Police not to see." He pulled Brand by his arm and dragged him down a little lane. Brand wrenched himself free. He had no intention of following the boy to some secret assignation.

"No! Let me go!"

"All right, all right," the boy said, still walking quickly. "Take your money back. Here."

Brand clutched the folded bank note and the youth was gone and out of sight within seconds. He looked down at his palm and saw that instead of his twenty dollars he had been given a one-dollar bill. He turned quickly but the boy was no more to be seen. Brand felt stupid and sick. Mark caught up with him. Brand did not dare to tell him what had happened. They walked slowly back to the bridge.

Mark said, "Let me take you to your hotel. You look ill. You need some rest. Take a bath and relax."

Brand flung around, the blood rising to his head. He

reached out violently and struck Mark on the face. Then everything collapsed within him.

"I'm sorry, Mark," he sobbed. "I'm sorry. I don't know what came over me."

Mark rubbed his cheek. His clear blue eyes were large and slightly darkened. "I understand."

* * *

"I'm afraid I have discouraging news," Steiner said.

"My family? Oh my God!"

"No, no. It is a cable from Jerusalem. Shertok is delayed."

"But you said you expected him any moment."

"He should have arrived on last night's plane from Cairo. But he could not get a Turkish visa."

"I don't believe it!"

"It's true."

"He is not a stateless refugee! Why won't they give him a visa?"

"I don't know, Brand. I don't know."

"And without this visa he cannot come to Turkey?"

"Of course not."

"We get hundreds of people out of Poland! We smuggled Jews out of Auschwitz! And you are telling me that Shertok can't travel to Turkey?"

The last words came as a cry, but even as he uttered them Brand remembered that he had used the argument too often before and to no avail. The silk upholstery on his chair felt slippery and hot. Steiner put his hand gently on his arm. Brand pulled away. It appalled him, this terrible dependence on Steiner, this need he had for him and the rest of them—here and in Jerusalem—all with their petty concerns for legality and status, and visas.

"Shertok wants to come here and he *will* get here," said Steiner. "They can't refuse him for long. It means a few more days."

"How many?"

"I don't know."

"There are only four more days. I must go back to Budapest on the first of June."

"Shertok wanted to take the risk and fly here even without a visa. He asked the British Embassy to send a man to meet him at the airport. But the embassy said no, he should on no account travel without a visa. It's too risky they said."

"Risky? They won't shoot him on arrival."

"They may turn him back."

"They haven't yet turned me back. He could . . . tip them at the airport."

"He isn't Gyorgy. Brand, please . . ."

"But it's incredible."

"It's the Turks. They are a strange lot."

"Or else it's the British," Brand snarled. "Too risky. I'll be damned!" What unseen hands were pulling the strings? Was this a British attempt to sabotage his mission? No, it couldn't be. It could not be that Britain, the only champion of freedom in Europe, which had alone fought the Germans, would sacrifice the weakest, the most pitiful of the oppressed.

"We really don't know," said Steiner quietly. "We keep trying. I telephoned the American Embassy in Ankara this morning, just as you asked. The ambassador wasn't in but I left word and he'll call me back as soon as he returns. Maybe he can help."

* * *

"Mark, about those leaflets you wanted the RAF to drop on Salonika . . ."

Roberts and Mark were in the colonel's room in the British Consulate. Outside, in the Horn, a Turkish cannon boat was cruising slowly by.

"Yes, sir. It's very urgent."

"I've been in touch with Baker about it . . . at the RAF Wing Command in Bari. He's made some inquiries. There are apparently some technical problems. But they'll let us know next week."

"What kind of problems, Colonel? We have had nearly absolute air superiority over northern Greece for months."

"I don't know. I can't think of any problems either. Baker is a decent chap. Hampshireman like myself. He doesn't run the RAF though."

"There is very little time left, Colonel," Mark said. "The Germans are packing up their main installations. They must be threatened with heavy reprisals if they continue with the deportations. By next week the Greek Jews may be finished."

"I know," said Roberts. His pale, tired eyes gazed at the cannon boat in the waterway below. "I'll get in touch with them again today. They have so many other things on their minds. But you're right. They really ought to drop those leaflets. Baker will put the heat on them. It isn't that they don't want to help."

"I know," Mark said bitterly. "It's just that they still think we exaggerate. They are good people and they still can't believe the horror. They have nothing like it in Hampshire or Surrey, so why should things be different in Auschwitz or Dachau?"

Roberts said nothing. Everybody's so nervous, he thought, and so quick to raise their voices. This bloody war has been going on for too long. He looked up at Mark, then out of the window again. The cannon boat had passed. The silvery waterway was shimmering in the sun. Little wisps of mist hung over the houses on the opposite side.

The colonel cleared his throat. "I do think they ought to have dropped those leaflets by now," he said wearily. "Honestly, Mark, I can't tell you how upset I am by this delay."

"So am I, sir," said Mark. "It's not your fault."

"It's decent of you to say so."

"Would there be anything else, sir?"

"About that fellow Brand. I understand Shertok is flying out from Jerusalem to meet him."

"We very much hope so," Mark said. "So far the Turks have refused to give him a visa."

"What? But he was here twice last year, wasn't he?"

"This time they're still considering his request."

"The bloody Turks. He must be in a rage."

"Rage is probably not the right word."

"I know. He's such a touchy little man, usually."

"We all are."

"Relax," Roberts said. "It's nobody's fault. It's the bloody war. Brand is still here, isn't he?"

"Yes."

"I understand you've been making a few little deals with Kuzuk."

"I wouldn't say . . . deals, sir."

"Don't apologize. It's all right with me. But do me a favor. Keep him inside the hotel as much as possible."

"Thank you, Colonel. I very much appreciate your help."

"We are not Turks," Roberts said.

* * *

Brand leaned against the balustrade facing the Golden Horn. The hotel terrace was red-tiled, and covered by striped awnings. Under the pergola of painted forged-iron leaves, a four-piece orchestra was playing a string of old-fashioned Viennese tunes. The hotel guests sat in cane chairs at small marble-topped tables. Waiters in starched white jackets were serving drinks and small sticky bits of Turkish confection from huge copper trays. The terrace was bathed in the gentle light of an afternoon sun. The orchestra was playing the "Waltz of the Blue Danube."

Below the terrace a fruit vendor was pushing a cart across the cobbled stones, hawking his cherries in short, staccato cries. The cherries were a deep crimson. Their smooth skins sparkled in the sun.

Two little boys were playing hopscotch on the sidewalk. They wore bright blouses and shorts so brief they barely reached over the tanned thighs. Brand looked at them intently. It had been a long time since he had seen children at· play in the sun. The orchestra reached a crescendo. Then the high screech of the violins mellowed in a melancholy mood. *"Donau so blau, so blau, so blau. Durch Wald und Au."* Brand looked up across the Golden Horn. The water had taken on a pale greenish color, and on the hill beyond, the mosques and palaces were carved into the rock in a thousand shades of red, blue, gray and yellow. In the soft and translucent light the distance was foreshortened and the palaces and their towers seemed unnaturally close.

One of the boys on the square below suddenly fell forward on his hands. Brand leaned over the railing. The boy scrambled up and laughed. His body was slim and muscular, sculptured under the tight blouse and pants. He might have been of the same age as his own little son. His hair was honey-colored and curled on the nape. Brand sipped the remainder of his coffee. He lit a cigarette and inhaled deeply. This made him feel slightly dizzy. A train rolled out of somewhere across the Horn, came nearer, grew louder and for a moment its clatter and roar drowned out the orchestra and the boys' cries and laughter below. Then it died. Brand's cigarette hung from his taut dry lips. The orchestra finished its presentation with a flourish. Brand struggled to his feet. The cane chair fell over as he moved. His head spun. *"Donau so blau, so blau."* A ghastly calculation was running through his mind. *"Donau so blau, so blau. Durch Wald und Au."* How many trains were pushing through the woods in these few moments, between the first movement of the "Blue Danube" and the last?

He rushed across the terrace and entered the hotel dining room. People were standing about sipping drinks and munching canapés. Brand pushed his way through. The crowd chattered and laughed. A waiter offered him a drink. Brand rushed past him. The noise in the crowded room sounded distant. He looked at his watch. It was five-thirty. He held his wrist to his ear to make sure the watch was working. He lowered his arm. The ticking continued to rustle in his ear. *"Donau so blau, so blau."* He rubbed his ear with his hand. The rustle would not stop.

The hotel lobby, too, was jammed with guests, departing and arriving. As he rushed through breathlessly, he bumped into a heap of luggage. He heard voices as if from a great distance and ran out through a side door into the busy street. The detective was nowhere to be seen. Brand headed directly for the post office. He was walking more calmly now. Steiner will be raving mad when he hears of this, he thought. I must do something to keep Eichmann expectant.

HERZL CONTINENTAL VIENNA: MOSHE SHERTOK HEAD OF POLITICAL DEPARTMENT JEWISH AGENCY JERUSALEM ENROUTE TO ISTANBUL AFTER CONFERENCES WITH BRITISH GOVERNMENT ON PROPOSED AGREEMENT. EVERYTHING HINGES ON EFFECTIVE CESSATION OF DEPORTATIONS. WILL HAVE INTERESTING PROPOSALS WHEN I RETURN BUDAPEST JUNE FIRST. RESPECTFULLY BRAND.

When he had finished he pulled out his copy of *The Three Musketeers*. He raced through the pages and slowly copied out three lines of numbers on another cable form, which he addressed to himself at his Budapest address.

The clerk looked at him suspiciously. "Each digit counts as a word," he said.

* * *

Brand heard footsteps in the corridor. He turned toward the door. There was a brief knock and Captain Kuzuk entered. He was in civilian clothes.

"I do hope I am not disturbing. I was in the hotel and thought I might pass by for a little chat." He peered through the open door leading into the bathroom. "I see we are alone. That's a nice change."

Brand lit a cigarette. "I never smoke," said Kuzuk. "If I may say so, you Jews smoke too much. Mr. Mark smokes forty a day. Much too many. I'll take this chair if you don't mind. Ah, it is comfortable. I run around a good deal. My feet hurt."

"Put them up, by all means," Brand said. Kuzuk had already placed his shoes on the table. Kuzuk smiled. "I hope you are getting a chance to see something of our city. May is our best month."

"I saw only the Hagia Sophia."

"A great pity. You should not have missed the mosques. And the bazaar." Kuzuk leaned forward to eye the sleeve of Brand's jacket.

"Flannel?"

"What? Oh . . . uh, yes."

"English? Of course. It is the best. Very difficult to obtain these days. So expensive."

"I bought it before the war."

"Of course. The war. It will soon be over."

"When it's over, there'll only be another."

"You are ironic. I like ironic men! But you are going back to Hungary, are you not?"

"I hope to go back as soon as Mr. Shertok arrives."

"Then you are going back. Good!"

"Good? Why?"

"I have had a few thoughts since our last meeting. There is still this little problem with your *permis de séjour.*"

"I thought you said it was merely a technicality."

"Dear sir, you are quite right. But life is filled with little annoyances. Now I have been thinking. And I have hit upon a solution. No, don't thank me. It is nothing."

He picked up *The Three Musketeers*. "Jews are bookish. Now take Mr. Mark. He reads dozens. You only have this one?"

"Yes, it's my favorite."

"It must be. Now, I've been thinking. If we came to an understanding, my superiors might relent—and permit you to stay on after all. Temporarily."

"An understanding?"

"Oh, a very amicable one. Strictly between friends. Don't tell Mr. Mark about this, or you'll spoil everything. When you go back to Hungary you might want to stay in touch with us. Render us an occasional service. Wouldn't you?"

"I am here on a rescue mission. I don't deal in intelligence."

"Oh, please don't be frightened by the word."

"Everything I know I pass on to Mr. Steiner's office here. You could be in touch with him. Or with Mr. Mark."

"They are both excellent men. But we would rather work with you directly."

"I see."

"I promise we shall not impose upon you. Now, as a start, would you be ready to take back a little parcel? We expected Mr. Gyorgy to take it. But his plans have changed."

Kuzuk looked at him expectantly. "It would be in everybody's interest." He smiled. "I knew you would be willing to co-operate. Thank you. We'll talk again before you leave." The last words were said more brusquely. With his left hand, Kuzuk made a little military salute. It was not clear whether he meant it in seriousness or mockery. He strode out of the room, leaving the door ajar behind him.

Brand remained seated. After a while he stood up and began to pace the room.

Steiner found him an hour later still walking back and forth in a cloud of smoke.

"The American Embassy called," Steiner said excitedly. "The ambassador is back. I spoke to him this morning. He wants to see you as soon as possible. He will help. He is very close to President Roosevelt."

Brand's throat was hoarse from too much cigarette smoke. "When can we go?"

"The best train is in the morning. I'll pick you up at the hotel entrance at six."

"I'll be ready," said Brand.

* * *

Late that night a telegram arrived. It had been forwarded through Berne by the Swiss Consulate in Budapest:

BRAND CARE JEWISH AGENCY ISTANBUL: DE-
PORTATIONS INTENSIFIED LAST FIVE DAYS STOP
URGE ACCELERATE NEGOTIATIONS STOP EVERY
MINUTE COUNTS. KASTNER KOMOLY HANSI.

* * *

The railroad station was crowded. The noise reverberated in the dim sphere of space under the cast-iron dome above. The air reeked of sweat and sulfur. Steiner was irritable and fussy. He posted Brand at the barrier and went to buy the tickets for Ankara.

Brand's hands were clasped behind his back. His palms were perspiring. Kastner's telegram was in his pocket. Why had Hansi and Komoly signed it too? Undoubtedly to give it a greater sense of urgency.

On the platform a steam engine was hissing and people were rushing through the small wooden entrance gate loaded with luggage and provisions. Everyone was hurrying and in the damp and stupefying air they all looked sick. Brand glanced impatiently through the diminishing crowd wondering what was keeping Steiner. A hand touched his shoulder from behind.

"Mr. Band?"

Brand turned around abruptly. The detective from the hotel coughed and rested his right hand heavily on Brand's arm. He was flanked by two dark-looking men in police uniforms.

"Your *permis de séjour* is restricted to Istanbul," said the detective. "Strict orders."

"I am only going to Ankara for the day."

"That is not permitted. Come with us now."

Steiner suddenly materialized out of the crowd. His gray mane trembled in the air and with his hands he gesticulated nimbly.

"Mr. Brand will be back tomorrow. We have an appointment with the American ambassador."

"Ah? Only tomorrow? No. You cannot go. You come with us, Mr. Band."

"The American ambassador is expecting him!" cried Steiner.

"I take orders from Lieutenant Azid, monsieur. Follow me now." He led Brand to the main exit, escorted by the two policemen.

"I will go to Ankara to keep the appointment!" Steiner shouted. "I'll see you tomorrow!"

* * *

Brand was taken around the block to the harbor police station and locked in a small cell together with a seedy-looking bearded man who squatted on the floor. There were no chairs or benches. Brand leaned against the damp wall. There was a vague smell of urine in the air, mixed with some disinfectant. The bearded man spoke to him in Turkish, shaking his bandaged fist. Brand moved his hands

wearily in a gesture of incomprehension. The man raised
his voice. His growls filled the little cell. The door was
pushed open. A guard barked in a few throaty words and
the man, who had fallen silent instantly, slumped back
onto the floor.

Brand pressed against the wall. His feet burned. After
perhaps an hour he sat down on the floor with his elbows
propped on his knees and his hands covering his face.

Two or three hours later he was taken from the cell,
handcuffed roughly and pushed into a motor launch. The
launch raced across the strait and docked underneath
Galata Bridge, where a police car was waiting. A plainclothesman took the seat beside him. The car sped through
the streets and drove up to a modern office building.
Uniformed guards stood at the door, and in the middle of
the vast hall rose the heroic granite statue of Kamal, Father of all Turks. The huge head—twice life size—was lit
by an unseen spotlight. Brand was led into an office. A
stocky man in a dark double-breasted suit was sitting at a
desk. Brand remained standing.

"Eugen Band?"

"My real name is Joel Brand."

"Who are you working for? The full truth now. No more
stories."

"I am in Istanbul to meet with Mr. Shertok from Jerusalem. He is expected to arrive at any moment."

"You are a German agent."

"No, I am a Jewish emissary."

"You wish me to believe you are here on a religious mission?"

"I am not."

"Out with it. How much is Andrew Gyorgy paying you?"

"I am not working for him."

"Surely your kind does not work for nothing?"

"I just happened to arrive on the same airplane as Mr.
Gyorgy."

"What business do you have with the American ambassador?"

"He asked me to come to see him."

"Did Gyorgy introduce you?"

"No, he did not."

"We know you are not working for the Americans."

"I did not say I was."

"Who are you working for?"

"I am a Jewish emissary from Budapest."

"I urge you to co-operate, Mr. Band. Or whatever your name is. We have less polite ways to obtain the truth from you."

The door opened. Captain Kuzuk came in, followed at a little distance by Teddy Mark. The interrogator stood up.

"Those will not be necessary," Kuzuk said curtly, pointing to the handcuffs. He turned to Brand. "A misunderstanding." He smiled. Then his face turned grim. "I believe I was very clear that you should not leave Istanbul. I was able to prevent your deportation only on that basis. You should not have tried to deceive me."

"I was only going to Ankara for the day," Brand said, rubbing his wrists where they had been chafed by the irons. "The American ambassador was expecting me there. It is part of my mission."

"I don't know what your mission is, Mr. Brand. I only know you are making things very difficult for me."

Mark spoke. "It will not happen again, Captain," he said. "Mr. Shertok is arriving from Jerusalem. As soon as *he* leaves, Brand leaves."

"We do not want Turkey to be the site of these intrigues. You are well aware that we are neutral."

"That is precisely why I came *here*," Brand flared. "Where else?"

"Leave this to me, Brand," Mark said.

"Perhaps I should have deported you right back to Germany," Kuzuk said. "You remember our little understanding of the other day? . . . Good. You have one more week in Turkey. Afterward you leave. It doesn't matter to where."

"I'm sure I'll be able to leave sooner."

"Fine. Now go. Remember you are not to leave the Pera Palace Hotel without my permission."

Mark drove Brand to the hotel. "What did he mean by understanding?" Mark asked.

"Nothing. Just that I should not leave the city of Istanbul."

"I see."

"Do you really?"

"Please, Brand, none of your sarcasms. We're trying to do the best we can for you."

"Didn't you tell me you paid the detective a retainer? Or perhaps you don't pay him enough. He arrested me at the station."

Mark said nothing. Steiner had called him from the station and he had spent the day shuttling between Colonel Roberts and Captain Kuzuk trying to secure Brand's release.

"Let's not go back to the hotel," Brand said. "I'll go into hiding until Shertok arrives. Put me somewhere the Turks won't find me."

"No."

"Please . . ."

"You have no right to endanger our entire operation here."

"That would be the least danger. Others can take your place. But if I fail, a million Jews will be thrown away. And not to Palestine like you. To Auschwitz."

"Brand, believe me, it wouldn't work. It's impossible."

The lobby of the Pera Palace Hotel was dimly lit. Gyorgy came toward them carrying a suitcase and accompanied by another man. "Hello, Jo. How are things with you?"

"Thank you."

"I'm leaving. See you sometime, somewhere, I hope."

"I thought you said you are not returning to Hungary."

"Who said I was going to Hungary? But my job here is finished. Is yours?"

"Up to a point . . ."

"I'm flying to Egypt tonight. Courtesy of the British Government. Let's meet there one day."

"I doubt it. I am going back to Hungary. Then, after the war—maybe to Palestine."

"Dear boy, you really are an idealist."

"It is the land of our forefathers."

"My forefathers haven't done much for me lately," Gyorgy said lightly. "I'll let them have it."

* * *

Brand passed another interminable night. He lay on his bed staring at the ceiling. His eyes burned. He dared not shut them for fear of the visions lurking in the recesses of his feverish mind. Four days left. Three. A party of guests passed through the corridor outside his door to an adjoining suite. A woman squealed. The corners of the yellowish ceiling seemed foggy. Brand put out his cigarette and lit another.

He thought of Hansi. No, she hadn't looked relieved when he left. It was her way of hiding her tension. Once, years ago, they had been together in a sailboat on Lake Balaton. A storm had come up, the boat had capsized and sunk. They had swum with great difficulty to the distant shore. When they finally reached land, Hansi had said, "To know how to swim is more important than to know how to sail."

He thought of Gyorgy. Gyorgy should be in Cairo by now, and, as always, in pursuit of no telling how many flags of convenience. Brand was not angry at Gyorgy. He sensed that he too did things with mixed feelings, for a variety of motives, some noble, some sordid. For any man to realize this was a form of modesty. He suddenly remembered that he had forgotten to pay Gyorgy his two hundred and fifty francs. Swimming was more important than sailing.

There was a knock on the door. Brand dragged himself up, and as he walked toward the door he felt a dreadful itching and tingling in his legs. But it was only a waiter with a large tray of bottles and glasses who had mistaken the room number.

He sank back on the bed, burying his hands under the pillow. He tried thinking of his youth. An afternoon long ago in the vineyards of Buda, the sun, the taste of freshly plucked grapes, his mother's voice. The distant lights and sounds and smells before the world broke down, blew up. Hansi before they were married. He won an hour or so of dreamless sleep shortly before dawn. When the first street noises began to filter in, he got up, and, with the assurance of a sleepwalker, showered, shaved, dressed and sat down at the desk facing the awakening city.

"Dearest Hansi, children," he wrote, "this letter will likely reach you after my return. I miss you and think of you constantly. The strain of the past two weeks . . ."

The telephone rang.

"Hello! Hello! Is that you Brand?" Steiner was calling from Ankara. "Are you all right?"

"Yes."

"Are you sure?"

"Yes."

"Good." Steiner coughed. He was taking the early morning train, he said, and would be back in Istanbul after lunch. "Will you be at the hotel?"

"Yes," Brand said hoarsely.

"Good. I'll come straightaway."

"What happened? Did you see the ambassador?"

"Not on the telephone," said Steiner and hung up.

But it was not before midnight that Steiner arrived at the hotel. Brand sat up in his bed.

"The ambassador is very upset. He is not at all surprised that Shertok was refused a Turkish visa. Nobody gives a damn here about anything but Turks. The Turks had their own Jews once. The Armenians. They've slaughtered them by the millions. It's one of the great crimes of history, said the ambassador."

"Very interesting. Did he say anything else?"

"Yes. The ambassador said that in his opinion the British are obviously afraid to upset the Arabs."

"Why don't you put that into your next report?"

"Hear me out, please. The ambassador is very serious about this. He thinks you should be sent back to Budapest with some sort of delaying answer. It's his private opinion. For his official opinion he has cabled Washington."

"And that will take weeks, of course."

"You are wrong," Steiner said triumphantly. "The Americans are very efficient. The answer came back within an hour. It's a good answer. Roosevelt is sending out a special emissary to meet you. Ira Hirschmann of the War Refugee Board."

"How soon will he get here?"

"I wish I knew," said Steiner.

"I hope the Turks will give him a visa."

"There is another thing, Brand." Steiner's voice came across as if from a great distance. "I am sorry I must tell you. We've heard from Budapest. They have arrested your wife."

29 May 1944

The mass deportation to the Polish death camps began almost everywhere in Hungary on 16 May, the day of Brand's arrival in Istanbul. Eichmann's special troops swept like a cyclone through the eastern regions, most exposed to the Russian line of advance, then through the south and southeast. The arrests were made mostly by Hungarian gendarmes. The Germans merely co-ordinated.

The Jews of Budapest were still left untouched. In the provinces, everywhere, Jews were rounded up with ruthless efficiency and herded into closed ghettos. From there, according to a timetable telephoned daily from the Budapest Hotel Majestic, where Eichmann alternated between his desk, his bottle and his horses, the inmates of the ghettos were loaded into cattle trains and sent north. Few of them knew where they were going. Most thought they were being sent for "resettlement" in the east. Their pengö were exchanged for reichsmark. This made them think they were going to labor camps in Germany. To bolster the deception, they were encouraged to take personal belongings with them, books and jewelry, food and—although it was May—winter clothing.

During the first ten days, while Brand was lingering at the Pera Palace, it seemed that the overwhelming size of the operation, as well as the panic it generated in some localities, would defeat its well-planned efficacy. Tens of thousands of Jews were fleeing the small towns into Budapest, while others were fleeing Budapest for the small towns. But Eichmann's special squads quickly developed a knack of redirecting the chaotic flow of human traffic and channeling it to their demands. Those streaming out of Budapest to the east, where they hoped to reach the Russians, were assembled at Klausenburg. Those fleeing toward Budapest from the south were gathered up at Komárom. The vast open plains of eastern Hungary offered little if any opportunity to hide. Once the fugitives were gathered it was mostly a matter of co-ordinating railroad schedules to keep up a steady daily flow of twelve or fifteen thousand to the death camp of Birkenau.

The speed and efficiency of the deportations were unintentionally abetted by the official Jewish community councils. In their timid commitment to a notion of law and order that had survived from a different age, they aided in the destruction of their flock and in their own destruction as well. Like rabbits confronted by a snake, dignitaries, rabbis and communal leaders were mesmerized into docility. Between the two poles of total obedience and open rebellion, they never found an intermediate area, and settled for the former. It is easy, but cruelly unjust to blame them for it in retrospect. All rebellion carried with it the risk of savage countermeasures. Total obedience in the end proved even more destructive, but to say that obedience precluded whatever slight chances there were to manipulate or delay implies that they were aware of such chances. It was less a lack of courage than of intellect and imagination. The communal leaders were for the most part conservative businessmen, not strategists of resistance. As a rule they shunned Brand's colleagues of the illegal Aid and Rescue Committee. Instead they meekly passed on the German orders to move into ghettos, and saw to it that this was done with a minimum of friction. Those among them who knew where the trains were going did not tell the deportees. Through fear or ineptitude they let themselves be absorbed into the scheme of subterfuge and deception which Eichmann and his henchmen had perfected over the years, and by which the Nazis often destroyed their victims even before they laid hands on them. The extermination machine seemed almost to be running by itself. If this was a horrifying fact it was merely another cause of self-congratulation for the Nazis. To Eichmann and his slave drivers and executioners it proved that the Nazi system was superior to all others.

Brand's wife, Hansi, was among the few who preached resistance. Her entreaties were dismissed as the inventions of an inexperienced housewife. After Brand's departure she spent much of her time forging baptismal certificates for the few with the courage and possibility to go into hiding. She awaited a signal from Istanbul, but none arrived. Eichmann's adjutant telephoned to ask if she had heard from her husband. Hansi said, "Not yet."

"We shall not be waiting for very much longer," said the adjutant and hung up. Hansi ran to consult Baron Philip von Freudiger, co-chairman of the Central Council of Hungarian Jews, who had signed Brand's letter of introduction to Steiner.

Freudiger was a man of considerable dignity and a pious Jew. Like the others, he had been counting the days for Brand's return. But nothing had been heard from Brand. There was a rumor that he was dead. Eichmann's inquiry struck Freudiger as a meaningless gesture. The Germans were not waiting anyway, and the deportations were continuing, not to Waldsee as Eichmann had promised, but to Auschwitz. The Jews of Budapest had also been ordered to move into proscribed quarters of the city.

"We must resist," Hansi said.

Freudiger shook his head. "It is impossible."

"Tell them to scatter and flee."

"How can I tell them to flee? Where would they go? Where could they hide?"

"In the countryside."

"They would be killed by the peasants. Or turned in."

A few days later, Freudiger himself fled east. He paid
Krumey ten thousand dollars to drive him to the Bulgarian
border. Before he left he saw Hansi Brand again. "You
must run too. You can manage it," he said. "Save yourself
and the children. While it is still possible."

"I must be here when Jo returns," she said, although she
hardly believed in it anymore.

"I don't think he will return," said Freudiger. "If he
does, it won't be before we are all dead."

It was 29 May. Brand was still idling at the Pera Palace
Hotel. Hansi walked home. It was not the entire truth that
she was only waiting for Brand's return. She wanted to stay
in Budapest where Kastner was, even though she had not
seen him. She was also a hostage in Eichmann's hands; his
deputy would never drive *her* to the Bulgarian frontier.

She walked quickly through the darkening streets. The
special pass that Brand had left enabled her to move about
more or less freely. The chestnut trees were in bloom.
There were few people about. But as she passed Grundel's
Restaurant on the park, the orchestra was playing, a great
crowd was eating and drinking on the veranda, attended by
waiters in immaculate black dress.

She hurried through the park. Swans were cruising in the
pool under the willow trees. The grass was freshly cut. The
flower beds were neat and fragrant. The gravel was raked
and dry. She walked up the stairs of the apartment house
and let herself into the flat. The children were playing with
a neighbor in the living room. She did not allow them out
of the apartment for fear they might be seized. They ate
a meal of beans and rice. Food rations for Jews were scarce.
But Dr. Schmidt—he had just been transferred to Berlin—
had sent her a case of tinned food before he left. (Some
said he had been arrested.)

At eight the children were in their beds. Soon afterward

Hansi lay down too. She longed to sleep. She had never really believed that Brand's mission would succeed. But she understood that he had to undertake it. And yes, she had been relieved to remain alone, and her skin turned to goose flesh.

As she lay on her bed feeling sick, feeling trapped, she reflected that at least he was safe. There was for her a kind of consolation in this thought, and a belated expurgation of guilt.

At about eleven she was awakened by a banging noise. In her half-conscious state she thought at first that a wall had collapsed and buried the children under it. By now she was well practiced in tearing herself out of nightmares. She forced her eyes open and sat up. The noise continued. Heavy boots and fists and sticks were beating against the entrance door. The children in their room screamed. Hansi rushed to the entrance and unlatched the front door. A group of Hungarian policemen pushed inside.

"You are Hansi Brand? Come with us!"

"I cannot. There are two small children in the house."

"That's too bad. You come with us. Quickly now!"

"But no!" she cried. "Look here. I have a special paper." She produced Krumey's pass from her wallet. The policeman examined it carefully. He nodded and put it into his pocket.

"Now you no longer have it. Come. On with you, bitch! Be quick!"

They allowed her to put on shoes and throw a coat over her flimsy nightgown. Then they led her down to a waiting car.

* * *

She was thrown into a bare and windowless room. The floor smelled of animal droppings. A light dangled on a wire from the ceiling. Hansi was strapped to a wooden chair. Her hands were tied behind her back. Her swollen left cheek was bleeding where she had been struck by a leather whip.

A man in shirt sleeves towered over her. The whip hung loosely from his hand. "Now talk, you filthy bitch. Where is he? Where did your husband go?"

"I don't know. I told you. He went on a business trip."

"When?"

"Two weeks ago."

"You are lying. He went abroad."

"He didn't."

The man seized her by the hair and forced her head back. The light exploded in her eyes. She pressed them shut. He pulled her forward by the hair.

"You are lying! He is in Istanbul!"

"He is not . . ."

"Who do you know in Istanbul?"

"No one."

"Who is sending you coded telegrams from there?"

"I did not get any telegram . . ."

"Of course you didn't. We intercepted it." The man held a piece of printed paper up to her swollen eyes. "Read, you bitch!"

The pain raced through her neck and chin and cheeks. Her eyes burned. The small piece of paper was covered with four-digit figures. Behind the paper the room whirled and turned.

"What does it mean?"

"I don't know. I've never seen anything like it."

"You are lying."

"Perhaps it is from one of my husband's business partners. An order for telephone parts."

"Your husband is in Istanbul. What is he doing there?"

"It cannot be my husband. This must be somebody with whom he is doing business."

"You are lying. But we'll get the truth from you."

"I tell you . . . it may be something to do with the Budapest Telephone Company."

"Where is your code book?"

"I have none."

"You'll have plenty of time to remember."

The man stepped back. His heavy foot shook on the wooden floor. She heard the slam of a door, then nothing. The overhead light was switched off. The room was pitch black. When the light went out, the stench grew stronger. Hansi pulled at the straps that tied her knees to the chair. They loosened slightly. Her arms remained twisted behind the back of the chair. She rose slightly and tried to lift them out. Her left foot slipped, the chair fell, she crashed sideways on the floor. Her left arm was squeezed under the heavy wood. The pain paralyzed her hand. The whipped cheek rubbed against the rough boards. She passed out.

30 May 1944

Very much later, the light was turned on. Hansi was lying on her side tied to the chair, with her cheek on the ground. She saw a pair of heavy boots. A man bent over her and untied the straps. She felt his breath of alcohol. Another pulled her up roughly, kicking the chair out from under her with his foot. She was pushed out into a yard. It was morning. A light rain was falling and wet her burning face. The two men lifted her into a closed van, which immediately drove off. She could not see where they were going.

Some fifteen minutes later the van stopped. Hansi was pulled down and found herself in a cellar. She was led up a few iron steps. It seemed to be a freight elevator. The elevator rose and stopped. She stepped out into a corridor carpeted in purple red. A door opened. Hansi noticed a lit crystal chandelier. The men removed her handcuffs and left. She looked around. It was some sort of office, but hunting prints in gilded frames hung on the wall, and the windows were draped in silk. The chairs were upholstered in fine needlepoint. Hansi was still wearing the coat she had thrown over her gown the night before. She tried to peer out of the window, but the view was blocked by heavy green shutters. She heard steps behind her and wheeled around.

"My dear Frau Brand, are you feeling well?" A German

officer, dressed in riding habit, stood in the middle of the room. He looked at her lacerated face and shook his head.

"I am so sorry. They are wild people. I am glad we discovered you in time. A strange coincidence in fact. We were anxious to speak to you this morning anyway."

"Yes?" Hansi held her breath. She stared, bewildered, into the man's pale dyspeptic face.

"Ah, I am afraid we have never met before. I am Hermann Krumey, Colonel Eichmann's first deputy. Will you follow me now? The colonel would like to speak to you."

She followed Krumey into another room at the far end of the corridor. Eichmann was leaning against a desk. He was also in riding habit. In his left hand he held a little leather crop which he was tapping nervously on his boot. Another officer sat in an armchair by the window. The room smelled of eau de cologne.

"How is your dear husband? I hope he is well."

Hansi's knees shook. She searched for something to hold on to.

"Where is he?"

"As far as I know, he is in Istanbul," Hansi said in a low voice. With her left hand she touched her bruised neck. Eichmann hit the table with his crop.

"He ran away. He used me. The damned swine, I am not accustomed to facilitating Jewish tourism in first-class German passenger planes."

"The Hungarian police who arrested me last night showed me a telegram from him that they intercepted."

"What did it say?"

"I don't know. It was in code."

"Aha! Who has the code?"

"Dr. Kastner. He might have received other telegrams directly."

"Aha. So that's why he was here yesterday with his honeyed phrases and three cases of French champagne. But he had nothing real to say."

"I know my husband. He is keeping his side of the bargain."

"Did you tell the Hungarians about it?"

"No. I told them nothing."

"They beat you."

"Yes. But I didn't tell them anything."

"Congratulations, *gnädige Frau*. If you had opened your pretty mouth you would have been a corpse by now."

"If he has cabled it means the negotiations are proceeding. He will be back on time."

"Bah! I also had a telegram from him. Very clever. Anybody can send a telegram. He should be sending trucks, not telegrams."

"Obviously it takes time. We knew that in advance. Anyway, the two weeks are not over yet."

"He's got one day left. What the devil has he done so far?"

"I am sure he is doing his best. He will be back as soon as he can."

"Is he having a good time meanwhile? Enjoying the sights of Istanbul?"

"These things take time," Hansi repeated. She had regained her composure. Her voice was firm and cool. Her mind raced feverishly forward to anticipate Eichmann's reactions. It seemed he still wanted to deal, and as long as he wanted to deal there was hope.

She said, "I'm sure he is waiting for word from London and Washington. He intended to contact the highest Allied authorities."

"Rubbish! Your husband is a phony. The Turks didn't want to let him in. His Jews couldn't even get him a visa! The German Embassy had to intervene! I should have known better than to trust a Jew!"

"Yes, he lied to us," echoed Krumey. "He told me Professor Weizmann was flying to Istanbul just to meet him.

But the man is still in England. He gave a speech in Margate the other day."

"Even if he is still in England, I'm sure that Weizmann knows what is happening. He is most probably taking the matter up with Churchill and Eden at this very moment."

"Is he now?" Eichmann crossed his legs comfortably. "And who tells you they want to take in any Jews? Of course they don't." He turned to Krumey. "There you have it. I offer them a million Jews, give or take a few. Do they want them? No. They don't like them any more than we do."

"You are wrong!"

"At bottom the English and the Americans are pleased as punch that we are ridding the world of its Jews."

"That's not true."

"Don't you shout at me!"

"There is a delay because you continue the deportations. If you had stopped the deportations my husband would have been back here last week with an agreed offer."

"What do you take me for, Frau Brand? Of course the deportations are continuing. If your husband is not back by the day after tomorrow, we'll start cleaning up Budapest too. . . . You still have that special pass we gave him, don't you?"

Hansi shook her head. "The Hungarians took it."

"Never mind. We'll send you another. Because you kept your mouth shut to the Hungarians."

"Thank you."

Eichmann turned to Krumey. "That *was* courageous. One might almost think she is a German woman."

"I assure you my husband is doing his best. I ask you. At least spare the children for now. It will be a sign of good will and would greatly facilitate my husband's efforts in Istanbul."

Eichmann laughed out loud. Under the receding forehead, the nose pointed up sharply. The eyes betrayed an expression almost of content.

"So now you are appealing to my humanitarian instincts. My good nature. Ha, ha! Really that *is* rich!"

Hansi waited calmly for the laughter to subside. Then she said, "Sir, I am not appealing to your good nature. I am appealing to you as a business partner. A gesture of good will at this point will enable my husband to get you what you want more quickly."

Eichmann's eyes suddenly turned cold and furious. "I will not be lectured by you, Frau Brand. You are permitting yourself too much. That might prove dangerous."

"You are not frightening me. One only dies once."

"My dear Frau Brand," Eichmann said in an icy voice. "You are clearly succumbing to your nerves. You are overwrought, aren't you? Perhaps a little trip to Auschwitz will do you good."

"I am fully aware of such a possibility. If you send me to Auschwitz you will have nobody left to deal with. And my husband will never return."

"Don't worry," Eichmann said lightly. He turned to Krumey. "If we'd known that she wears the pants in the family . . ."

"Yeah," echoed Krumey, "we might have sent *her*."

"You have nothing to fear personally," Eichmann continued. "We are German officers. We keep our word. However"—like all dedicated bureaucrats he tended at difficult moments to console himself with a cliché—"*Ordnung muss sein*."

"Thank you."

"You have two more days," Eichmann added. "Then the party begins. So far we've been leaning over backward to accommodate you people. What are you standing around for? We have work to do. You may go."

Hansi turned slowly and walked out into the corridor of the Majestic Hotel. She went down the stairs and crossed the lobby, gathered her coat about her and stepped out to the terraced entrance. The doorman looked surprised. She ran down the hill. The light rain soaked her thin gown. Sodden leaves were lying in mounds on the steep ground. The drizzle was everywhere, encasing in its cold net not only the city, it seemed, but the whole world.

2 June 1944

Shertok went through his morning mail. His fine oval face was tense. The dark eyes, under their bushy brows, glanced out through the open window. The office was in the east wing of the Jewish Agency Building, a horseshoe-shaped stone structure in the heart of the suburb of Rehavia, which only a generation before had been a bare expanse of rock and shrub a mile or so outside the Old City of Jerusalem. Through the open window he looked out on the trees that had been planted in his youth. They were now reaching the rooftops and shading the neat little terraces from the sun.

He pushed his mail impatiently aside and rang his secretary. "Anything from the Turks?"

"No, not yet."

A week had passed since his first request for a Turkish visa. In the meantime Brand's two-week period had expired.

In the colorful band of pioneers and labor leaders who had worked their way up to the political leadership of the Jewish national home, Shertok was something of an exception, a loner. Ben Gurion and the other Labor Party leaders were self-taught men. Shertok was a graduate of the London School of Economics. The others were flamboyant, stubborn and strong-willed in the service of their romantic cause. Shertok believed in compromise; he was a circumspect and sober man regarded by many as a pedant, and by some as a bore, who tended to confuse the vital with the incidental, with too great a reverence for bourgeois correctness and symmetry of form, too bureaucratic, too fussy, too pious in his commitment to abstract notions of morality in what the cynics regarded as a world of cruel power realities.

Shertok's colleagues on the Executive had migrated to Palestine as young or middle-aged men. Shertok was a child of the country, brought up in its new kindergarten and schools, in the first class of graduates of the new Herzlia Gymnasium of Tel Aviv. The others had grown up in the Jewish diaspora of Eastern Europe. Shertok's roots were in the new land. And yet, in some way, he seemed more obsessed with the disaster that had come upon the Jews of Europe than they were. All were deeply struck, but Shertok was less fatalistic, more tortured by the thought that they could do more to help.

In his office this morning Shertok pondered this difference, with but a shade of self-righteousness. The reaction of his colleagues to Raskin's report from Hungary was a case in point. They had vented their horror in public speeches, and then had turned to other matters.

In Shertok's nature there was something like a feeling of personal guilt. He kept saying, "There must be a way, there must be *some* way." The others viewed him with perplexity, for however much they wished there were some way, they could not find it. They were engrossed in many other urgent matters. Ben Gurion had spent most of the week in a furious effort to prevent a split in the Labor Party, and, failing in this task, had lashed out against the dissidents in public and in private. In the evenings he was closeted in his home.

"He is like Achilles sulking in his tent," Shertok told his wife. No, more like an overgrown child. Their enemy was the Devil incarnate and all his hosts, but they were still picking at one another like scrapping children.

The Brand mission was constantly on Shertok's mind. He had lived through the past week in uninterrupted anguish, counting each day as it passed. And he conferred with leaders of the clandestine Jewish defense organization *Haganah*. Their secret links within Allied intelligence organizations gave them a point of view entirely their own. One of them urged Shertok to contact the Germans directly. The suggestion struck him as irresponsible. "You are mad," he said. "We have no choice but to work through the British."

The Turkish visa did not arrive. Shertok tried another course. On Wednesday, 29 May, he visited the brigadier in charge of British Military Intelligence in Jerusalem. The brigadier knew vaguely of Brand's mission. Shertok explained that it was vital that he meet Brand—a great many lives might depend upon it—but that for some mysterious reason the Turks were preventing the meeting by refusing him a visa. He pleaded with the brigadier to permit Brand to come to Jerusalem for a few hours.

The brigadier shook his head. He was sorry, but if Brand came to Jerusalem he could not guarantee his return to Hungary. No, he could not offer him safe-conduct. It would set a dangerous precedent incompatible with the proper conduct of the war. Moreover, the security authorities would definitely be against it.

"Brigadier, with respect," Shertok said, "this isn't reasonable at all. What possible damage could a man like Brand inflict upon the security of this country?"

"He would see quite a few Allied installations while he is here, and carry vital information back to Germany. Even if he is not a spy"—the brigadier was ready to take Shertok's word for that—"the Germans might later extract information by torture."

Shertok argued doggedly and politely. The brigadier listened patiently but did not change his mind. "There must be a way out of this absurd impasse," Shertok said. Thousands of lives were at stake. Couldn't they blindfold Brand at the airport? He need not leave the terminal. British security officers could be present at all stages of his interrogation. The brigadier thought that this would not be feasible. While it might be agreeable to him personally, he was sure the security authorities would never agree. They were likely to relent only under pressure from London.

"There is no time for that."

The brigadier said he was very sorry indeed, but he did not see another way out.

"I am simply aghast that this should be your final answer," Shertok said. The brigadier was taken aback by the desperate tone of his voice. He was not a bad man, only slightly phlegmatic. He cleared his throat and promised to look into the matter further. Would Shertok please contact him on the following day?

* * *

All this had taken place yesterday. In the afternoon a mystifying telegram from Steiner had arrived. "SENDING DRAFT INTERIM AGREEMENT FOR BRANDS PARTNERS. CABLE APPROVAL SOONEST." Shertok was confounded by this. Were they sending Brand back to Budapest after all? He rose from his desk and walked out through the corridor into Ben Gurion's room. A small delegation of Haifa merchants was there, protesting the recent introduction of new taxes. Ben Gurion asked Shertok to join the conversation. Shertok mumbled an excuse and retreated to his room. With slow mechanical movements he gathered his papers in a neat pile and carefully screwed on the cover of his fountain pen. He called his secretary on the internal telephone.

"Anything new from the Turks?"

"There is still no word."

"Have you reached the brigadier?"

"He was not in his office. We'll try again."

Shertok slammed down the receiver. The brigadier had probably left for the weekend. And on Monday it would still be only talk. The British had all the time in the world. They temporized. They were fighting the Germans with all their might. But in the face of the Jewish tragedy they were bystanders. It was not their kin being shoved into the gas chambers. Perhaps the wild men of *Haganah* were right after all. No, not possibly. To contact the Germans directly in the middle of the war would jeopardize the entire future of the Jewish national home.

The telephone rang. The brigadier was on the line. "A solution has been suggested that may satisfy everybody. I was wondering how you felt about it."

"Yes, sir?"

"We cannot give this man a safe-conduct to Palestine. But if *you* met him on the Turkish frontier, say in Aleppo, it would be another matter."

"You mean he would be free to go back?"

"Yes, sir, that's right. I realize it's a long way for you to go . . ."

"I don't mind that at all. As long as Brand can go back."

"Well, it's practically on the border. If he does not go farther Security say they will not touch him. I'm sorry about the inconvenience. Security are rather bores at times."

"I can't blame them," Shertok said. A tremendous weight was lifting. "Thank you very much."

"Not at all. When do you expect to go?"

"We shall cable our people in Istanbul to put Brand on the train on Monday. I'll wait for him at Aleppo station and take him off."

"Right. I'm sorry I didn't think of this sooner."

"Thank you very much anyway."

Shertok put on his jacket. He was suddenly feeling almost lighthearted.

On the stairs he met Raskin. "You are still here?"

"I'm leaving day after tomorrow."

"Any trouble with your Turkish visa?"

"No trouble at all. They gave it to me immediately."

Shertok nodded and walked on. A fierce *khamsin* wind was blowing up from the stone wilderness of Judea and its hot fury was aflame with dust. Shertok wiped his brow and quickly walked home. The melting asphalt road clung to his soles. From a mosque in the Valley of Hinnom the sound of a muezzin's voice wound itself in coils over the rooftops. The distant wail rose in the hot air, ghostly, like smoke from an as yet invisible brush fire.

Brand went down to the dining room. The detective posted himself in the doorway. Steiner was waiting at a little side table. Brand ordered lunch.

Steiner was making conversation. He had been speaking with the American Embassy in Ankara earlier in the day. In their opinion, the British, while not actually blocking Shertok's visit, had made no move to facilitate it. Brand glowered. His own mission too would run aground in a quagmire of indifference and red tape.

"Where is the American emissary? Hirschmann?" he asked. "He was supposed to fly here right away, wasn't he?"

"He was detained by another commitment in New York," said Steiner. "Then he ran into some trouble getting a seat on the plane." He began a long discourse on the difficulties of air travel in wartime. Brand stared vacantly at his plate. Priorities were flexible, Steiner explained, anyone could get bumped off the plane, and yes, even high-ranking officials were at the mercy of wily junior transportation officers. The American ambassador was forced the other day to give up his seat to a roving colonel with a higher priority rating, or perhaps just pull in the right quarters. "But Hirschmann will certainly be here within the week."

"Kuzuk wants me out of here."

Steiner said, "In Turkey nothing is ever final. We may yet change his mind. There is a meeting this afternoon of the Interdenominational Committee, and afterward . . ."

Brand was on his feet. "Enough!" he cried. The guests at the other tables looked at him curiously.

Steiner colored. There was nothing he disliked more than a public scene. "Please, Brand. Sit down . . ."

"Excuse me," said Brand. "I am going up. I want to be alone." He turned to go. Steiner remained sitting in a pose of offended dignity. Brand rushed upstairs. The detective was by his side. Brand locked himself in his room. He dozed in his chair by the window.

The telephone rang. An unfamiliar voice said, "Herr Band, at long last I've finally reached you!"

"Who are you?"

"Dr. Hoffmann." There was a pause. "Werner Hoffmann of the German Legation. I've been waiting to hear from you."

"I'm sorry. I have been very busy. One meeting after the other."

"Oh? I look forward to hearing. For some reason I haven't been able to reach Mr. Gyorgy either. Do you know where he is?"

"I am afraid I don't."

"Well, no matter. I happen to be downstairs at the bar. Please join me."

"Right now?"

"Why not? There is much to discuss."

"Yes. Of course," Brand said quickly. "I shall be right down." He walked numbly across the carpet and out the door. The detective looked up from his newspaper. Landau was just coming out of the elevator.

"Where are you going?"

"Down."

"No! Not just now!" Landau said, pressing his heavy frame against the elevator door.

"Let me pass. You have no right."

"I am only advising you. Don't go down now."

"I am not your prisoner!"

"I know that Hoffmann called you. Don't go down to see him."

"Out of my way, damn it," Brand said. He pushed his foot through the doorframe and seized Landau's arm. Landau grabbed him by his collar. For a moment they glared at one another in a tense embrace. The detective came closer to look. Landau tore his arm free and pushed Brand away brusquely. Brand reeled back and kicked Landau in the shins. Then he wheeled around and started for the stairs. Landau heaved forward and fell upon him heavily. They rolled over one another on the floor. Brand was on his back now, pushing with his hands and knees. He was weeping with rage.

"Let me go, let me go!" The detective was watching them with a smirk. Brand's knee hit Landau very hard on his left cheek. Landau pushed his full weight down and pressed Brand's wrists firmly to the floor. Brand heaved and pushed. Landau's grip remained hard and firm. As Brand writhed, Landau brought his knee down and struck him with more force than he intended in the abdomen. Brand's muscles slackened and his face turned sideways. Landau held him firm for another moment. Then he let go and rolled off.

"I didn't mean to hurt you," he said as he scrambled up. "But you shouldn't have tried to go see the Gestapo man."

Brand rose shakily to his knees.

Landau said, "Do you hurt?" Brand dragged himself up. Landau said, "I am sorry."

Brand's lips trembled. He walked slowly back toward his room. The detective grinned. In the doorway Brand turned. Landau was standing at the end of the corridor straightening his jacket and tie. In the room the telephone was ringing. Brand walked in and fell into an armchair, humbled and self-loathing. Why did I begin all this, he thought. I am not up to it. The telephone continued to ring and then stopped. Across the Golden Horn the mosques hung on the hill, pink and opaque, completely still.

Mark came next morning soon after ten and knocked on Brand's door. There was no response. He turned to the detective. "No, monsieur, he's not gone out. Not since—ah—yesterday." The detective smiled knowingly.

Mark knocked again. The detective took a key from his pocket and let him in. Brand's inert fully clothed form was lying on the bed. He seemed hardly to breathe at all. Mark raced over. He shook Brand by the shoulders. Brand did not move. A sour smell hung in the air.

Mark cried, "Brand! Brand!" The detective opened a window. Brand raised his head heavily and fell back. Mark shook him again and brought up his head with his hands. Brand's eyelids opened to two narrow slits of white. He muttered something incoherent. Then, very slowly, he came to. He had taken a strong sleeping tablet the night before and had been unconscious for almost twelve hours. Mark ordered coffee and sat with Brand while he drank.

"You should not take these things," he said. "Where did you get them?"

"It's none of your business."

"Landau told me of your little encounter yesterday."

"Why don't you employ the brute to beat up Nazis?"

"He didn't mean to hurt you. He is sorry and feels badly. He just wanted to keep you . . ."

"Get out, please. Leave me alone. Oh, for God's sake, why don't you all just leave me alone."

"All right, all right," Mark said. "I'll come back in the afternoon."

Brand staggered out of bed. He showered but did not feel refreshed. Then he sat down at the desk staring vacantly at the telephone. He did not go down for lunch. Steiner came, fussy and apologetic.

"I was very sorry to hear what happened. And, yes, make no mistake about it. Landau will be severely reprimanded. The agency in Jerusalem will hear about this. But you did promise me, Brand, not to contact that German."

"Forget it. I've decided to go back to Budapest."

"What will you offer them? You have nothing and you know it. And the Germans know it."

"How? Have *you* told them?"

"Brand, this is Istanbul. They have spies everywhere. You'll be arrested the minute you cross the frontier."

"That's why I was going to meet Hoffmann. We must make a move."

"You are right. I've thought about that."

"I know. You do a lot of thinking."

"I merely meant to say we are not just sitting on our hands. Sit down. Let me tell you what I have in mind."

Brand sat down and looked at him wearily. Steiner turned on the radio.

"I have composed a little memorandum," he said through the noise, "which I think we might pass on to the Germans—if Jerusalem approves. It may keep them quiet until you meet Shertok and return with a more concrete offer. Here it is. I have called it an interim agreement. Brand, do you follow me? I am talking to you. Brand!" He handed Brand two typewritten pages.

Brand went wearily through the text. It was couched in the form of a "minutes of agreement" between the "plenipotentiary of the Central Council of the Jews of Hungary, Mr. Joel Brand, and the representatives of Moledet." *Moledet,* the Hebrew word for "homeland," was one of the code names for Steiner's office, used in the past for communications with Jews in Budapest.

The gist of the "agreement" was an offer to pay the Germans one million Swiss francs for each month that the deportations were suspended, pending a final agreement.

"If Jerusalem approves—and I hope they do—we'll find a neutral courier to bring it to Budapest."

"This letter won't satisfy the Germans," Brand said. "For God's sake, why Moledet? Say it's the Jewish Agency! Two weeks ago Mark was ready to sign Weizmann's name."

"Mark is a child. Even Moledet is too clear an identification. We must think of the British, too."

"Steiner, I tell you this letter won't satisfy Eichmann. Not for any time at all."

"But you will soon be back in Budapest anyway. With Shertok's precise instructions. It's only a question of time."

"Why don't I return with this right away?"

"You must see Shertok first. You said yourself the Germans will not believe you if you don't."

"Then send this memo over to Hoffmann right away. He's waiting to hear from me."

"First I must get Jerusalem's approval. I have a man who is flying there this week. Trust me, Brand."

"What choice have I?" Brand said. His voice was hoarse. "Kuzuk wants me out on Monday."

*   *   *

An hour later he was still sitting by the window. Mark came in. "You look a little more cheerful."

"Maybe."

"I'm glad."

"Steiner has shown me some kind of memorandum we can give them."

"Has he been here with his legal stuff? Well, it can't do any harm."

"I'm not sure it will do any good. Maybe, if I go with it immediately . . ."

"Ten days ago, maybe. Not *now*."

Brand said bitterly, "It's not for *now* anyway. Before it gets approved by all the bureaucrats and busybodies in Jerusalem and London, weeks will go by."

"Forget the memo, Brand. I have good news."

"Shertok is arriving?"

"No. You are going to Jerusalem to meet him."

"But that's in British territory. You said they'll arrest me."

"No. Everything is fixed. You'll be free to come back. They are guaranteeing you a safe-conduct. Colonel Roberts just told me."

"You trust him?"

"There's no choice, Brand. We have to trust him."

"But do you?"

"I tell you, he promised you a safe-conduct. You'll be free to return."

"But do you trust him?"

Mark paused. "Yes, I trust him," and he masked his own hesitation with a reassuring nod that obtained an instant response in Brand's broad and open face. He is like a boy, Mark thought. He cannot be a fake. Landau is wrong. Aloud he said, "I will go with you. As long as I am with you nothing can happen."

"What about a visa? You forget, I don't have a visa."

"Give me your passport. Roberts will have a military visa stamped in by tonight. It will all be easier from now on."

"What does Steiner think?"

"Forget Steiner. You know how he thinks."

"Are you sure it's all right?"

"Absolutely. Everything is fixed and arranged with Colonel Roberts."

"How soon can we leave?"

"In the morning. We'll be in Jerusalem on Thursday. You'll be back in Budapest within the week."

* * *

On the following morning, Monday, 5 June, Brand and Mark boarded a ferry at the foot of Galata Bridge. The sea was frothy in the salt wind. The boat turned the point and the Old Seraglio came into full view, and the islands and hanging gardens and the lone tower of Leander. For the first time since his arrival in the city, Brand eyed it with something less than guilt. A thin layer of mist hung over the water, and through its melting shreds the white palaces and minarets and mosques gleamed in the morning sun. Mark pointed with his thumb. "The Blue Mosque."

"I know," said Brand. "I was here before. As a young sailor. I'd almost forgotten."

"You were a sailor?" Mark looked surprised.

"I wasn't always in this business," Brand said.

The boat turned sharply to the left and edged its way slowly past the breakwaters to the railway pier. A swarm of porters came aboard with wild shouts of *"Bagajji! Bagajji!"*

Brand and Mark followed the stream of passengers into the station hall. The platform was drowned in steam and smoke. Brand and Mark squeezed through the crowd. The sleeping car was at the head of the long train, just behind the locomotive. The conductor led them to their compartment, number eight. The detective, dressed in a yellow suit, was standing outside the door.

"Bon jour, monsieurs," he said with a broad smile.

"I was already wondering where you were," Mark said. The detective opened the compartment door and helped them to store their luggage.

"I travel in the next car," he said in an amiable tone. *"Bon voyage, monsieurs."*

"He'll go as far as the frontier," Mark said.

"I shouldn't have thought they'd really go to such lengths," said Brand.

"Don't worry. He is harmless."

"Do they think I'd jump the train in the Taurus Mountains?"

"He won't give us any trouble," Mark repeated. "Relax. Sit back. It's going to be a long trip."

The train moved out of Haydarpasa in jolts and jerks and wound along the seashore, slowly gathering speed. Brand stood at the window. The stony beach was littered with the debris of past summers. In the narrow channel the islands floated in a greenish mist. The train shook. The gulls swooped down on the dead fish that had been washed up on the shore. Brand's face was flushed. "I am very tired," he said.

"It must be the anticipation," Mark said. He looked up from his newspaper and saw the hard expression on Brand's face, and it suddenly occurred to him how little he really knew him.

* * *

Ten hours later the train rolled into Ankara station. It was just becoming dark. The conductor rapped on the door and stuck his head in.

"Monsieur Mark, there are two gentlemen to see you."

Two men in dark overcoats huddled in the corridor.

"Ah, it's Griffel," Mark said. "Come, we'll walk outside with them."

They climbed down to the platform. The detective lingered a few feet behind. Mark introduced Brand. Griffel nodded. He was the Ankara representative of a refugee relief organization and knew all about Brand's mission. Brand wondered how he had found out. The man with him was a businessman from Jerusalem residing in Ankara. They strolled over to the station restaurant. Mark ordered drinks. Griffel was upset.

"I don't understand you," he said. "In my opinion you're taking a very great risk."

"That's just one point of view," Mark said soothingly.

"No," said Griffel. "I tell you, Brand, you are being lured into a trap."

"That's not true," Mark said with visible annoyance. "We have a guaranteed safe passage."

"Fairy tales. The British will throw both of you into prison. You won't get out before the end of the war."

"I tell you they have promised Brand safe-conduct," Mark said.

"They break promises," Griffel said solemnly as though he were quoting a well-known text. "It would not be the first time."

"The high commissioner in Jerusalem gave us a guarantee," Mark said, "and Colonel Roberts in Istanbul. Roberts has never lied to me."

"It's a trick, I tell you. The British first made sure that Shertok would not get a Turkish visa. Now they lure Brand into British-controlled territory where they can arrest him."

Griffel's companion spoke. He was a small man with large spectacles. "Brand should try to reach America. In America we have a chance. He can rouse public opinion. Through speeches. Interviews."

"Nonsense," Griffel said. "How could we possibly get him there?"

"We can try."

The two men continued to argue the point heatedly, as though Brand and Mark were not there. "Well, maybe he should go to America," Griffel finally said. "He certainly shouldn't go into British territory."

Mark said, "Our friends here exaggerate the dangers, Brand. The British are not the villains Griffel thinks they are."

Brand looked at Mark, and then back at Griffel. He could not really bring himself to believe that the English would plot in cold blood to block him and his mission. He had spent the darkest years of the war glued to the Voice of Freedom on the BBC, the opening bars of Beethoven's Fifth Symphony, followed by "This—is—London." Aloud he said, "Maybe you are right about the British. But I must continue anyway. The Turks are throwing me out. I can either go back to Budapest empty-handed, or I can go to Jerusalem. Between the two, Jerusalem seems the lesser risk. Shertok is waiting for me there."

The sleeping-car attendant came into the restaurant and asked them to return to the train, which was about to leave. They walked back to the platform. Griffel continued his heated appeal. Brand's face was frozen. They settled back into their compartment. Their beds had been made up. Brand lay staring at the springs and coils above. Griffel's warnings had had the curious effect of making him feel much surer than before that he was doing the right thing. The train rumbled through the night and began the long ascent toward the Taurus Mountains.

They were just leaving Kayseri when Brand awoke. Behind the low station building the mountains were covered with snow. The attendant came in with coffee and cakes. Mark had gone to the restaurant car. Brand drank his coffee and watched the scenery roll by. A second locomotive had been added at Kayseri. The train wound its way slowly through the forests and narrow valleys and little picturesque villages precariously perched on the rocky slopes. Brand opened the window. The air was cool and full of fresh fragrance. The train stopped at every little station. Mountain people got on and got off, loaded down with huge baskets and animals and provisions for their journeys. Brand walked out to the corridor. The detective stepped aside to let him pass.

He entered the next car, which was the restaurant car. A tall young man, sitting at a table by the window, looked up. A smile of recognition spread across his pink owlish face. Brand shrank back. Then he remembered Vitin, the Swiss Red Cross official he had met on the plane.

"Goodness," said Vitin, "it's a small world. Do sit down please."

"Thank you," said Brand as he took the seat.

"May I order you a coffee?"

"I'd like a brandy as well." The mountains had become bare as the train climbed higher and higher, almost parched, crystalline and covered with long patches of white snow.

"I am taking a week off. Away from my work," Vitin said. "Are you too? Had enough of machines?"

"Ah . . . yes . . . I am off for a while."

"I am getting off at Adana. I'll try and find a nice sunny spot on the beach."

Brand echoed mechanically. "A nice spot on the beach."

"When are you going back to Germany, Herr Band?"

Brand started. Vitin looked surprised. Brand looked into the clear eyes and felt a sudden wave of warmth. "Listen, Vitin," he said hurriedly, "I am not German. I am a Jewish emissary. On a special mission. Can you understand?"

Vitin's eyes had opened wide. He leaned forward across the narrow table and placed his hand on Brand's icy fingers.

"Of course I understand," he said. "Of course. Can I help?"

"Help?" Brand forced himself to smile. "You are very kind. Will you be going back to Germany for the Red Cross?"

"I am going back in two weeks' time. Not to Germany. To Hungary most probably."

"I am Hungarian," said Brand. "Will you try to find my wife in Budapest? The last I heard was that she had been arrested. Do you think you can help?"

"I'll certainly do my best."

The paid bill had been returned with change and was lying upside down on a little porcelain plate. Brand scribbled his name and address on it. "Thank you very much," he said. "You see, at this moment, I don't even know . . ."

He stopped short. Mark was hovering over them. "Good morning. You know one another?"

"Yes," said Brand. "We met some time ago on an airplane. Mr. Vitin, this is Mr. Mark. We travel together. Mr. Vitin is with the Red Cross."

"By the way, what happened to Mr. Gyorgy?" Vitin said. "I expected to see him in Istanbul. But he never showed up for our dinner together."

"I did not see him either," Brand said.

"I thought you were traveling together. Weren't you?"

"It's a long story," Brand said. The coffee and brandy had cleared his head. "Let's talk about something else."

He leaned back. Vitin folded the bill and put it in his pocket. Mark noticed, but said nothing. The snow patches on the mountain were turning gray with mud.

*   *   *

In Istanbul early that morning, Roberts called Steiner at his hotel. Steiner was still in bed.

"I understand the bird has flown."

"You mean Gyorgy?"

"No. Brand. He's gone."

"Impossible."

"Didn't you know?"

"What? Back to Budapest? I assure you, I knew nothing about it."

"Actually he has left for the Syrian border. Young Mark went with him. How odd you didn't know."

"This is the first time I heard of it. Why in God's name did they leave without telling me?"

"To meet Mr. Shertok, I suppose. Well, I must be off. Good-bye."

"Colonel, I don't understand . . ." But Roberts had hung up. Steiner rose from his bed. He was at a loss to understand what had happened and why. He thought, I have been short-circuited again by the wild men. I have been made a fool.

He phoned the Pera Palace receptionist, who confirmed

Brand's departure. Then he called Landau. "Oh yes. There was no time to tell you. They left for Jerusalem to meet Shertok."

"Jerusalem? Roberts didn't mention Jerusalem."

"That's odd. Well, he should know. He fixed it."

I have been made a fool, Steiner thought. And not for the first time. But this insolence tops everything else. Running off like thieves. Without telling me a word.

I ought to hand in my resignation, Steiner thought. In protest. Yes, I will cable Jerusalem today. Things must not be allowed to go on in this way.

* * *

In the afternoon, when they were alone in the compartment, Mark said, "Please don't be upset with me for asking, but I must know. You didn't ask that Swiss to cable Eichmann for you, did you?"

"I asked him to find my wife. He is going to Budapest in two weeks."

"You trusted him? He is a complete stranger."

Brand snapped, "I have all the friends I need just now. I'm ready to trust a stranger for a change."

"I'm sorry, Brand. I shouldn't preach. Don't get mad now. We'll soon be in Jerusalem and everything will be under way."

"You didn't sound so sure in Ankara."

"Griffel annoyed me. He is another Steiner."

"Why were you so annoyed when Vitin mentioned Gyorgy?"

"I wasn't annoyed."

"You still don't trust me."

"Don't say that, Brand."

"But you don't."

"I am in a very difficult position, Brand," Mark said. "Gyorgy is only one part of it. By the way, the day after you arrived in Istanbul, Gyorgy warned me against you. He said you were a phony. Peddling a fairy tale."

"Poor old Gyorgy."

"Don't say 'poor old Gyorgy.' He also insinuated that your wife and Kastner . . ."

"He did?" Brand's face was expressionless.

"I'm sorry. I shouldn't have mentioned it."

Brand said nothing.

"He is a slimy character."

Brand said, "I wonder where he is now?"

"In prison, I'm sure. Where he belongs."

"I wonder," Brand said.

Mark suddenly felt that he owed Brand a confidence. "Perhaps he isn't. Did you know that Gyorgy was also an American agent in Hungary?"

"No."

"He smuggled a radio transmitter in for them. It was quite a feat."

"I'm not surprised," Brand said. I'll yet surprise you, he thought. He turned away and stared out the window.

*   *   *

The train had begun its sharp descent toward the Mediterranean plain. The hills on both sides of the track were ablaze in the brilliant red of a billion poppies. The train shook badly on the uneven track. Torrents of water came gushing down from great heights into riverbeds below. Then the rocks opened abruptly and they were rolling through rich farmland and vineyards and olive groves. Oxen moved slowly across the fields, dragging wooden plows and harrows. The flat plain extended south to the Gulf of Alexandretta, but the sea could not yet be seen. It was close to five in the afternoon when they pulled into Adana. The conductor announced there would be a three-hour stop.

Mark and Brand wandered through the dull and dusty

streets followed by the detective a few steps behind. The detective was annoyed by the delay, which meant that he would not start back to Istanbul before the next evening. It was growing dark, and when the train finally pulled out of Adana the night was black. Brand sat quietly by the window. They were due at the border before dawn.

"I say," Mark's voice came at him through the rumble, "I say, I don't think anything will happen. But just in case we get separated at the border . . ."

"You mean if the British do arrest me?"

"No, I didn't mean that. But understand, Brand, we must be ready for anything. You can never be sure when you cross borders."

"You swore they gave me a guarantee."

"I'm not saying they'll arrest you. But if something happens . . . one never knows . . ."

"You know something!" Brand cried. "Griffel was right!"

"I don't. I swear! I only want to . . ."

"You did this deliberately. You want to destroy me! You knew it all the time!"

"Brand, please. I don't know anything. I swear Roberts promised you a safe-conduct. The border has been informed. Relax. I'm not saying they'll break their promise. But this is their war. It's their army, not ours. I only want to say that if there is a mix-up—don't talk to them. Don't answer any of their questions. Always insist that one of us is present."

Brand was very pale. The train trembled. "Relax, Brand," said Mark. "Most probably everything will work out all right. You'll see. Let's try to sleep now. We need it."

At three in the morning the train slowly ground to a stop. There were voices outside. A Turkish border policeman came in, glanced at their passports and left. The train began to move again. A few minutes later it screeched into

the British checkpoint of Meyden Ekbez. Dawn was break-
ing in the wooded hills. A British official passed slowly
down the corridor, knocking politely on each door. Brand
handed him his German passport. The British official carefully inspected every page. There was a sound of rifle butts
knocking against the paved station platform outside. The
Englishman handed back the passport.

"Thank you, sir," he said. "Have a nice trip. Good
morning," and turned to leave. Brand lit a cigarette. His
heart was still pounding and his hands were slightly trem-
bling.

"You see," Mark said softly, "nothing happened. Everything is all right."

Presently the train began to move again. Brand shaved
and put on a fresh shirt. His gray face stared at him from
the small mirror above the sink. Then he sat down silently
at the window watching the hills and forests in the pale
morning light. He lit another cigarette and inhaled deeply.
A light dizziness spread through his head. He threw away
the cigarette. We'll be in Jerusalem by tomorrow afternoon, he thought, and he felt a slight contraction in his
chest. The two days in the train had been like a suspension
from life, a voyage out of time. It was not just the mystery,
after the long journey, of regaining in Jerusalem a missing
fragment of reality, but also the haunting fear in Brand's
heart that it might prove to be trivial.

Mark said, "Everything will be all right from now on.
You'll see."

The train entered the outskirts of Aleppo. Brand looked
over a low wall into a small yard where a man was pulling
a bicycle out of a tin hut. Farther on a massive citadel rose
over the rooftops and silvery spirals of smoke. The train
crept into the Aleppo station and jerked to a stop.

Mark gave him a broad smile. "Here we are," he said in
a cheerful voice. "Everything will be just fine from now on.
You'll see."

Brand pushed down the window and looked out. It was a station like all others early in the morning. The platform was nearly deserted. The train to Jerusalem was on the opposite track and seemed still unoccupied.

"I hope there won't be a long wait," Mark said. "I'll call a porter. Wait here." He disappeared on the platform.

Brand lit another cigarette. He heard footsteps. A stranger was standing in the doorway.

"Are you Mr. Brand?"

"Yes, I am."

"Is this your suitcase?"

"Yes."

The man motioned to a waiting porter who picked up Brand's valise. "This way, please," the man said.

Brand turned around to look for Mark. The stranger took him by the arm. "No, this way." Brand pulled his arm free, frantically looking around. But Mark was nowhere to be seen.

"I don't understand," Brand began and turned left sharply to where the porter was standing with the luggage.

The stranger said, "Take him." Two soldiers drew up on either side and seized him by his arms. Brand tore back. The two soldiers dragged him into the corridor. A jeep was standing on the platform and its engine was running. The two soldiers lifted him up like a package and forced him into the back seat of the jeep.

Brand cried, "Mark! Mark!" But Mark had disappeared. The jeep raced off into the street.

LET OUR CRY BE HEARD: HASTEN AID
TO OUR BRETHREN IN THE HOLOCAUST

The general work stoppage called to alert the
conscience of the world was solemnly observed
by Jews everywhere in the country.

Factories employed in the war effort closed for
half an hour of solemn observance.

* * *

LET OUR CRY BE HEARD: HASTEN AID
TO OUR BRETHREN IN THE HOLOCAUST

Adults above the age of eighteen observed the
fast called by the Chief Rabbinate. The meetings,
held in the main cities, were attended by thousands of citizens. Solemn appeals were addressed
to the great democracies, who, even in this hour
are . . .

* * *

LET OUR CRY BE HEARD: HASTEN AID
TO OUR BRETHREN IN THE HOLOCAUST

* * *

(an editorial)

. . . we should be sinning against ourselves if
we do not ask whether the continuing prolif-
eration of meetings (to protest and appeal) is not
self-defeating as a measure . . .

* * *

ROME LIBERATED

Allies advance on Orvieto

* * *

Charges that the government is going back
on its word that train service to Jerusalem will
be . . .

* * *

. . . in Jerusalem the mass meeting at the Edison
Hall erupted in a stormy scene when a small
group in the audience protested against the presence on the stage of Mr. Yitzhak Gruenbaum of
the Jewish Agency Executive. . . . Their ire was
raised by the fact that Mr. Gruenbaum was bare-
headed. . . . Screams of "Apostate!" . . .
"Down with the Atheist!". . .

Mr. Gruenbaum cried back, "I will not put on
a hat. If you don't like that leave the hall." . . .
Order was restored with great difficulty.

* * *

LET OUR CRY BE HEARD: HASTEN AID
TO OUR BRETHREN IN THE HOLOCAUST

* * *

(Text of the Resolution Adopted)

". . . the occupation of Hungary places the last remnant of the Jews of Europe in danger of utter destruction . . . one million Hungarian Jews and three hundred thousand in the Balkan countries are facing certain death.

"The general convocation of the Jews of Palestine refuses to believe that the democratic powers whose great victories and achievements recently . . . cannot find effective means to arrest the evil hand of murder. If only their resolve be in conformity with their growing capacity to rescue . . .

"In this last hour the Jews of Palestine raise their voice to sound a desperate plea . . .

* * *

BUY WAR BONDS

* * *

LET OUR CRY BE HEARD: HASTEN AID
TO OUR BRETHREN IN THE HOLOCAUST

* * *

. . . Mr. B.L. broke through the ring of orderlies, seized the microphone and cried: "Sitting here you will not save a single Jew!" He refused to surrender the microphone. . . .

* * *

BLACKOUT REGULATIONS RELAXED FURTHER

At about the same time as Brand and Mark boarded the Taurus Express at Haydarpasa, Shertok was attending one of the solemn mass meetings in Jerusalem held to protest the massacre of the Jews of Hungary. A long resolution was passed. Shertok had the entire text cabled to London, New York, Ottawa and Johannesburg.

Soon after, he left Jerusalem by car and headed north for Aleppo. Aleppo was at the northern tip of Syria, across two frontiers, some twelve hours away on narrow, bumpy roads that had much deteriorated since the beginning of the war. With his usual precision, Shertok was timing his arrival in Aleppo to coincide almost exactly with Brand's and Mark's. He would meet them at the Aleppo railroad station and take them off the train.

He spent the first night in Haifa in a hotel overlooking the sea. The bay curved into the shore and lay enclosed like a shining river, dotted with ships and boats. Shertok was tense with expectation, and then night fell and nothing could be seen below in the blacked-out harbor except a huge dark void. He read himself to sleep with a Russian novel. Early next morning he set out for the border at Ras el Naqura, fifty kilometers due north. Shertok glanced through the morning papers, which were filled with reports of the mass convocations of the day before and banner headlines: "Let Our Cry Be Heard: Hasten Aid to Our

Brethren in the Holocaust." Every few minutes he fiddled
with the car radio. For during the night a momentous event
had taken place, too late to reach the morning papers. The
long-expected invasion of France had begun. Shertok wondered what effect the invasion would have on the fate of
the Jews in Nazi-occupied Europe and on Brand's mission.
The Russians might now move into Hungary much more
rapidly than expected.

He was eager to meet Brand face to face. Before leaving
Jerusalem he had co-ordinated everything once more with
the head of Military Intelligence and with the high commissioner's adjutant. He was going to Aleppo with their
full knowledge and consent. The meeting there had been
their idea, not his. He would have preferred to meet Brand
on the neutral soil of Turkey. But he had been assured by
the British that there would be no impediment whatsoever
to Brand's returning to Turkey and from there to Hungary.
He still wondered why he had not been granted a Turkish
visa and his anger at the consequent loss of precious time
had not abated. But at least he would meet Brand. If
Brand was as serious and convincing as Raskin claimed, he
must go back to Eichmann with some sort of an answer.

The Australian troops manning the border checkpoint at
Ras el Naqura were celebrating D-Day with beer and song.
The car was waved through with a minimum of fuss and
they drove on along the Phoenician shore. Outside of
Beirut the car broke down. Shertok found a taxi to take
him into town while his driver and a local mechanic dis-
mantled the radiator. He passed the afternoon on the terrace of the St. George Hotel, in the heart of old Beirut,
fretting nervously. If the car was not fixed soon, he would
miss Brand's train. Officers of the Free French Army were
toasting one another, celebrating the liberation of France
from the Nazis. Evening came. The car had still not arrived. Shertok's stomach was burning from too much black
coffee. The car finally arrived at 8:00 P.M. They raced into

the night on narrow mountain roads that were often blocked by long military convoys. At the Syrian-Lebanese border station they were held up and their luggage was searched. No one knew exactly why, for Syria and Lebanon were both French puppet states and both were currently under British rule. They stopped at Choms, searching in the dark for a restaurant that would serve the driver a meal at this late hour. He had not eaten all day. When they finally reached Aleppo it was three in the morning. Brand was due at seven. Shertok retired to the Hotel Baron, where rooms had been booked. Wanting very much to be rested for his conference with Brand, he asked the driver to fetch Brand and Mark at the station and bring them to the hotel. He would nap awhile and be up when they arrived.

At seven he was awake and rested. He had that gift of public men to overcome fatigue easily as though in politics they find the secret, if not of everlasting youth, at least of endurance. He showered and shaved and listened to the radio. The morning news from France was very good. The Allies were widening their bridgehead in Normandy and the city of Bayeux had been taken. Shertok felt eager and energetic, in that impatient youthful mood in which everything seems possible and sometimes is.

At seven-forty-five the driver was at his door. Shertok said, "I'll join you in a minute. We'll all have breakfast together."

The driver shook his head. He had been at the station and the train had arrived. But Brand apparently was not on it. Nor was Mark. The next train from Istanbul was not due before Friday. Shertok pondered this unexpected reversal. He booked an urgent telephone call to Jerusalem. He was told that it would take about four hours to come through.

He was just ordering his breakfast on the terrace when he saw Mark rushing up the steps.

"Finally," Shertok called. "We were looking for you at the station."

Mark stopped short abruptly. He seemed completely bewildered. "You? Here in Aleppo?"

"But of course," Shertok said with some irritation. "We were supposed to meet here with the emissary from Hungary. Where is he?"

". . . Here?"

"Where is Brand?"

"Forgive me. I don't understand. Brand and I were on our way to Jerusalem to meet you there. Colonel Roberts . . ."

"For God's sake, where is the man now?"

"Brand . . . he has vanished. I left him for a moment at the station. We were changing trains for Jerusalem. When I came back he had disappeared."

"He was your responsibility."

Mark swallowed. "Yes, sir."

"He couldn't just disappear."

"Well, apparently he didn't." Mark wiped his brow. "I was told that a couple of British military policemen kidnaped him from the station platform." He swallowed. "It's my fault. I shouldn't have left him alone."

"We'll talk about that later. Do you know where they've taken him?"

"I'm sorry. I don't. I rushed over here to telephone and find out."

* * *

The British army barracks were in a palm grove behind the great bazaars. Shertok sent his card in and was shown to the field security office. The officer in charge was a young major. He received Shertok politely and offered him some tea.

"I understand a Mr. Joel Brand was arrested this morning on the train," Shertok began.

The young major was toying with Shertok's card. "Why do you want to know, sir?" he said. "I hope you don't mind my asking?"

"I had an appointment with him here this morning," Shertok said in an urgent but quiet manner. "Everything was cleared and co-ordinated with the chief of Military Intelligence in Jerusalem."

The young major said he was very sorry but that he knew nothing of such a meeting. They had had clear orders to detain Mr. Brand. "Perhaps we are not talking of the same man?"

"I am afraid we are."

"I am very sorry."

"I must see him."

"I am afraid, sir, we have had no instructions at all about that. I am sure you will understand."

"I don't."

"I cannot allow you to see him without orders, sir."

"Why was he arrested?"

"He is a German national, don't you know? He was intercepted on his way down to Palestine."

"He wasn't going to Palestine. He was coming only as far as Aleppo. To meet me."

"That's not our understanding, sir. I am sorry."

"This is obviously a misunderstanding," Shertok said calmly. "It can be cleared up very soon. Would you be kind enough to call the high commissioner's office in Jerusalem?"

The officer again said he was very sorry but his orders came from Beirut. He had nothing to do with the civilian authorities in Jerusalem.

"Well then," Shertok said, still patiently, "will you please telephone headquarters in Beirut?"

The officer considered this. "It might take some time."

"How long?"

"It is difficult to say." But he promised to call Shertok as soon as he had an answer.

Shertok returned to the hotel. He was experienced enough not to flare up at a complication of this kind. The military machine was too vast for smooth co-ordination. He had no reason to doubt the high commissioner's integrity. Mark's performance was another matter.

Mark was waiting for Shertok at the hotel, looking meek. "Let us begin at the beginning," Shertok said, the calmness in his voice betrayed by an icy edge.

"Colonel Roberts of M.I. Eleven assured me Brand had a safe-conduct for Jerusalem," Mark began. "I should not have believed him. But he has always been honest with me before. He said it had been arranged that you and Brand would meet in Jerusalem."

"Not in Aleppo?"

"No. In Jerusalem."

"Are you sure there was no misunderstanding?"

"Absolutely."

Shertok took a deep breath. "Geography has never been a strong point with them," he said slowly. His voice had lost its characteristic nasal tone and the zest had gone out of it.

"Yes," Mark said, "but when it comes to arresting a man they are very precise."

"Don't jump to conclusions. It's a misunderstanding."

"It's my fault. I should have known better."

"You had no reason not to believe Roberts," Shertok said.

"They are callous."

"It is just a misplaced sense of goodness," Shertok said wearily. He was still hoping that the misunderstanding would clear up. "We must wait for word from Beirut."

* * *

In the evening there was still no word. They were sitting in the hotel lobby.

"Of course I had my doubts about Brand at first," Mark

said. "They have been dispelled. We must send him back. He is all we have."

"But can we depend on him? Is he a reliable sort?" Shertok persisted. "Can he negotiate? Is he sound? Is he sober?"

"It's hard to say . . . he is a strange man. There is something odd about him. Almost eccentric."

"That's not what I meant."

"I thought you wondered whether he was sober . . . ?"

"My dear Mark, you are forgetting your brother Karamazov. Eccentrics and dreamers built the Jewish national home. The rest of us almost don't seem to belong. We're just as though we'd been cast up by the tide. . . . I hope we'll get our clearance during the night."

But they did not. Shertok waited restlessly at the hotel. In the evening of the second day the English major stopped by. "I have some news for you," he said, a little timidly, "though I'm afraid it isn't very helpful."

"Oh?"

"I spoke to Beirut. They cannot tell me when you will be able to see Mr. Brand, or whether you'll be allowed to meet him at all. I *am* sorry. I understand it is up to Lord Moyne in Cairo."

"Are they trying to reach him?"

"I think so," the major said with some hesitation. "I hope we'll hear from them in the morning. If you'd care to wait. It's up to you."

"Where is Brand now?"

"I'm afraid I'm not at liberty to say, sir. I *am* sorry."

In the morning the major returned. They had reached Lord Moyne, he said, but the matter had been referred by Moyne to the Foreign Office in London. Further instructions were now being awaited from there. Lord Moyne wished to assure Shertok that he was doing everything in his power to speed the decision.

* * *

Brand was led into a large army barrack. The two military policemen ordered him to sit down on a bench at the far end. Then they left. Soldiers came into the barrack and went, paying little attention to him. He wondered whether or not he was under arrest. He certainly was not free. At midday a couple of soldiers sat down at the lunch table and invited Brand to join them. From them he learned for the first time that the Allies had landed in Normandy and were moving toward Paris. The young soldiers at the table were friendly and full of easy childish humor. He spooned up a dish of lukewarm bully beef and imagined for a moment that his detention was a mistake, soon to be corrected.

A few hours later, the military policemen reappeared. Brand was led out to a waiting jeep. He noticed his luggage stacked on the back seat. He was driven to the far end of the walled-in compound and escorted into a wooden hut. The luggage was brought in after him, and the door was locked and latched. Brand hammered at the closed door. "Why are you locking me up? Open up! Damn you, open up!"

The policeman's voice came back through the door. "Calm down, friend. Calm down."

The air under the tin corrugated roof was stale and hot. An army cot stood on the right, slightly removed from the drab wall. He lay on his back, hot and perspiring. The days of waiting in Istanbul, even his arrest and confinement by the Turks, seemed only a bad dream, even painless in retrospect. The real pain came now. He felt a curious, smarting ache in his head, like sharp needles piercing through the scalp, and for a moment he thought he was actually feeling his own hair grow.

He should never have gone to Turkey, a corrupt state that hovered between Nazi sympathies and opportunistic flirtations with the winning Allies. He should have gone to Switzerland instead. Eichmann wanted him to go to Switzerland. The very thought that Eichmann had been right— "prescient" was a better word—made Brand shiver.

He stared at the electric bulb suspended from the ceiling. Something seemed to have happened to his eyes. He blinked rapidly as if to clear them from some fog. The perspiration was running down his face.

He remembered Kastner's words after the meeting with Eichmann: "You had better be on your guard in Istanbul —against the British."

Gyorgy had been right too. Gyorgy had said, "You are too tame for this kind of job. You are an innocent." From outside came the noise of heavy trucks moving in the dark and hammering and shouts. Brand's watch had stopped. He didn't know what time it was. He knew it was Wednesday. Twenty days. No, twenty-one. He remembered Hansi saying, "Hurry back, every minute counts." And although she had been skeptical, less hopeful, she had said, "It's time, high time, we tried something. It's high time." And then she had said it again and again. "High time, high time . . ." No time. Only split seconds were left for rescue and escape.

He moved his head sideways and stared down at the floor as if to see through it. A sensation of weariness and filth seeped through his body. He forced his eyelids shut. A veil shrouded his mind, but a moment later he was again wide awake and bathed in his fear.

He remembered Mark saying he should be not only courageous but shrewd. Yes, he had been shrewd enough to make his own escape—in high time, like Gyorgy. But he had not reckoned with the guilt born in the circumstance of his rescue. His sense of guilt mounted in self-loathing. He had saved himself, but at what cost?

His sleep, when it finally came, was haunted by dreams, and too short. He forced his eyes open. He was covered in sweat. The folded blanket under his head scraped against his cheek. He unfolded it and covered his chest, and he could feel his heart beat through its rough cotton texture. The beat grew slower and then virtually stopped. He did not know how much later it was when he awoke. He looked around the room without raising his head. A pale half-light seeped in through the window. The yellowish walls seemed to be floating. At first he could not make out where he was. Then he remembered and sat up abruptly as if to combat the sinking feeling in his stomach. He rushed to the door and rattled the knob. He beat his fists against the wooden boards and kicked them with his shoes. There was a sound of steps outside, then the sharp clang of the latch bar being heaved back. A uniformed man came in.

"Who are you?" Brand demanded.

"Calm down, it's all right."

"You cannot keep me here! Let me out! I was promised a safe-conduct!"

"I don't know about that. Let's have a nice cup of tea now. You'll feel much better."

Later he was led out into the courtyard and told to wash at a battery of wooden sinks. Afterward he was marched to an adjacent Nissen hut. A narrow balcony, supported by painted wooden pillars, ran its entire length. The doors all opened out onto it. The man who had arrested him the day before was sitting in a small room. He wore khaki shorts and his pink knees were thrust against the wooden bar under his desk.

"Good morning," he said. "Have you slept well?"

Brand took his words as mockery, a threat to be deflected. He glowered. For a moment they looked at one another. Then the man said, in clipped English tones, "Very well. No pleasantries. What is your name?"

"Joel Brand."

"Your real name."

"I told you my real name."

"You are German? Your English is fair enough."

"I am a Jew. On an urgent rescue mission."

"You carry a German passport. I don't see any letter 'J' in it. You cannot be Jewish."

"I am a Jew. There is a valid visa in my passport. I am on an urgent rescue mission."

"What was your business in Aleppo?"

"I have no business in Aleppo. I was on my way to Jerusalem when you pulled me off the train."

"Why were you going to Jerusalem?"

"I have an appointment there with Mr. Shertok and other Jewish leaders. They are waiting for me."

"Who is Mr. Shertok?"

"The Jewish leader. Don't you know?"

"Waiting for you?"

"Yes. Everything was cleared with the British authorities."

"We have heard nothing of this."

"Then go and find out, damn you. I have no time to lose."

"No time to lose, eh?"

"I have nothing more to say to you," Brand said. "I am a Jewish emissary and will say nothing. Except in the presence of Mr. Shertok."

"Let us start at the beginning. You were born in Erfurt?"

"No, in Budapest."

"It says here you were born in Erfurt."

"I did not write that. The Gestapo did."

"You work for the Gestapo?"

"No."

"Listen, my friend. We have the entire day, and the night too. And tomorrow. And the day after. Now, let's begin again. Do you work for military intelligence?"

"I told you. I am not a German agent. I demand to see Mr. Shertok."

"You never worked for any German Government agency?"

"No."

"The Hungarian Government?"

"No."

The man looked at a piece of paper in front of him. "You served as a cadet officer in the army in 1940, didn't you?"

"Who told you that?"

"You did serve in the army then?"

"I was conscripted."

"As a Jew? I find that difficult to believe. I ask you again . . ."

So it went. The interrogator spoke in a calm low voice. "What is your mission?" "Who sent you?" "Why did you come to Syria?" "What are you after?" "Why do you want to see Shertok?"

Brand's replies were as unvaryingly monotonous. "I will not make any statement except in the presence of Mr. Shertok."

The interrogation continued until late in the afternoon. Periodically the interrogator refreshed himself with a steaming cup of tea.

When it got dark Brand was led back to his prison hut. "I demand to see Moshe Shertok. I demand to see a representative of the Jewish Agency!" he shouted as he was marched through the yard. "I demand to see a Jewish representative!" The guard pulled his door shut. Brand banged on the thin wooden panel.

"Easy now."

"I demand to see a Jewish representative!"

"Easy now. Calm down."

Brand took off his shoe, jumped on the bed and smashed the fly-specked window pane. The splinters crashed on the asphalt outside. He banged on the door again. "I demand to see a Jewish representative!" The room turned around

him in circles. He heard voices outside. "Murderers!" he
screamed. "Murderers!"

The door opened and the guard came in accompanied by
another man who carried a small case.

"Roll up your sleeve."

"No."

"It won't hurt. It's only a sedative."

"No!"

"It would be better if you complied. Otherwise I must
put you under constraint."

The guard held him from behind. The orderly rolled up
Brand's sleeve and pushed the syringe needle into his upper
arm. The two men pulled him to the cot. Brand fell onto it.
For some time he was only dazed. Then the floor collapsed
under him. He careened down into a pit so black, so deep,
he could no longer force open his eyes to escape his nightmares.

10 June 1944

Shertok and Admiral Sir Andrew Cunningham were having tea in the lobby of the Hotel Baron. They knew each other from Jerusalem and had met by accident in the hotel bar. The lobby was large and covered in soft carpets. The heavy brocaded armchairs had been brought from a seaside pension in the Bretagne; the copper trays and wall hangings were Turkish. The waiter was Armenian. The admiral was in good spirits. His fine subdued voice exuded confidence and cheer. They were talking of the war.

"The invasion of France changes everything," the admiral was saying. "In Italy we tackled their soft underbelly. Now we shall crack the hard shell."

Shertok said, "I take it that the invasion is going well."

"We caught them by surprise. With the high winds that blew on Sunday they never imagined we would attempt the landing. The Germans will be on the run in a month's time."

"For us even a month might be too late," Shertok said.

"I beg your pardon?"

"I mean for the Jews."

"Ah, yes. Of course. I understand. Until a short time ago one hardly believed it at all."

"One still doesn't, really."

"Milk?"

"Thank you."

"It's hard for most people to believe in the unbelievable."

"I daresay they have had much practice recently," said
Shertok.

The admiral nodded. "It's beyond all imagining. The
Nazis are even botching their own war effort to pursue this
. . . this war against the Jews."

"You see, Admiral, it isn't like their war against you.
They attacked England and France and Poland for territorial and economic reasons. But their war against us is an
act c.f faith for them, a kind of Messianic ideology."

"I hadn't thought of it this way. How utterly horrifying."
The admiral paused awkwardly and drank his tea. His
cheerful mood was gone. Shertok, too, felt uncomfortable.
He disliked these conversations that reeked of pathetic self-
pity and always exposed one to the suspicion of seeking
special favors. It was distasteful to force others to listen to
elaborate accounts of one's own misery; and for a man of
Cunningham's background, in particular, nothing was so
un-English.

Cunningham sensed his embarrassment. He asked
gently, "What brings you to Aleppo at this time of year?
It's a bit far from your constituency."

"I am waiting to meet one of our men from Istanbul. A
small conference. There has been a delay, I'm afraid."

"There are always delays, sir, there always are. Take an
old sailor's word. I am glad we have had a chance to chat a
little. In the navy we tend to lose touch with events on
land."

The admiral bade him good-bye and went upstairs. Shertok walked out to the veranda. French colonial officials
and their wives were sipping apéritifs under the striped sun
shades. He wandered aimlessly between the potted plants
and cane armchairs and tables. Four days had passed since
his arrival in Aleppo. There was still no word from the
Foreign Office on whether he might meet Brand. He

walked back and forth. Shertok was a connoisseur of Moslem art. But although he had nothing else to do in Aleppo, he had not had the patience to revisit the Seljuk mosques and palaces he knew from previous visits.

He thought about this now as he stood on the veranda, gazing idly across the grand square. He spotted Mark coming up the steps. Mark's large eyes met his inquisitive gaze. Yes, he had just seen the major at Army Security. No, there was still no reply from London. London was busy with D-Day and its aftermath.

"Which means more delays," Mark added.

"Yes," Shertok said absentmindedly. "Delays on land and on the high seas."

"I'm afraid I don't quite follow."

"Pay no attention. It's something I just learned from Admiral Cunningham."

"Ah. Yes."

"He does not believe in unbelievable things. But he is happy with the way the war is getting on."

Mark shuffled. "The major said he thought he would hear from Cairo tonight. And he gave me his word of honor that Brand is still in Aleppo. They are questioning him. He said it's purely routine interrogation."

"I am beginning to wonder," Shertok said. "Come. Let's have a walk in the square."

"They aren't going to do anything to him," Mark said. "At least not while you're here waiting."

"I hope not."

"Let me go to Budapest in Brand's place."

"That is impossible, Mark."

"Why?"

"No."

"We don't know how long they'll keep him in jail. Maybe forever. Let me go back to Budapest in his place. With your instructions. I'm certainly better than Brand at bluffing the Nazis."

"How would you get there?"

"I'll find a way. Eichmann will be impressed by the arrival of an official negotiator for the Jewish Agency."

"You can't go there in any official capacity. It would be treason."

"I don't need any official title. You'll disown me if the British find out. Meanwhile we gain time. And lives."

"You are a British subject. And you are tied to British Military Intelligence on our behalf. You could not possibly go without their approval."

"I don't intend to ask them."

"But you must. If you didn't it would be a gross breach of faith."

"They never consult us!"

"That's not true, Mark. And you know that we are dependent on them in every way."

"A bit too much, I'd say."

"They are fighting the Germans."

"Not to save any of ours."

"We are all in the same boat. If they don't win this war, we are all lost."

"They are not going to lose the war because I go to Budapest. I know I can get there within a week. Let me go, please."

"I am sorry. It can't be done." Shertok's eyes were dark and cloudy. He accelerated his stride. The large square was teeming with strollers. Mark's shirt sleeves were rolled up. Shertok clasped Mark's arm. He felt its warmth under his palm. He moved closer to the younger man. He gripped his hand and pressed it tightly, as though mere touch meant that he was not alone, and if he was not alone now he never would be.

He dined by himself in the hotel. A call came through from Jerusalem and he spoke to Ben Gurion. "When are you coming back?" Ben Gurion asked. His voice sounded very distant.

"It's hard to say," Shertok said. "I'm still hoping they will let me see Brand. Though I'm no longer so sure. It is up to the Foreign Office."

"They have other things on their mind," Ben Gurion said.

"I am waiting for their reply."

Ben Gurion filled him in on current matters and hung up. Shertok stared at the dead telephone. With some bitterness he reflected that Ben Gurion was not supporting him in this particular task as strongly as he should. The telephone rang again. The young English major was downstairs waiting to see him.

A message had finally come through from the Foreign Office. "I am happy to say, sir, that you may see Mr. Brand at your convenience."

"Thank you. I should like to—first thing in the morning."

"Very well, sir. I am sorry about the delay. I understand they were waiting for Mr. Eden to give his personal approval. But now he has done so, and everything is in order."

"It was important as all that?" Shertok said. "So high an affair of state?"

"I wouldn't know about that, sir. We also have an order that Mr. Brand be moved south. After you see him, of course."

"To Jerusalem? Good. He will travel with me."

"I am afraid that is not where they meant, sir."

"Cairo?"

"Most likely."

"Mr. Brand was guaranteed a safe-conduct back to Turkey after he had spoken with me."

"I am sorry, sir. I am simply carrying out my orders."

"This rather complicates matters—a good bit," Shertok said.

"I'm sorry, sir. I hope you'll understand."

"Yes, I am quite used to it by now."

"How long do you expect your interrogation of Mr. Brand to take?"

"I suppose I could finish within the day."

"Fine. I'll make arrangements for him to leave directly afterward."

"I understand he has been under constant interrogation for the past few days."

"I would not say constant. He has been questioned. But he has refused to talk unless you were present."

"I see."

"The first day was rather difficult for everybody. But he is all right now. He was given a sedative and felt much better afterward. He expects to see you. Would you mind very much if a British officer were present?"

"Of course not," Shertok said. "But let it be someone who speaks German."

"His English seems quite good."

"I prefer to speak with him in German. I think it's his mother tongue. I also want a verbatim report of his conversations with the Nazis, not a translation. At least as far as is possible."

"Very good, sir. That can be arranged."

11 June 1944

On the following morning Brand was taken from his cell and driven to an Arab villa on the outskirts of Aleppo. In the main room a little water fountain played in a basin of glazed pottery. He noticed several officers seated in heavy silk-embroidered armchairs. A man of medium stature, dressed in dark, formal civilian clothes, rose from a couch at the far end of the room and walked toward him in small, measured steps. The others remained seated. Brand recognized Shertok. Mark had shown him his picture in an illustrated magazine. Shertok shook his hand silently. The dark eyes, under the heavy, knitted brows, rested firmly on Brand's face. He said nothing. Brand pulled back his hand.

"Why am I under arrest?" he said. "I must go back to Hungary immediately."

"I am . . . very sorry," Shertok said. "It's not likely that you'll be able to return right away. Believe me, I have tried my best. You will be able to return at a later date."

Even as Shertok was speaking, Brand had begun to shake. "What!" he gasped. "No. It cannot be." He clasped his hands before him with such vehemence that his knuckles turned white. Then he grasped Shertok by the shoulders.

"You are condemning them to death! My wife, my children! Eichmann will never believe that I am detained by the British. He will think I've run away!"

Shertok's brows narrowed to form a line across the bridge of his nose. He eased himself from Brand's grasp and took his hand soothingly into his own. "I promise you. I will do everything in my power. You will go back."

"When?"

"As soon as possible."

Brand covered his face with his hands.

"You must believe me," Shertok said sharply. "I beg you. Collect yourself now. Please calm down. Try to give us a full account."

The English officers looked ill-at-ease. The steady dripping in the fountain ticked like a metronome through the room. A young captain sat at Shertok's side with an open notebook on his lap, and a sharp pencil in his hand. He had flown in especially for this meeting from Middle East headquarters in Cairo. Brand raised his head slowly and began to speak.

He spoke haltingly at first, but calmly, and only his face, his eyes, his hands betrayed his emotion. He began at the beginning and gave them a full account of all that had happened to him, and to the Jews of Hungary in the past few months.

It soon transpired that none of the Englishmen present properly understood German. Shertok had to act as interpreter. He swallowed his annoyance at this needless distraction and loss of time. Brand's story was not new to him. But as he listened tensely to it in Brand's own words it was as though he was hearing it for the first time. He breathes honesty, Shertok thought. He had half expected an adventurer, an intriguer. He found a man overwhelmed by a sense of urgent destiny and with a winning simplicity of manner. Brand gave a quiet, almost dry, factual account of his conversations with Eichmann and the other Nazis. He emphasized his own doubts where he had them. But he insisted that a negotiating tactic could be found that would at the very least cause a delay in the timetable of the slaughter. He spoke of the corruption and chaos within the Nazi hierarchy. There were means to exploit those and save lives, without jeopardizing Allied interests. When he finished he bowed his head slightly and said, "For all these reasons I must go back."

Refreshments were brought in. Brand ate some fruit. Then Shertok began his interrogation. He first asked Brand what he thought of Gyorgy's story.

"It's quite probable. There certainly are German officers who seek a separate peace. I agree it throws a suspicious light on my mission. But it need not distract you from the main purpose"—he looked around the circle—"the main purpose is rescue."

"Do you really think the Germans are so stupid as to believe that the Allies will give them trucks?"

"I am sorry," Brand said firmly. "Don't think I am being impertinent. But your question betrays a lack of understanding of the Nazi mentality. They really believe the Jews are a power in the Allied world, and own at least some of the great trucking firms. They believe we appoint and dismiss American congressmen and senators. They are convinced it would be a mere trifle for us to send them ten thousand trucks."

"For use on the Russian front only?"

"But we don't have to send them any trucks. Let us just dangle trucks—and money—before their greedy eyes. There are many Nazis who simply want to get into the good books of the Allies. Maybe Eichmann too. They know they're not winning the war. They want a sanctuary for themselves. And perhaps they even hope you'll be easier on Germany as a whole after the war."

"They want to be rewarded?"

"Yes," Brand said. "Yes. Let's exploit their delusions."

"You think you can outfox them."

"Keep in mind we are dealing with thieves and murderers. Suppose you catch a thief stealing a hundred dollars. He says, 'Here's twenty for you and keep quiet about the eighty.' That's how they think. A million Jews are still alive in Europe. Eichmann offers to release them in the hope he'll get away with having murdered the other five million."

He looked around at the stunned faces. "You must believe me!" he cried, rising to his feet. "They really have killed five million Jews already!"

"Brand!" Shertok said. He sensed that Brand was thinking they did *not* believe. "Please sit down, Brand. We know."

Brand yelled, "You must believe me! They have really killed five million!" There was dead silence. The officers exchanged looks. Brand slumped back and continued in a lower voice. "Now they come to you and say, 'Take the million.' By this they think they'll be able to exonerate themselves."

"Where do they want this million to go?"

"Eichmann made only one condition," said Brand. "They mustn't go to Palestine. He doesn't want to antagonize the Arabs. Other than that he doesn't care where they go."

"What will happen if you go back with a favorable reply?"

"At first I thought that if I went back immediately with a positive reply it would mean we would all be saved. The death camps would be closed. The survivors would be released. But we lost three precious weeks. In the meantime at least three hundred thousand Hungarian Jews have been deported to Poland. I am not sure anymore what will happen. But there is still an outside chance we can save a great many."

"What if you go back with a negative reply?"

"It would mean the wholesale slaughter will continue. Perhaps I and my family and my close friends won't be sent immediately to the gas chambers. They might want to keep some way open for further negotiation."

"What if you don't go back at all?"

"In that case, all our people, all my friends, will be killed at once. The men and women of our committee. Nobody will be left with the courage to speak up, to negotiate for delays. It will be the end."

"What about your wife and children?"

"It's almost certain they'd be killed too. I say *almost* because it's just possible they would leave my family alone. Just to make a show of them. 'These are the people of the Jew Brand, whom we sent on a mission and who ratted!' I must go back immediately!"

"Dear Joel," Shertok said. "The military want to interrogate you further. I have tried desperately to convince them to send you back. So far I have failed. I swear I will not rest until I have changed their minds."

"But this is plain murder!" Brand cried in a strange, metallic voice. "Our best people will be slaughtered! Their blood is on your hands! All of them! My wife! My mother! My children!"

"Brand, I'll do all I can."

"If I don't go back they'll all die!" Everybody was standing now. Brand turned to the English officers and shouted, "You have no right! Why have you arrested me? What harm have I done you? What harm have I done— England?"

"Brand!" Shertok said, "Brand!"

"What do you want from me? What do you want from us?"

The officers said nothing. Brand began to weep. Shertok put his arm around his shaking shoulders. "I promise you. I won't rest. I'll fly to London immediately. I'll take this matter up at the highest level." And through clenched teeth he added, "We are powerless. But not that powerless."

The English officers were preparing to leave. The young captain who had been taking notes cleared his throat. He said timidly that Brand would have to be on the train to

Cairo the same evening. Shertok pleaded for permission to drive Brand at least as far as Haifa, or Jerusalem.

"I am very sorry. My orders are to bring him to Cairo myself."

* * *

Brand was driven back to the prison compound. He walked heavily into his cell, as though his feet were shackled to a weight. In the villa, while he had been speaking, he had felt a kind of relief, as though after a long arduous climb he was inhaling fresh invigorating air on the summit of a high mountain. Now he breathed with difficulty, and from his chafed throat and lungs came a hollow cough.

His inquisitor from the day before appeared in his cell accompanied by the young captain from Cairo who had taken the notes. "This is Captain Sutherland," he said. "He will be your travel companion. He has all the necessary travel orders to get you across the frontiers."

The station was teeming with soldiers. The train was due to leave in a few minutes. It was a long train, several passenger cars and a dozen freight cars filled with bleating animals. They were given adjacent compartments in the sleeping car. Sutherland was kind and helpful, and polite as he eased Brand along, like an invalid on his way to a sanitarium.

"May I bring you something?" he inquired before he left Brand alone.

"No."

"Good night, then."

Brand's bed was already made up. He looked out the window. It occurred to him that he might still escape. For one brief moment he imagined himself actually doing it. Jump off the train—kill the guard—dive into the crowds that filled the station—run for the Turkish border. Then he realized the utter hopelessness of it all. He would be caught within two minutes. He knew he was not capable of murder. He slumped down on the berth. Andrew Gyorgy was right, he thought, he was too tame for the job.

Sutherland was walking back from the station waiting room, where he had bought a magazine, accompanied by a fellow officer.

"You are traveling alone with that man? No other guard?"

"None."

"What if he's another Hess! He'll jump the train."

"I doubt it," Sutherland said. "He is a good man, I think. He was thrown by chance into this boiling pot. He is also a disciplined Jew. Which means he lacks the courage to defy Shertok."

* * *

Shertok drove back to the hotel in deep gloom. Mark was waiting in the lobby.

"They are releasing him?"

"No."

"Let me go to Budapest in his place."

"No."

"But the Germans will assume there is no deal."

"I'll fly to London immediately and get him released."

"In the meantime . . . let me go."

"No."

Shertok went straight to his room. He was shaken by the long encounter with Brand. He had talked with others in the past who had come out of Nazi-occupied Europe. It had always been talk, little more. He sharply realized that now. Ultimate reality can be understood only intuitively, he thought, through an act of the emotions. Brand had forced him to experience this. He had triggered within him a wave of feeling, and of fear, so powerful and shattering that it seemed to Shertok that he himself had just come out of hell with a message from the devil.

_____

Early next morning Shertok began the long drive back to
Jerusalem. Brand's destiny had become his own. He was as
convinced of the need to explore Eichmann's offer as he
was terrified of the indubitable consequences if they did
not.

He arrived back in Jerusalem late on Tuesday night. At
eight the next morning he was in his office. The first thing
he saw on his desk was a cable from Steiner. Steiner was
protesting Mark's high-handedness and was tendering his
resignation. It was not the first time Steiner had resigned.
Two months earlier he had issued a similar threat if his expense account was not immediately approved. Shertok
turned to his aide. "Cable back. Tell him to take it easy."

He intended to compose a long memorandum on his
meeting with Brand. But he was continuously interrupted.
The telephone rang endlessly, bringing all sorts of petty
problems that purported to be urgent and demanding his
instant attention. After an hour Shertok slammed down the
receiver and yelled at the switchboard girl that he would
take no more calls. The secretary came in with the draft of
Shertok's reply to Steiner's cable. She was stunned by her
chief's violent temper. She remembered nothing like it in
the past.

"What do I do about this cable?" she said. "There is no
such thing in the code book as 'take it easy.'"

"For God's sake," Shertok moaned. "Send it *en clair*." Later on in the day he called Government House and demanded an urgent meeting with the high commissioner. He was told that Sir Harold was in Cairo. The adjutant could not promise him a meeting before Thursday.

Ben Gurion came into his room. Shertok briefed him on his meeting with Brand.

"A million Jews!" Ben Gurion exclaimed. "If a million Jews came here, it would be the beginning of a Jewish state."

He thinks of only one thing, Shertok thought. He concentrates on one thing only.

Ben Gurion stomped around the room and his hands were clenched behind his back. "A million immigrants could be the basis of a Jewish state!" Shertok was captivated by the idle speculation and at the same time irritated by it, but Ben Gurion did not waste much time on it and soon he was fuming at the British for having broken their word. He fairly screamed at Shertok, venting his anger at the continued detention of Brand. The white tufts of hair shook on his massive head. Shertok listened in awe, as he always did in the presence of his leader. He feared Ben Gurion's fury might be counterproductive. Shertok was still assuming that Brand's arrest was the inadvertent result of a bureaucratic mix-up. Ben Gurion insisted it was deliberate; for if he had a one-track mind, it was at most times singularly free of pious illusion. The two men walked together to the board room in the other wing of the building, where the Executive was meeting to hear Shertok's report. The members of the Executive listened to his speech in silence. There were none of the objections and doubts and jealousies that had marred the previous meeting on this topic.

"I am convinced Brand is completely trustworthy," Shertok concluded. "I was enormously moved by the force of his personality, and by his spirit. I am flying to London as soon as the British let me. We'll take up Brand's mission at the highest level."

Later in the day he dictated a telegram to Chaim Weizmann in London:

> JERUSALEM 14.6.44
> NLT WEIZMANN 77 GREAT RUSSELL STREET
>   LONDON
> 208 WAITED ALEPPO FOUR DAYS FOR AUTHORITY
> SEE FRIEND WHO ARRIVED WEDNESDAY 7/6 STOP
> INTERVIEWED HIM SUNDAY SIX HOURS FOUND
> HIM ONEHUNDRED PERCENT RELIABLE WAS
> DEEPLY IMPRESSED BY HIS PURITY CHARACTER
> SPIRIT SELFSACRIFICE FACTUAL EXACTNESS
> SOBERNESS STOP CAME CONCLUSION ACTIVE
> STEPS NOW IMPERATIVE VIEW EXPLORING POSSI-
> BILITY ACHIEVING PRACTICAL RESULTS STOP AF-
> TER INTERVIEW FRIEND TRANSPORTED CAIRO
> MYSELF RETURNED JERUSALEM TUESDAY NIGHT
> STOP REPORTED EXECUTIVE TODAY STOP REQUIRE
> YOUR INTERVENTION SECURE AIR PRIORITY FOR
> MY FLYING LONDON SOONEST STOP SECONDLY
> ARRANGEMENTS FOR FRIENDS RETURN HOME STOP
> WE MUST KEEP DOOR OPEN THIS MAKES FRIENDS
> RETURN ABSOLUTELY IMPERATIVE STOP PLEASE
> DO UTMOST EXPEDITE MY JOURNEY STOP INFORM
> NEWYORK
>
> SHERTOK

Thursday afternoon he met with the high commissioner. Sir Harold had just returned from Cairo. Shertok was his first caller. He gave the high commissioner a resumé of his talk with Brand. The high commissioner had already received his own report of the meeting and was quite prepared for what was coming. Shertok pressed his demands. Brand must be allowed to go back and propose a meeting later in the month in Switzerland to discuss terms for the release of the Jews.

"Who do you suggest should meet with the Germans?" Sir Harold asked.

"It need not be government representatives. Red Cross officials perhaps. Or agents of the American War Refugee Board. Nonpolitical people. That would prevent it being misrepresented as a peace feeler."

"I can't voice an opinion on that," said the high commissioner. "This is a decision for the Foreign Office. But even if they agree, I doubt very much they would let Mr. Brand be an intermediary."

"Your Excellency, I have spoken to this man. I consider him absolutely reliable."

"That remains to be seen," the high commissioner said darkly.

"Brand himself is of no consequence. What matters is the offer he brought out."

"If it is acceptable."

"We don't have to accept it as it stands. The very fact of his arrival—and that an offer was made—is itself highly indicative. If we handle this skillfully we might save lives. This is the point I should like to impress upon the Foreign Office."

"The Foreign Office has been alerted to the problem," the high commissioner said. "Dr. Weizmann saw the Foreign Secretary last week. They discussed this affair at some length."

Shertok was surprised. It was the first he had heard of such a meeting.

"Dr. Weizmann was not so single-minded about this as you are." The high commissioner smiled thinly. "Of course he has not talked to Brand himself. Mr. Eden agreed to avoid anything that might look like a slamming of the door."

"I am very pleased to hear that, Your Excellency. Yes, let us not slam the door."

"It doesn't mean that this man will be allowed to go back."

"If he does not go back the Germans will take their revenge on his family."

"I am surprised you take this view. Suppose one of our people managed to penetrate into Hungary. Do you think the Germans would let him out again? The Germans will probably credit us with the same intelligence. They won't blame Brand for it, or his family."

"Brand did not *penetrate* into Syria. We assured him safe-conduct."

The high commissioner seemed not to hear this remark. "The Germans will understand why he was detained."

"If Brand does not return it would mean a complete breakdown," Shertok said heatedly. "It would be the very course Mr. Eden has agreed to avoid. It would slam the door."

"I agree, you have an argument. There are, of course, other considerations which might outweigh it."

"Brand would not have come from Turkey into Syria were it not for . . ."

The high commissioner interrupted him in mid-sentence: "Don't go on! I know what you are going to say. You are going to say that there has been a breach of faith. The answer is very simple. *This is war.*"

Shertok said nothing. He was a natural diplomat, experienced in the art of negotiating with hostile colonial officials, and deft in the use of reticence. He could not remember another exchange with the high commissioner that had cost such effort at self-control. Sir Harold seemed not to notice. A lean figure in repose, his bony face was chiseled finely in delicate lines of pink and silver. He intoned again, "This is war."

Shertok made a final attempt. "We don't have to work

through Brand, if he himself is unacceptable. Our men in Istanbul might make direct contact with the Germans. We would ask them to be extremely cautious. They would not commit the Allies."

"We cannot allow private citizens to negotiate with the enemy."

"In that case I must go to London as soon as is humanly possible," Shertok said tightly. "We are not gaining time by doing nothing. We must take action."

The high commissioner was not displeased at the prospect of passing this delicate issue on to the Home Government in London. He promised Shertok to cable Whitehall, and request priority seating for him on a flight to London.

Shertok settled down to wait. On 19 June, Steiner cabled that Kastner had telegraphed from Budapest asking anxiously when Brand would return. Shertok instructed Steiner to respond that Brand's mission "was under consideration in the highest quarters." He cabled Weizmann once more:

240 (ACCORDING TO TEXT OF TELEGRAM FRIENDS IN BUDAPEST TRANSMITTED ISTANBUL) UNLESS BRAND AND OTHER PERSON WHO ACCOMPANIED HIM TO ISTANBUL RETURN IMMEDIATELY EVERYTHING WILL BE LOST STOP BOTH BRAND AND THE OTHER PERSON ARE NOW IN CAIRO STOP WE HOLD NO BRIEF FOR THE OTHER PERSON AND MUST LEAVE HIS FATE TO BE DECIDED BY COMPETENT BRITISH AUTHORITIES STOP BUT BRAND CAME AS EMISSARY OF THE REMNANT OF EUROPEAN JEWRY STOP IN THE INTEREST OF ITS RESCUE HE ACCEPTED THIS MISSION ON THE CLEAR UNDERSTANDING THAT HE RETURN WITH REPLY STOP ALTHOUGH REALIZING THAT HIS RETURN ALONE AND WITHOUT DEFINITE ANSWER MAY CAUSE HIS DEATH IMMEDIATELY HE IS DESPERATELY ANXIOUS TO CARRY OUT THE BARGAIN AND

RETURN IN THE HOPE THAT HIS REPORT ABOUT
THE DELIVERY OF MESSAGE AND ITS CONSIDER-
ATION IN HIGH QUARTERS WILL HELP GAIN TIME
AND PREVENT PRECIPITATION OF CALAMITY
STOP WE CONSIDER HIS RETURN IS IMPERATIVE
IF THE SLIGHTEST CHANCE OF RESCUE IS TO BE
PRESERVED AND PURSUING LINE AGREED TO BY
MR. EDEN, OF GAINING TIME AND NOT SLAMMING
THE DOOR

There was no answer from Weizmann to either of the
two telegrams. But communications with England were
slow and erratic. He could not be sure that Weizmann had
received them.

On Wednesday, 21 June, almost a week after his meeting with the high commissioner, Shertok was still awaiting
a seat on one of the daily flights to London. None had been
available so far. In the afternoon he received a call from
the American consul in Jerusalem. Ira Hirschmann of the
American War Refugee Board had just arrived in Ankara
from Washington in connection with the Brand mission
and was flying on to Cairo to meet with Brand. He wanted
very much to see Shertok too. Shertok happened to have a
valid Egyptian visa in his passport. On Thursday afternoon
he met Hirschmann at the American Legation in Cairo.

Hirschmann was in a state of high excitement. He had
already seen Brand in detention. Hirschmann told Shertok
that Brand's arrival in Istanbul had raised quite a stir in
the State Department. He himself had been in Cincinnati at
the time and the War Refugee Board had immediately sent
for him. He had been told, "As long as we talk there is a
chance for these people to survive."

Then Hirschmann had flown to Ankara only to find that
Brand, in the words of the American ambassador, "had
been spirited over the border into Syria by British agents."

"How is Brand?" asked Shertok.

"Suicidal," said Hirschmann. "He is in a military prison and under constant interrogation."

"What do you think of him?"

"He seems honest. Gyorgy is another cup of tea."

Hirschmann was furious at the British for having perhaps, through intelligence intrigues, foiled an opportunity to save lives.

Shertok implored Hirschmann to make a direct appeal to President Roosevelt. Hirschmann replied that this would be too difficult. He would, however, return to Ankara immediately and cable his recommendation to the War Refugee Board. "I hope it will not be too late."

"I am waiting to go to London myself. I pray I shall not be too late either," said Shertok.

In his heart he already felt he would be. He wiped his forehead. The heat was heavy and oppressive and on the seared lawn outside the embassy residence the desert wind was whirling up a cloud of burnished dust.

Before Shertok drove back to Jerusalem on Saturday, he learned that although Brand was under heavy interrogation, counterespionage officers no longer considered him a "security risk." He was stunned. Why then was Brand still kept in detention? He rushed to see Lord Moyne, the British minister-resident (a member of the War Cabinet), and realized that instead of security problems there was now a serious political question. Moyne told Shertok frankly that the status of Brand's person would have to be determined by the Foreign Office in London.

Shertok's request to see Brand in Cairo for a short talk was refused by Lord Moyne without an explanation.

"But your air priority to London has been granted," Lord Moyne said.

Shertok also discovered that his most recent message to Steiner had been held up by Lord Moyne. In Moyne's view, Shertok had gone too far in writing that the Brand matter was "under consideration in the highest quarters."

It might imply to Steiner that Eichmann's request for trucks was actually under consideration.

"Such a suggestion is premature, to say the least," Lord Moyne said. Shertok offered another version, which Moyne approved:

AM FLYING LONDON TAKE UP MATTER HIGHEST QUARTERS.

He motored back to Jerusalem in a dejected mood and remained there only a few hours. On the following morning, Sunday, 25 June, he drove to the flying-boat terminal on the Dead Sea. The short drive through the desert depressed his spirit even further. The heat soared out of the Jordan Valley and singed his skin. Above the vast desolate expanse of parched dead soil the sky rose in a blinding glare. In the wasteland between Jericho and the mountains there were only blacks and whites, as in the mind of a fanatic, no shadows or muted colors in between.

The air terminal was at the Potash Works of Kaliah. A stench of sulfur hung over the limp surface of the Dead Sea, where Sodom and Gomorrah had once stood before they had drowned in a rain of brimstone and fire. The passengers were herded into a launch, stooping for their shadows in the high noon. The seaplane was rocking gently on the water, in which there was no fish nor any other form of life. Shertok strapped himself into his seat. His head was aching from the sudden change in air pressure. Two hours later they were circling over Cairo and came down on the Nile. Shertok peered out at the river citadel where he assumed Brand was being held. The passengers were ferried ashore and offered supper. Shertok did not eat. In the sweltering heat he paced impatiently back and forth. Then they flew on through the night to Tripoli and Rabat. The plane was detained in Morocco because of enemy movements in the air over the Bay of Biscay. On Tuesday, at 9:00 A.M., they landed at Swindon. As he passed through police control, Shertok was handed a message:

"Weizmann expects you at 3:00 P.M. at the Dorchester Hotel."

He wondered wryly whether it would be for tea or politics. The leaden sky was dun and low. A cold drizzle came down. Dazed with fatigue, Shertok struggled into the London train. In the monotonous rumble of the wheels he seemed to hear Brand's metallic voice rising to a pitch:

"Their blood is on your hands."

* * *

(Document)

Ira Hirschmann to John W. Pehle, Executive Director, War Refugee Board, Washington, D.C.

Brand impressed me as honest, clear, incisive, blunt and completely frank. In short, his disclosures are to be accepted in my view as truthful, without reservation. My advice is that he be sent back to Hungary at the earliest moment with promises of money and immunity but that there be no mention of trucks.

(Random note by unknown hand): "The President agrees to continue negotiations if possible, in order to gain time."

Chaim Weizmann was the most prominent Jewish leader in the West. In 1906, as a young biochemist fresh from Russia with but a smattering of English, Weizmann had sparked Lord Balfour's first interest in the idea of a Jewish state in Palestine. In 1917 he had been the architect of the so-called Balfour Declaration, which was said to have been "the greatest act of diplomatic statesmanship of the First World War" and in which the need for a Jewish national home in Palestine was first recognized by a great power.

He was the last in a long line of eloquent continentals who, in the nineteenth century, had made freedom-loving England their home and power base from which to liberate their own peoples. He was infatuated with England as only a foreigner could be. His English, otherwise perfect, came with a heavy foreign accent. He impressed his Tory friends because he would not assimilate, and always maintained his pride as a Russian Jew from the Pale. As a famous scientist he was well established in English society. One of the secrets of his charm, which many found irresistible, was that in England he was both the outsider and the insider at one and the same time.

In recent years, however, he had become increasingly isolated. Winston Churchill, one of his oldest friends, was avoiding him, for personal and political reasons, perhaps also because of a sustained guilty conscience. For Church-

ill had made solemn promises of support to Weizmann that
he had been unable or unwilling to fulfill. "Whenever I
meet Weizmann," Churchill was said to have exclaimed on
more than one occasion, "it gives my heart a twist."

Weizmann was still the foremost spokesman of the Jews
of the free world, their president even before they had
gained a state. His main appeal was still directed to the
conscience of mankind, but it was no longer what it had
been. In a world that he watched slip into a nightmare,
where the unthinkable was imposing itself on the ordinary,
he could no longer cope. His essential decency and good
faith seemed outmoded and ineffective, and his pro-British
policy bankrupt. He was frail and ailing, and slowly going
blind from an incurable eye disease. At sixty-nine, he
looked older than his years. His persuasive power, once so
great it was said he could charm birds from trees, had
dwindled and worn down. He was a bitter and disillusioned
man. Above all he was stunned by the apathy he encoun-
tered, even in England, toward the fate of the European
Jews. He was one of the few who had seen the coming disaster, speaking (as early as 1936) of "six million Jews
. . . for whom the world is divided into places where they
cannot live and places into which they cannot enter. . . ."
Yet his warnings had gone unheard. He pounded helplessly
at walls of incredulity, impenetrable to persuasion, testi-
mony or document. The most he would hear were expres-
sions of sympathy and shock.

A tall and imposing figure, as a young man he had been
endowed with almost Mephistophelian good looks. At
sixty-nine, the great forehead, nose, the pointed beard, lent
his face a certain resemblance to Lenin's, but, unlike
Lenin, his harmonious nature eschewed all extremes. The
means, Weizmann felt, must always justify the end. In his
moderation he often clashed with extremists, both left and
right, whose streak of bigoted nationalism bred harsher
creeds and a belief in final solutions. For Weizmann, as for

the liberal nationalists of the nineteenth century, Zionism was a never-ending quest for justice and civility.

He addressed his argument to reason rather than emotion. He believed in science, human effort, honesty, moderation, compromise. Above all he believed in England. For years he had squeezed the juice of hope out of the vaguest promises of his English friends. He loved an England that perhaps never really existed, moved in the last resort by moral considerations rather than by self-interest, greed or passing fashion. And when the England of his dreams began to fail him, it shattered his political base and broke his spirit. The bitter dissappointment knocked him awry. By 1944 he was but a dim shadow of his former self. His predicament was compounded by personal tragedy. His younger son, Michael, had been killed in action over the English Channel in 1942. The famous blend of eloquence, warmth and common sense was still there, but the optimism, tenacity and skill of his younger days were gone. The robust earthy sense of humor had given way to wry self-irony and bitter, gloomy *Galgenhumor*. He always carried with him a vial of poison, which he intended to use should the Nazis invade England.

His face was pale, almost yellowish, and like that of a tragic clown. He still believed in the justice of his cause, but was no longer sure of its triumph. His policy of caution emanated from a consciousness of his own weakness. His immense natural authority among the Jews of Palestine and America was fading. He was being eclipsed politically by the powerful Jews of America, and in Palestine by David Ben Gurion, whom he despised and feared as an irresponsible rabble-rouser and fanatic. In a state of increasing grief and isolation, he was crippled into the role of a passive observer of events.

Weizmann first learned of Brand's mission on 2 June. The subject came up in a meeting at the Foreign Office with George Hall, the Undersecretary of State. Weizmann disliked Hall. In his eyes, Hall was a caddish sort of fool. He much preferred to deal directly with Foreign Secretary Anthony Eden. But Eden, pressed by more urgent problems of foreign policy in the middle of a war, often asked Hall to substitute for him. Hall was annoyed by the task, imposed upon him from above, of dealing with a foreign representative of no formal diplomatic standing. Weizmann was a private citizen, after all. Hall regarded the need to placate him constantly as somehow personally degrading. He also resented Weizmann's efforts to browbeat him. What sympathy he had mustered in the past for Weizmann's recurrent appeals to permit this or that little group of refugee children into the safe haven of Palestine —or England—he managed to drown in a barrage of interoffice memoranda filled with reservations of an administrative, technical or legal nature.

On that particular morning Hall was again voicing the government's concern at the re-emergence in Palestine of dissident terrorists who threatened to attack British installations unless the gates of the country were immediately opened to European Jews.

"You will agree, they hurt your cause more than even the Arabs could," said Hall piously.

"They hurt and damage our cause, I agree," Weizmann said. He did not say this for the sake of politeness. Weizmann did not share Ben Gurion's view that they could extract political capital out of the acts of dissident terrorists whose violence they publicly deplored, and his failure to change Ben Gurion's mind was an index of his growing impotence. Weizmann was a nationalist of an older, more humane order, a pacifist with an ingrained abhorrence of all violence. He had staked his entire career upon the peaceful creation of a Jewish state in close alliance with Great Britain. He was horrified by the use of terror, which he saw as a fascist aberration and a mortal threat to his life's work.

As so often in the past, he promised Hall the full support of the Jewish Agency to hunt the terrorists down.

There was a short exchange between the two men on the proposal to form a Jewish army, which the War Cabinet was to discuss shortly. It was known that Churchill strongly favored allowing the Jews to "fight under their own flag." There was still opposition, however, in the Foreign Office and in the War Office.

Hall was elaborating on the latter. "What is it so many people have against the Jews?" he said facetiously at one point.

"Undoubtedly it is our own fault," Weizmann snapped back, "because it has been going on now for two thousand years."

"The trouble with Jews is that they are bad mixers," Hall continued in the same half-serious tone. "Why don't they enlist in British units?" He was only being a little facetious. Weizmann knew there was nothing evil in his meaning. He shot back:

"There are thousands of Jews already fighting in the British Army. Would you ask such a question of the Free Poles? Or the French? Or the Czechs?"

"Of course not," said Hall, a little taken aback. He switched to a more serious tone and told Weizmann that a mysterious emissary had arrived in Istanbul from Hungary with an offer to barter a million Jewish lives. "The phrase he apparently used was *Blut gegen Waren*. Blood for goods."

"What?" Weizmann gasped. "What goods?"

"I think it means lorries, and foodstuffs."

"Who is this man?"

"He says he is a Jew," Hall said. "But he came in the company of a Gestapo agent."

"When was that?"

"About two weeks ago."

"Where is this man now?" Weizmann asked.

Hall did not know. He might still be in Turkey, or perhaps he was already back in Hungary.

"It reeks of unacceptable blackmail," said Hall. "The S. of S. has had a report on it directly from Istanbul. The Jewish Agency in Jerusalem appears to be pursuing the matter on their own. They have approached the high commissioner about it and have asked that the information be passed on to you."

Weizmann made no immediate comment. He asked Hall for a written memorandum. Hall said that it could take a few days to pass through the various channels. Weizmann took his leave and returned to his office at 77 Great Russell Street, across the street from the British Museum.

On first hearing, and in such an offhand manner, the matter seemed incredible enough, even preposterous. Less so, on reflection. Weizmann shut himself into his room and called in Lewis Namier, his chief counsel. Professor Namier, the great English historian, was at that time a political adviser to the Jewish Agency. A man of great erudition, of Polish birth, who, like Conrad, had become a master of the English prose style and, like Weizmann, enamored of the English aristocracy, Namier was Weizmann's closest confidant. And although he himself was cruelly at odds with his Jewish origins (in what he called sneeringly the "kosher crowd") he loyally served the Jewish cause as a diplomat, though not as a historian.

(His friend Lord Derby once asked him, "You are a Jew. Why do you write English history? Why don't you write Jewish history?"

Namier answered, "But Derby, there is no Jewish history. There is only Jewish martyrology. And that is not at all amusing.")

Namier strode into Weizmann's office and heaved his large frame into a chair.

"Lewis . . ." Weizmann coughed. Namier looked at him

with alarm. The old man's face was white, his hands trembled.

Before Weizmann could continue, Namier cried, "Are you all right?"

"Yes, yes."

"Perhaps we ought to call a doctor."

Weizmann lifted his hands. "No," he said, and then in a barely audible voice he told Namier what he had just heard.

Namier spoke. In his opinion Brand's mission was a cynical German trick to discredit the Jews of the Free West and generate anti-Semitism there. Namier was appalled at the evil intelligence of the Nazis. The devilish cunning behind their offer was shrewdly calculated to spread disunity among the Allies.

"It is directed to us," Weizmann said with some hesitation.

"No," said Namier. "Don't you see how it fits the savage efficiency and science of the Nazi death machine? They have set a trap for us. While the Allies are fighting the Nazis on the battlefield, they wish to insinuate that we are secretly sending them trucks and ammunition."

"Perhaps they only want money," Weizmann said, but with little conviction. No dilemma more monstrous had confronted him in fifty years of public life. "We cannot accept this offer," he said, "and we cannot reject it either." Instinctively he feared that by even considering the offer he might be thought unmindful of Allied interests by his English friends.

"I must read Hall's memo before we say or do anything," he said. "There has been nothing from our own people in Istanbul?"

"Nothing."

"Jerusalem?"

"Nothing."

Weizmann fumbled through his drawer in search of his

pills. A photograph of his dead son, Michael, fell out. Namier bent to pick it up. The old man swallowed a pill and leaned back wearily. "Please cable them," he said hoarsely.

Namier urged him to go home at once. It was a Friday. Hall would not do anything over the weekend anyway. Weizmann went back to his suite at the Dorchester Hotel. His wife, Vera, insisted he go to bed. In the early evening he coughed up blood. The hotel doctor was urgently summoned and gave him an injection. The doctor recommended complete rest. The air-raid sirens sounded. The old man hobbled down to the cellar. André Maurois, the famous writer, clad in the smart uniform of the Free French, rose to greet the Weizmanns with a pleasant bon mot. Lady Diana Cooper and Helen Kirkpatrick were on a bench beside the door, offering to share a bottle of champagne. Richard Tauber, the singer, wandered around in blue dungarees. Lady Cadogan called, "Sing Danilo's aria for us. Please!"

"But I am a tenor!"

"Please!"

In a far corner the Foreign Secretary's wife, Mrs. Eden, was waiting for her husband, who was held up at a cabinet meeting. Tauber sang:

> *"Dann geh ich ins Maxim*
> *Dort bin ich sehr intim*
> *Dort kenn' ich alle Damen*
> *Bei ihren Kosenamen*
>
> *Mimi, Lulu, Fru-Fru . . ."**

Weizmann's face was pale and the large eyes were sunk into their furrowed sockets. But he smiled. The *Merry Widow* was Hitler's favorite opera. Tauber continued to sing.

* "I'll visit Maxim, There I'm so *intime,* There I know all the ladies, and call them all my babies, Mimi, Lulu, Fru-Fru . . ."

"You are my only love,
    Where you are, I long to be."

Weizmann reached into his dressing-gown pocket. For
the next hour or so he read Isaiah from a Hebrew Bible.

* * *

On the following morning he was feeling better. Vera
made him stay in bed. On Sunday their close friend
Blanche (Baffy) Dugdale—Lord Balfour's niece and biog-
rapher—came for dinner. They ate upstairs at Weizmann's bedside. He confided his dilemma to her. If they
were to ignore the Nazi offer, thousands of Jews might die.
If they were to show an interest in pursuing it, the Jewish
community would lay itself open to accusations by the Allies of undermining the war effort.

"You are tearing yourself apart needlessly," Baffy said.
"Why do you worry so what the English will think? They
know you well enough. They will never think you unmindful of British interests."

Baffy was an energetic woman of great warmth and
compassion, in her early sixties. From her maternal grandfather, the eighth Duke of Argyl, she had inherited the
fierce independent mindedness of the Scots Highlanders;
from Lord Balfour, an uncle on the paternal side, a pas-
sionate interest in Jews.*

Nurtured as she was on the Scriptures, she had a pro-
found understanding of the roots of Zionism. For some

* It was not the only cause she endorsed in a lifetime at the hub of
London political society. She was as close to the Czech leader Jan
Masaryk as she was to Weizmann. Harold Nicolson recalled a moment
during the Munich crisis. Chamberlain had just sold Czechoslovakia to
Hitler for "peace in our time."
"The morning begins by Baffy Dugdale ringing me up. She said she
had been sick twice in the night over England's shame. Then at breakfast
she read *The Times* editorial and came upon the words, 'the general
character of the terms submitted to the Czechoslovak government, could
not in the nature of things be expected to make a strong *prima facie*
appeal to them.' Having read these words she dashed to the lavatory and
was sick for a third time."

years now she had been one of Weizmann's closest intimates, a member of the inner circle of his London policy-making committee.

"You must not hesitate," she said firmly.

"Ah, Baffy, you are so sure." The old man smiled wanly.

"Be firm," she said. "If they try to stop you don't give up. But I don't think they will. Find out what this offer is all about! Forget the English Government! Your record of thirty years banishes any suspicion of you."

Weizmann was very moved but still in great doubt. On the following afternoon Baffy and the others met twice at 77 Great Russell Street to agonize at great length over the affair. The advisory group was an informal body. It included full-time aides like Lewis Namier and the Palestinian Berl Locker as well as independent men of influence or wealth, Lord Melchett, Lord Rothschild, and Simon Marks and Israel Sieff of the Marks and Spencer department stores, whose generosity had sustained Zionist affairs through many a lean year.

Hall had not yet sent the memorandum. Baffy Dugdale urged Weizmann to demand an urgent meeting with Anthony Eden. Weizmann still hesitated. He could not be sure of even being received at such short notice.

"Tell Eden it is a matter of life and death."

Weizmann still wavered. His hesitation was rooted in long and bitter experience. For years he had harrowed the feelings of Eden and the others, and he had more than exhausted their patience with tales they only half believed about the horrible fate of the European Jews. He was reluctant to test Eden again, and with an affair so ostensibly dubious as this. Dugdale argued with great vehemence. The others were divided. Weizmann decided to wait.

On Tuesday morning, 6 June, George Hall's letter finally arrived. Twenty days had passed since Brand's arrival in Istanbul. For the first time Weizmann learned that Brand's mission was bound to a two-week deadline. He withdrew to his room with Hall's letter. The staff was gathered in Professor Namier's room listening to radio bulletins, for during the night the Allies had landed in Normandy. Everybody rejoiced in the news of the invasion. While all around him soared to flights of enthusiasm, Weizmann was plunged into a deep gloom.

1626/109/6

FOREIGN OFFICE
S.W. 1
5 June 1944

STRICTLY PERSONAL
AND CONFIDENTIAL
Dear Dr. Weizmann,

As promised at our meeting on June 2nd I write to confirm, in the strictest confidence, what I told you about a suggestion reported to us by the Jewish Agency for the evacuation of Jewish victims of Nazi persecution.

On May 19th Joel Brand, a trusted and well-known Zionist representative in Hungary, arrived in Istanbul from Vienna in a German aircraft. He was accompanied by a Hungarian Gestapo agent. High German Gestapo chiefs in Budapest sent Brand to Turkey, with this man as watchdog, to place before High Allied authorities and Jewish leaders in England, America and Palestine the following offer.

Instead of completely annihilating all remaining Jews in Rumania, Hungary, Poland and Czechoslovakia, the Nazis, it was stated, would agree to evacuate from those countries 1,000,000 Jews to Spain and Portugal (but not to Palestine). The delivery of 10,000 motor lorries and certain quantities of tea, coffee, cocoa and soap was required in return. Once the offer has been accepted in principle, the Germans were prepared, as an earnest expression of good faith, to release the first batch of 5000 to 10,000 Jews before receiving any corresponding consideration. They would also consider exchanging Jews against German prisoners of war. The programme of wholehearted liquidation will be carried out if the offer is rejected. Brand must return with a reply to Budapest within two weeks from 19th May.

The Agency has expressed the fear that unless they can be saved in time, the fate of these Hungarian, Czechoslovakian and Rumanian Jews is sealed. They hope that High Allied authorities will not be deterred by the seemingly fantastic character and magnitude of the proposition from making every possible effort to save the greatest number possible. While fully realizing the overwhelming difficulties, they believe that if the task is faced with the boldness demanded by such an unprecedented catastrophe these might not prove insurmountable.

Shertok is proposing to proceed to Istanbul as soon as he can obtain a *Turkish visa* to discuss the matter with His Majesty's Ambassador.

The Agency stated that they would keep all the foregoing information strictly secret and wished us to do so too, but they requested His Majesty's Government to communicate it to the United States Government and this has been done.

Yours sincerely,
[signed] G. W. Hall

Weizmann was still pondering Hall's letter, agonizing over what he could do and what he could not do, when Dugdale came in flushed with the latest news of the invasion. She had been listening to Winston Churchill's speech in the House of Commons.

"How wonderful for Winston," she cried exuberantly. "He planned and failed once, with Gallipoli, but now he has carried through the greatest enterprise of this war."

Weizmann looked at her absently. The high dome of his forehead was shiny with perspiration and the heavy lids drooped over his glassy eyes, which seemed feverish.

"Are you all right?" she said worriedly. He handed her Hall's letter.

"The two-week deadline is over," she said after reading

it carefully. "Perhaps it can be extended. The invasion has put the Germans on a spot. They may be more anxious than ever to discuss terms."

"Shertok wants to go to Turkey. We ought to do something to expedite his visa."

"We must do even more," Dugdale said. She urged Weizmann again to go straight to the heads of the British Government. Weizmann was still doubtful of the good it would do. He wondered whether Anthony Eden would even find the time or patience to consider such a doubtful intrigue, and at this tense moment. But Dugdale prevailed and in the evening a letter went off to the Foreign Office.

6 June 1944

The Right Honorable Anthony Eden, P.C., M.P.
Foreign Office
Whitehall, S.W. 1
Dear Mr. Eden,

I first have to thank you for causing to be communicated to me the message from Mr. Shertok in Jerusalem about the German suggestions with regard to Jews in Hungary, Poland, Rumania and Czechoslovakia which Mr. Hall told me of last Friday. The story related in the telegram naturally gave me a great and most painful shock, and I have allowed a short time to elapse in which to think it over with such calm as I can muster. As the upshot of my reflections I write now to ask whether you could possibly spare me a few minutes for a personal talk on the subject? It appears to me that questions of policy in the highest degree critical and delicate may be involved, and I am most anxious that anything to be done by the Jewish Agency should be with the knowledge and approval of H.M. Government. At the same time, it is of course my paramount duty to try and discover the course of action which offers the best hope of saving Jewish lives.

It would therefore be of very great assistance to me at this juncture to have the benefit of your personal advice. Meantime, might I ask you to do me the favor of asking the British ambassador in Ankara to do all he can to expedite the granting of a Turkish visa to Mr. Shertok who wants to go immediately from Jerusalem to Istanbul to make further investigations into this extraordinary story?

Yours sincerely,
Chaim Weizmann

Neither Weizmann nor, apparently, Hall was aware how dated their information was. Shertok no longer wanted to fly to Turkey. Within a few hours Brand would be a British prisoner in Aleppo. The letter to Eden, however, helped Weizmann to overcome his depression. It was his way to agonize a great deal before reaching a decision, and to be carefree, almost gay, once he had acted.

Eden responded to Weizmann's letter within a few hours, asking him to the Foreign Office on the following afternoon. They were all pleasantly surprised. Weizmann took Blanche Dugdale to lunch at the Carlton Hotel.

"You are in an expansive mood," she said, relieved.

"My dear Baffy," he answered somewhat apologetically. "The world has very much shrunk since we first met twenty years ago. And so have I." As usual he was holding the world—and his own doubts—at bay with rather mordant humor. He was pleased to have followed her advice. The meeting with Eden would at least bring the matter to the highest levels of government. And it would put him personally on a better footing.

After lunch they strolled briefly through St. James's Park. Dugdale watched Weizmann disappear behind the wall of sandbags at the entrance to the Foreign Office. Anthony Eden received him very warmly, listened very intently, showed great sympathy, but said:

"The enemy is playing a very devilish game. We must be extremely careful."

"I could not agree more," Weizmann said. "That is why we thought it would be best if Mr. Shertok interviewed

Brand as soon as possible. I very much hope the ambassador in Ankara will convince the Turks to grant him a visa."

"What possible good can come of this monstrous intrigue? We cannot send the Nazis motor lorries. The only thing to do is to win the war."

"Britain is already winning the war," Weizmann said gloomily. "But the Jews may yet lose it. Perhaps we have already lost it. Unless we take a risk now to save lives."

"How could we do that without jeopardizing Allied interests?" Eden asked. "And the war is far from finished. I am afraid you are ignoring the enormous difficulties that yet remain."

"Perhaps I am," Weizmann said. "What I cannot ignore is the people who do not want to be gassed. I wish we could explore this offer, at least in order to gain time for them."

"I do not see how," Eden sighed. The skin on his fine face quivered slightly. "The only way to change the situation is to win the war. After the war, the perpetrators of these terrible crimes will pay the penalty."

Weizmann gazed at him with blank eyes. Is it vengeance he thinks we want? What good would that do for anybody behind the barbed wire of Europe? Would it help them to have their suffering and death avenged in the future? Weizmann sought rescue now, not revenge later. If it would save lives, he was even ready to forgive.

"The Prime Minister is in favor of handing these murderers over to you after the war for punishment," Eden added.

"It would not be much of a consolation," Weizmann said. "I know the criminals will be punished after the war. I never doubted it. I am only beginning to doubt there is still a will here to save the victims."

"The first rule is not to submit to blackmail," Eden said.

"But if it is to save lives?"

"Dr. Weizmann, surely the Jews, of all people, cannot compromise their honor by dealing with the Nazis?"

"I render the account of Jewish lives, not of Jewish honor."

There was an embarrassed silence. Weizmann changed his tactic. "You have known me for many years," he said quietly. "I would never suggest that we send them lorries in the middle of the war. But clearly there are people over there who want to deal. Let us at least not slam the door closed on them."

He has aged considerably, Eden thought. In Weizmann's voice there was a tremor he had never heard before. Eden greatly respected the old man, and being half his age he felt he could not totally dismiss his earnest plea.

"Let this man go back to Budapest," he said, "as long as he does not take any lorries with him. I agree. We should keep the door open."

Weizmann was relieved by this limited result. "Your attitude is a great comfort to me in my distress," he wrote Eden on the following day. Two weeks passed. Weizmann spent most of this time in the country working on his memoirs. The staff at Great Russell Street was engrossed in other matters. Brand's mission remained in limbo. Shertok's report on his meeting with Brand arrived. Weizmann wrote to Eden reminding him of his promise that Brand be permitted to go back. He received no answer. Shertok cabled that he was anxious to come to London immediately. On 23 June, Weizmann wrote to Hall at the Foreign Office.

". . . May I beg again that all which is in the power of the Foreign Office to do, be done to give facilities for Brand's return to Hungary and to expedite Mr. Shertok's arrival in this country."

The answer arrived on the same day.

". . . It seems to us unthinkable that retaining Brand in Cairo should be held to indicate that His Majesty's

Government are not giving earnest attention to any practical scheme for assisting Jews now suffering under German threats.

Yours sincerely,

A. W. Randall (in Mr. Hall's absence.)"

Shertok continued to send frantic cables asking that they obtain permission for him to fly to London.

"He obviously takes it very seriously," Doris May, Weizmann's secretary, said to Namier.

"It sounds more to me like a Phillips Oppenheim thriller."

May shook her head. Calling it a thriller, she thought, is a kind of defense mechanism. We all assume this attitude, thankful for the relief it provides. The horror is repressed by euphemizing it, she thought. In a sense, of course, it was a Phillips Oppenheim thriller. Life everywhere was imitating the worst fiction, but the glimpses it provided through the barbed wire of Europe, and worse still on the assumptions on which life there was based—*Blut gegen Waren*—were horrible beyond belief. It was a world in which one could rely on little save an all-pervasive hatred.

27 June 1944

Shertok's train rolled into Paddington Station at 1 P.M. Soldiers and uniformed air-raid wardens crowded the platforms. Namier was awaiting him at the barrier.

"You got here in fewer than forty-eight hours!" Namier marveled. "That makes you frightfully VIP."

"After two weeks' waiting," Shertok said.

They drove directly to Great Russell Street. Shertok had been in London only two months before. Namier noted immediately how much he had changed in the interval. Shertok's eyes, darting about, reflected a strange disquiet. The agitation within him was evident in the inflection of his voice. It seemed unfamiliar to those who had known him for many years. The prodding, patient, polite diplomat of the Palestinian Jews was gripped in an overwhelming urgency. The pedantry had given way to breathless, nervous, desperate haste. He is a possessed man, Namier thought. The phenomenon interested him as a historian with a psychoanalytic outlook.

Shertok asked at once, "How much do you know of this matter?" They knew only what the British had told them and what they had gathered from Shertok's cable after his talk with Brand in Aleppo.

"When can I go to the Foreign Office? We must not lose time."

"You have an appointment tomorrow morning. But brace yourself. They don't believe in this scheme, not in Brand, nor in his motives."

"They cannot dismiss it so summarily. It's not rational."

Namier gazed at him calmly. The shrewd eyes sparkled behind the large oval horn-rimmed glasses. "They seem to have found support in unexpected quarters," said Namier. "According to the Foreign Office, Ben Gurion told the high commissioner that the whole business was quite likely a trick."

"What?" Shertok turned in anger. "It must be a misunderstanding." Ben Gurion would never say anything so specific to the high commissioner. Especially after Shertok had raised heaven and earth to get here.

"Of course," said Namier, but he was not sure. Misunderstandings and lack of co-ordination and vanities of all kinds and one man always knowing better than the next were regular features—and a main handicap—of Jewish diplomacy. There was little difference in this respect between vast empires and a small voluntary organization like their own.

"How is Weizmann taking this affair?" Shertok asked.

"Badly. He's terribly nervous, but he lets only us notice it."

Shortly after five, they gathered in Weizmann's suite. The small group Weizmann had called in for the occasion included Gershon Agronsky, editor of the *Palestine Post* of Jerusalem, who was visiting London; and Weizmann's friends Simon Marks and Israel Sieff; Lord Melchett (director of Imperial Chemical Industries), and Leo Gestetner, the office-machine tycoon.

Melchett said he was writing the Prime Minister at Weizmann's request to ask for an early appointment. "If anything can be done for the Jews of Hungary, Churchill will do it," said Melchett. "But can we be certain of the accuracy of these reports?"

"There is little doubt that at least one hundred thousand have already been exterminated," Shertok said testily. "We have a reliable report from Geneva as well."

"According to today's Manchester *Guardian,* this report is still unconfirmed," said Gestetner. "It occurs to me that it should not, perhaps, be taken at face value."

"Unconfirmed reports!" Shertok retorted bitterly. "Does the *Guardian* expect us to send over the death certificates and coroners' reports?"

"Let Shertok give his account," Weizmann said hollowly. Shertok unfolded the amazing story from the beginning, just as Brand had done so often. He concluded with a description of his meetings with Brand in Aleppo and with the high commissioner in Jerusalem. It was the first time that Weizmann and the others heard it in full detail. Six weeks had passed since Brand's arrival in Istanbul.

Shertok vividly described the man. "He is solid," he said. "Not at all naïve. Rather shrewd and experienced. He seems very courageous. I expected some sort of adventurer. But he breathes honesty. I trust him."

It was becoming dark. The rain was beating gently against the windowpanes. The treetops in Hyde Park were barely visible. Vera Weizmann drew the blackout curtain. Weizmann slumped in his armchair. His large frame seemed weighed down by the bald and bony head that had once suggested so much energy and now seemed shrunken by age and frustration. The eyes, squinting behind the thick glasses in their heavy frames, were straining relentlessly toward Shertok during his long discourse.

Little was said afterward. They agreed that Weizmann and Shertok should call at the Foreign Office in the morning. It would be a preliminary step only. Weizmann did not believe they would get anywhere before seeing Anthony Eden once more. They decided to request another urgent meeting with the Foreign Secretary. Melchett would make a separate approach to the Prime Minister.

* * *

(Document)

Ian C. Henderson (Foreign Office) to Anthony Eden, Secretary of Foreign Affairs, 27 June, 1944, on the subject of Shertok's mission in London: "[We must be on guard against] total capitulation to Jewish pressure unmindful of the political consequences."

28 June—4 July 1944

On the following morning, Wednesday, 28 June, Shertok and Weizmann drove to 3 Cleveland Row, in St. James's Place, to confer with A. W. G. Randall at the Refugee Department of the Foreign Office. Randall was a wispy man of medium height. He offered them tea.

"You look worried, Dr. Weizmann."

"Worry is my daily bread."

"We too have our worries," Randall said.

"I know."

"Why is Mr. Brand so anxious to return to Budapest?" Randall asked. "Doesn't he feel safe where he is now?"

The inappropriateness of this remark outraged Shertok. At the very least he had expected some understanding, even if no help.

"He did not come to save himself. He came on a mission on behalf of the Jews of Hungary. And he has been detained like a common thief."

"I am sorry. I did not mean to sound unconcerned," Randall said quickly. "By the way, the counterintelligence people have cleared Mr. Brand. There are no further security reasons for detaining him."

"I am happy to hear that," Shertok said. "He must go back to Hungary. He has a wife and family there. They will be put to death if he does not return."

"I shouldn't think there would be any serious objections to his return," Randall said brightly, as if the thought had just occurred to him.

"It's not enough to send him back. He must be able to tell the Nazis something that will cause them to delay."

"Yes . . ." said Randall. "That is certainly the main question. You will want to discuss this with the S. of S. himself. What bothers me is, why the Germans are all of a sudden offering to release the Jews? We've been asking them for years to let them go. There was never a response."

"The situation has undoubtedly changed," Weizmann said. "They are ready to let them go on a *quid pro quo* basis. Similar exchanges have taken place, most recently in Rumania. Eichmann's offer to Brand is just the biggest."

"It's very big, I agree," Randall said. "Very big. That's just the point. I ask you, where would we be if we let the Germans pour a million Jews on us?"

Weizmann peered at him through his heavy glasses. The thick lenses enlarged his eyes and reinforced the expression of shock at the words he had just heard. The telephone on Randall's desk rang. Randall answered it in a strained voice. "I am very sorry. I cannot talk right now. I'm sorry, I'm in conference." He turned to Weizmann. "What a dangerous precedent that would create."

"If the Germans are really prepared to release Jews, who would otherwise most certainly die, it should be possible to accommodate them somewhere."

"A million people?"

"Hundreds of thousands of German prisoners of war have been transported and housed fairly inconspicuously here, and in America."

"Transport is not the only problem. The main problem is —where do you put them? We've run into enormous difficulties with only a few thousand in the past."

"There are empty army camps in North Africa. They might be put up there temporarily," said Shertok, furious that rescue was being reduced to this banal level of convenience. "Or they might go to Palestine."

"I expected you would say that," Randall said with something of a triumphant smile. "But you know there is no room left there to swing a cat."

"There are many other places, I am sure," Shertok said. "Let us at least make the Germans a concrete offer."

"It would mean giving in to blackmail. Give in once and they'll never stop. Next thing, they'll try to dump all their undesirables on us. Where would it end?"

* * *

In Mr. Ian Henderson's office a short while later, Weizmann said, "I realize that as a government, you cannot deal with them officially. But we might find a discreet middleman for the purpose."

"Not without first bringing in the Russians."

"The Russians have no reason to suspect us. By all means, invite them to send an observer. The mere fact of an offer would give the Jews of Hungary a respite."

Henderson pulled himself up in his chair and assumed the tone of a lecturer summing up. "We fully realize that the Jewish problem is an important problem. But please understand. It is by no means the only one. The trouble with Mr. Brand's mission is that it might be calculated to prejudice our victory. Therefore I would even doubt that it is in the interest of the Jews of Europe."

* * *

They were riding back to the hotel in a taxi. Shertok bristled with anger. Weizmann slumped in his seat. After a while he said, "It is of no use. They have written us off as war casualties."

They drove on in silence. The recent execution of fifty Allied officers by the Germans had had a greater public impact than the murder of four million Jews, Weizmann thought. Maybe it was their uniforms that so inflamed the public. Their buttons. A flag was nothing more than a rag of cloth nailed to a stick, but to have one made all the difference.

The taxi drove along the edge of Hyde Park and stopped at the entrance of the Dorchester. Gray fumes drifted through the misty haze. Ivor Linton, one of Weizmann's aides, was waiting for them in the lobby. He handed Weizmann a message that had just arrived, through the Foreign Office, from Richard Lichtheim, the Jewish Agency representative in Geneva.

W 10264/15/48

FOREIGN OFFICE
(Refugee Department)
3 Cleveland Row
St. James S.W. 1

28 June 1944

Dear Linton,

We have received the following message for you from Lichtheim: "Urgent. Received fresh reports from Hungary stating that nearly one-half total of 800,000 Jews in Hungary have already been deported at a rate of 10,000 to 12,000 per diem. Most of these transports are sent to the death camp of Birkenau near Auschwitz in Upper Silesia, where in the course of the last year over 1,500,000 Jews from all over Europe have been killed. We have detailed reports about the numbers and methods employed. The four crematoriums in Birkenau have a capacity for gassing and burning 60,000 per diem. In Budapest and surroundings there are still between 300,000 and 400,000 Jews left including those incorporated in labour service, but no Jews are left in eastern and northern provinces and according to a letter from our manager of Palestine Office Budapest, the remaining Jews in and around Budapest have no hope to be spared. These facts, which are confirmed by various letters and reports from reliable sources should be given widest publicity and present Hungarian Government should again be warned that they will be held responsible because they are aiding the Germans with their own police to arrest and deport and thus murder the Jews. In addition, the following suggestions have been made: first, reprisals against Germans in Allied hands; second, bombing of railway lines leading from Hungary to Birkenau; third, precision bombing of death camp installations; fourth, bombing of all Government buildings in Budapest. Please consider these or other proposals, also inform Jerusalem and New York about situation."

> Yours ever,
> A. Walker
> (for I. L. Henderson.)

* * *

Winston Churchill, in the margin of his own copy of this message, 29 June 1944: *"Foreign Minister: What can be done? What can be said?"*

* * *

Later in the evening Shertok was walking back to the hotel through the blacked-out streets. He was crossing Queen's Gate when the air-raid sirens sounded. A few seconds later came the deafening noise of an explosion. A flying bomb had crashed into an empty lot farther down the street. Shertok crouched down. A blast of air swept across the road, knocking a double-decker bus against a tree. The few passengers were struggling out the doors and windows. No one seemed to be hurt. An elderly gentleman had slipped onto the pavement. Shertok helped him to his feet. From far away came the faint boom of other explosions; on the blackened street there was now only an eerie silence. The man thanked Shertok for his help.

"I should say the situation calls for a spot of whiskey,"

he said. "Will you join me, sir?" They walked briskly around the corner to a pub, which was just closing. The old gentleman shrugged his shoulders. "Well, next time perhaps," he said, and bade Shertok good night. He was completely unruffled.

Shertok gazed after him as he passed serenely down the empty street. He envied the man's quiescence. It seemed so English, and yet almost a kind of zeal. The fanaticism of calm, he thought, given only to certain peoples. The roof caves in on them. They feel at home. Completely at ease. If the lives of a million Englishmen were at stake, would they be so adamant against ransoming them for lorries and bars of soap? And he walked on to the park, where he found a taxi back to the hotel, to his turbulence and his pain. The incident with the old gentleman lingered in his mind. It had the unreality of a country he was leaving forever.

> You gentlemen of England
> Who live at home at ease
> How little do you think
> Of the dangers of the seas
>
> Martin Parker (b.?—d. 1656)

* * *

(Documents)

Jerusalem 27.6
NLT Shertok 77 Great Russell London
ACCORDING CABLES RECEIVED ⁚ . . PARTLY CORROBORATED BY POLISH REPORTS . . . OVER 450,000 HUNGARIAN JEWS MOSTLY YOUTH DEPORTED SILESIA REMAINDER EXPECTING SAME FATE . . . IN MY VIEW YOUR EFFORTS [in connection with the Brand mission] GRAVELY IMPERILED STOP MATERIAL MAY DISAPPEAR.

GRUENBAUM

Jerusalem 29.6
NLT 77 Great Russell London
ISTANBUL ON BEHALF OF KASTNER [in Budapest]
INFORMS US DETENTION OF BRAND IS DIRECT
CAUSE FOR SPEEDED UP AND INTENSIFIED
DEPORTATIONS.

GRUENBAUM

* * *

Shertok said, "Can't we be a bit bolder?"

"I am all for being bold," Weizmann retorted testily, "but not for being reckless."

"What if they don't release Brand soon enough? Shouldn't we send another man to Budapest instead?"

"We can't. Not unless the government concurs."

Namier interjected, "The only serious measure suggested so far is the proposed air raid on the gas chambers."

"The Executive in Jerusalem has decided against proposing this to the Allies," Shertok said. "In an air raid the inmates might be hit. They don't want to be responsible for the death of a single human being."

"Not even if it means saving tens of thousands?" Namier said. Shades of Ivan Karamazov, he thought.

Weizmann kept his gaze riveted at a point above Shertok's head. "I understand how they feel," he said slowly. "I do not regard myself bound by their decision. We'll make the proposal when we meet Eden. And we'll ask to bomb the railway approaches as well."

Later, when the two men were alone, Shertok returned to the theme of dependency upon the British. "Why not move our office to America and work from there? America is the great power of the future. After the war not much will be left of the British Empire anyway."

"You are wrong," the old man said angrily, for Shertok was suggesting the impossible. "The British Empire will not disappear. Good God, it would be a disaster if it should."

* * *

(Document)

Anthony Eden, in the margin of Weizmann and Shertok's urgent request to see him: *"Must I? Who of my colleagues is dealing with this matter. M. of S. [Richard Law] or Mr. Hall? At least one of them ought to be there if I am to see the two Jews. Weizmann normally does not take up much time."*

5 July 1944
(In the House of Commons)

The Right Honorable Anthony Eden: "The attitude of the Hungarian Government towards the Jews of that country fills Britain with loathing.

"I greatly regret that there are strong indications that the German and Hungarian authorities have begun barbarous deportations in the course of which many persons have been killed.

"Unfortunately there are no signs that the repeated declarations made by His Majesty's Government, in association with other United Nations, of their intention to punish the instigators and perpetrators of these frightful crimes, have moved the German Government and their Hungarian accomplices to allow the departure of even a small proportion of their victims, or to abate the fury of their persecution. The principal hope remains a speedy victory."

Mr. Silverman (Labour), asked whether Mr. Eden could in any way confirm the report that the number deported amounted to 400,000 while those already killed totaled 100,000.

Mr. Eden: "I would rather not give figures unless absolutely sure. It is bad enough, God knows, without doing that."

Mr. Hopkinson (Independent): "Is it not the first step in these matters to ascertain the real facts?"

Mr. Eden: "I agree. That is why I was reluctant to give figures. But I am afraid there is little doubt in the main as to what is going on."

* * *

6 July 1944

On 6 July, Shertok and Weizmann finally carried their plea to Foreign Secretary Anthony Eden himself. It was the day after Eden's speech in the House of Commons. Weizmann was suffering from a cough. Shertok had a bad cold. Eden received them with great courtesy. There was little trace of his initial reluctance "to see the two Jews." His oval face was cool and smooth, with just enough pallor to suggest the long ancestral line of lords and admirals behind him.

He pulled up an armchair for Weizmann, who was leaning unsteadily on a stick. Weizmann began. He was appreciative, he said, especially of the *tone* of Eden's statement in the Commons on the previous day. (Its operative content, "The principal hope remains a speedy victory," left something to be desired.)

"There is simply no precedent to what is happening now in Hungary," he said. "When I spoke with you about the Brand mission a month ago we thought that we might still gain time. Now the catastrophe is upon us. Four hundred thousand Hungarian Jews have already been deported to the death camps. Another three hundred thousand in the Budapest area await their certain deaths."

As he spoke, Eden's pale mask slowly moved, the lips tightened and the brows knit. Eden said, "These crimes are outrageous, beyond all human comprehension, loathsome." He reassured Weizmann of his fullest sympathy.

Weizmann introduced Shertok as the man who had seen and interrogated Joel Brand in Aleppo. "I came away convinced of his honesty," Shertok said. "He should not have been detained further."

"Is he still in detention?"

"Yes, sir. He ought to be sent back immediately. Each day we lose, thousands are going to their deaths. Perhaps even he cannot save them. But he is our only hope. At least we would have tried."

"There is no objection in principle, I think, to his going back. I agree we must not slam the door on them as long as there is some hope. But is there, really?"

"We think that yes, there is," Weizmann said. "There has been a new development. Last Monday the Germans in Istanbul contacted Mr. Bader, one of our men there, and asked him to come to Budapest to continue the negotiation. This shows they are serious. We would prefer that Joel Brand go back as soon as possible. But perhaps it would be a good thing if Mr. Bader went with him."

The Foreign Secretary met these remarks with a dubious look. He again expressed his deepest sympathy, but added, "We must be extremely careful. The enemy is playing a most devilish game with us." In careful phrases he suggested that the Germans might be floating trial balloons to see if they might disengage the Western powers from their Russian ally.

"Would they really send out a little Jewish businessman for that?" Weizmann said. "Surely they have other means to contact His Majesty's Government?"

"Perhaps," Eden said. "But remember, it is a vicious game they are playing with us. We must be on guard. When I told the War Cabinet that I favored sending this man back, the feeling in the Cabinet was that I had gone too far. This is the problem. And we cannot act without the Americans and the Russians. We have cabled them and are now awaiting their reply."

"But that was two weeks ago," Shertok said in a high-pitched voice. (Control yourself, he thought. Nothing can be gained by making him angry.) "The Germans' invitation to Mr. Bader shows us the matter is still alive. They obviously want to strike a bargain."

"What kind of bargain?"

"Perhaps it is simply money they want. If that is so, we believe the ransom should be paid."

The Foreign Secretary shook his head. "We mustn't have financial dealings with the enemy."

"Couldn't we, so to speak, merely go through the motions in order to gain time? If Brand cannot go back we think it important that Bader go in his place."

"It might be a trap."

"He is prepared to take that risk."

"I admire Mr. Bader's courage," Eden said. "But we cannot permit a British national to go into enemy territory."

"I realize that our proposals are unorthodox, even unprecedented," Weizmann said. "But they are warranted by the tragedy. The disaster is also without precedent or parallel."

"We will make every *possible* effort to save lives," Eden said, and again reiterated his deep sympathy. His tone and manner were kind, even understanding. There was no doubt how he felt. Yet a gulf separated Eden's emotions from his sense of statesmanship and responsibility as he perceived that responsibility in his cool and orderly mind.

"If you insist on Mr. Bader's going," he said, "I would have to refer the matter again to the War Cabinet. Mr. Brand is something else. He is not an Allied subject. Therefore he could go back as soon as we have Soviet consent."

"But we must decide what he will say when he gets back," Shertok said. The conversation seemed to be going around in circles. Eden's mind was like a rubber ball, quickly bouncing back to shape after each argument.

Weizmann said, "The Germans want a meeting. At least this particular group. Unless Brand offers them a meeting there is little point in his going back at all."

"Any meeting would have to be through neutral intermediaries," Eden said. "The Swiss. Or the Swedes." And he added that for this, too, prior agreement would have to be reached with Washington and Moscow.

They had brought with them an *aide-mémoire* to leave with Eden. Weizmann quickly went through the other items in it. He asked that the Allies declare their readiness to admit Jewish refugees to all their territories. Eden promised to consider the proposal. He would not commit himself.

"We also ask that the neutrals—Switzerland, Sweden, Spain, possibly Turkey—be requested by the Allies to grant temporary shelter to Jewish refugees from the massacres. In particular, let them instruct their consulates in Budapest to issue visas to all applicants." Eden promised to consider this proposal too.

"We also ask that Hungarian railway workers and policemen be warned not to take part in the roundups and deportations. Otherwise they will be considered war criminals."

Eden promised to consider this proposal too. Only one suggestion seemed to appeal to him greatly. Weizmann asked that Marshal Stalin be approached to issue a stern warning to the Hungarians on the part of the Soviet Union.

Eden immediately said, "A very good idea!" Something sparked in his wan face. "I will take this up with the Prime Minister at once."

Finally Weizmann came to the last item. "We propose that the railway line from Budapest to Auschwitz and the death camps there be bombed from the air."

"That suggestion is not altogether new," Eden said. "I have already spoken with the Air Ministry about the bombing of the death camps. I'll add the suggestion about bombing the railway."

"It is so terribly urgent," Shertok reiterated.

"Believe me, I am fully alive to the urgency. I will call the Air Ministry today."

"A decision on Brand is also extremely urgent."

"I am fully alive to that as well," Eden said. "But we *must* have the agreement of the Russians. We shall cable Moscow again."

"There is a conclusion one must draw from this entire tragedy," Weizmann said as they were preparing to leave. "The need to create a state of affairs—especially for the Jews—which would make a recurrence impossible. I hope that we shall soon have an opportunity to discuss this aspect."

"I very much hope so too," said Eden. He held Weizmann's hand. "Dr. Weizmann, I fully appreciate . . . I fully appreciate the enormity of the tragedy. We shall meet soon."

8 July 1944

Lord Melchett said, "It is very kind of you to ask me to come out here. At such short notice. We all know how busy you are."

"The busier I am, the more free time I have," Churchill said. It was two in the afternoon. The Prime Minister had just risen from his morning bath. They were sitting in the library at Chequers. Churchill was wearing a dark jumpsuit. He offered Melchett a cigar.

"It's the Hungarian massacres I must discuss with you. Weizmann has the full details. We ask for your guidance."

"How is Weizmann? It's a long time since I've seen him."

"It's been a long time for him too."

"He gives me a guilty conscience each time I look at him. Don't tell him that. After we crush Hitler we shall establish the Jews in their rightful position."

"There may not be too many Jews left to enjoy it. An emissary arrived from Hungary recently bearing the most horrible tale. He came out with an offer of ransom for the Jews there. Weizmann takes it very seriously. He is quite shaken."

"The feeling in the War Cabinet is that he ought not to play at these intelligence games."

"Weizmann isn't keen on games. He is keen on rescue."

"I know. There has been no worse crime in history. After we crush Hitler we shall establish the Jews in their own land. It will be the biggest plum of the war. The Jews who suffered will be compensated. And, if I have anything to say about it, they will judge the criminals themselves."

"The prospect of retribution isn't much of a consolation right now. Weizmann feels something should be done immediately. We all place ourselves in your hands."

"I won't let you down, tell Weizmann I won't. I have an inheritance left me by Balfour, which I shall not forget."

"Weizmann knows you won't change your mind. He is afraid others are working against him within the Cabinet."

"I'll speak to Eden about this emissary and let you know."

(Documents)

> 10 Downing Street
> Whitehall
> 13 July 1944

The Lord Melchett
My dear Henry,

I have spoken to the Foreign Secretary [about the German plans for the massacres of the Hungarian Jews] and fear that I can add nothing to the statement he made in the House on 5 July in replying to Silverman's Question.

There is no doubt in my mind that we are in the presence of one of the greatest and most horrible crimes ever committed. It has been done by scientific machinery by nominally civilized men in the name of a great State and one of the leading races of Europe. I need not assure you that the situation has received and will receive the most earnest consideration from my colleagues and myself, but, as the Foreign Secretary said, the principal hope of terminating it must remain the speedy victory of the Allied Nations.

> Yours sincerely,
> Winston Churchill

FOREIGN OFFICE, S.W. 1
15 July 1944

(WR 102/10/GL
Moshe Shertok Esq.
The Jewish Agency for Palestine
77 Great Russell Street, W.C. 1
Dear Mr. Shertok,

I have to inform you that after the most careful consideration His Majesty's Government have decided that they could not agree to Mr. Bader's proposed journey to Hungary which, it is felt, would have no practical value but on the contrary would be open to the most undesirable interpretations.

I am to add, with reference to Dr. Weizmann's latest appeal to the Secretary of State, that his suggestions regarding bombing [the death camps] are receiving attention with the appropriate authorities, and that the suggestion of a special approach to the Soviet Government has been accepted and that a personal appeal has been made from Mr. Eden to Mr. Molotov.

I should be grateful if you would inform Dr. Weizmann accordingly.

Yours sincerely,
A. W. G. Randall

NEWS AGENCY REPORTS

Budapest, 15 July—The Hungarian Minister of Interior has announced that there is no reason for concern over allied "threats" that those participating in the solution of the Jewish problem will be penalized. Such threats coming from England or America, he said, are nothing but bluff.

In answer to a question in the House of Commons, the Foreign Undersecretary of State Mr. George Hall said that

the proposal to grant British nationality to the remaining
Jews in Nazi-occupied territories had been carefully considered. The British Government were convinced that to
give what in fact would be merely a verbal British protection would bring no advantage to Jewish individuals.

Although the Germans had attacked Jews, he said, they
have also attacked and murdered many thousands of non-
Jews in Poland. The British Government were prepared to
aid and rescue as far as consideration allowed all victims of
German tyranny, and they were pursuing this with every
means available in close collaboration with the other governments concerned.

                                        Waterhouse, Bath
                                        15 July

The Lord Melchett
My dear Henry,
    I am very glad you have drawn the P.M.'s attention to
the terrible tragedy of the Hungarian Jews, though whether
we can really do anything to help I do not know.
                                        Much love,
                                        Chaim Weizmann.

* * *

Weizmann withdrew to his summer cottage at Waterhouse, near Bath. Shertok stayed on in London, grasp-
ing desperately, here and there, at every thin thread. The
city was buoyant with news of the Allied advance toward
Paris. Shertok moved about uneasily, a mourner at a wed-
ding. He was unhappy that Weizmann had chosen this moment to closet himself in the country to work on, of all
things, his memoirs. But as always, loyal and disciplined in
the extreme, he hid his puzzlement from the old and ailing
leader.

He went to the Foreign Office almost every day, sick at

the stuffy atmosphere of accredited mendacity that was prevailing there, and at the moral vacuum. On his daily trips to Whitehall in a taxi he might have seemed to a by-stander as one more stockbroker on his way to the City, alarmed by no greater calamity than the sudden collapse of tin on the futures commodities market. Brand remained their only link with the bureaucracy of death, the only vague hope to circumvent and to perhaps delay. The third week in July passed. Brand remained in the Cairo jail, and there was still no word of his release. Hall and Randall assured Shertok that the matter was not fizzling out. He continued to pursue them with dogged persistence. There was still no word on when—or whether—the gas chambers and railways would be bombed. Wherever he turned he had the feeling he was groping in a void. He was being led, carried along the circuitous route of unfathomable civil and military administrations.

The sympathetic were powerless to help. At the Atheneum Club, one day, he met Victor Gollancz, the well-known socialist publisher.

"For the Germans, the *destruction* of the Jews is a major war aim," Gollancz argued. "To stop them, the *rescue* of the Jews of Europe should be a major war aim of the Allies."

"We've been preaching this for years," Shertok said. "But it's precisely what they don't want. They are afraid to make it seem like a 'Jewish' war."

"Perhaps it is partly your own fault," Gollancz suggested. "Instead of crying 'Save the Jews,' you have been crying, 'Save them by opening the gates of Palestine!' It's like saying there are people in this burning house, but instead of calling for rescue you tell the Allies, 'You must let them move into the Ritz Hotel.'"

It was too late now for such sophistries. Too late also to draw any comfort from the apparently imminent breakthrough on a different score. Jan Masaryk, the Czech foreign minister in exile, consoled Shertok that he had heard from Winston Churchill himself, with whom he had just dined, that a Jewish army would be established within the month to fight the Nazis in Europe under its own flag— like the Free Czechs, the Free Poles and the Free French.

"It is your last step before independence," Masaryk said. "We also received our independence after the First World War—because we had a Czech legion fighting the Austrians in Russia."

The establishment of a Jewish fighting force in Europe would be Shertok's very own success after years and years of futile pleading. And yet he now feared that the rejection of Brand's initiative might be the price they would pay for the formation of a Jewish army. When that thought first occurred to him, late one night at the hotel, he trembled. Flags and badges were paltry exchange for hundreds of thousands of lives. The words of Isaiah were forever with him. "Only a remnant shall escape . . . and the remnant shall be very small and feeble . . . only a remnant shall return . . ."

The Return. Half a century before, Shertok's father had settled in the hills outside Jerusalem, fired by the dream of the Return, a dream so ravenous it had devoured all his strength, so radiant that every doubt and every regret had paled in its wake. And now where were they? A small and feeble remnant. Shertok was a conscientious man, with a penchant for acute self-criticism, and he looked at the various parts of his character with perplexity. Probing back at the interlacing coils of the past, he wondered where he— and others—had gone wrong.

Was Gollancz right? He agonized over this. Or had he been wrong in the handling of the Brand affair? Could they have asked Brand to go back directly from Istanbul? Should he have let Teddy Mark go to Budapest on his own? These were useless questions now. Nevertheless they tormented him greatly. He was a very lonely man, unfailingly loyal to his colleagues yet without a real friend. Namier watched him in his anguish. He had a sharp eye for human weakness and wondered whether Shertok was not lacking in "personality."

The Prisoner

In the train down from Aleppo, Brand was a free man, or almost. He had a first-class compartment to himself. Sutherland occupied the adjacent one. The sleeping-car attendant was Cypriot, slim and suave. He treated the two like traveling royalty. In the restaurant car a table was reserved for them. Sutherland tactfully refrained from imposing on his prisoner. At Choms station he bought him the French newspapers and a flask of whiskey, which he placed with a shy smile on the seat next to Brand. The attendant kept him supplied with ice and mineral water. In Beirut the train journey came to a temporary halt. Sutherland drove Brand to a hotel on the seashore where they spent the night in a luxurious suite. The English and the Germans had this in common, Brand thought, they afforded him with excellent travel facilities.

In the morning their train crossed into Palestine. The landscape changed, imperceptibly at first, from browns to greens and pale yellows. Brand gazed at it silently. There was a bastard quality to it. The architecture was a cross between *Mitteleuropa* and the Levant. The train made its first stop outside Naharia, a seaside colony that had been settled by Jewish refugees from Germany a decade earlier. The houses had twisted and slanted roofs and gables, but were surrounded by palm trees and dunes. On the station

platform a man in lederhosen was selling ice cream and
dates. The signs were trilingual: German, English and Hebrew. NAHARIA. A VACATION PARADISE. BLUE SEA. VER-
DANT CHARM AND RURAL FLAVOR.

An Arab boy was just adding another: HAUS COHN,
ERSTKLASSIGE KÜCHE, KOSCHER. "I spent a weekend here
this spring," Sutherland said. "They've quite a few nice
guest houses and pensions. Friday evenings they do ama-
teur theatricals . . . in German."

"The young probably speak Hebrew by now," said
Brand.

"I mentioned it only as a curiosity."

The train continued down the coastal plain toward
Haifa. The warm air had a peculiar scent of sea and sand
and dry grass, and acid humidity. Captain Sutherland was
hot and uneasy in his tight-belted uniform that had been
designed for other wars in more comfortable climes. His
bashfulness came as a polite stammer.

"Do you intend to set—to settle in this country—uh—
after the war?"

"I think so. I can't believe I would feel secure anywhere
else."

"If the Arabs—let you."

"They'll have nothing to say after the war. They sided
with the Nazis!"

In Haifa they changed trains. There was a long wait.
Sutherland walked out of the station into the Kings Road
to cash a check at Barclay's Bank. Brand waited alone on
the empty platform. A man dressed in workmen's overalls
walked by. On a sudden impulse Brand rushed up to him.

"Help me," he whispered hoarsely. "I am a Jewish emissary from Hungary. I am held by the British. Help me!"

The man stared at him blankly. Before Brand could say
anything more Sutherland came striding up the stairs. "Our
train should be leaving now," he said, looking at the work-

man. And with strained pleasantness: "Can I bring you anything before we leave?"

The train rolled south through the orange groves and the dry heath and the sand dunes, and when they reached the desert it was night. The sparks in the trail of smoke flickered in the dark. Milling through the train were packs of soldiers in creased uniforms traveling down to Egypt, smelling of sweat and shoe polish. Their tanned faces were shiny with fatigue and youth. The train shook badly on its uneven desert bed.

It was still night when they rolled into Cairo station. Brand's short semblance of freedom was not yet at an end. They drove through the dark streets to a large office building. Sutherland disappeared inside. Brand waited in the taxi. Beggars were sleeping on the pavement and wild cats strayed through the empty square. Sutherland reappeared, they continued through the blackened streets to another destination and finally stopped at a tall gate. The outlines of a fortresslike structure were dimly visible. It was still dark. Through the heavy, hot, humid air came the chirping of a million crickets. Brand was led into a room. A uniformed man was sitting at an elevated desk. His pen was poised on a large ledger.

"Name and surname?"

"Damn," said Brand. "You know very well who I am."

Sutherland said, "Mr. Joel Brand."

The man at the desk stood up. "Empty your pockets here," he ordered.

Brand looked at Sutherland. Sutherland nodded uncomfortably.

"Take your jacket off."

The man's hands ran down the back of Brand's shirt and the legs of his trousers. His luggage was stacked in a corner.

Sutherland said in an embarrassed voice, "I'm very sorry about this . . . I am sure it's a temporary measure."

"Where am I? Why am I here?"

"Here *we* ask the questions," the man said. "This way!" He led Brand through a corridor down a spiral staircase. They came to a narrow passage with iron doors on either side. The guard unlocked number five.

Brand entered a small square room. The door slammed behind him. He leaned against the wall and searched his coat for a cigarette. Then he remembered that his pockets had been emptied in the anteroom. He looked around. A bare electric bulb hung from the ceiling, covered with dark encrustations of dust and dead flies. In the dim light the walls looked yellowish and uneven, like packed sand. A large tin can stood in the corner smelling of disinfectant. There was a narrow bedstead. Brand collapsed on its hard surface. It smelled sour.

Then the light went out. He heard the warder's footsteps in the corridor slowly receding into the Egyptian darkness, and then nothing, except a faint buzzing far away, like bees.

* * *

He awoke two or perhaps three hours later, covered in sweat. A faint light came from behind, and as he turned his head he noticed a small window blocked by thick iron bars. He pulled himself up and looked out across a greenish river at a vast expanse of sand. The Nile, he thought. He had been in Egypt fifteen years before, as a sailor on shore leave. The air was hot and stuffy. He sank back on the bed and waited.

When they came for him, he did not know when, he had lost all count of time, Brand said, "I would like to wash and shave."

"You'll have plenty of time for that later on," said the warder. He had a thick Irish accent and wore military overalls. Brand was led back up the spiral staircase and into the anteroom. His luggage was still piled against the wall. They passed out into a little courtyard. A row of prisoners was marching around and around. They crossed the yard and entered another corridor. The warder knocked on a door. A bright voice rang out:

"Come in! Come in!" The door opened and closed behind Brand. An officer was sitting at a desk covered in bright green felt.

"Please sit down, Mr. Brand. Would you care for some tea?" He clapped his hands. A black servant appeared through a curtain behind him. "Or coffee?"

"No. Why am I under arrest?"

"You are not under arrest, Mr. Brand. You are here for your own welfare. I hope they did not treat you too roughly last night. They were told not to."

"They treated me like a common criminal."

"I am very sorry about that. It won't happen again."

"Why are you keeping me here? What wrong have I done?"

"None at all."

"Then let me go."

"We cannot. It's in your own interest."

"What?"

"Since you'll be going back to Hungary eventually, being here is in your own best interest. You'll be able to tell the Germans in all honesty that you saw nothing in Egypt since you were behind bars. Otherwise they might even use strong-arm tactics."

"When am I going back to Hungary?"

"That is not for me to decide. I'm sorry."

"Who is it up to?"

"Higher-ups, no doubt. I'll let you know as soon as I receive orders." The servant came in with a tray. The officer poured himself a cup of tea. "In the meantime we have much to do, Mr. Brand. It is my duty to obtain all possible information from you, and send daily reports to London. We shall meet here every morning and afternoon. We'll try to make you as comfortable as we can. Let us begin at the beginning. You were born in . . ."

* * *

The interrogations were long, from eight in the morning until six in the afternoon, with brief intermissions for lunch, every day of the week except Sunday, when the officer was off duty. A secretary kept notes. The interrogating officer wanted to know everything, and at least twice.

"Your parents know where you are?"

"I told you my father died in 1921."

"Was it a natural death?"

"What? Yes, he was diabetic."

"Are you?"

"No."

"Where is your mother?"

"She is with my wife and children in Budapest."

The morning of the third day was spent on Hansi's family background and upbringing.

"I'd rather talk about my mission. It's very urgent," Brand said on the fifth day. But the interrogation officer first wanted to know of his political activities in the past.

"You were a Communist?"

"No. Why do you say that?"

"You were arrested as a Communist in Erfurt in 1933."

"I was never a Communist."

"Why then were you arrested?"

"As a Jew."

"Ah."

"It's true I was a Socialist."

The interrogation officer wanted to know everything about that too. "Every detail is important," he said.

Brand explained that after the Nazis had come to power he had joined a Zionist Socialist party, Ichud. He was requested to explain the difference between Ichud and another Jewish Hungarian Socialist group, Shomer.

"Does that have something to do with Mizrachi?" the officer asked.

No, Mizrachi was a religious party, although it also had a Socialist faction. Jewish politics were very intricate, the interrogation officer complained. What other political groupings were there among the Hungarian Jews? Who were the leaders? Were there any in the pay of German Intelligence?

"None."

"Are you sure?"

"Positive. Jews would never collaborate with German Intelligence."

"You might be surprised!"

Many hours of interrogation were devoted to what Brand knew, or did not know, of the workings of the Jewish Agency in Palestine, in England, in America. The interrogation officer was surprised and incredulous that he knew so little. "But you are a Zionist of long standing, are you not?"

"Yes. Well, no."

"Yes or no?"

"I am a rescue worker."

"But as a Zionist, surely you ought to know more of the Jewish Agency?"

"I am not interested in the Jewish Agency. I am interested in rescue."

"When did the Germans first contact you?"

"They did not contact me. I contacted them."

"On your own initiative?"

"No. On behalf of our committee."

Thus, on the sixth day of interrogation, very slowly, they began to discuss Brand's mission. Who was on the Rescue Committee? Names and addresses. Wasn't Gyorgy on the committee?

"No!"

How could he be so sure?

"I am positive. We all know one another."

"He used you."

"No. We used him."

Did the committee have any arms?

"Yes. One hundred fifty pistols, forty hand grenades, three small rifles."

"Were you planning an insurrection?"

"Of course not. We were too weak."

Why the arms, then? Brand did not know, it had been Kastner's idea.

Everything he said was carefully written down. The interrogating officer was anxious to learn as much as he could about the current political situation in Hungary. Was there much opposition to the government? How was Eichmann's Special Command structured? What was its relationship with the Hungarian police? How deep was the antagonism between the Wehrmacht and the SS? What were Eichmann's intentions? Krumey's motives? Who was Schmidt? Winninger? What did he know about their private lives? So Schmidt was a sex maniac? Details, please. Krumey cared only about money? Winninger a cheat? Eichmann drank?

"Yes."

How could he bring himself to deal with such human refuse?

"Perhaps to you, an Englishman, it seems incomprehensible. To me it was a question only of finding means to send money and food into the ghettos. I never stopped to think about the morals of it."

"But you would trust them on a deal?"

"We must deal with them if we hope to save lives."

So it continued. Brand spoke, theorized, explained. Every so often the officer would say, "Let's go back now. . . . What did Eichmann mean when he said he would stop the deportations? Is he his own master now? Surely he is under instruction from Berlin?"

"Yes. Himmler's office."

How come Brand knew so much about the Nazi hierarchy? If the Nazis did not get trucks would they still release the Jews? How would Eichmann arrange the transport of two hundred thousand Jews to Switzerland. Or to Spain. By rail? Or by truck?

Brand answered patiently, day after day, in the sweltering heat, over innumerable cups of bittersweet black coffee. He was shown photographs of German intelligence agents and asked to identify them. He could not. He was given a map of Budapest and asked to point out possible military targets. He could not, except for the most obvious. This struck his interrogator as odd, and hours were spent in explanation.

The edges of Brand's temper had softened, but his frustration at the delay prevailed. "Has Auschwitz been bombed?" he asked the interrogation officer. "Have the rails been blown up?" The interrogator did not know. The news broadcasts he allowed Brand to hear on his radio spoke of massive air raids; every day and night, thousands of Allied planes were flying sorties over the continent, as far east as Prussia, Silesia, Rumania. The cities of Germany were said to be in ruins, but there was no mention of Auschwitz.

He was led out twice a day, to walk in the yard alone. The other prisoners were kept on a different schedule. He knew they were mostly Spaniards and Italians; he could hear their voices through his cell door. The interrogator told him they were spies and saboteurs.

One afternoon the schedules had apparently been mixed up and when he came out into the yard there was another prisoner walking around and around. It was his friend Saul Kleinmann, whom the committee had sent out in March to warn Steiner of the impending disaster in Hungary. The two prisoners fell into one another's arms.

"Steiner told me you had gone to Palestine!" Brand cried.

"That shit Steiner."

"Didn't you go?"

"No. I was arrested."

"But why?"

"Ask Steiner. They took me off the train. In Aleppo."

". . . In Aleppo?"

"Yes. First they said I was a German spy. Now they grill me every day with questions about—*you!*" Kleinmann stopped. A guard was running toward them, shouting.

"Hey! No talking there! Move apart, you two!"

The schedules were never mixed up again. When he asked his interrogator where Kleinmann was, the officer said, "He is all right," and then, "No, I am afraid you cannot meet him. You see, we use him to verify your statements. It is in your own interest."

Brand's living conditions were improved somewhat. One of his suitcases was brought into the cell and a washstand set up. A straw mat was laid on the stone floor, and he was given a little table and chair. Every other day an Arab prisoner came in to shave him. He was given newspapers, and a few books.

The cell was hot and in the evening stuffy, though the window was open, covered only by bars. He would pace back and forth until he would feel dizzy. The air was humid. His shirt was wet and clung to his skin. He would look out of the window for hours. Boats floated up and down the Nile, their pink sails swollen in the hot breeze like huge balloons. Beyond the river and trees lay the barren desert, a dim, vast, lackluster, almost glassy surface. Later on he would lie on his bed, staring into the darkness that enveloped him, straining to keep his eyes open for fear of the visions lurking under his heavy, burning lids. He would lie bound, immobile, in a pit of palpable gloom. And always he was gripped in the gnawing tension of trying to grasp something, an idea, a scheme of salvation, that might yet turn things around and make his mission a success. But he could find nothing. He dreamed of Hansi, and the children. These dreams were confused, full of wild deeds and inchoate sounds and sights he could only partially remember when he awoke. Except, somehow, their violence in his bones.

*　*　*

On the twelfth day of his imprisonment the interrogating officer told him they would be going out after lunch. "An American gentleman wants to meet you. He has flown in from Ankara."

Brand rose from his lethargy. "Ira Hirschmann?"

"I think that's his name, yes. He is with the Yank Refugee Board. A very insistent man, and apparently of some importance. Lord Moyne himself decided he should see you."

The interrogation that morning centered on the rivalries between the Gestapo and German Army intelligence units. Brand tried to be alert and helpful. The officer made copious notes. They broke off earlier than usual. Brand went back to his cell to eat his frugal lunch. In the afternoon they drove out the prison gates, down a wide esplanade along the Nile. The river was brown and rising, filling the air with a dank moisture.

They entered the spacious grounds of a large secluded villa, surrounded by palm trees, jasmine and oleander. A few marble steps led up to a large veranda. Sutherland was standing by a little table looking at Brand with an embarrassed smile. He introduced Brand to a tall man dressed in white whose deep voice and solemn manner suggested a man of the cloth. A giant Sudanese servant shuffled across the stone floor and offered cool drinks.

"President Roosevelt has sent me to talk to you," Hirschmann began rather pompously. "I flew to Istanbul, but you had already left. So I followed you."

"All this would not have happened if you had come to Istanbul in time."

"I had to stop in Washington to receive my instructions."

"Did they tell you my mission was being sabotaged?"

"I know how you feel. I know," Hirschmann said gravely. "I would like to help."

"Help me to get back."

"Believe me, I am doing all I can."

"I have done no harm. Why are they keeping me here like a criminal?"

"The American Government is not in accord with the way the English are handling this matter. Now, tell me everything."

"What's the use? I have done nothing but talk for weeks."

"Believe me, I would have come earlier if I could."

"Do you realize how many people went to their deaths during this time? I must go back. How often do I have to say it? They don't realize what they are doing!"

"I am sure they don't."

"The Nazis are murdering everybody!"

"Women and children too?"

"Damn it, are you really so naïve?"

"I . . . understand."

"You don't!" Brand said. He covered his face with his hands. Hirschmann shuffled uncomfortably. Sutherland was frozen in his seat. Then with an enormous effort, Brand collected himself. And again, as so many times in the past weeks and with as much calm as he could muster, he gave Hirschmann an account of his mission, his adventures in Turkey, his interview with Shertok in Aleppo, his imprisonment in Cairo.

Sutherland spoke. He was looking at Hirschmann. "Mr.

Brand's detention is a temporary measure, sir. I was a bit surprised by it myself. In Aleppo I assured Mr. Shertok . . ."

"I think you will soon be released," Hirschmann said. "I will do everything I can to enable you to resume your mission. Shertok is working on it too. He is in Cairo today. I'm seeing him later on. I know he is on his way to London to see what he can do."

"Charming! I hope he's got the proper visa."

"I beg your pardon?"

"I said I hope they'll let him in."

"But of course they will."

"His travel plans always get waylaid at the last minute. He told me he was going to London two weeks ago."

"Mr. Brand, he is not a free agent. He depends on the authorities. Like all of us. I don't have to tell you, he is a very decent man."

"He is the victim of his own decency, then. He should not have lured me into this trap."

"You are being very harsh."

"I am simply counting the days," Brand said in a choked voice. "I should go back with an answer. Instead we sit here talking. And the British are at me without let-up. They want to know the number of every goddamned tram in Budapest. In the meantime . . ."

"I am sure it's only a matter of days now. The American Government is taking an active interest in this case. And in a few days Shertok will be in London and clear up everything."

Sutherland said, "In the meantime, as I'm told, you'll be moved to more comfortable quarters. You'll be freer to move about." The cane chairs creaked. On the lawn outside the sprinklers whirled and swished.

The soft-footed servant returned with more ice and cool drinks. Brand waved him aside. A heavy scent of jasmine wafted through the air. Brand lit another cigarette. The shadows were beginning to retreat behind the flowered wall and the sun struck Brand's face, hot and blazing, like the eye of an enemy. He shaded his eyes with his hands and looked around and for the first time he raised his voice.

"Where are we? Is this the American Embassy?"

"No, it's one of the British houses of assignation," Hirschmann answered with unexpected sarcasm. "It's where they entertain their . . . more important visitors." The glass in his hand was dripping icy moisture. "We'd better go inside," he said, wiping the perspiration from his pink jowls.

He wrapped his arm gently around Brand as they walked back into the house. Inside, the half-light seeped through the shutters, and it was cooler. The servant turned on an electric fan. The interrogating officer was sitting on a couch looking at a newspaper.

"I promise you," Hirschmann said with finality, "I shall not rest until you resume your mission. You will soon be out of here."

* * *

But he was not. He was moved to a more pleasant room in the administration wing across the prison yard. The window was not barred, but the door was locked at night. His meals were brought in on a tray from the mess kitchen and the warders began to say "sir" to him. The daily interrogations continued as before.

"When will I be sent back?"

"I am sorry. I don't know."

"Who will make the decision?"

"Lord Moyne, I should say."

"I must speak to him."

"It is not an easy thing to arrange."

"I must speak to him. Otherwise I shall refuse to co-operate anymore."

"I'll put in a request. Now, let's go back to where we were . . ."

They were plodding through much of the same ground now for the second and third time. The interrogator's passion for detail was insatiable. He checked and rechecked everything again and again. On Sundays he rested. Brand was left alone to brood in his room. On the third Sunday following Hirschmann's visit he awoke very early. The room turned gray, then mauve, and ablaze in the light of the rising sun. He lifted himself up to close the shutters and lay back on the hot sheet. The odor of his body offended him. It was damp and sour. He pulled himself up again and opened the shutters. The burning sky was white as zinc. Huge dust clouds rolled in over the rooftops. The river was buried under a burnished haze. The warder came in with his breakfast.

"Take it away."

"Sir?"

"Take it away, I said."

"You are not hungry?"

"Tell them I am on a hunger strike."

"Sir?"

"You heard me."

He sank back on the bed. At noon the warder returned with his lunch on a tray.

"Take it away."

"It's kidney pudding and veg, sir. They only do it on Sunday." The warder was standing in the open door. Brand took the tray into his hands. The warder looked relieved.

"You'll like it, sir. No use getting excited. It's the heat that's getting us all down."

Brand smashed the tray on the floor outside his room. "You heard me!" he yelled. "I am not eating! Go and tell them!"

He turned and walked to the window and wiped his brow on his sleeve. A yellowish dust was blowing in, powdering the wooden sill. He removed his shirt and lay down on the stone floor to cool off. The smooth tiles soon grew hot under his damp skin. He rolled sideways to another spot. He was still in this position when the interrogating officer walked in accompanied by an army doctor.

"Do you feel ill?" The two men were towering over him.

"No."

"It might be the heat. Or perhaps something he has eaten," the doctor said, feeling for Brand's pulse. Brand pulled his hand away.

"What's all this about not eating?"

"I won't touch any food until you release me."

"I am sorry. You know that decision is not mine to make."

"I won't eat until you let me out of here."

"There are ways to make you eat, you know," the doctor said.

"Try."

The interrogating officer said, "I have written to Lord Moyne that you wanted to see him."

"When you hear from him, let me know. Now, get out of here! Get out!"

* * *

(Document)

EXCERPTS FROM THE CONCLUDING PART OF THE OFFICIAL REPORT OF BRAND'S INTERROGATION. G.H.Q., M.E. Forces, Cairo. Security Branch.

. . . the problems which follow logically out of Brand's contacts (and purported mission) are:

a) whether he has been sent to the Middle East on a secret mission for the Abwehr* or the S.D.† or whether his ostensible mission of bargaining for goods in exchange

---

* German Army counterintelligence
† Sicherheitsdienst (Security Service of the SS)

for blood is in fact the real one—i.e., is Brand telling the truth or has he a second mission?

b) whether Brand's professed mission was seriously intended by the German authorities or whether there was some ulterior motive behind it.

c) How far have the Germans penetrated Brand's organization?

d) To what extent is the Jewish Agency implicated with the German Intelligence Service?

Brand gives the impression of being a very naïve idealist. He has at the moment one aim in life—to save as many of his fellow Jews as he possibly can.

There seem to have been certain indications that the Germans have not been as sincere as Brand thought. Only on one occasion were numbers of articles or foodstuffs (for barter) specified and then only casually. If they were sincere they would have been more thorough.

Conclusion:

That Brand has not been sent to the Middle East with any mission other than the business deal of "goods for blood" which he had come to openly negotiate but that the sincerity of the German offer is very disputable.

Recommendation:

a) that Brand should be interrogated further on his knowledge of the Jewish Agency and other institutions about which a Zionist of Brand's standing should know more than he has shown.

b) that otherwise Brand be regarded as cleared from the security point of view.

W. B. Savigny, Lt.
Interrogating Officer

2 July 1944
S.I.M.E.
G.H.Q., M.E.F.

* * *

In the following days Brand was left alone. Food was brought into his room three times a day. He touched none of it except an occasional sip of water. The ordeal was less difficult than he had imagined. He smoked heavily. The spasms of hunger of the first two or three days disappeared on the fourth.

A kind of mist seemed to have lifted from his mind. His recollection of things past sharpened. He was suddenly able to remember long-forgotten faces and past conversations with a clarity that amazed him. Distant scenes paraded through his mind. A Chinese teahouse in Surabaya, on the island of Java . . . Ramdas Gonzales, half-Indian, half-Portuguese, the ship's doctor with whom he had served in 1929 as a telegraphist. In the teahouse by the harbor, smoking opium. He remembered the sudden lifting sensation in his mind. It was like the lightness he was feeling now. He remembered Gonzales' saying that in his native city of Calcutta the Indians believed in successive incarnations, not in one death but in many. It was possible through concentration of the mind not only to choose one's next species, but also one's nationality. In his next incarnation Gonzales would be an Englishman. . . .

Brand pondered this now. What would it be like to be an Englishman? He did not know many Englishmen. Then he thought, to be a Swiss would be better. In Switzerland they make chocolate and live in peace with one another. He remembered an evening in Budapest with Kastner two years ago. They had been walking through the snow. Kastner had just returned from a meeting in Switzerland with the representative of an American relief organization. Near Zurich he had seen skiers queuing up at a little ski lift. There had been a sign on the little wooden shed: ERBAUT 1941. The whole goddamned world was going up in flames but the Swiss were building ski lifts. The Swiss were lucky.

Thinking of luck made him remember his father. The inexorable fatality of a particular father. Mothers gave you affection, the need to love. Fathers burdened you with an origin, an identity, a race, a religion, a name you can never cast away.

His father had been a stern man. Remembering his father made him think again of his failure. He reached for the clay jar where he kept his water and downed a few tepid gulps. He resolved to think of his mission no more. It was, after all, only bad fortune. To be angry at himself now was unjust. Yet no matter how he rationalized, no matter what he promised himself, the self-torture and self-loathing grew stronger, as do some poisonous plants, and on the eighth day of his fast he began to think about suicide.

The idea of suicide triggered no particular emotion, except some vague anticipation of release. The inevitable pain did not frighten him and the next world could be no worse than this one. There was no life after death anyway, only oblivion.

He calmly contemplated the means. They seemed plentiful enough. Nothing would be easier, any vein in his body would set him free, and there was the window. He opened the shutters. But there was a flat asphalt roof only a few meters below. He must find a rope. But there was no rope. The prison authorities had taken away his suspenders, and his razor. He shuddered. He recalled a man who had escaped from a concentration camp in Poland and had told him of a strange phenomenon in the Warsaw Ghetto. The more irrelevant life became in the ghetto the fewer the number of suicides. There were fewer suicides among the Jews of Warsaw than before the war. The secular among them had been reduced to animal existence. Dogs never committed suicide. The pious would not even consider it. Suicide was a sin, the desertion of God's army. They were God's chattel, He would be angry with them if they destroyed His property. In the Roman Empire, too, it had been a crime for a slave to try to kill himself. He thought about this as he twisted on his bed, trapped in the concentration camp of his mind, tormented by guilt, and he suddenly felt very hungry.

Later in the afternoon he heard voices outside his room, then a knock on the door. They were treating him gently now, like a terminal patient. He said, "Come in." His mouth felt dry.

Teddy Mark stood in the door. "How do you feel?"

"What do you think?"

"May I come in?"

"If you wish."

"I know what you think," Mark said. "There was nothing I could do. I should never have left you in the station. Not for a minute . . ."

"Don't apologize."

"I had nothing to do with your arrest."

"I haven't yet said you did."

"May I sit down?"

"Sit down."

"Brand. We were all trapped."

"Or perhaps you were just playing your part?"

"I must have played it very badly if you see through it so easily."

"I didn't say I see through anything—easily."

Mark said, "I'm told you're on a hunger strike."

"Yes."

"How many days has it been?"

"Six—seven. I don't know anymore."

"I understand how you feel."

"You understand?"

"Please don't be sarcastic."

"I am very far past sarcasm."

"Listen to me. I have good news. Steiner has made contact with the Germans in Istanbul. They're asking one of our men to fly to Budapest to resume your negotiations. They're offering him safe-conduct."

"Safe-conduct, eh?"

"Yes. What do you think?"

"I think, Mark, that I am going mad."

"Hold on, Brand. We need you and we need you clear and sane. If we send someone to Budapest he'll be sending us back reports. Only you can evaluate them."

"I must go with him."

"Of course. We think so too. If it were up to us . . ."

"Where is Shertok? I hope he hasn't been arrested in London as a German spy."

"Don't be sarcastic."

"Goddamn it, stop telling me what I am being."

"Shertok is in London . . ."

"They may arrest him yet. My interrogator is hot on the scent of a German spy ring inside Shertok's office."

"Stop it, Brand."

"I'm not fooling."

"Listen to me. Shertok has been in London for two weeks. He's had a series of meetings with Eden and others. Good meetings. Our basic requests are as good as met."

"Do you mind if I ask what our basic requests are?"

"We asked that you go back to Hungary. Eden did not say no. He is consulting the War Cabinet. They take the matter very seriously."

"Do they?"

"Very seriously. The Americans too. Hirschmann has been leaning on them very hard."

"He is a pompous ass."

"He's a worker. And tough."

"We shall see."

"Don't give up. We haven't."

"You haven't?"

"Brand, there is just so much we can do, and so much more that we can't. Give up this hunger strike."

"It's the only weapon I have."

"They'll force-feed you."

"What good will that do them?"

"What good would it do if you starve?"

"I will not be shelved away."

"We'll get you out of here."

"I spent all last night trying to figure out a way to kill myself. Even that is a problem."

"Brand!"

"Don't worry. With my luck it would probably be a temporary solution anyway."

"Give Shertok another week. He is turning Whitehall upside down to get some action."

"What about the bombing of Auschwitz?"

"We've asked this too."

"There were a thousand planes over Berlin last week. I heard it on the radio. They are blowing up whole cities and factories that produce shoes, but they still don't bomb the factory where they make death at the rate of twenty thousand corpses a day. Doesn't that tell you something?"

"Yes, Brand. It does."

"I tell you they care more about shoes than about Jews!"

"Damn it, Brand!" Mark yelled. "You know bloody well we have no air force of our own! All we can do is ask. We're only a couple of old Jews who run around the world crying for help!"

A long silence followed. Finally Brand said, "Couldn't Steiner contact Budapest about my wife and my children?"

"I think he can, yes. We'll let you know as soon as possible."

"Thank you."

"Give up this hunger strike."

Brand stood up and walked to the window. He was drowsy. He pushed open the shutters. The sun was setting and lay over the roofs, sallow and jaundiced as though it had rolled through the dust. A weird light hung in the dry palm trees and oleanders. Brand turned around. Mark noted how haggard his face had become and it seemed that his hair was thinning.

"All right," Brand said wearily. "I'll wait another week."

* * *

A mile or so away, in an old rambling villa by the Nile, Lord Moyne was reviewing the Foreign Office minutes of Eden's conversation with Weizmann on 6 July. It was just after lunch. The temperature hung at 100 degrees in the shade. Walter Moyne was accustomed to working through the afternoon, even in July, when others escaped the heat sleeping, or in the swimming pool of the Gezirah Sports Club. It gave him the leisure to think, he said, and time off from the endless procession of callers.

An electric fan suspended from the ceiling whirled slowly. Moyne was in shirt sleeves. His exterior was uncomfortable, even sweltering, but within he basked coolly in the corporate pride of his office. He was Minister of the Crown, Resident in the Middle East, a former Colonial Secretary and Leader of the House of Lords. The Foreign Office minutes, immaculately typed on stiff, embossed stationery, crackled in his hands. Moyne shook his head. This third-rate spy thriller, he thought. He could not understand why it had been permitted to drag on for so long. The ransom offer should have been rejected at the very outset. Instead, false hopes were raised and new areas of contention opened with both Arabs and Jews. The Arabs would never believe that the final destination of the ransomed Jews was *not* Palestine.

Moyne's secretary came in to recite the afternoon agenda to his chief. It was fuller than Moyne had hoped. The secretary read the list out in a voice so solemn it sounded rather like the incantation of a prayer.

"At three, the conference with Air Marshal Tedder. At five, Nahas Pasha calls, at his request. He will be accompanied by Mr. Jamil Husseini of the Arab High Committee in

Jerusalem. At six Mr. Haddock of the War Production
Board. At seven-thirty, dinner at the Residency for the Air
Marshal . . ."

"I shall barely have time to change," Lord Moyne said
with a sigh.

"And Captain Sutherland of Intelligence Branch is still
waiting for permission to see you. At your convenience, my
lord. He has called twice."

"Did he say what he wanted?"

"No, my lord. I didn't ask. I'm afraid I've been remiss. I
assumed he wanted something of a private nature."

"I doubt it. He *is* my cousin, but we try not to let that
come between us."

The secretary regarded his chief with admiration. "Very
good, my lord."

"Do you know if this man Brand, who was arrested last
month, is still being held here in Cairo?"

"The Croat spy?"

"No, the Jew. His name was Brand."

"I daresay I'm not sure. He is a War Office body."

"Thank you."

* * *

It was Lord Moyne's fate as Britain's pro-regent in the
Middle East that he found himself saying "no" more often
than "yes" in his dealings with both Arabs and Jews. It had
little to do with his character, but was in the nature of his
task. Moyne's main purpose was to diffuse the Palestinian
conflict for the duration of the war. There were moments
when he disliked himself for having to say "no" so often,
especially to the Jews, who were always pleading to allow
their persecuted kin into Palestine. But since there was
nothing he could do about it, his incapacity became principle and he ended by congratulating himself for his pro-
ficiency.

"I sit in Pilate's seat," he would say resignedly. "In the

end I shall be blamed by everybody." He did not wash his hands of the matter, however. He was an able administrator and he believed that in the Near East, British policy suffered not from too little imagination, but from too much. Eden's latest plan to forge a new Arab league of independent nations in close alliance with the British Empire was a pathetic error in Moyne's view. A chimera, just as Balfour's dream in 1918 of a Near East restored to its ancient glory by the returning Hebrews had been a romantic illusion.

The Jews regarded Moyne as pro-Arab and hated him for it. The Arabs considered him pro-Jewish because he dared envision the partition of Palestine into a Jewish and Arab state as a possible postwar solution. The Arabs, however, being a more polite people and feeling that they had the upper hand anyway, made less a show of their resentment.

Facing his two Arab visitors a little while later, in the bay of his study, Moyne wondered once again why it was that nine out of ten Englishmen in the East came away enamored of the Arabs while actively disliking the Jews.

The two visitors bowing from their seats accepted the proffered cups of coffee and the cigarettes. Nahas Pasha beamed. "I trust we shall have the pleasure of your company at Aboukir for the hunt this fall."

"If it is at all possible, I should like very much to come." They are a very graceful people, Moyne thought, easier than the Jews, who are always picking away at their consciences, and at ours, and in their misery become petty and vindictive. "Yes, I should like that very much."

When the pleasantries were done and the mutual inquiries into their welfare and the wishes for an agreeable summer vacation had been completed, Moyne and his visitors arrived at the business at hand—slowly. Nothing was ever done abruptly in Egypt. Nahas Pasha, the great Egyptian statesman, and Jamil Husseini, the prominent Palestinian Arab leader, had come to inquire of Lord Moyne what truth there was in recent press reports that the present restrictions on Jewish immigration to Palestine might shortly be relaxed.

"It is true that they speak only of a limited number of additional entry permits, and only after the war. But surely, my lord, a question of principle arises here. And good faith. We have always been assured that the remaining quota was the final one. To extend the quota further would be a breach of faith. Every Arab, inside and outside of Palestine, must take a very serious view of this. And the consequences, I need not stress, my lord, would be unpredictable."

Nahas finished his little speech. His smile, made more brilliant by its darkness, was not reflected in his eyes. Moyne cleared his throat. In the strain of universal expectation even the coffee quivered in the small Turkish cups.

"Nothing has yet been decided," Moyne said, "and nothing shall be decided without full consultation with you. We must recognize, however, that there is a serious problem here of overwhelming human import. We cannot overlook it. It was a different world in 1939 when the immigration quotas were last fixed."

"It is my understanding," Nahas Pasha said, "that Britain recognized in 1939 that the Balfour Declaration had been a mistake. Surely you are not going to commit another mistake now by reversing that decision."

"I would not put it that way," Moyne said carefully. "We recognize our responsibility to both sides. But what of the serious problem of the homeless Jews? What should we do about them?"

"Britain will win the war," Nahas Pasha said. "Then she can do anything she pleases."

"I see your point," answered Moyne. "But we must also keep in mind the tremendous suffering inflicted on the Jews. We must help to make life a bit sweeter for them."

"Not by making it bitter for the Arabs," Husseini said. He was the current head of a feudal family of Jerusalem that traced its ancestry to a Moslem prince who had come out of the Arabian peninsula with the Caliph Omar in the sixth century. The return of the Jews had haunted him for years. He saw it as a terrible danger. It was also the name he gave to his own fears and blunders. Earlier in the century his family had sold enormous tracts of land to the Jewish colonists. In the process the Husseinis had become richer and more powerful than before.

"We certainly do not want to make things bitter for the Arabs," Moyne said. "But I reiterate. There remains a serious problem with the homeless Jews. His Majesty's Government cannot overlook it."

"The Jews you speak of aren't really Jews at all," Husseini said. "They were our cousins once, a long long time ago. But they come back as strangers. They are Poles now, Germans, Rumanians, Hungarians. They descend from the Khazars, the Tartars, or whatever. What right have they to replace us now? We are not insensitive to their suffering. But after all, we did not cause it. The Germans must pay for it. Not we. That would be only just."

"It would all be much simpler if it were only a question of abstract justice," Moyne said with a sigh. Not without a certain pleasure as well; he enjoyed his role as devil's advocate. "But it isn't quite so. As the imperial power, we face a choice between a lesser evil and a greater evil, not between absolute right and absolute wrong. The Jews would argue that the Arabs have many sovereign countries and vast territories, whereas they have only one. They want to build their home there."

"It is not their home. It's ours. Their claim is based on legend."

"My dear pasha, we don't have to believe that legends are facts. But the existence of a legend is a very great fact."

"The biggest fact is that Palestine is now an Arab country. After the war the Jews should go back to where they came from."

"Many will go back, I am sure. But many will not. Can you blame them? After all that has happened?"

"It must not be at our expense."

"Certainly not. Perhaps the best solution would be to partition Palestine between the two of you."

"The Arabs will never agree to partition," Nahas Pasha said. "Never! My lord, I do not wish to sound dramatic. You know me. I am a man of peace. But Palestine cannot be partitioned except through terrible bloodshed. More terrible than anything that sacred soil has seen since the Mongols."

The discussion continued in this vein. The sacred river flowed outside, in browns and reds and pinks. Sails drifted past, and barges and feluccas. Lord Moyne made another effort to reassure his visitors. Their fears were unfounded. Britain was fully aware of her responsibilities toward them. Britain would not let them down.

They parted amicably, however, with smiling faces and warm handshakes. Afterward, Moyne gazed out the open window. A dry, hot wind blew in. Moyne thought about Nahas' threat of a bloodbath more terrible than that of the Mongols. The Moslems, he thought, were at least honest. The Christians preached a religion of love even as they killed. But Islam had always come openly with a sword. And yet they've done less killing than we have, Moyne thought. And they've been kinder, more tolerant to minorities than we have been—Papists, Huguenots, Jews. He shuddered a little at the thought. A Mongolian bloodbath! All that sacred blood and soil talk; the mixing of the two always produced tetanus. It was not a serious threat, of course, and especially coming from Nahas, the kindest, most civil, most pro-British of all the pashas of Egypt. Even if he meant it seriously, which was unlikely, he had to keep in mind that Britain was still the paramount power in the Near East. Moyne believed so strongly in the myth of British power he could not imagine there were others who did not.

He was interrupted in these thoughts by the arrival of Captain Sutherland.

"Oh hullo, Stephen. Do you hear from your mother?"

"She seems quite all right from all I gather. She's had to close the London house."

"Too difficult to keep up?"

"She didn't much mind though."

"M.I. keeping you busy?"

"Can't complain, sir."

"Was there something special you wanted to discuss with me?"

"Well, sir . . . yes, sir. It's about this Hungarian Jew Brand who was detained in Aleppo."

"What's he to you?"

"I was the escort officer who brought him down here. An interesting man, sir. Quite straightforward. Very intelligent, too."

"He came with a scheme that sounds quite mad."

"Well, sir, it does. But there is something to be said for it."

"Where is he now?"

"He is in Cairo Prison. Not quite as a prisoner. He is in very bad shape. Physically and emotionally. That's what I wanted to talk to you about."

"He is in the care of Military Intelligence. Aren't you treating him kindly?"

"He has made various requests to be permitted to speak to you."

"Whatever for? He is out of my hands. I have told London what I think."

"He can't go to London, sir. He is locked up in a cell."

"What good would it do if I saw him?"

"You see, sir, he has come out of hell, really. On a mission he considers important."

"He must be mad if he thinks we'll send the Nazis motor lorries."

"He isn't a bad sort, if that's what you mean. But he is in despair. He is convinced he has been betrayed by everyone. By the Jews too."

"Good. It shows they haven't lost all reason yet."

"He has gone on hunger strike this past week. And he has threatened suicide unless he can speak to you or someone in authority."

"Rubbish," said Moyne. "Nobody kills himself for political reasons."

"I'm not sure you are quite right. I mean, in this case, sir. I am sorry. I know it sounds presumptuous on my part to suggest—to ask—that you—see him. If only for a minute. It would mean a lot to him. He has been through hell."

"Does he still want to go back to Hungary?"

"I think so, yes."

"Doesn't he like being where he is, safe from the Nazis?"

"He thinks of his family. And the others."

"He is mad if he thinks that by going back to Hungary he can save a single life."

"You are possibly quite right. Still it would mean a lot. If you would see him just for a moment."

"Why do you take such an interest in him? Do you mind if I ask?"

Sutherland was taken aback.

"I didn't mean to pry."

"It's just that I think he is a very decent chap. I feel very sorry for him."

"You are your mother's son," Moyne said. "She was always big on lost causes."

"You mean to say, sir, that his cause is lost?"

"I fear it is." Moyne paused. Sutherland, in his armchair, was fidgeting self-consciously. Moyne extinguished his cigar. "If you think it's that important, I don't mind seeing the man. But not here. He is a War Office body, isn't he? There is too much friction already. Do you think you can get him out of his—uh—confinement for an hour or so? I'll meet him—let me see—how is Monday? After tea, at the Gezirah Club."

* * *

He had agreed to meet Brand as a kindness to Sutherland, in a moment of weakness at the end of a long day. Nahas' Mongolian massacres were still ringing in his ears. He was also a bit curious to see the man who had come out of hell and wanted to go back.

But when he actually met Brand, on an especially torpid afternoon, three days later, he was unexpectedly petulant. Sutherland was astonished. Perhaps it was the heat. Moyne himself wondered why. He thought, I mustn't let this affair get under my skin. He was angry at himself and at Brand. This naïve man, aflame with zeal and ignorance, and gripped by a towering sense of self-importance! By all means he should look for ways to save his kin! But the remedy he advocated was useless! It would not save anybody. The Nazis wouldn't let any Jews leave anyway. So why did he have to come here and meddle? Arouse the suspicions of the Russians, who smelled a rotten fish everywhere? The silly blundering fool! And his crackpot scheme of salvation! What salvation? There could be no salvation before Germany was crushed. The very people he wanted to save would hate him for it!

Brand was cowed. He countered all argument by timid suggestions of a tentative nature, qualified "maybes" and "possiblys" and "perhapses" and "we shall never know before we try," wringing his hands and lowering his eyes all the time.

"Perhaps they only want money," he said at one point,

"and hundreds of thousands might be allowed to leave. Even a million!"

Moyne's eyes grew large. "What would I do with a million Jews? Where should I put them? Switzerland will let in a few thousand children and people with numbered bank accounts."

"If there is no place for us on this planet," said Brand, "then there really is no alternative for our people but to go to the gas ovens."

"But who said there is no place? I agree, they should have a place of their own. We must establish a Jewish state. But we can't do that before the war is won."

"Why not now?"

"Because we have not yet *the space!* We will have it after we smash Hitler. After the war we'll establish a Jewish state in Europe."

"Not in Palestine?"

"Palestine cannot take in all the homeless Jews. Oh, I know—history and all the powerful legends. But it's an Arab country now. You can't get around that fact. After we destroy Hitler we'll expel the Germans from East Prussia and set up a Jewish state there."

Brand shook his head. "I don't doubt that you can drive the Germans out of East Prussia. But even with machine guns you can't force us to settle there."

Moyne looked at his watch. Sutherland was embarrassed by his great kinsman. Some men admit mistakes on occasion. Bureaucracies never do. They legitimize their errors by administrating them later on.

Concert of Nations

Shertok was waiting for the British Government's decision. The British Government was consulting the American Government, which was consulting the Russians. The Grand Alliance was resolved to act in concert. Meanwhile, each day, between fifteen and twenty thousand people went into the gas ovens.

The American Government first learned of the Brand mission on 5 June. Lord Halifax, the British ambassador to Washington, officially informed Undersecretary of State Edward Stettinius of Brand's arrival. It would not be entirely true to say that he was upset, for he was an ambassador of the old school and he believed it best never to expose too obvious feelings. Perhaps he was ruffled.

"Assume for a moment that this ransom offer was really made by the Gestapo," Halifax told Stettinius. "Do they expect us to house, clothe, feed, another million people? This is tantamount to asking us to suspend essential military operations.

"Even worse," he went on, "what sort of flotsam and jetsam might come through, once we opened this door. Nazis posing as refugees. Fifth columnists. All kinds of spies. Do we have the manpower to screen them before they enter Allied territory?"

Another aspect of the proposition worried Halifax even more. "If only Jews are freed under this scheme," he said, "we shall face a serious problem of public opinion."

What about Allied subjects, civilians and prisoners of war, who suffered the most terrible conditions in Nazi hands?

"If British and American prisoners and internees are left to the Nazis, it would lay our governments open to very serious protest."

His Majesty's Government, Halifax said, took the view that the ransom offer should be rejected outright. (He was acting under specific instructions from London, where Eden would solemnly assure Weizmann twenty-four hours later that they were definitely not "slamming the door.") In keeping with diplomatic custom Halifax handed Stettinius a written *aide-mémoire* to emphasize the importance of his *démarche*.

Stettinius did not immediately commit himself. His first reaction was considerably more sympathetic. On the following day he received Dr. Nahum Goldmann, Weizmann's representative in Washington. Goldmann wrote Weizmann:

> . . . Stettinius intends to give the Germans the impression that the matter is being considered, and to drag out the talks so as to win time.
> He is hopeful that in a short time the Russians will be in Hungary . . . and save the Jews there. . . . If only food were involved [Stettinius thinks] it might be feasible . . . naturally trucks are out of the question. Prolonging the talks is certainly the right idea.

Goldmann was jumping to conclusions. Before reaching a decision, Stettinius solicited the Russian point of view. Ten days went by before an inquiry was actually sent to Moscow on 15 June. The answer came back, with uncommon alacrity, on 18 June.

> . . . the Soviet government does not consider it permissible or expedient to carry on any conversation whatsoever with the German government on the question. . . .

Three days later American Secretary of State Cordell Hull cabled the American embassies in Moscow and Ankara: ". . . *take no action concerning this matter pending further instruction.*"

As experts in human engineering, deft in the art of luring an adversary into traps of his own making, the Russians may not have been insensitive to the importance of spreading disorder and confusion in the rear of the German line of retreat. For the victims, the railroads to Poland were the horses of the apocalypse; for the Russians, the clogging of the lines was of strategic value. Trains that carried Jews to the gas ovens could not carry tanks and troops to the Russian front. And, emptied for the return trip, the same trains might more easily accommodate retreating German forces.

Eden's personal plea that Marshal Stalin threaten Hungarian police and railway officials with reprisals (Soviet troops were about to enter Hungary) went unanswered. No reply came, either, to an American request that Marshal Stalin join with President Roosevelt in declaring that the butchers of European Jews would be severely punished as war criminals. Stalin's own hands were stained with the blood of millions killed or deported to certain death in Central Asia and in the concentration camps of the polar zone. He did not feel strongly about a mere few hundred thousand Jews.

The possibility of opening talks only to bluff and gain time was not even considered in the Anglo-American-Soviet exchanges. The alternative of suggesting that the ransom money be deposited in blocked Swiss bank accounts was not mentioned either. The Russians lived in a nightmare of fears that the Western powers would conclude a separate armistice with the Germans. Weizmann's suggestion that they participate in mock talks, or send observers, was never conveyed to them. The Soviet veto was firm and unequivocal. On the diplomatic level it doomed the Brand mission.

Disclosure

Three weeks after the Russian veto, Shertok was told that Brand's return was still being considered. On a sunny day in July, between two air-raid alarms, Undersecretary of State for Foreign Affairs George Hall assured him that the matter was definitely not fizzling out.

"Certainly there are complications," Hall said, "as we always knew. We are in consultations with Washington and Moscow to see what can be done."

The bombing proposal too was still under study at the Air Ministry. The main reason for the delay was said to be that the death camps of Auschwitz were very far from Allied air bases. Shertok said, "We know that a number of fuel dumps in the immediate vicinity have recently been bombed."

"We are only diplomats," Hall said wearily. "We only propose. We do not dispose."

There was also the very delicate question of securing landing rights for RAF bombers on Russian airfields. The bombers would have to land there to refuel. "We can't gate-crash them, can we," Hall said.

* * *

On his arrival in England on 27 June, Shertok had been a possessed man. Three weeks later he was more like an automaton. He plodded on, driven by the kind of nervous energy that sustains the loser, the naïf or simply the man of routine. He suffered from chronic headaches and insomnia. He would try to read himself to sleep at night, with Russian or French novels. The table in his bedroom was covered with them. In the mornings he would drag himself out of bed, dizzy with fatigue. He plodded on through the offices and clubs, to the visitors gallery in the House of Commons, the luncheons and engagements and casual encounters.

He had a new idea. Two hundred armed Jewish volunteers should be parachuted into Europe to organize resistance among the doomed. The War Office favored the scheme but the Foreign Office vetoed it. The "political drawbacks" of this scheme were said to outweigh its "military advantages."

He plodded on. He sometimes went for a few hours to the reading room of the British Museum, across the street from the agency's offices on Great Russell Street. It was his only distraction. One afternoon he entered the library again, weary after a long day at the War Office. He settled under the great dome of the reading room among his fellow readers, pale soldiers and youths, and elderly Poles and Czechs and Austrian refugees, poring over the desks, seeking their lost patrimonies in the books.

While he was waiting for his order to be brought up, he glanced at the books lying on his table. One was Dostoevsky's Gothic tale, *Bobok*. He opened it at random.

> . . . something strange is happening to me. My character is changing and my head aches. I am beginning to see and hear some very odd things. Not exactly voices, but as if somebody close to me was going bobok, bobok, bobok.

He stopped reading. The musty smell of books was everywhere and he felt sick. The attendant came with his books. Shertok mumbled an apology and walked out. As he pushed open the door into the pillared portico, he came upon a small crowd gathered in a circle by the wall. There were cries of "Poor dear! . . . Poor dear!" "He's obviously crawled in here to die." "Oh, the sweet little thing." "Has someone called the RSPCA?"

Shertok walked down the wide steps out into the street. Books, books, books; he was going "bobok, bobok" himself. Books full of learning and advice and opinion. All the varieties of the human experience. One might think they would generate a greater empathy for the suffering of others. When, in fact, empathy seemed to shrink the more one read or knew. Ecclesiastes was wrong: "Knowledge increaseth not sorrow." The same people he had just seen bending over the little dog in the portico did not really believe in the tale of horror he had been peddling all over London for the past month. Weizmann had been telling them for years, and what had he proved? What results had it brought? And if they could believe what would they feel? Less than in the museum portico just now. And who was calling for the RSPCA?

Only we are calling, Shertok thought. And he reproached himself again. We should have cried louder. Screamed. . . . Yes, perhaps. But would it make a difference? Yes. No. Why torture himself then? This self-reproach was merely another form of boasting. Hubris of the weak.

He walked back to the hotel. The park was ablaze in the pinks and yellows of a brilliant summer day, and filled with young conscripts and their sweethearts. And children. Heirs to all the ages. Dogs. Horses. Riders were trotting smartly down the bridle path. He could hear gay, carefree voices. That night he was visited by an affliction which had tortured him at irregular intervals for years, and for which no doctor had yet found a cure, an unaccountable cramp in his right foot, sending up sharp spasms to his calf and

loins. It was long past midnight when the agony slowly
began to recede and he slept.

* * *

On the following morning he rose drowsily and dressed
slowly, meticulously for a duty lunch with a conservative
M.P. at a club. The tea in his breakfast pot was lukewarm.
He picked up the morning newspaper, turning the pages
mechanically, more with a sense of duty than of real interest. Suddenly he froze. His eyes rushed through an item on
the "Home News" page:

They promised to keep it secret, he thought in impotent
rage. Only two days before Hall had assured him that
Brand's mission was still under consideration. And now
this. This senseless leak would finish the last chance to gain
time, to use Brand to achieve a delay. Unless this had been
their intention all along, and the senseless would begin to
make sense.

He went over the text again, more calmly. It reeked of
official inspiration. He could visualize the confidential
briefing behind the tall cream doors of Hall's room, the
group of select journalists sitting in the crepuscular light
around the stately desk, from which it had undoubtedly
originated. He had been there himself only a few days before. "I assure you, Mr. Shertok, the matter is most definitely not fizzling out . . . we are well aware of the importance of making it appear we are not slamming any door
. . ." And now this. But why? "From our Diplomatic Correspondent"! For what purpose, except to oil the creaky
joints of the bureaucracy? And ease the diplomatic social
rounds?

He walked to the window. It was a glorious summer day.
No, he thought, no, I am becoming paranoid. I must not
become paranoid. They are not evil, only sloppy—we are
sloppy too—and absentminded. He clung to this thread.
Sloppiness had always been a part of their charm; now it

THE TIMES THURSDAY, JULY 20, 1944

HOME NEWS

A MONSTROUS "OFFER"

German Blackmail
Bartering Jews For Munitions

From our Diplomatic Correspondent

It has long been clear that faced with the certainty of defeat, the German authorities would intensify all their efforts to blackmail, deceive and split the allies. In the latest effort, made known in London yesterday they have reached a new level of fantasy and self-deception. They have put forward, or sponsored, an offer to exchange Jews for munitions of war—which, they said, would not be used on the Western front.

The whole story is one of the most loathsome of the war. It begins with a process of deliberate extirpation and ends, to date, with attempted blackmail. The background is only too well known. As soon as the German army occupied Hungary in March of this year anti-Jewish measures were applied with a brutality known, until then, only in Poland. At the end of last month, 400,000 of the 750,000 Jews in Hungary had been "liquidated"—which means that the younger ones had been put into labour camps, where they work under conditions of appalling harshness, and the older ones were sent to the lethal camps in Poland. After reports had come that more than 100,000 had already been done to death in the gas chambers which are known to be there, both Mr. Eden and Mr. Cordell Hull expressed the horror of the civilized world and promised punishment for the guilty.

A short time ago a prominent Hungarian Jew and a German official whose job obviously was to control his actions and movements, arrived i Turkey and managed to get a messag passed to British officials. The Hun garian Jew said that he had "ever reason to suppose" that the Germa authorities were prepared to spare th lives of the remaining 350,000 Jews Hungary and even let them leave fc abroad, if the British would sen Germany important war stocks, includ ing 10,000 army lorries. These stock he said, would not be used on th Western Front.

THE ONLY ANSWER

Such were the terms of the offer reported to London. The British go ernment know what value to set on an German or German-sponsored offe They know there can be no securit for the Jews or the other oppress peoples of Europe until victory is wo The allies are fighting to achieve th security; and they know, as well as t Germans, what happens when one b gins paying blackmail. The blackmail increases his price. Such consideration provided their own answer to the pr posed bargain.

Whether the German authoriti seriously believed that Britain wou heed the offer cannot be known at th stage. Probably even before making they had decided for one reason or an other—perhaps for transport difficu ties—to drop the deportations Poland; yesterday, in fact, the Intern tional Red Cross announced that t Hungarian Government had agreed put a stop to the deportations and ev allow some Jews to leave. In the light that announcement (which will judged by events) the German off seems to be simply a fantastic attem to sow suspicion among the allies.

Fantastic though it was, Lond made sure that Moscow and Washin ton were quickly in possession of the facts.

was our undoing. The leak was not officially inspired; more likely it was the upshot of a casual talk between one or another garrulous official, perhaps after a drink, and an eager reporter pining for his scoop like a little boy rushing off to pee.

He picked up the paper and looked at it once again. A few key words danced before his eyes. ". . . JEWS FOR MUNITIONS." *What* munitions? Who had spoken of munitions? "A process of *extirpation . . .*" A fine word, this, suitable for a gardening column. They were great wordsmiths. "Liquidated" was in quotation marks, as it should be, of course, if "liquidation" merely meant that the young were being put into labor camps. . . .

And the Germans had "probably decided" to drop the deportations to Poland anyway, even before making their "offer"—the quotation marks again—"THE ONLY ANSWER." Why, Eden himself had assured him that Brand could go back. The only question had been Brand's answer when he got back. This had now been spelled out for him by "our Diplomatic Correspondent." The door Eden said he would leave open had been slammed tight in a roar of destructive publicity.

He left soon for the office at 77 Great Russell Street. Reporters had been calling all morning for details, or comment. Weizmann was in the country. Namier, Linton and Dugdale were gathered in Shertok's room. The telephone on Shertok's desk rang. It was the writer Arthur Koestler saying that he had been told by the journalist Michael Foot that the leak had come from the Foreign Office. It had been on the Reuters wire last night, and in some of the American newspapers and on every BBC newscast since. By now the Germans knew all about it.

Namier stood at the window gloomily shaking his head. He was not surprised, he said, not at all. He had been expecting something like this for days. Shertok noticed that he was no longer referring to a "Phillips Oppenheim" thriller. For the Foreign Office, Namier said gravely, the disclosure made sense. He had heard somewhere that the Russians had been fussing about this for days. "The Foreign Office simply had to throw them a bone."

"Poor Brand," Dugdale said. "Now they'll kill his family."

"What do we know about this supposed promise that no more Jews will be deported from Hungary?" said Linton.

Shertok took up this last straw. "Could it be true?"

"It's an AP wire from Berne. Apparently the Hungarian Government also promised the Red Cross that children under ten years will be released to neutral countries."

"I doubt it," said Dugdale. "If the Hungarians made such a promise it means they are no longer powerful enough to carry it out." And she added bitterly, "But I can easily imagine the interoffice memo that will make the rounds now in the Foreign Office. 'While it is true that the Germans continue to massacre the Jews of Hungary, nevertheless the Hungarian Government has taken our warnings to heart.'"

* * *

Weizmann and his wife were in the little cottage near Bath, at Waterhouse. It was a pretty house lent to them by Lord Melchett, with flowers and thatch and gleaming timber beams. The rooms were bright and airy. "He knows a good 'ole when he sees one," Dugdale said when Weizmann first came there in the spring. The house was comfortable and for the ailing man there were good doctors in the Bath area. He was working on the first chapters of his memoirs, dealing with his youth in the province of Pinsk, "the darkest and most forlorn corner" of the Jewish pale of settlement in Russia.

The news of the disclosure reached him here. Weizmann was sitting in the garden. He read the newspaper report with a stony face, and asked at once that a call be put through to the office in London. Before the telephone call came through he had a sudden seizure. In an instant, he could not breathe properly. Terrible pains developed in his shoulder and chest. He was carried into the house coughing up blood.

Presently the doctor arrived and spoke of pneumonia, with a bleeding from the lung. The old man was pale and running a high fever. The call to London came through. Weizmann's wife spoke to Lewis Namier in tones that bordered on hysteria. Namier promised to come down by the first train next morning.

In the afternoon, under heavy sedation, Weizmann's pains receded and the coughing stopped. But the feverish chills continued. Vera remained by his bedside. In the evening he felt slightly better and drank a cup of tea. He was able to chat a little.

"Rest," said Vera. "Rest." He was still running a high fever.

"Have you spoken to London?" he demanded.

"Yes. Namier is coming down in the morning. Now, rest."

His head was turned a little sideways on the cushion and his eyes were wide open. A little while later he suddenly sat up in a hallucination of high fever and cried, "Call Lord Balfour! Call him now! I must see him immediately!"

"Chaimchik, darling boy. It's all right. Chaimchik!"

He stared at her with glistening eyes.

"Chaimchik, you've been dreaming. Balfour has been dead for many years."

He looked at her and his face fell a little. Dropping back on the cushion with a sigh, he muttered, "Well, in that case I'll have to delay seeing him for a little while."

* * *

Walter Moyne heard the news on the radio. He was in the bathroom of his house on the outskirts of Cairo, and

had just finished shaving. So it's out, he thought. He stared
at his face in the mirror. This thing had been left hanging
for much too long. Eichmann and Brand. Both believed
they could outmaneuver one another.

The shrewish iterations of too many minds had toyed
with this scheme for too long, raising false hopes and needless suspicions. A good thing it was over. But Moyne had
not expected it to be made public. Why in God's name did
they publish it? The Nazis will take their revenge on
Brand's family. Why all this publicity? There was always
some damned fool in Whitehall who spoke out of turn.

The mirror was humid and the reflection in it stared
back at him through a haze. He wondered whether the
young Sutherland was still as interested in Brand, and
why? And he suddenly felt saddened, and sorry for Brand.
Odd details of their meeting came back to him. Brand's
voice, the strange manner he had of wringing his hands,
saying there was no place for them on the entire planet.
Moyne suddenly had to admit to himself that he had been
following Brand's case with absorbed attention, and with
something like awe, and if they met again he would feel
ashamed in his presence. No, Brand's failure had not been
by chance. It was more like a destiny.

Was he still in detention? Moyne could not remember. I
must find out, he thought. There was light music on the
radio now. He snapped it off. The valet behind him noticed
his abrupt manner and ascribed it to the rising heat. He
held out the light jacket for his chief. Moyne turned to go.
He walked through the vestibule. The valet held the door
open. Lord Moyne stepped into his waiting car. The pen-
nant hung limp in the hot air. It was nine o'clock and the
sky above was already burned white by the rising July sun.

* * *

The interrogation officer told Brand of the disclosure as
they were settling down for their daily session. "It has been

on all the news broadcasts. Motor lorries and all." He spoke with a certain amount of amazement, as though until now he had only half believed in the whole story himself. "Doesn't this throw an entirely new light on the question of your return?"

Brand nodded heavily. The expression on his face shifted ever so slightly. He said nothing. The shoulders slumped. The interrogating officer was struck by his numb passivity. Brand lit a cigarette. The charade had come to an end. Everybody had played out his part. The curtain was down.

With no further comment he looked up at the interrogation officer, ready to face his questions. The officer was a little surprised but did not pursue the subject. He picked up the thread of the interrogation where they had left it on the day before. They were going over the same material— Brand no longer remembered how many times it had been. The interrogation officer noticed that Brand was unusually co-operative, almost anxious to accommodate. But his voice was inert. There was no hysteria in it, nor any appeal for sympathy, as so often in the past. Only a certain passive gloom.

Later on Brand was sent back to his room for lunch. Led back, rather, for he seemed to be carried along not by his own volition but by some invisible belt moving silently under his slack feet, with all the science and illusion of a dream. His eyes were vacant.

He entered the room and slowly closed the door. When he sat down on the bed his limbs felt light, and with their seeming weightlessness came a quickening sense of relief, almost a reprieve. It was over. He was free. He was hot. He took off his shirt. His suspenders were hanging on the back of the chair. The fact that they had been returned to him a few days before was suddenly charged with special meaning. He buttoned them on with slow, mechanical movements. The broad leather bands rubbed against his bare skin. He rubbed his fingers down their length. Then, moving more quickly, he unbuttoned them again. The light in the room was intolerably bright. With the suspenders in one hand, he moved to close the shutters with the other. The shadow was a foretaste of oblivion, and felt good. He moved the chair to the center of the room, where the light bulb was suspended on a wire from a hook, and climbed onto it. He pulled one end of the suspenders through the hook and tied it into a knot. The other end he slung as a noose around his neck. He felt almost festive. He tied the noose carefully. His fingers moved slowly, as in one of his inchoate dreams. Then he kicked the chair. With no dread, limp, he let go, expertly, as though he had done it many times before. The noose cut into his flesh. His head jerked sideways, then upward and back. His feet shook violently in the air. The elastic strap lengthened and snapped. Brand's head slumped forward and he crashed heavily onto the floor.

The warder coming in with his lunch tray found him there a few minutes later. Brand was lying on his side. His face was a dark red. He was breathing heavily, with eyes shut. He had not lost consciousness and was writhing in pain. He had broken an ankle.

*   *   *

(Documents)

Dr. Edmund Veysenmeyer, German Minister in Budapest, to Foreign Minister Ribbentrop, Berlin:

Top Secret

No 2055 22.7.44 . . . I was given to understand in confidence that the broadcast from London is true and that in fact two representatives of the SS are now in Turkey [to negotiate the ransom] on secret order from the Reichsführer SS [Himmler].

Legation Counselor Grell informs me the negotiations in Turkey are proceeding well and that the Reuters dispatch was probably issued only to camouflage the matter vis-à-vis the Russians. In reality, however, the western powers are prepared to enter such a *Geschäft* [deal].

Statement by Zikalahi Gebess, spokesman of the Royal Hungarian Government, 26 July 1944:

In connection with reports that have appeared in the English press according to which, under German leadership, a delegation of Hungarian Jews was negotiating with the Allies for the exchange of 400,000 Jews against an equivalent number of trucks and other consumer items for the German Army, I am authorized to state that these malevolent rumors are of course free inventions.

The Hungarian Government is willing and resolved to arrive at a solution of the Jewish problem. Anglo-Saxon circles can rest assured, however, that this will be done in the spirit of Humanism. Such ridiculous canards are yet another proof of the naivete with which Hungarian conditions are now viewed in the enemy camp.

Veysenmeyer to Ribbentrop: Cablegram: July 28, 1944
The phrase "Jewish problem will be solved in spirit of Humanism" was excused by Herr Zikalahi Gebess as a regrettable faux pas which unfortunately slipped through.

* * *

"Bad news, I fear," Linton said, fidgeting with a piece of paper.

"What is it now?" Shertok said tiredly.

"This letter arrived yesterday for Weizmann," Linton said with some hesitation. "I don't know if I should forward it to him. He might have another attack."

"Is it the bombing proposal?"

"They are rejecting it."

Foreign Office S.W.1
Permanent Undersecretary of State
September 1, 1944

My dear Dr. Weizmann,

You will remember that on the 6th day of July you
discussed with the Foreign Secretary the camp at
Birkenau [Auschwitz] in Upper Silesia and the atrocities
that were committed there by the Germans against
Hungarian and other Jews. You inquired whether any
steps could be taken to put a stop to, or even to mitigate,
these massacres and you suggested that something might
be achieved by bombing the camps and also if it was possible the railway lines leading to them.

As he promised Mr. Eden immediately put the proposal
to the Secretary of State of Air, the matter received
the most careful consideration by the Air Staff, but I am
sorry to have to tell you that in view of the very great
technical difficulties involved we have no option but to
refrain from pursuing the proposal in present circumstances.

I realize that this decision will prove a disappointment
to you but you may feel fully assured that the matter was
most thoroughly investigated.

Yours sincerely,
[signed] Richard Law

Shertok put the paper down and clutched his head in his
hands. "I don't understand it," he said. "I don't understand
it." In the past two months Allied planes had ranged more
or less freely from Normandy to East Prussia. It had been
in the newspapers. "I don't understand them."

"He says there are 'very great technical difficulties,'"
Linton said.

"For all I know there aren't *any*," Shertok said grimly.
"They have bombed German fuel deposits less than twenty
kilometers from the death camp."

"Perhaps it isn't so easy to pinpoint the camp. It is a case
of precision bombing, after all."

"Rubbish! Huge pillars of smoke are rising constantly from the crematoria. Brand said they were visible for miles. And what about the railway line? There is not a word about it in this letter. It's the one railway line in Europe they don't seem able to bomb." He shook himself. "The villainy." Shertok was shouting now. "He reminds *us* that on the sixth of July . . . as though we had forgotten!"

"It's the way we all write letters," Linton said soothingly.

"Damn him!" Shertok shouted. "This is not about some overdraft in the bank!" He sank back in his chair. He hated himself for yelling so. He had been feeling remiss and guilty all along. What else might he have done but to plead and plead.

Then he said in a lower voice, "We had better talk to Weizmann's doctor before we show this letter to him."

Linton nodded silently.

"There are only the Americans now," Shertok said. "Maybe we'll have more success with the American Air Force. Has there been any word from Washington?" he added, although he knew well the answer and he turned his face to the wall as Linton shook his head slowly and gravely.

I should go home, Shertok thought, I have been away for too long. I should fly back as soon as possible. He turned to Linton. "Cable New York. Ask them to redouble their efforts."

* * *

This was also in vein:

(Documents)

Memorandum for the Files
　　　　　　(by John W. Pehle, Executive Director of the
　　　　　　War Refugee Board, Washington, D.C.)
　　　　　　June 24, 1944
I saw Assistant Secretary Macloy today on the proposal that arrangements be made to bomb the railroad line

between Košíce and Pressov being used for the deportation of Jews from Hungary to Poland. I told Macloy that I wanted to mention the matter to him for whatever exploration might be appropriate by the War Department but that I had several doubts about the matter, namely:

1) whether it would be appropriate to use military planes and personnel for this purpose;

2) whether it would be difficult to put the railroad line out of commission for any long enough period to do any good;

3) even assuming that this railroad line were put out of commission for some period of time, whether it would help the Jews in Hungary.

I made it clear to Mr. Macloy that I was not, at least at this point, requiring the War Department to take any action on this proposal other than appropriately explore it. Macloy understood my position and said he would check into the matter.

[signed] J. W. Pehle

The meeting between Pehle and Macloy led to the following response:

WAR DEPARTMENT
Office of the Assistant Secretary
July 4, 1944

Mr. John W. Pehle
Executive Director, War Refugee Board
Treasury Department
Washington, D.C.

The War Department is of the opinion that the suggested air operation [against the railroad lines between Hungary and Poland] is impractical. It could be executed only by the diversion of considerable air support essential to the success of our forces now engaged in decisive operations and would in any case be of such doubtful efficacy that it would not amount to a practical project.

The War Department fully appreciates the humanitarian motives which prompted the suggestion but for reasons stated above the operation suggested does not appear justified.

J. J. Macloy
Assistant Secretary

In October 1944 the representative in Switzerland of the War Refugee Board renewed his appeal for the bombing. By now Pehle had overcome his early hesitation about employing military planes and personnel for the ostensibly "civilian purpose" of saving lives. Pehle wrote the War Department urging Macloy to order the air raid without delay. And he attached a copy of the chart Brand had brought out with him. This elicited the following reply:

WAR DEPARTMENT
Office of the Assistant Secretary
November 18, 1944

Dear Mr. Pehle,

I refer to your letter of November 8 in which you forwarded the report of two eye witnesses on the notorious German concentration and extermination camps of Auschwitz and Birkenau in Upper Silesia.

The Operation Staff of the War Department has given careful consideration to your suggestion that the bombing of these camps be undertaken . . . [and] the following points were brought out:

a) Positive destruction of these camps would necessitate precision bombing employing heavy and medium bombardment or attack by low flying or dive bombing aircraft, preferably the latter.

b) The target is beyond the maximum range of *medium* bombardment dive bombers and fighter bombers located in the U.K., France or Italy.

c) Use of *heavy* bombardment from U.S. bases would necessitate a hazardous round-trip flight unescorted of approximately 2,000 miles over enemy territory.

d) At the present critical stage of the war in Europe our strategic air forces are engaged in the destruction of industrial target systems vital to the dwindling war potential of the enemy from which they should not be diverted. The positive solution of the problem is the earliest possible victory over Germany to which we should exert our entire means.

Based on the above as well as the most uncertain if not dangerous effect such a bombing would have on the object to be attained, the War Department has felt that it should not at least for the present undertake these operations.

I know that you have been reluctant to press this activity of the War Department. We have been pressed strongly from other parties, however, and have taken the best military opinion on its feasibility and we believe that the above conclusion is a sound one.

> Sincerely,
> John J. Macloy
> Assistant Secretary of State

Item: In September–October 1944, American and British heavy bombers twice flew sorties over the Auschwitz area but dropped only food parcels to Allied prisoners of war held in an adjacent camp. The nearby I. G. Farben chemical plant had been bombed before. In both cases, the "technical difficulties" were not apparently insurmountable.

Item: The diversion of huge strategic bomber forces from vital industrial targets to stage indiscriminate raids on civilian centers continued throughout the fall and winter. Eight weeks after Macloy's letter, hundreds of Allied planes attacked the city of Dresden killing approximately 220,000 civilians.

Cairo

The warder, upon finding Brand on the cell floor after the unsuccessful suicide, rushed out to call for help. A medical orderly arrived, who loosened the noose around Brand's neck and helped him to a sip of water. Brand was lying on his side. The room was turning around him in circles. His lips moved lightly and his short breath came hissing through his teeth.

The two men tried to lift him. He groaned. They hovered over him undecidedly. Brand blinked. The room was slowly coming into focus. He shifted his head. The orderly said, "Take it easy now." Removing the noose from Brand's neck, he turned to the warder. "These things never work as simply as they think."

The cell was suddenly filled with people. The interrogating officer came in and the chief warden and another man and an army doctor who felt Brand's pulse and fingered his chest with a stethoscope. The others stood around with their hands in their pockets. A stretcher was squeezed through the narrow door. Brand was lifted by many hands and carried out to a waiting ambulance in the yard. The others remained inside but the interrogation officer walked behind the stretcher, and after it had been shoved into place and the ambulance had driven off in a cloud of dust, he remained standing for a while in the sun, perspiring.

He was conscious suddenly of the affinity that had grown between Brand and him in the long hours of interrogation, a curious intimacy they shared like an uncomfortable, or carnal secret. He wondered about this. For a moment he felt vaguely guilty, as if he had just almost lost a dear old mate.

The military hospital was on the edge of town in a Coptic monastery, requisitioned by the army for the duration of the war. Its wards were filled with wounded or sick prisoners of war. There were ikons on the dark walls. The nurses were English, young, cheerful and efficient. Brand's foot was bandaged and blocked inside a wooden frame and hoisted up. Flies buzzed about the room in black clusters. The nurses spread a mosquito net over the bed. Through its fine mesh Brand stared up at the vaulted ceiling. His mind was blank. He drifted in and out of sleep and was visited by nagging dreams with no sequence—he was digging, or running for no reason, or falling—and when they came at dawn with charts and thermometers he was wide awake and aching all over. He asked for a sedative and finally sank into a deep, dreamless sleep. It was what he had been aiming for all along.

* * *

Back at the prison, meanwhile, the chief warden (a major in the military police) was facing a ticklish problem.

"It isn't so simple," he told the interrogation officer. "Suicide is a criminal offense." Even though the attempt had failed, Brand was punishable under the law. "He will have to answer charges."

"You can't be serious. Not after what he has been through."

"I understand how you feel. Still, I must hand in my report."

"He might try to kill himself again."

"I don't think so. Nobody ever does it twice. He is just like a little boy crying 'If I kill myself you'll all be sorry.'"

"Look here," said the interrogation officer. "He is an M.I. body. Let *us* decide what's best."

"If he is charged it doesn't mean that Military Intelligence can't go on with their interrogation."

"The interrogation is more or less finished."

"Well, in that case M.I. suffer no harm. I'll write my report. Now it's up to CCCS."

On the following morning, the chief warden's report was on the desk of the colonel in command, Cairo-South, who had jurisdiction over military prisons and detention camps in the area. A legal adviser was consulted. He complicated the matter further. There was a question whether Brand's case came under Egyptian penal law, since he was a civilian, or under British law, since the offense had been committed within a British military establishment. Under CCCS tended to apply British law. But the question of ju-Egyptian law the punishment would be more severe. The risdiction was not simple. Brand was an enemy alien and therefore fell under martial law. On the other hand he was not, strictly speaking, a prisoner of war, or even—it was discovered—a prisoner. The warrant for his arrest could not be found. The decision was postponed.

*   *   *

On his third day in the hospital, the swelling began to subside. Brand was told to sit up in bed; he did so for short periods only, staring blankly into space, slumping back on the pillow as soon as the nurse was out of the room. The young nurse tried to humor him. He merely nodded. He did everything they told him to, with slow, mechanical movements. His facial expression remained blank. A part of him seemed to have died. He drifted in and out of sleep. He was examined by a neurologist, who found nothing wrong. The neurologist tried to engage Brand in conversation. Brand said "yes" or "no" or "I am tired." On the seventh day the foot was back to its normal shape. He was rolled into an operating room and given an anesthetic. His limbs grew heavy, and then numb, and when he was unconscious his face was frozen in a smile. The foot was set and put into a cast up to the knee.

On the following morning when he awoke, the interrogation officer and Captain Sutherland were standing by his bed. Brand shifted his body. There was no pain. He heaved himself up on his elbows. The interrogation officer said brightly, "Hello there!"

Sutherland said, "How do you feel?"

Brand said, "Thank you, I think it's all right." He looked at the interrogation officer. "Thank you very much for coming."

"Not at all."

"Thank you anyway. How are things back at the Old Bailey?"

"We were worried about you."

"It's very kind of you to say so."

"Not at all," said the interrogation officer.

They were perfectly pleasant to one another, like two conspirators after the act. Sutherland watched them with a certain amount of amazement. He had first thought that Brand's attempt to kill himself had been a kind of scream, a cry for help. It struck him now that maybe it had been an appeal for personal approval. Nobody killed himself for political reasons. He needed this lopsided proof that he had done all he could. The interrogation officer offered Brand a cigarette, and then, as though Brand were just another tourist who had suffered a light accident, he said casually, "What are your plans?"

Brand eyed him a little absently.

"Your interrogation is finished. You've been cleared, from the security point of view."

"I want to go back to Hungary."

"Yes. You'll be going back. Quite soon."

"Are you serious?"

"Yes. First you must get well. As soon as you can stand up, you move into St. George's."

"What's that?"

"It's a convalescence center. Very pleasant. You'll like it."

"Thank you very much," Brand said.

"Don't thank me, thank Sutherland. There were some idiotic legalities to overcome."

"Legalities?"

"Lawyers' stuff. Penal charges. Sutherland took care of it."

"What kind of charges?"

"Never mind. It's all right now."

* * *

On Monday, 28 August, he was discharged from the hospital and told to come back in three weeks' time to have the cast taken off. Sutherland drove him to his new quarters. St. George's was a rest camp for British officers. It was on the southern edge of Cairo, not far from the pyramids, on the grounds of a former sports club by the Nile. The main house was surrounded by lawns and tennis courts and wooden barracks that accommodated some two hundred officers.

Brand limped across the brittle grass, dragging the cast behind him like a chain. He had lost much weight and his face was drawn. An orderly showed them to the room. Brand's suitcase was standing against the wall, and its contents had been laid out on the bed. The shirts were freshly laundered, the suits cleaned and pressed.

Sutherland said, "If you need anything there is a NAAFI store on the grounds. Your money is in the receptionist's safe. You can have it at any time."

"Thank you."

"I live not far from here. I could come by occasionally to keep you company."

"Yes. I would like that very much."

"If there is anything else you might need . . . ?"

"No, thank you. . . . Yes—perhaps you could find me some newspapers. The Jewish papers from Palestine if you could possibly get them . . ."

"Of course. I'll see that you get them in the morning. You'll probably find the English papers in the library here. You ought to relax for a while . . ."

"There is no time to relax. I am going to resume my mission. You heard it! I must prepare myself!"

* * *

First of all there was the change in scenery. From the confining humiliation of prison and the sickening discomfort of hospital to the luxurious spaciousness and easy clubbiness at St. George's. He had a telephone in his room, and although there was nobody he could call he luxuriated in the feeling that he was once again in touch with the outside world. There was a veranda, which no one was using at this season, with potted plants and wooden deck chairs for sunbathing. It was so hot that even in the shade the air was thick as woolen vapor. From the veranda one saw the pyramids.

In the main clubhouse servants shuffled across polished floors, carrying drinks on gleaming platters. The walls were hung with hunting trophies and oil paintings, and over the huge stone mantelpiece the King and Queen were framed in gold. There were leather armchairs everywhere, and the bar was beamed and paneled in dark wood. There were squash courts and a large swimming pool. Young men in elegant uniforms played croquet on the lawn with women officers of the ATS. Many were convalescents like Brand, some amputees, others recuperated from wounds or shell shock. Two young officers were blind, waiting for passage back to Australia.

Brand hobbled to the office and fetched his wallet. He noticed a sign announcing a regular bus service into the center of Cairo. Tickets were on sale for performances at the Cairo opera house. He bought himself some socks, a shirt and a few books. Apart from the ample personnel he seemed to be the only civilian in the place; he was treated by everyone with politeness and consideration. Nobody asked any questions. The change was abrupt, beyond all thought and belief only a short time ago.

* * *

Then, there was the expectation of imminent release, the return to Hungary and the resumption of his mission. He was in no position yet to think about it very clearly. He merely sensed something like a vague thrill. The interrogation officer had said clearly that he would be going back soon, and Sutherland had confirmed it. Were it not for this damned foot he would be going back today. He did not know the reason for this unexpected change. How did it tie in with the public disclosure of his mission? (He must read the newspapers, he thought, they might give him a hint.) The disclosure had not apparently undercut his mission. On the contrary, it was probably meant to prepare the ground for the proposed deal. If he was going back something undoubtedly had happened. Something important. Perhaps one of Steiner's men had gone to Budapest alone, as Mark had told him. Perhaps they were already negotiating with the Nazis. His patient collaboration with the interrogator had been worth something after all. He had convinced them of his honesty and sincerity. They have realized that his presence in Budapest was necessary after all. He knew Eichmann and his collaborators. The others did not. They needed him. Or was it the attempted suicide that had awakened them? In that case, it had not been in vain. Perhaps it was still not too late.

Such thoughts, and others, were passing through his mind in disorderly fashion. They were sweet illusions freeing the soul from its painful cares with something almost like sensual pleasure. He hobbled through the lobby to the dining room. He was shown to a table, which he shared with a middle-aged major recovering from malaria. The food was served on crested plates of English bone china. Brand dined, more leisurely than he had perhaps intended. After dessert he ordered a brandy and watched a bloodshot moon rising over the river. The scene had a hallucinatory quality about it, and again he felt something like a thrill.

He rose and limped over to the reading room. Air-mail editions of the Australian, South African and English newspapers were stacked up on a long library table. He leafed slowly through the *Mail,* the Manchester *Guardian* and *The Times.* A large picture gave him pause. General de Gaulle striding down the Champs Élysées. Paris had been liberated. He had not known that. In the background the Arc de Triomphe. Then a quick succession of headlines. The Russians were on the outskirts of Warsaw; the civilian population there had risen up in arms. Dissension in Germany—Wehrmacht officers make an attempt on Hitler's life. He must read about this later—did it not tie in with the resumption of his mission? Of course it did. The satraps were ready to deal. He felt his heart beat wildly. He turned a few more pages. The long piece in *The Times* ("Bartering Jews for Munitions") struck his eye. His mouth dried up as he raced through it. No. This did not herald the resumption of his mission; nor this comment by Weekham Steed, the famous liberal journalist in the Manchester *Guardian:*

A rich Hungarian industrialist, accompanied by two German officers, has arrived in Turkey to

negotiate the ransom of Jews. . . . There is no
need to point out that this humanitarian blackmail
was rejected by the Allies.

He shifted his cast and reached for the handle of his
crutch. It dropped noisily on the wooden floor. The silent
faces at the writing tables looked up. He scrambled up and
hobbled out as quickly as he could. The foot hurt, but
more than the pain he felt its inert weight pulling him
down. A part of him seemed dead and buried in that cast.
Outside the main house the lawn was damp and the air
thick and heavy and filled with the chirping of crickets, or
perhaps frogs. He dragged himself to his room. He put up
his foot as he had been told to when it hurt. "A rich industrialist . . ." What a mess he had made of it. The interrogation officer was a liar, of course, but he himself was
inept. He blamed himself for everything. He had rendered
his people a disservice. What a tragedy that of all people in
Budapest he had been picked to negotiate their rescue! Another man would have impressed Shertok, Moyne or the interrogator. Another man would have convinced them of his
honesty. "A rich industrialist." Someone else should have
been chosen for the journey. Kastner, he was a much
shrewder man, and politically experienced. Yes, even
Gyorgy. Gyorgy was a man of parts who knew his way
around. "Accompanied by two German officers." Another
man would have fared better. The thoughts raced through
his feverish mind and he continued to tear at his own flesh,
ferociously, for not having been shrewder or more talented.
It was by now almost a form of self-indulgence. If he had
only been more skillful, more persuasive. Of all the devilish
temptations, an insufficient talent is the cruelest, the most
painful of all addictions. And when he finally fell asleep
the nightmares came back—he was holding a flower to his
nostrils and felt it slowly, voraciously eating his face. In the
middle of the night he imagined he was waking up and

looking out of the window. The clubhouse was situated in a bombed, ruined, burned-out city. In the pale moonlight he saw smoke rising on all sides. But that too was a dream.

In the morning a waiter entered the room with a small tray. Brand sat up abruptly. The waiter spoke. Brand heard his voice but could not make out what he was saying, and in what language. He cried, "What? What?"

The waiter had only been saying, "Good morning, sir." He brought Brand a large manila envelope. It contained week-old Hebrew- and English-language newspapers from Palestine, which Sutherland had bought as he had promised in a bookstore in downtown Cairo.

Brand took up the English-language papers first—six or seven recent issues of the Palestine *Post*. The *Post,* he knew, was the unofficial voice of the Jewish Agency. Shertok was on its board of directors. Its role was to propagate the Jewish cause among English-speaking readers in the Near East, members of the armed forces and officials of the British administration. In the Palestine *Post,* one might have thought, the news of the mass killings in Europe, which so rarely found its way into the English papers, would be displayed prominently . . . accompanied by editorial comment. Yet there was no mention in any of these issues. Brand could not believe his eyes. Nor could he find any reference to his mission anywhere, not even in a distorted form. Could it be that nobody there knew? Nobody, that is, except Shertok and Mark and their cronies in the pay of the British rulers? Could it be that they were afraid to let the truth be known? Could it be that the news was expunged by British press censors for fear of a public uprising in that country? It seemed improbable, since the distorted version had been on the BBC news too. But there it was. The improbable seemed the rule these days.

Then he turned to the Hebrew papers—there were many more of those—some issues of the independent *Haaretz* and a thick batch of *Davar,* the Histadrut daily and organ of the leading labor party. Before he began the difficult task of reading a language he still only barely understood (and in a script he had to labor haltingly to decipher) he was struck by a curious graphic feature. The front page of every single issue of *Davar*—there were more than ten—was framed in black, a thick, funereal line of black. They were obviously in deep mourning.

But as he began to read, slowly, he realized with a chill that this extraordinary display of public grief, day after day on the front page of the leading paper, was not for the slaughtered of Europe as he had thought, but for a labor leader named Berl Katznelson, who had died (the result of a traffic accident) on 15 August. Brand vaguely remembered the name; he did not know from where. It meant nothing to him.

He leafed through the black-bordered pages, and finally found what he was looking for, in small print, with no comment, a small item that "two Nazi or Hungarian agents have come out of Occupied Europe to offer the British Government a barter deal which has been rejected." So that was what *they* too thought he was. He dropped the papers and let out a harsh, crackling noise. Brand laughed.

* * *

He spent the early part of the morning in the library casually looking through illustrated magazines, or staring out at the muddy river and the sand bars beyond. He limped to the office and inquired about the bus service into Cairo. He hobbled back out toward the main gate. There was a sentry on guard there asking everybody for their passes. He had no way of telling whether he was still under arrest or free. He was in no shape to try his luck. He found a shady spot on the lawn and settled on a bench. The tip of a pyramid was visible behind the dusty palms. It was like a man-made mountain. A great depressing flatness surrounded it. Brand gazed at it, drowsy with tiredness or heat, and suddenly, for no reason he could think of (he found it rather difficult to think anyway), he imagined the pyramid melting down in the sun and becoming plains. The fantasy filled his mind with a wild, absurd exaltation. He shook himself. The sweat was pouring down his back. He hobbled back to the main house and went in to lunch. He ate slowly. Afterward he was curiously at peace with himself and no longer thinking grim thoughts. Only . . . I must take care of myself. The major who shared his table spoke to him. He told Brand of his attacks of malarial fever. Then he said that in his barrack was a convalescent, a man in his early twenties who never left his quarters. He suffered from a rare war injury. A bomb had exploded near him, too far away to blow him up, but close enough to scramble his insides in the air pressure. His liver, his heart and his intestines had been jolted out of place even though the skin remained intact.

Then, changing the subject abruptly, the major said, "And how do you like Egypt?"

"I've seen little of it so far," Brand said. "I had this accident, you see."

"How did it happen?"

"Oh, it was a . . . a fall."

"I once knew a man in Glasgow who broke his arm shaving," the major began. "He used to say . . ."

Sutherland, who came by a little while later, found Brand in the main lobby reading the local French daily, *La Bourse Egyptienne*. "You look tired," he said, "but otherwise much better than yesterday. How do you feel?"

"I have stopped noting how I feel," Brand said. "It was once a habit. But I have decided to break it."

"Ah, you are getting back to your old self. I am pleased to hear it."

"I'm finished playing heroics."

"Don't say that. You'll soon be out of this cast. You'll need both your feet when you get back to Budapest."

"You know they won't let me go back."

"But you are going back. Positively. It's been decided."

"I am too tired for these jokes."

"I wouldn't dream of joking about this."

"Please. You don't have to pretend."

"I have it on very good authority. You are going back."

"On what terms?"

"We don't know yet. But you are going."

"When?"

"As far as I know it's now all up to the Jewish Agency in Jerusalem."

"Ah, the Jewish Agency."

"Yes. They've been after us for weeks to get you released."

"I should not have thought they were so interested in me. They lured me into this trap."

"That's not true. On the contrary, Mr. Shertok has been pressing your case in London for over a month. He has talked to everybody from the Foreign Secretary down."

"It's not done me much good so far. The newspapers say I'm a Nazi agent."

"Pay no attention to the newspapers. You have full security clearance."

"But they haven't released me. They've just moved me to a nicer cell."

"Not true. You are no longer under detention."

"You mean, I could just walk out of here—and run?"

"Certainly. But why should you? You couldn't anyway. Not with this cast."

"I am a free man?"

"Yes. Naturally to employ your freedom usefully, you require a little more preparation."

"I see."

"I'm not sure you do. I am not trying to be coy, Brand. We'll have definite word from Jerusalem within a few days.

As soon as you get rid of this cast, you'll go back to
Budapest. Until then, try to relax."

"I don't understand . . ."

Sutherland gently insisted, "Try to rest."

Brand slowly inhaled his cigarette. "Yes, I think I am
going to rest."

"Fine."

There was a long pause. Then Brand said, "Thank you
for sending those papers. It was very kind of you to take so
much trouble."

"No trouble at all. I'll put in a regular order for you if
you wish."

"You are very kind."

"Would you like me to drive you into Cairo today?
You'll enjoy a little outing."

"Do I have a pass for the gate?"

"It's no problem. I'll get you one."

"I don't understand why you are taking so much trouble
over me."

"No trouble at all. Shall we go?"

"I am still quite weak. Could we do it some other day?"

"Anytime you like."

"Don't you have regular hours at . . . at . . . ?"

"Military Intelligence? Yes. They're not stringent. I can
always get away."

"Thank you."

After tea they somehow began to talk about their fam-
ilies. Sutherland had a five-year-old daughter. Brand said
he had had no word from his family in months. Hansi had
been arrested and he feared the worst. "You see, they were
keeping her hostage against my return."

"But you will return, and quite soon."

"I was supposed to be back on the first of June. It's September now."

"You must not give up."

"I keep telling myself that. But I have deluded myself

too often. The worst is this feeling of guilt. To be here. Having tea."

"I know. It will soon be over."

"I hope you are right," Brand said. "But I don't believe it."

* * *

Sutherland asked, "Any word from Jerusalem about Brand?"

"Not that I know of," said the interrogation officer. "They are taking their time, quite clearly."

"I can't believe that."

"Why not? The Jews' bureaucracy isn't likely to be more efficient than ours."

"I don't think that's it. More likely they are still haggling with the high commissioner about what Brand should say when he goes back."

"It's certainly not a very easy problem."

"Must they make it so difficult?"

"You seem quite fond of him."

"If I'd been in his shoes I think by now I would have gone out of my mind."

"Why make such a drama? Nervous, yes. But otherwise . . . ?"

"You see, he thinks he's guilty for the deaths of hundreds of thousands."

"But he isn't. The Nazis would have butchered them anyway."

"He is sure it's his fault. He thinks that if he had only been more convincing, no—if he had been a better man—he might have saved them."

"I think he is wrong."

"Perhaps," said Sutherland after a pause. "You see, he thinks . . . he thinks he has survived his own damnation. Not because he was virtuous, but because he was inept."

"I would not say inept. Just naïve."

* * *

He did think about killing himself, even after his arrival at St. George's. He thought about it quite a lot, tormented as he was by self-doubt, and disoriented by an isolation no less cowing for all the apparent brilliance of its creature comforts. But the first attempt had misfired so badly, so absurdly, so humiliatingly, that he began to rationalize it as an omen. In suicide, as in everything else, the odds were against him. He did not have the strength, or the courage, to test the fates again.

His physical condition improved. He walked more easily, gaining strength all the time. After the first week he threw away his crutch and walked with only a stick. Some of the officers in the club heard that he had come over from the other side. They teased him—"Hello, Mr. Hess"—and he laughed. To Sutherland he spoke of his mission with wry detachment, even something like wit, mocking and deflating his former pretensions.

Sutherland was now coming by often. They would have tea and talk. Brand complained of his headaches. Sutherland said they were probably psychosomatic and would cure themselves in time. Time, time, time. Sutherland drove him into Cairo. They strolled along a main thoroughfare. The shop windows were lit up, filled with the handiwork of peace—lace, linen, lacquered luxury automobiles, Indian teas, English perambulators, Cuban cigars and, in Groppi's pastry shop, a giant Eiffel Tower in spun sugar to commemorate with all the rich gourmands of Cairo the recent liberation of Paris.

They stopped for ice cream at a sidewalk cafe. The air was damp and smoky, and filled with the screech of streetcars and the cries of little boys selling newspapers and pistachio nuts. It was the same evening hour that—it seemed ages ago—he had so often sat in a cafe, feeling reasonably pleased with life. Then Sutherland went to fetch the car and drove him back. At least he had no more nightmares. The answer from Jerusalem, Sutherland said, was due very soon.

Brand was trying hard not to think about it. He hung about the club, reading, playing billiards or chess, and chatting with the others. He got into the habit of ordering a bottle of wine with his meal, and a cigar after dessert. Every morning there was a croquet match; every evening a movie. He learned a new card game and read a book about ancient Egypt.

One day Sutherland drove him south to see the pyramids. Because of the cast, Brand could not climb them or enter the dark recesses and chambers. At the foot of the Great Pyramid they joined a group of Australian officers who were being lectured by an English-speaking tour guide. The guide spoke of weights and measures and of gods. There were many gods. They even had a God of the Dead here, who was also an ox, or a cow, and at the same time the sun and the stars. Brand did not quite get it. The pyramids were sharply outlined in the bright sun. Their walls were pale as bones—and they were all tombs. Mountain ranges of death, made of timeless granite. And in the desert where they stood, which was flat as a sheet, there too there was no sense of time. As soon as they walked on, the wind blew away their footprints, as though they had been a flock of passing crows.

When he came back that night to St. George's, he found a letter from Mark. They had heard through a Swiss Red Cross official, Mark wrote, that Hansi and the children were safe. About Brand's return, there was not a word in Mark's letter.

* * *

At the end of the month the cast was taken off. "Exercise a little every day and in a short while you'll be as good as new," the doctor said. Brand still limped. But the weight had been lifted and with it the shackle that had tied him to this ground. Or so he thought. There was no word yet of his release. Sutherland came to congratulate him on what he called his liberation from Egyptian servitude. He had a request to convey to Brand, from the interrogation officer, who was facing a problem, he said, and was wondering if Brand could possibly help him out.

"Oh? But how?"

Sutherland continued with some hesitation. "He is having trouble with Andrew Gyorgy."

"Where is he?"

"In the same prison that you were. He's been there all the time."

"What do you want from me?"

"It's not my idea. They're wondering if you would have a word with him. You've known him for years, haven't you? Perhaps if you spoke to him he would be more cooperative. He is lying all the time."

"He won't listen to me."

"You don't have to if you don't want."

In the afternoon Sutherland drove him to the prison. Gyorgy's cell was on the lower floor. Brand went in alone. Gyorgy was lying on a plank hinged to the wall. He looked thin and sick. It seemed that his mournful face had not been washed for weeks. At first he did not recognize Brand. Then his gray face broke into a grimace.

"Aha, the savior of mankind is here. And to what do I owe this unexpected pleasure?"

"Hello, Bandi," Brand said.

Gyorgy sat up. "Is your cell as nice as mine?"

"I am free."

"Don't pretend to me, old boy."

"Well, I was here. Before. But now I am staying at a convalescent center. It's quite nice."

"How much did you pay?" Gyorgy rubbed his thumb against his fingers."

"I didn't pay."

"Come on, now. Who spreads his legs around here?"

"I didn't bribe anybody."

"Don't pretend."

"I am staying at a place called St. George's. It's on the Nile."

"Very chic. Make no mistake about it, they won't let go of you so quickly. You'll see."

"Why?"

"They're afraid you'll open your big mouth. I know."

"What do you know?"

Gyorgy fairly yelled. "I know everything, you stupid fool! They are keeping me here because of you! It's your fault. They need me to double-check on everything you said. They pester me all the time about you and your goddamn scheme of tanks and ammunition!"

"Ammunition?"

"Yes, you goddamned fool!"

"I doubt that," said Brand gently. "My interrogation was finished over a month ago. They want other things from you. Why don't you tell them all you know?"

"Damn you, did they send you here?"

"Yes."

"Go away."

"Speak freely to them. It's the best thing you can do. Believe me."

"You bastard! I don't believe any of you. You're all crooks. Your Jews have cheated me too! And after I risked my life for them."

"Gyorgy, you'll get your commission. They won't cheat you. No, listen, Gyorgy. Please. You are making a mistake."

But Gyorgy was already stretched out on the plank with his back toward Brand. The striped shirt he was wearing was dark with sweat and torn under the collar.

Sutherland was waiting at the entrance. "I am sorry," said Brand. "I am afraid I blundered this too. He won't talk to me. He is in very bad shape."

"Thank you for trying."

"What are they holding him for, anyway?"

"I'm not sure I know exactly. It has something to do with what he did for the Americans."

"Why don't they leave him alone?" Brand said. "He is a poor fool who tried to save his skin in a very difficult situation, that's all. And he did a lot of good, too."

"You don't know all the details," Sutherland said. There was a certain coolness between them as they drove back to St. George's. But on the following day the incident was forgotten.

Sutherland came in the afternoon beaming. "We have word from Jerusalem," he said. "You'll be flown back to Budapest via Jerusalem. In Jerusalem, you'll be joined by a Jewish Agency official. He will brief you and give you exact instructions."

The date set for Brand's departure was Tuesday, 26 September. On Monday, 25 September, a little farewell party was given at the club. Sutherland came, and the interrogation officer, and they were joined by some of Brand's new acquaintances, the major (who was about to return to his base in Lebanon) and two Australian officers. Champagne was ordered and the interrogation officer gave a little speech in which he said how much he had learned from Brand, how they were all grateful to him and how brave a man he was. He hinted vaguely that Brand would in the near future render even more important contributions to the war effort and "to the cause nearest to his heart, and rightly so—the cause of his own people."

It was past midnight when they broke up. A cool breeze was wafting in from the river at the garden's end. On the following morning Brand woke up with a hangover. He packed his things and waited on the veranda. Shortly before lunch Sutherland came. He stammered a little as he spoke.

"I am . . . afraid there will be a little delay."

"What?"

"The Jewish Agency cabled. Apparently they don't want you back in Budapest right now. They want you to wait a little while."

"What?"

"It seems they've received a signal from your colleagues in Budapest saying that your return right now might cause some inconvenience."

"I don't believe it," Brand said. A month ago he would have yelled. "Not my friends in Budapest. No, not they."

"It says so in the telegram."

"The truth is that in Jerusalem they don't think I am the right man to negotiate. Why don't they say it openly?"

"Look, it's only a delay. They say so themselves. We'll hear from them again soon."

"I must go to Jerusalem right away."

"I quite understand that. I should think it can be arranged."

* * *

But it was not arranged, not right away. They hated letting go. Sutherland tried his best on Brand's behalf. He dared not approach his powerful relative Lord Moyne. But he made discreet inquiries with the security people at Middle East headquarters. They had no objections in principle to Brand's removal to Palestine. Some paper work remained to be done, though, before they would receive the necessary agreement from the authorities in Jerusalem. There was no hurry. Was not Brand comfortable where he was?

He was, in fact . . . at least part of the time. With each further day at St. George's he alternated between extremes of energy and depletion, charged and sapped in turn by the heat, the cigarettes, innumerable cups of coffee, cold showers and pills. The heat fell from the sky every day, like a weight. The evenings were more pleasant. He waited for the situation to clear up. The Jewish newspapers from Palestine, which he received regularly, gave him few clues. The copies of *Davar* were framed in black, they were still mourning the late trade union leader. A strident election campaign was going on over there and its issues were as far from those agitating Brand as was humanly imaginable. He thought, they have forgotten me, they have forgotten my mission. Or maybe they are afraid I might open my mouth when I get there. It might be bad for the elections.

On 1 October 1944 he wrote a letter to the chairman of the Executive of the Jewish Agency in Jerusalem. It was a wild letter, full of invective. He threatened to escape unless he was free to leave immediately for Palestine. The letter was intercepted by British military censors. It caused no great stir, but perhaps it accelerated his release, which was being processed anyway. On 7 October, Sutherland told him he was free to leave. He would be driven to Jerusalem, and remain there for the time being. "I'm afraid it's the end of your mission," Sutherland said quietly.

"No!" Brand flared up with an intensity Sutherland had not seen in him for weeks. "For me there will never be an end!"

"When do you want to leave?"

"Tomorrow," Brand said. Then he remembered. "I am the only civilian here. How do I ask them for the bill?"

"No need for that," Sutherland said. "Besides, you are no longer a civilian. I haven't yet told you the terms of your release. You must not reveal your true identity. Your new name is Jacobson. Lieutenant Jacobson of the British Army. It's a temporary commission. . . . Why are you laughing?"

Jerusalem

His journey was ending as it had begun: on a false identity. His new pass, however, was genuine enough, the other was still in his briefcase, and both were duly signed and stamped with all the appropriate accouterments of legitimate authority. He was pondering this oddity with but a trace of confusion when the sleek staff car came for him in the morning and he settled in the front seat next to the uniformed driver. Two hours later, at the border control station on the east bank of the Suez Canal, the guard saluted and said, "Thank you, Lieutenant." He handed Brand back his papers with a certain amount of awe, for officers in civilian clothes were a rarity in wartime.

The long drive through the desert was hot and monotonous. At Beersheba, Brand stopped at an officers' club for lunch while the driver went off to look for fuel. North of Beersheba the desert melded into parched farmland. The dusty undulating hills were bare and dry, with only a few weather-worn fig trees and olives between the rocks and the dry shrubbery. In the distance he saw the clustered mud houses of a few Arab villages. He thought, so this is the land of Jewish dreams. His eyes strained through the windshield to catch every little green patch. It was still distant, and at the moment there was no pain, only the faintest melancholy.

In a vague sort of way, of course, the land had been part of his inner life for years. He remembered his grandfather talking about it; he may have been five or six years old then. His grandfather had spoken of it in a possessive sort of way. A land of roses and sun, where the rivers never froze, for they flowed directly from paradise and the river Sambatyon threw up stones into the air all week, except Saturday when it rested, for it was a Jewish river. Dreams, dreams. It was an arid land, bleak and bathed in a harsh light. They drove through a dusty little hill town. A little road sign said HEBRON. Arab boys in rags were hawking pumpkin seeds and in the hot wind the dust rose in spirals. The higher they climbed in the stony hills, the hotter it became, and when they reached the outskirts of Jerusalem Brand unbuttoned his shirt and wiped his shoulders and chest even though he was not perspiring. It was as though his insides had dried up. The driver said, "It's the *khamsin*, sir. It's always worse up here than in the plains."

The driver nosed the car through the city traffic and entered the walled grounds of a former hospital and orphanage—Talitha Cumi, so-called because on that spot Jesus had said, "Talitha, *cumi*," and the dead maid had risen. The half-ruined building now served one of the branch offices of British Military Intelligence. Before the war it had been the seat of a Lutheran order. There were still signs in German everywhere, in elaborate Gothic script.

Brand was led into a small office. An officer waved casually at a chair. "You must be tired," he said. "It's a bad *khamsin*."

Brand remained standing. "You are not going to keep me here, are you?"

"Have no worry. Just until you tell us where you are going to stay."

"I am not going to stay in Jerusalem at all, if I can help it. I must get back to Hungary."

"My dear Mr. Brand," the officer said in a strained

voice, "this is something neither of us is able to decide. Would you like me to call the Jewish Agency? They have to vouch for you before we allow you to leave."

"I thought I was now an officer of the British Army."

"Yes . . . Cairo often has these imaginative ideas . . . but your commission was just a temporary convenience. To bring you over here without too much legal fuss, since the Jewish immigration quota is closed. As of now, you're a civilian again."

"I see."

"Shall I call the agency then?"

"Yes."

"With whom would you like to speak?"

"Mr. Shertok."

"I believe he's in London."

"Teddy Mark, then."

"As you wish."

The officer dialed, and in a minute Mark was on the line sounding excited and surprised. "Where are you?"

"In Jerusalem."

"You must be joking."

"I am not."

"Since when?"

"I just arrived."

"What? From Cairo?"

"Yes."

"They let you go?"

"They haven't yet. They want to know where I'll be staying."

"Stay where you are. I'll be right over!"

A short time later he was in the car next to Mark, who was still not over his surprise, and was treating him with a mixture of curiosity and fear, Brand thought, chatting a bit nervously of this and that, and his face was perspiring. Mark kept wiping it as he drove.

"It's hotter here than in Cairo," Brand said.

"You're telling me." Mark grinned. "Dear boy, Zionism is strictly a winter sport."

"You were always complaining that *I* was sarcastic."

"I'm sorry."

"When am I going back to Hungary?"

"Let's talk about it at the office," Mark said.

They were just pulling up outside the agency building. They walked up to the second floor. Mark noticed how much Brand had changed in the short time since their last meeting in the prison cell. The reddish hair had thinned; the gray eyes had sunk more deeply into their sockets and darted restlessly here and there. He walked with a slight stoop, and his gait, always a bit lumbering, was heavy and awkward, as though he were suffering from arthritis. They passed through a whitewashed corridor. Through the open doors Brand peered in on an assortment of clerks and secretaries. The little desks were cluttered with papers and files but their occupants seemed to be engaged in nothing more urgent than sipping tea or staring vacantly through the air, for it was close to the end of a long, tiring, hot day.

Gruenbaum, the head of the National Rescue Commission, was still in his office, talking on the telephone. It was a long conversation, conducted in Polish. When he finally put down the receiver, Gruenbaum sat up in his high upholstered chair and silently met Brand's gaze. After a while he said, very sonorously, as though he were addressing an assembly, "I have said it before. And I shall say it again. You have rendered an inestimable service to our cause. It is thanks to the information you brought out that the world has finally risen to understand our plight. We are no longer crying in the wilderness."

Brand colored. "Perhaps you are not. I am. I came out to rescue, not to cry! I am not in the propaganda business!"

"We are doing all we can," Gruenbaum said.

"The hell you are. You should have sent me back to

Budapest. Instead you lured me into a British trap. When the British were ready to let me go, you told them to keep me in Egypt even longer."

"That's not true."

"The British told me."

"They are lying. We tried our best to send you back. But they refused."

"I know we could have rescued so many, if only . . ."

"But we are doing all we can. I think I may tell you, and please, this is in the greatest confidence, we are already negotiating with the Germans. In Switzerland."

"Who is negotiating?"

"Ira Hirschmann."

"That old fool?"

The white streaks in Gruenbaum's little beard quivered slightly. "There are certain tasks," he said in a magisterial voice, "that perhaps are better suited to old experienced fools than to rash youngsters . . ."

"I failed, but not because of my rashness, or my age. I did nothing rash. You did. You betrayed me!"

"We did nothing of the kind."

"Without Mark I would never have gone to Aleppo."

"You are not going to be vindictive about that now."

Mark said, "I swear to you. I did not betray you."

"Let's say you didn't. But did you lift a finger to help me? You and Steiner worked at cross purposes. You were too busy feuding among yourselves to grasp the possibilities."

Gruenbaum said, "Don't be unfair to Steiner. He's not perfect, I know. Who is? But no matter, I may tell you in confidence, we are recalling Steiner. We are reorganizing the Istanbul office."

"Little good it does now. We had a chance to save . . . thousands. Maybe hundreds of thousands. We missed it. You should have protested my arrest. Publicly!"

"We can't go on protesting all the time."

"The world still thinks I am a Nazi agent. I read it in your own newspaper! You betrayed me, and those who sent me!"

"You mustn't overestimate your own importance, young man," Gruenbaum said. "You have rendered a great service, but please don't exaggerate. You must be tired after the long journey."

He was still treating Brand gently, but he was becoming impatient.

Brand repeated, "I must go back."

"The British won't allow it."

"What about my wife? My family?"

"They are safe. The Nazis haven't touched them . . ."

"Now they'll kill them! It's your fault! You killed them! You killed them! You are murderers! Murderers!"

* * *

Later on, in the car, Brand said, "I lost my temper. I shouldn't have called him a murderer."

"No."

"I'll apologize to him. I'll write a letter."

"Don't worry too much. He's got a thick skin."

"What shall I do now?"

"Find your bearings. They may want to consult you from time to time. But first settle down."

He settled into a little pension off Zion Square. There was a cafeteria across the street where the food was tasteless and greasy and made him miss the fleshpots of Egypt. The pension was in an old four-story building. The better rooms were occupied by soldiers on leave. The permanent residents were elderly refugees from Europe. They had somehow made it to the new country on the eve of the war, like salmon swimming back from the sea to the headwaters of their birth, in search of safety and the comfort of finding their own kind.

But it had not been quite so. They were lonely in the new country. It was a hard country, even though they no longer wore the yellow star and were no longer Jews but people like all other people. The landscape, the language were nothing they had ever known. Through the thin walls Brand heard their whining voices, in German, Polish, Rumanian. He remained shut in his room waiting, he knew not for what. There was no word from Mark.

In the adjacent room the windows were always shuttered. Through the crack of the door a vague smell of incense wafted to the corridor. The room was occupied by a white-haired woman in her late fifties who was said to have been a famous poet in Germany before the war. She was very poor, living from the charity of other German immigrants, who knew her hyphenated name that had once been a household word in avant-garde circles in Berlin. Something had happened to her mind.

"She is quite harmless," the innkeeper told Brand, who complained that she was tapping on his wall at night. "It's just that she thinks she is God's bride."

She would wander the streets by day, singing out in a high shrill voice, smiling, speaking comfortably to Jerusalem, and people would laugh. The street urchins threw orange peels at her and whistled and pulled at her hair. One evening she passed Brand on the staircase and hissed in his ear, "God loves Jerusalem! He clasps her to His heart!"

In the room across from him lived a dark little man from one of the Baltic countries. He told Brand that he was waiting for his immigration papers to the United States. His quota was due in seven years' time, but he was hopeful of getting there sooner. One night Brand heard him screaming, in a fit. He went out into the corridor. The man was standing in his pajamas pounding the wall with his fists. He seemed to have lost—or misplaced—his wallet. He was not crying for his money. "My passport," he whimpered. His

Lithuanian passport was the passport of a nonexistent country. But it was his past, his persona, his soul, his substance, his whole life.

Others came out of their doors to calm him. Brand turned back to his own room. He lay awake on the narrow bed. The hollow peal of church bells came in through the open window. In a little while a muezzin's voice rang out, harsh and tinny through the loudspeaker on the nearby minaret. "I praise the perfection of God, the forever existing, the perfection, the beloved, the Existing, the Single, the Supreme, the Perfect, the One and Only." It was 4 A.M. Brand was wide awake. As day broke the church bells rang again, the red streaks in the sky proclaimed the glory of God, for this after all was Jerusalem, His city, and the firmament displayed His charming handiwork.

The innkeeper was a short bald man who chewed unlit cigarettes. He also owned the cafeteria across the street. Brand came down in the morning to ask if he could use the telephone. The innkeeper said, "I see you've just arrived from over there."

"Yes."

"Where from?"

"Hungary."

"How are things?"

"Pretty bad."

"I know. People being killed, and starving."

"Yes, starving too."

"I know what it means," said the innkeeper. "We've gone through hard times ourselves. Only one hundred grams of sugar this month."

The telephone operator at the Jewish Agency switched him from one office to another. Finally a woman's voice came on the line and said she thought that Mark was out of town. She had no idea when he might be coming back. "Mr. Shertok? He is on another extension. Who wishes to speak to him? Who? Would you spell that? Did you say he knows you? He is in a meeting right now. Can he return your call? Yes. Yes. Thank you for calling."

He climbed back up to his room. It was small and dingy and even in the morning a little dark. The only bright spot was a 1936 wall calendar extolling the glories of sea travel. He leaned at the window and looked out at what he could see of the city. Beyond the tiled roofs there were other roofs covered with flagstones, and domes and church towers and minarets and pigeons turning in clouds of silver and amethyst. There was a smell of autumn in the air, and hot stones. In the distance, Mount Scopus hovered over the ramparts, pink, luminous and bare. Like every other spot in this mixed city, where all extremes of race and faith and habit met but never married, and destinies intersected only in death, Mount Scopus had another name: Mount Vulture. Brand gazed out at it for a long while. Whether one prayed or cursed, it was a gripping view. I must find something to do, he thought, and then he exhorted himself, be rational, be rational, much like Mark once upon a time, when he had admonished him to take another bath.

* * *

The world, having suffered an eclipse, emerged in his eyes more concrete than before, and shorn of all delusion. Or so he thought. There were also moments when he had the illusion less of safety than of permanence. Certain events, faces, voices ate into his memory like ticks. Trivial, banal little things. The shape of a door handle in Cairo. Schmidt's profile. The terminal building in Belgrade. Eichmann's fingernails.

He never left the pension in daytime, except to eat or buy the newspapers, which he devoured in great quantities, local and foreign. In the evenings he formed the habit of sitting at a corner table in the nearby Cafe Vienna, where earnest men were playing chess and youngsters were sipping lemonade and laughing and talking in gay, loud voices. The few elderly people he met seemed distant, their faces animated by a mysterious glee.

Younger people confused and embarrassed him. Their exuberance grated on his nerves. Their leaping energy never seemed to wear off. They seemed gullible, simple, and excited with their own problems and soaring expectations, for it was a time when the future of their country was being decided in London, Washington and Moscow, or so it seemed. They said there would soon be a Jewish state, and if not they would fight for it and it made them all feel taller, and good, and being also young, they felt they were in veritable heaven. They looked upon themselves as young heroes, blond new Jews—and upon those of Europe as cowards. Hadn't they marched to the slaughterhouse like sheep? They were embarrassed by their past. They wished to forget it. Brand wished himself far away from them and from the guilt that tinged his mood. One evening he was passing through the corridor of the pension. The little Lithuanian who had misplaced his passport was sitting in an armchair sipping brandy.

"Come in. Have a drink."

Brand said, "No, thank you."

"Why not?"

"I am tired."

The man's eyes shot up. "Try a little hatred," he said. "It's the best stimulant in the world."

* * *

One morning he saw a picture in the newspaper. Shertok, on a grandstand, was reviewing a parade of the new Jewish Army. He is too busy to call me, Brand thought, he has other things on his mind. The paper said that the Russian Army was on the outskirts of Budapest. Mark came to the pension on the following day and took him to the offices of a relief organization. He introduced Brand to the elderly lady in charge. She nodded knowingly when she

heard his name. A first list of survivors had arrived through
the International Red Cross, she said, and she offered him
the job of sorting out the names.

"No, thank you," he said quickly, "I am waiting to go
back."

"Think it over," Mark said.

"No."

"Be reasonable," Mark began. "You will soon need the
money."

"No," said Brand. No, he would not become their em-
ployee, no. They were trying to drag him into some sort of
complicity in which they were all involved. He ran back to
his pension through the thronged streets. The crowd parted
and people looked after him as he ran, shaking their heads.
A wooden crate was standing outside a shop. He tripped
on it and fell. Two men hovered over him to help him up.

One said, "You look ill. Rest awhile."

He shook them off and ran on. They want to think I'm
sick. Everybody thinks I'm sick. They need me sick, to
convince themselves that they are not. He reached the New
Gate and rushed down the narrow alleys of the Old City,
pushing his way through the multitude of street vendors
and donkeys and sightseers, monks and soldiers, Orthodox
Jews in long beards and fur hats and veiled Moslem
women. In the frosty shadow of the meat market, stripped
carcasses of mutton hung outside on hooks and little boys
were waving away the flies from the coagulated blood.

At the foot of David Street he came upon a black mass
of bearded men in skullcaps and silk caftans. The crowd
surged forward through the filthy lane, Brand with it.
Behind the maze of lanes and disemboweled ruins there
was a short flight of steps, a narrow paved passage and a
towering lone wall, which was the sum and meaning of this
motion. Brand looked up at the Wailing Wall. Try as he
would, no special feeling came. He edged his way slowly
through the crowd of crying men. Some were rocking back

and forth in prayer. Some leaned their foreheads against the wall, others clung to it with their fingers. The women howled. The Lord comforteth Jerusalem. An old man offered him a prayer book. Brand walked back up the flight of stairs and out into the open bare countryside beyond the Old City walls. Street vendors called after him, offering candles, prayer beads, crosses and Stars of David carved in olive wood with little thermometers attached.

He pushed on through, to be alone, into the open valley. The terraced sides were steep and hung with fig and olive trees, and date palms and gnarled vines and vegetable patches. He reached the end of a dusty path and climbed over a low stone wall. No matter where he trod there were graves—everywhere, all the way down the wide slope. It was that kind of place. Caves. Catacombs. Ruined battlements and bunkers of past wars. At the bottom he paused. He looked up ahead at the Mount of Olives, where yet another vast graveyard rose before him like a wall, almost perpendicular. An old guard came up and said it was the oldest Jewish graveyard in the world, ten million were buried in it. Then he held out his hand for alms. Some of the tombstones lay flat, some stood up, many had fallen down. It was unlike any other cemetery he had ever seen, bare and drab. There was not a single flower, nor any tree, not even a trace of green. Just a dusty jigsaw of crumbling masonry and dimly inscribed stone. Birnbaum, Rosenberg, Tannenbaum—names of flowers and fruit, strange in this arid soil on the edge of a great desert. Sternbach, Rastenburg—patronymic castles on the Rhine—turrets and spires of Tyrol. Preuss, Frankfurter, Ungar, Warsawski, Chomsky, Weichsel—faraway provinces, walled cities and frozen rivers of Poland. The geography of the exile. Brzezinski. Horns of Galicia. Schlonsky. Bugles of the Ukraine. Epitaphs of the dispersion. Sounds of passage. Yamani. Haddad. Abugadef. The East harmonious with the West on a mountain of dry bones.

The bells of the Church of Gethsemane at the bottom of the hill suddenly rang out brightly, *Jerusalem the Golden with milk and honey blest. Beneath thy contemplation rise heart and voice oppressed.* He started and shook himself and ran down the hill, stooped in the hot sun. His lips moved feverishly. The guard at the lower gate looked up. Brand was panting, running, muttering and wiping the sweat off his face with his sleeve. At the bottom of the hill the hot desert wind rose and struck him numb.

Postscript

Joel Brand eked out a meager living in a poor suburb of Tel Aviv and died in 1964 of a sudden heart attack in Germany, where he had gone to testify at the trial of a Nazi war criminal.

Hansi Brand was not molested by the Germans and survived the war. With her children she was among the 1,368 Jews who were permitted by Eichmann (against payment of a five-million Swiss-franc ransom) to leave Budapest on a special train via Bergen-Belsen for Switzerland. She is a schoolmistress in Tel Aviv. The ransoming of the 1,368 Jews was the only practical result of the negotiations that began with Brand's mission. We shall never know whether more might have been saved.

Moshe Shertok (later Sharett) became Foreign Minister of Israel (1948–53) and Prime Minister (1953–55). Shertok was haunted by the mission of Joel Brand throughout his life, and especially in the later years spent many hours obsessively going through the (then still classified) archive material making copious notes. Unlike other public figures who maintain they never erred and pretend there is nothing they would have done differently, this remarkable man never overcame the doubts that tortured him and tinged his most intimate feelings.

Chaim Weizmann became Israel's first President, 1948–52.

David Ben Gurion became Prime Minister of Israel (1948–53, 1955–63).

Lord Moyne was assassinated by Jewish terrorists in Cairo two months after his meeting with Brand, in November 1944. The assassins were hanged.

Andrew Gyorgy (alias Andor Bandi Gross) served a prison sentence in Turkey after the war, where he was charged with espionage activity and the distribution of counterfeit money. His name was linked with the so-called Cicero affair. After his release in 1953, he traveled to Israel to claim a debt of $100,000 he said the Israeli Government owed him. After several dramatic encounters, during which he was threatened with legal charges as an alleged collaborator with the Nazis, he was paid an undisclosed sum and quietly left for Europe, where he is said to be still living under another name.

Yitzhak Gruenbaum became Minister of the Interior in the first Israeli Cabinet, 1948.

Otto Komoly, senior member of the Budapest Committee who supported the choice of Brand as emissary to Istanbul, was killed by the Nazis.

Rudolf Kastner of the Budapest Rescue Committee, who participated in the negotiations with Eichmann, survived the war and became a senior government official in Israel. He was assassinated in 1953 on a Tel Aviv street after a district court judge—during a sensational libel case—had called him a Nazi collaborator who "sold his soul to the devil." The accusation had nothing to do with the Brand mission, and was reversed on appeal. The assassin was said to be a former agent of the Israeli Secret Service.

* * *

Adolf Eichmann was tried and executed in Israel in 1962. Joel Brand testified at his trial.

* * *

Anthony Eden (later Lord Avon) became British Prime Minister, 1955–56.

George Hall became Colonial Secretary, 1945, First Lord of the Admiralty, 1946–51, created Viscount, 1946.

* * *

It has been estimated that after 16 May 1944, the day of Brand's departure from Budapest, 70 per cent of the Jews of Hungary (more than 450,000) were gassed, shot, beaten or starved to death, or died under German Occupation.

Notes

I would like to thank all those who agreed to be interviewed and to share their memories of Brand and Shertok and their continuing sadness. The diplomatic negotiations have been reconstructed from the ample written reports prepared at the time by the officials involved and preserved in the various archives. Some dialogues, of course, had to be reanimated from the dry paraphrases of the bureaucratic records and some have been imagined, but always in keeping with the documented facts, the personality, views and attitudes of the particular character. Wherever possible I have inserted the actual words of the speaker. Letters and telegrams are reproduced verbatim. The main sequence of events in this book is historical and such liberties as I have taken occur mainly in the dialogue and in the attribution of motive. My good friends Ori Bernstein and Miranda Kaniuk read the manuscript and I am deeply grateful for their suggestions and efforts to improve the final text.

* * *

The documents and letters set in small-size type can be found in the Central Zionist Archive (CZA), Jerusalem; the Public Record Office (PRO), London; and in the National Archives, Washington. American diplomatic exchanges on the Brand affair can also be found in *U.S. Foreign Relations,* Vol. 1944.

Shertok's activities in London from July to September 1944 are in CZA files, Z/4 Nos. 15202, 10405, 10398, 15428, 14849, in S/25/5206 and S/26/1190.

The events in Aleppo are recorded in CZA S/26/1488. The deliberations of the Jewish leaders in Jerusalem are recorded in S/25 (Jewish Agency Executive Sessions), as are the negotiations with High Commissioner Sir Harold Macmichael. For the purpose of this narrative the material from three Executive sessions and three meetings with the high commissioner has been compressed into two sessions and two meetings. The Istanbul office files are in CZA L/15/244, 245, 327, 278080, 131 and 188.

The records and internal memoranda of the U.S. War Refugee Board are preserved under this heading in the National Archives, Washington. The material on Brand's interrogation in Cairo and the British Military Intelligence report can be found in PRO (Foreign Office) 371/42810/42807.

Use has been made of the transcripts of the so-called Kastner Trial (*State of Israel* v. *Malchiel Gruenwald*), Tel Aviv, 1953, and the Eichmann Trial (especially the Sixty-fifth Session, 29 May 1960; Testimonies III, pp. 865–935). And, of course, there are Brand's own recollections published in his (ghostwritten) *Desperate Mission* (London, 1962) against which I have double-checked the material in the official archives. *Desperate Mission* was heavily cut and censored by unknown hands at a time when the mere mention of Brand's mission touched upon so many open wounds that Brand himself agreed to excessive rather than judicious restraint. Despite the deletions, the book is an important aid to the understanding of his character; it conveys a shattering impression of his agony upon the failure of his mission. There are at least three earlier, unpublished, fragmented drafts to this book, two of which, in Brand's own hand, I have been able to consult. Another important source are interviews with Joel and Hansi Brand in Griffel's *HaSatan Wehanefesh* (Tel Aviv, 1954).

The written documentation has been expanded by interviews with most of the surviving participants in the drama and with the two main protagonists of this book, with Joel Brand himself, shortly before his death, and with Moshe Shertok, after his retirement from public office. Finally, I had a long interview with Hansi Brand, and with Dr. Nahum Goldmann, Weizmann's representative in Washington in 1944. The British War Office papers with regard to the deliberations (if there were any) on the feasibility of bombing the Auschwitz death camp are not available. It is worth noting, however, that during the Eichmann trial, when the British refusal to bomb first gained worldwide publicity, Sir Arthur Harris, formerly of the Air Staff, was quoted in the newspapers as saying he did not remember that the subject had ever come up in a discussion of possible targets.

Other Arrow Books of interest:

SOME OF OUR BEST FRIENDS ARE ANIMALS

Peter Spence

Life at Cricket St Thomas was never quite the same after the Taylor family converted the house and grounds into a wildlife park. Some very unusual animal personalities made their mark. Like Twiggy the elephant, or the barnacle goose who fell in love with a red deer – not to mention the sealion who hijacked a Range Rover.

'Life among the residents of a wildlife park seems to have all the ingredients of the Marx Brothers joining the Goons in an unscripted farce down on the farm'
Coventry Evening Telegraph

85p

TO CATCH A KING

Harry Patterson

His previous bestsellers include *The Eagle has Landed*, *The Valhalla Exchange* and *Storm Warning*. Now Harry Patterson (alias Jack Higgins) has transformed the facts of history into his most compelling thriller to date.

July 1940. While the world awaits the invasion of England, a plot unfolds in Lisbon that could change the course of the war. Its instigator: Adolf Hitler. Its target: the Duke of Windsor. Its aim: to catch a king. Only one man could have conceived of so daring, so deadly a plot. Only the maddest moments of history could have made it possible.

£1.25

THE VALHALLA EXCHANGE

Harry Patterson

Fact!
Dawn April 30th 1945. Russian radar reports a light aircraft
leaving one of the last strongholds in besieged Berlin –
passengers and destination unknown.

Fiction?
In a concret bunker beneath the burning city, Reichsleiter
Martin Bormann assembles a crack team to fly him out of a
tightening Soviet ring around the capital. Objective – the
medieval fortress of Arlberg where a group of VIP prisoners
are to be used as bargaining counters in the epic struggle to
come.

'Patterson is in his element here, with lots of fast, fierce
fighting, subterfuge and inside betrayals.'
Publishers Weekly

£1.50

THE GRAVE OF TRUTH
Evelyn Anthony

First there was the dream . . .

It was the dream Max had been having since the war. The dream of those horrifying, final moments in the Führer's Bunker – images of that night of terror, of the brutally beaten, dying man and his last desperate words; dreams of a past from which Max can't escape.

Then there was the nightmare . . .

Suddenly, it starts all over again – but it is no longer a dream. And now Max finds himself caught in a chilling search for Hitler's last legacy.

The Grave of Truth is the story of a deadly race to discover the Führer's final evil bequest to mankind.

'Ms Anthony knows how to thrill and chill' *Observer*

'Brilliantly convincing' *Evening Standard*

£1.25

THE RETURN
Evelyn Anthony

In 1945 the Yalta Agreement committed 3 million Russians to forcible repatriation – and certain death. It was a cruel double-deal that led to mass suicide and unspeakable horror. It also led to the formation of a group of exiled relatives – a group dedicated to justice, and revenge. They called themselves 'The Return'.

To them, no life was too dear to be lost; no risk too awesome to be taken; and nothing was sacred – save their work to expose the crimes of one man – Grigor Malenkov. They had waited for years. Soon the time for vengeance would come.

'Exciting, well written . . . one of the year's top ten thrillers'
Allan Prior in the Daily Mail

£1.60

BAPTISM OF BLOOD

K. N. Kostov

Traitors, reactionaries, pimps, whoremasters, black marketeers, murderers and perverts – the worst the labour camp had to offer . . . they called them the gulag rats.

Punishment Battalion 333 was the roughest, wildest band of fighting men ever to draw blood. Yet they fought like the hounds of hell.

Driven by an embittered and sadistic commander against the Nazi push towards Moscow, the gulag rats face a desperate conflict of fury and brutality: their baptism of blood.

£1.25

BLAZE OF RIOT

James Tucker

Robert Lawrence isn't a secret agent, he is a partner in a cutlery firm. Robert Lawrence knows how to mind his own business, and how to play along. He knows enough to salute when the Brownshirts march by, and he can even manage to look pleased if he has to. If there is one lesson that he has learned since coming back to Germany on this trip, it is to stay out of all trouble – especially at night.

But then the girl upstairs is murdered. And Robert can't quite put it out of his mind. Slowly and inexorably, he is drawn into an entanglement of plots and counterplots as the Nazi hierarchy develops its plans for one of the most dramatic political manoeuvres of the century: the Reichstag fire.

£1.50